Moonshine Jar of Diamonds
~ ~ ~ ~
Buried Secrets at Big Creek

Ramona G Kearney

All rights reserved.

Copyright © 2020 Ramona G Kearney

This is a work of fiction. Names, characters, places, and incidents are the product of the author's imagination or are used fictitiously

ISBN: 978-1-7331619-7-8

Dedication

This book is dedicated to my sister-in-law, Mrs. Sallie Grant, who has always been like a grandmother to my boys Clifton and Timmy. She is an encourager and a cheerleader. At 96 years old, she is a staunch Christian and a prayer warrior, much like Lillian of this story. Thank you, Sallie, for the million memories and the blessing you have been to me.

ACKNOWLEDGEMENTS

When I saw the beautiful picture Nicole Secrest took, I knew it was Big Creek at Davie's Landing. Thank you, Nicole, for allowing me to use your photograph to depict the setting of Davie and Jenny's story. And thanks to Unsplash for the picture of Davie and Jenny.

I want to thank the special members of my Oars in the Water Facebook group for their opinions, suggestions, and support. And a big thank you to my family and friends for giving me ideas. Thank you to the readers, I hope you will be blessed by the Wellsly family's stories.

Thank you to my wonderful husband Doug Kearney for taking care of all the things I neglect while I am writing and never complaining about what might appear to be a waste of time. He would never say that.

And most of all, thank you, God, for being real to the characters and being real to me.

"But those elusive diamonds drew them in like the sirens of Greek mythology luring sailors to their destruction."

Contents

Chapter 1 Night Noises 1
Chapter 2 Gristmill Landing 8
Chapter 3 Pine Ridge Landing 12
Chapter 4 Davie's Landing 17
Chapter 5 Beauty Shop Talk 21
Chapter 6 Night Light 23
Chapter 7 April Fools or Aliens 30
Chapter 8 Vandalized 34
Chapter 9 At the Day Spa 37
Chapter 10 Cleaning Up 44
Chapter 11 Renee Renoir 52
Chapter 12 Davie's Dilemma 55
Chapter 13 The Soup Kitchen 67
Chapter 14 The Agency 72
Chapter 15 Loose Lips Sink Ships 84
Chapter 16 Man in the White Suit 95
Chapter 17 Identifying a Body 99
Chapter 18 Breakfast at Tiffany's 106
Chapter 19 Clues from the Hymnbook 114
Chapter 20 More Radio Talk 120
Chapter 21 Who Goes There? 123
Chapter 22 Current Resident 128
Chapter 23 Burgundy Blues 134
Chapter 24 Jo Swan 139
Chapter 25 The Letter 147
Chapter 26 Deciphering the Letter 151
Chapter 27 Man in the White Suit 157
Chapter 28 Counterfeit 163
Chapter 29 Regrouping 168
Chapter 30 Country Club Hills 173

Chapter 31 Nancy Drew, the Accidental Sleuth 183
Chapter 32 Gray Tower 189
Chapter 33 Through the Looking Glass 195
Chapter 34 Second Thoughts 204
Chapter 35 Pictures and Proof 213
Chapter 36 Davie's Secret 217
Chapter 37 Reckoning 226
Chapter 38 Confession 232
Chapter 39 Isaac, Lillian and Old Times 237
Chapter 40 The Parking Lot 243
Chapter 41 Gray Tower Revisited 251
Chapter 42 Game Plan 253
Chapter 43 At the Yellow House 256
Chapter 44 Reflections and Plan B 261
Chapter 45 Spring Festival Begins 267
Chapter 46 Chesapeake Horses 269
Chapter 47 Spring Festival in Full Swing 272
Chapter 48 Game! 277
Chapter 49 The Fish Box 279
Chapter 50 Reprieve, Review and Regroup 287
Chapter 51 The Red Shoe 293
Chapter 52 Davie's Surprise 301
Chapter 54 And They're Off! 310
Chapter 55 The Good Samaritan 319
Chapter 56 Hospital Visit 324
Chapter 57 Dr. Zoey Rosenberg 329
Chapter 58 Relief 336
Chapter 59 The Mystery Man 338
Chapter 60 Petals in the Wind 344
Chapter 61 Crest Lawn Rest Home 348
Chapter 62 Into My Heart 354
Chapter 63 Memory 362
Chapter 64 Testimony 370

Chapter 65 Tough Decisions and Forgiveness..381
Chapter 66 One More Thing..390
ADDENDUM..399
ABOUT THE AUTHOR..**400**

Chapter 1 Night Noises

Sunday about 3 am, March 31, 2013

"**D**id you hear that?" **Jenny shook Davie.** "I do now," he said. He sat up in bed and cringed as the sound wailed again. "Sounds like a wolf howling at the moon," Jenny said. Then a crash, like it was coming from downstairs, made them both shriek.

Davie jumped out of bed and reached for the gun he kept on the top shelf in the closet. He felt for bullets without turning on a light and inserted them as his heart pounded.

Jenny reached for her robe and crept near Davie. They stood together, silently listening for footsteps or any other noise an intruder might make. But it was quiet, as though that crash had never happened. They would have thought it was only a dream, except that they both had heard it.

It was dark outside. The moon was barely a sliver, and clouds shrouded what light it gave. Through the bedroom window, Davie peered out into the night. Lit by a security light across the street, he could see his parent's mailbox. Though he couldn't read it, he knew it said Jessica and Jimmy Wellsly. Their yard appeared undisturbed. He noticed a bathroom light was on, but then it went out. He heard the clock downstairs strike three chimes. There were no unusual noises now. Aside from the soft bump of the heating system coming on, it was silent.

After a few seconds, Davie whispered, "I'm going downstairs."

"I'm right behind you," Jenny said. "Don't shoot me."

Cautiously, Davie crept downstairs with Jenny behind him. At the bottom landing, he stopped. From that vantage point, he could see a nightlight on in the kitchen to his left and a nightlight on down the hall toward the front door on his right. "Who's there?" He called, not that he wanted an answer, but he wanted them to know he was there. The only sound was his own heart beating too fast, he leaned against the wall and accidentally bumped the light switch. "Don't shoot!" yelled Jenny. He was so startled, he shot and the bullet hit the wall above the front door. Jenny screamed.

With the light on, they could see that nothing was disturbed. Davie took a deep breath and walked around flipping on lights in all the rooms downstairs. Even the porch lights in front and back. Nothing seemed to have been touched. He looked up at the bullet hole above the door. "Now I've got to fix that," he shook his head.

Jenny was still sitting at the foot of the stairs shivering even though her robe was warm. Davie sat down beside her and put his arm around her. "Well, this is weird. But I know we heard a crash."

"And a wolf howling," Jenny said.

"No. I don't think it was a wolf," Davie said. "Maybe a dog. But while we're up, we might as well get a snack." He stood up and reached for her hand. In the kitchen, he laid the gun on the table and pulled a Mountain Dew from the refrigerator and a box of crackers from the pantry.

Jenny laughed, "You and your Mountain Dew." She poured herself a glass of milk to settle her nerves. As they sat at the table trying to regroup, Jenny said, "I was having trouble sleeping anyway. I kept thinking about the Smythes."

"Yeah, me too," Davie said, remembering the activities of the past few weeks. From his office at WDGW Oars and Boats, he had made one more call to Jeffry Smythe about the yacht still waiting to be delivered.

Davie built boats. His ambition was to be the best in the south, but he built small boats, fishing boats, dinghies, and deck boats. He never planned on building yachts.

However, Jeffry Smythe of Chesapeake, Virginia, had made a special trip to Claxton, South Carolina, and pleaded with him. He had heard of WDGW Oars and Boats and wanted that quality in his yacht, he said. He had pictures of what he wanted and he had the money to back it up. But Davie gracefully declined. His plant was busy enough and he didn't need to take on such a daunting project.

A week later, Mr. Smythe returned with his wife Julie. He would not take no for an answer. His beautiful wife was as convincing as he was. The first impression they gave was down-to-earth, wealthy, a sharp-looking pair. Smythe was a classy, blondish gentleman who turned heads, and with his wife on his arm, the charm was doubled.

They were a couple who could get what they wanted. Davie and Jenny debated the issue at length. He had the degree and the skills, she had the interior design degree which was part of the package. It was a lot of money and it would be a boost to their businesses. But it would change the focus of the plant, and Davie was not too happy about that. However, the Smythes were persistent. Davie told them he estimated three years and three million dollars. He would have to expand the shipyard and hire more staff and they could get the same boat cheaper if they went to a larger company.

Jeffry Smythe didn't flinch. He said he wasn't trying to save money. He wanted the best. He finally wrote a check for 500,000 dollars from a bank in Chesapeake, Virginia, to get the project started. Davie capitulated. He brought in Alex Wolf as the project manager. Davie would design the exterior and Jenny would design the interior. They all had the education and credentials. She owned and operated Burgundy Blue Boutique. Alex Wolf had been one of Davie's classmates at the University of South Carolina at Claxton. It had been a positive experience and a prosperous venture.

Three years later, the yacht was completed at $2.4 million, and Smythe had disappeared. He was supposed to come down on the first of March for the final inspection and payment for delivery.

"Why would a man so eager for me to build that yacht, not be as eager to get it?" Davie asked Jenny. "We need it out of our way now. I've called several times and left messages."

"We need it out of the shipyard or I'll have to start charging docking fees." He was half-joking, but as he thought about it, he said, "I should have listened to George when we were setting up this business six years ago. I'll have to address that on contracts from now on."

"I wonder if it's because...but it's his loss."

"What?" Davie asked.

"They invited us to join them on a Caribbean cruise this fall. But that was before...oh well, I didn't like their friends anyway."

"They made us think we were their friends. And we certainly went out of our way to be. But..."

"You should never mix business and pleasure!" Davie said.

Davie had worked closely with Jeffry Smythe, designing the ship like he wanted it, and Jenny designed the interior to Julie's classic taste. They were both thrilled with Davie and Jenny's work throughout the project.

"Now he's dumped us and left us hanging. That kind of makes me mad." Davie fingered the gun lying on the table.

"Take the bullets out," Jenny said.

"I guess I can now," he said and emptied the gun, handing the bullets to Jenny who dropped them in the pocket of her robe.

"Why did that man hang up on you?" Jenny wondered. "You suppose he thought Jeffry owed you money?"

Davie agreed. "Well he does, a little, just chump change to him, mainly delivery expense, but I have no idea. And if that guy was a friend of the family, he would most likely have known about the yacht."

"Maybe that wasn't really a friend of the family," Jenny suggested.

"That's what I'm wondering. Julie Smythe knew every step of the process, too. And she knew it was practically ready 3 months ago."

"It is strange." Jenny put her glass in the sink. "Let's try again tomorrow."

"I will. For now, I guess we need to get back to bed. Morning will be here soon."

"Yeah, but I won't be able to sleep. I want to know what that crash was."

"Maybe it was an animal turning over the garbage can," he speculated.

"It was inside the house, Davie," she insisted.

"We've looked in every room down here," Davie told her. Nothing's broken in the kitchen nor the dining room. The living room is fine, and our office is undisturbed. The only places with hard floors that would make that much noise are the kitchen, the bathroom, and the laundry room."

"Did you check the pantry?"

"Everything, and there's nothing in any of them."

"Oh," Jenny said. "Maybe it wasn't down here. We didn't check upstairs at all."

Davie beckoned for her to give him back the bullets, and he quickly loaded the gun. On impulse, she grabbed a flashlight from the pantry. They left the lights on downstairs and cautiously crept back up the same way they had come down.

At the top of the stairs, Davie turned on the hall light. Movement at the opposite end of the hall turned out to be their own reflections in a mirror. Except for their bedroom, all the doors on both sides of the hall were closed. The first door on their right opened into a bathroom. Davie flipped the light and chrome gleamed. The blue shag rug on the blue and white tile was undisturbed. Nobody was inside the glassed-in tub and shower.

Their master bedroom was dark. Davie flipped the light switch, and Jenny flashed her light under the bed.

Nothing was under the bed except a tray of shoes and a layer of dust. She winced. She blamed the beige carpeting for trapping dust. The floor-length royal blue draperies were neatly in place with no feet sticking out. She imagined having a heart attack if there had been.

The matching bedspread lay just as they had left it. Their bathroom was gleaming white with blue curtains and towels, Davie's favorite color. The shower stall was empty. In the dressing nook, the clothes she had worn yesterday were slung across a vanity seat. Davie's clothes were on the hamper.

Relieved, they moved across the hall. Davie opened the door and quickly flipped the light switch. The white French provincial bedroom suite with a rose garden bedspread and draperies to match looked like a little girl's room. It had been in Jenny's bedroom growing up.

Nothing was under that bed except the layer of dust trapped on the white carpet. "I have to get some cleaning done," Jenny admonished herself. But at least the room had no monsters and everything was in place even in the louvered closets.

The next room was directly across from their bedroom door, a smaller bedroom they intended for a nursery someday. It was nearly empty except for a rocking chair, a daybed, and artificial plants.

With nervousness mounting, they approached the last door, Jenny's craft room. Davie tightened his grip on the gun in his right hand, and with his left, opened the door and flipped the light switch with one swift motion. It was quiet and well lit. No need for the flashlight. There was no bed.

A love seat, sat on one wall accompanied by a couple of occasional chairs, end tables, and lamps. A coffee table, with a silver tea set, sat on a small oriental rug in front of the loveseat.

Across the room, a table sat against the wall with partial bolts of tapestry. Some baskets were stacked in the corner stuffed with artificial flowers. A sewing machine sat in front of double windows whose white sheer curtains let in ample light during the day.

A double closet was open with shelves of decorative boxes, rolls of ribbon in assorted colors, and various vases and trinkets. On the opposite side, an antique dresser that Davie's great-grandmother had given them was pressed against the wall. Its mirror lay shattered, face down, on the hardwood floor.

Jenny grabbed her heart. "Oh, my goodness!" Davie blew a huge sigh of relief, laid the gun down on the table, and squatted down to pick up the mirror frame. The backing was still intact but the mirror was in a million pieces.

When Jenny started picking up shards, the sight of blood on her fingers finished her off. She started crying.

"Oh, you're hurt, let me get some medicine." Davie jumped up. She leaned her head back against the dresser while he dashed to the bathroom for some ointment and band-aids.

"It doesn't hurt that much," Jenny pulled herself together. "It's just the sight of blood, the tension, and relief. But ouch! That does hurt," she winced. "That's too tight." Davie loosened the band-aid and kissed her fingers. She laughed at his chivalry and already felt better.

"Wonder why it fell off?" Davie asked, examining the dresser top. "I thought it was secure."

"I thought it was too," Jenny agreed. "It just decided to jump off the wall and fall on the floor. I'll take it to the shop and find another mirror for the frame. At least the wood frame is not messed up. Maybe you can reattach it and make sure it's more secure this time."

Davie swept the remaining slivers of glass into a dustpan and dumped it all in the trash basket. They closed the door and went back to bed, still unsettled, but at least thinking the mystery was solved.

Chapter 2 Gristmill Landing

Sunday about 3 am, March 31

A few miles away, shadowy figures worked stealthily. At first, the shovels made little sound, swishing easily into the sand as diggers worked rhythmically. A hole about six feet across deepened as the swishing continued. Shovels of sand built a growing bank of dunes.

Big Creek, which in the daylight was sky blue, was shimmering black with only a sliver of moonlight in the sky.

Three figures worked in unison, silently, with only the sound of the shovels accompanying the chirping of crickets and night frogs. One shovel at the time, the excavation grew deeper, and the semicircle of dunes grew higher. When one shovel struck a rock and then another, the crunching of shovel against rock was like fingernails on a chalkboard, silencing for a moment the chorus of night creatures.

But it spurred the diggers on. Below the topsoil, they chiseled away through a layer of rocky soil and roots. The crunching grew louder as the rocky debris made the shoveling harder. Grunts and graveling sounds were joined by a growling motor and the night chorus stopped again. Clouds hid what was left of the moon. A wolf howling close by unnerved the figures and they disappeared into the darkness.

About five o'clock, in the darkest hour just before dawn, the kitchen staff started arriving. Rebecca Wilson's first job was to post

Sunday's specials on the bulletin board outside the Gristmill Restaurant.

She didn't need a light. She had followed that path a hundred times from the back door, up the side of the building, to the bulletin board. The parking lot lights usually illuminated the area. But the parking lot was dark.

Her scream pierced the early morning quiet and brought staff running. Someone flipped on the emergency lights. Only then could they see the six-foot pit where she lay crumpled and quiet.

A quarter-mile away, Bud Littman was about to enter the door of the Gristmill to work his shift when he heard the scream. He knew it was Rebecca. He had just dropped her off. His girlfriend was a waitress at the restaurant, and he worked at the gristmill next door. They rode to work together. In a lightning sprint, he crossed the empty parking lots and sailed into the pit--a big mistake.

When one foot landed on a rock that twisted his ankle, he heard a crack and felt the sear of pain. He cursed himself for being so reckless. He crawled to Rebecca crumpled on the ground and felt blood on her head. "Get a ladder! Quick!" He yelled, "Rebecca's hurt bad."

Out of nowhere, it seemed, a six-foot ladder was slipped over the edge of the pit. "It's not enough," a voice cried. "Push the dirt back in the hole," another voice commanded. Several went to their knees and started shoving dirt over the edge. Bud sat beside Rebecca, talking to her, trying to ignore his own excruciating pain. She did not respond.

Jim, the head cook at the restaurant, climbed down the ladder. He felt for a pulse. She was breathing, but blood was seeping down her neck from the gash on her head. "Somebody call 911!" He yelled.

"I did," a voice answered back.

The group continued pushing dirt over the edge to build a mound. "Somebody, call Mr. Wellsly."

"I already did," someone else spoke out. "He's on his way."

Amid the confusion, someone asked, "What in the world was this hole dug for?" Someone wondered if Jimmy Wellsly had started another project on the property. "We would have known. Mr. Wellsly is always upfront about the resort's development."

The Riverside Hotel and Marina had been expanded a few years back. A helipad had been built on top of an extension to the hotel. And the staff always knew what was going on. Mr. Wellsly made them a part of the process. Sometimes, it meant promotions or new jobs available. Jimmy Wellsly looked after his people.

"He would not have done this."

"But who did? And why?"

"A buried treasure, I bet!" Someone cracked.

"Are you crazy? There's no buried treasure out here. Besides, so much of this property has been dug up for foundations, plumbing, and parking lots. Nah. There's no buried treasure here."

"Not now anyway," someone concluded. "If there was, they've got it and gone. They left nothing but this big empty hole."

"And blood on their hands if Becky dies."

The cook and a couple of helpers hoisted Bud up the ladder and put a makeshift splint on his leg. They had tried to help Rebecca but were afraid to move her. The sound of a siren announced the emergency team arriving from Merryville.

The EMT's hustled to the rescue. One strapping young man sat down on the edge and jumped down easily, then lifted Rebecca to the stretcher being lowered into the hole. Rebecca did not awaken as they hoisted her up and into the ambulance. Bud was helped into someone's back seat and followed the ambulance to Claxton Emergency.

Jimmy Wellsly barreled into the parking as the rescue squad screeched out. Other traffic trickled in with a changing of shifts at the mill. Drivers craned to see and wondered what was going on.

The restaurant staff drifted back to their stations abuzz with questions and speculations. Some said prayers for Rebecca and Bud and the whole mysterious situation.

Jimmy called the Phillips County Sheriff's Department who sent Deputies Johnson and Smith who took pictures and kicked dirt around looking for anything that could be a clue. They bagged the bloody rock that apparently struck Rebecca's head. They did not think it was foul play. They considered it a prank. It must have been teenagers.

After all, this was a place where parents brought their pets and children for picnics and fun days at the park. A road led up the bank from the dock where families left their boats. Everybody was familiar with the area. The statue of Bruiser Wellsly, the legendary black German shepherd, stood just a few feet from the hole. This was Bruiser's Park.

Deputy Johnson laughed wryly and said, "If the stories I've heard about that dog were true, he would have done something if it was foul play."

"He might have," somebody argued. "You don't know."

"Well, I'm not putting that in my report," the deputy said as he wrote, "Suspect teenage pranksters."

Jimmy called his Uncle Benjamin who owned the gristmill next door. Then he called Rebecca's parents. Someone had already contacted them, and they were leaving for the hospital. Jimmy assured them that the company would take care of her and asked that they call him back.

Benjamin met Jimmy in the restaurant and was joined by the deputies who asked questions. They talked with each of the staff separately. No one knew anything except hearing the scream and then finding Rebecca at the bottom of the pit. Someone had stuck some sticks in the ground with white napkins tied at the top as caution. Several had taken pictures and sent them to friends on their phones.

Even though they did not consider it a crime scene, the county deputies strung crime tape around the pit. Jimmy called the maintenance manager. "Jack, we've got a problem. A six-foot pit's been dug by the road that leads down to the dock. Soon as you can get here, get it refilled. It's dangerous."

"Who...what...how in the world?" Jack stumbled for information.

Jimmy was baffled. "The Phillips County deputies say they think it was a teenage prank. But there's no way. This is not a teenage prank."

Chapter 3 Pine Ridge Landing

Sunday about 6 am, March 31

Just a few miles up the river from the resort, Dick Vinton, a local fisherman, pulled into the landing off Pine Ridge Road and started backing his trailer down to the edge of the water as he had done a hundred mornings before. He slammed the brakes just before hitting a deep gully, like a huge well that almost grabbed the trailer.

"Thank God! He yelled aloud. "That's a disaster waiting to happen!" He started driving back out and hit the horn as another truck pulled in.

"What's wrong?" The driver yelled. Meadows pointed to the hole he had barely missed.

"What the heck is Isaac Wellsly doing?" The driver asked.

"Lord only knows," the fisherman said. "I'm pulling back out. Don't know what this is all about and don't want to get in trouble. I'll come back another day."

"I'm calling Isaac," the driver told him.

"No need. No signal out here," the fisherman said. "But we can call when we get back out to the highway."

Isaac Wellsly had built a dock at the small landing allowing fishermen to put boats in the water and leave their vehicles there. The only building was a shelter over some picnic tables.

Almost every morning there would be boat trailers and trucks waiting for their owners. On weekends, there could be up to a dozen. But not today; it was Easter. The landing was smooth sand sloping to the edge, easy to access. A short pier allowed small boats to dock. It was a popular spot for local fishermen. But today it seemed ominous. A hundred feet from the water's edge was a gaping hazard.

When Vinton called, Isaac had just hung up from a conversation with Benjamin and Jimmy.

"Who in the world's calling this early?" Lillian asked. "Are the kids alright?"

"It's weird," he said. "Jimmy called, and then Dick Vinton called. Something weird is going on. Somebody's doing some digging. There's been a huge hole dug at the resort, and Dick says there's a huge hole at Pine Ridge Landing. He almost backed into it. I'll have to run up there and check on it."

"Oh, my goodness. Give me a minute. I'm going with you. I'll make some coffee and we can take it with us." Lillian jumped out of bed and slipped into pants and a pullover sweater. Jumping out of bed was not easy anymore, but something was wrong and she pushed herself.

As they drove the few miles up to Pine Ridge Road, Lillian moaned, "So much drama over the years. I thought it was over. Is it starting again?"

The twenty-mile stretch of wooded land along the river from the gristmill to Claxton was part of Big Creek Plantation a hundred years ago. Isaac's grandfather, William Doran Green Wellsly, had parceled the land to his sons, Hinson and Antry, but tragedies had taken them. Hinson was murdered in 1943 and the WDGW Oars and Boatbuilding business had closed. Then Antry was killed in 1955, but Isaac had managed to keep his father's Gristmill going.

"You're remembering, aren't you?" Lillian asked as Isaac's jaw clenched. He just nodded and kept driving.

The coroner had called Antry's death suicide, but it wasn't. And a year later, when Isaac thought he had proof, and took it to the Phillips County Sheriff's Department, he was almost killed, too. It was 2003 before Isaac's sister Bernell was instrumental in solving those murders and bringing down the criminal empire of Roger

Riddick. The Sheriff of Phillips County had been arrested as part of the sting.

"We finally learned the truth, didn't we?" Lillian reminded him. He nodded but didn't say anything.

Before Riddick died, he confessed his role in taking over the Wellsly Sawmill and WDGW Oars and Boatbuilding in the forties and his attempt to take over the Wellsly Gristmill in 1955. It wasn't their businesses he wanted. It was the property and control of the river for his international criminal operations, drugs, gun smuggling, and human trafficking. Big Creek was his highway. But he was no Robin Hood. For sixty years he had reigned and left a trail of blood.

"God has answered so many prayers," Lillian said. Isaac nodded but didn't say anything. His mind drifted to that day when he awoke in the hospital. His car had been rammed over a cliff, and Isaac had miraculously survived. Even now he thought it was an angel who pulled him out of the burning wreckage.

Though he was badly burned and broken, it was that stay in the hospital that brought Lillian Del Vecchio, the beautiful Italian Jewish nurse, into his life; and good things had happened after that. He reached over and patted her hand. She could read his mind.

"I know," she agreed.

He had managed to salvage his father's gristmill and, turned it over to his younger brother Benjamin. Then he and Lillian followed their dream which they felt was directed by God. They envisioned a restaurant offering Italian, Jewish, and Southern cuisine, without discrimination, serving all who would come. Their restaurant was avant-garde in the sixties and maintained a five-star rating for fifty years. They had added a park, and a hotel, and built a renowned resort.

When Isaac and Lillian retired, they turned the resort over to their only child Jimmy who along with his wife, Jessica Greyson, had continued to maintain its five-star status. Their son Davie, the apple of Isaac's eye, was a dreamer and a doer. When he finished college, he became the new WDGW with a goal of resurrecting the old Wellsly Oars and Boatbuilding brand which had ranked number one in the south from the turn of the century until 1943. Two fishing boats, symbolic of the past had lain for years on Big Creek Landing. When Davie refurbished them, they were stationed as showpieces in front of Oarlocks and Bagels, Isaac's sporting goods store on the waterfront in Claxton.

And Davie's boatbuilding plant now dominated the landing at the end of Big Creek Road, just five miles up from Pine Ridge where Lillian and Isaac were heading to investigate a mysterious hole in the ground. Fishermen and friends, Dick Vinton and Gene Wexler, were waiting.

"We thought we'd see if there was anything we could do," Dick said as the two men met Isaac getting out of his truck. Lillian took out her phone and snapped pictures of the gigantic hole.

"Looks like somebody was searching for something; what you reckon it was?" Dick asked.

"Good question," said Isaac. "You reckon you and Gene can help me block this off? We can move some picnic tables over here."

"Yes, that'll work. Want us to help rake the dirt back in?"

"No," said Isaac. "I think I need to call the sheriff. I'll run back by Sheriff Ritchie's office. Lillian can show him the pictures and maybe he'll know what to do."

"Yeah," Gene said. "That's what I'd do."

With tables placed around the hole to prevent anyone from accidentally driving in it, Isaac thanked them both for letting him know and for coming back to help him. "Y'all go on, catch a lot of fish today. I hear they're biting good."

When Sheriff Ritchie and his deputy saw the pictures, they just shook their heads. "With nothing but a hole in the ground, it's hard to report a crime," The sheriff said. "I think it's all just vandalism, and we have no clues who's doing it. Looks a lot like the one up at Bruiser's Park."

"Yeah," Isaac said. "I've talked with Jimmy and Benjamin. At least nobody was hurt here like Rebecca was at the restaurant."

Lillian gasped. "What? Oh, my!" She knew Rebecca as one of their waitresses, but she did not know Bud. "I'll be praying for those kids. Jimmy must be in a tizzy," she groaned. "I have to call him."

"Right now we need to go back out there and fill up the hole," Isaac said. "It's a hazard and we don't want anybody else getting hurt."

"I'll send a couple of guys out there to help," the sheriff offered. "And we'll look around for clues. But don't count on anything."

Chapter 4 Davie's Landing

Monday about 7 am, April 1

As the sun rose over **Davie's Landing** on Monday morning, employees of WDGW Oars and Boats filtered in. The landing at the end of Big Creek Road had always been called Big Creek Landing until Davie built his boat plant. Then it became known as Davie's Landing.

The sun rising across the river was an awesome vision of pink, orange, and yellow streaks between a blue sky and the blue-green river. Asher Ingles had painted many pictures of those sunrises and some were on display at Jenny's Burgundy Blue Boutique.

In the morning splendor, the gaping hole by the parking lot hardly drew attention until Joe Miller almost drove his car into it. He slammed on brakes just in time.

"Whoa!" he yelled. "Did Davie do this? It's mighty stupid! Somebody's gonna get hurt. He should have put up a barrier."

Joe strode into his work station, found two boards, and made a cross which he drove into the ground in front of the pit. A couple of men came out and helped, wondering what this was all about as other employees gathered around the pit.

"What's going on?" Davie yelled as he pulled up beside them.

"That's what we want to know." Someone chimed in, "We thought YOU did it."

"Me! Well, I didn't know anything about it."

As he talked, he was dialing the Claxton Police Department. "Edna, could I speak to Chief Stanton?" After a pause, he asked, "Well, can you send a deputy to Oars and Boats on Big Creek Landing? Yeah. It's sort of an emergency. We've been struck by vandals."

The Police Department of Claxton took the situation seriously, unlike the Sheriff of Phillips County. Big Creek Landing was in the jurisdiction of Claxton Police Chief Jeb Stanton, and as soon as he heard about it, he suspected more than vandalism.

Deputies strung crime tape around the perimeter of the hole and searched more closely for any evidence left by the perpetrators. Two police cars guarded the hole. Officers sifted sand and picked up every scrap or smidgen of interest to examine further.

A lady in black shorts and a gray tank top jogging along the river approached curiously. "What crime has been committed?"

"Don't know as we can say," the policeman told her. "Maybe just vandalism. But we don't have anyone to charge yet."

The lady rearranged her headband and then jogged back up the river toward town.

Chief of Police Jeb Stanton pulled into the parking lot and asked Davie. "What happened here, Buddy?"

"Danged if I know," Davie blurted. "But the guys are telling me they're hearing about it everywhere. It happened up at the Gristmill Restaurant and at Pine Ridge Landing Saturday night and now here. Somebody is certainly intent on searching for something. But what?"

Davie talked with the chief about some options. "We can fill it back up and you can just remove the crime tape," Davie suggested. "Curiosity seekers are driving down here and turning around on our parking lot. Some people get out and take pictures. All these cars coming down here just to gawk at a hole in the ground, they're getting in our way—and on my nerves. I'd appreciate if you could stop it somehow. Maybe you could put a barrier down the road?"

During the past twelve years since Jeb Stanton had been hired by Claxton as its police chief, the Wellsly family had been his strongest supporters and he had tried to look after them. It wouldn't hurt to put up a roadblock. It was a dead-end road that ended at Davie's parking lot anyway. Nobody had any business down here except employees and customers of the business.

"Alright," he agreed. "We'll put up a barrier. We'll leave one lane open for your employees, but you know how people are."

"I know," Davie agreed. "But it's better than nothing; I appreciate it."

Within an hour, a barrier of black and white striped boards blocked one lane about a mile up from the river. A sign on the barrier boards said WDGW EMPLOYEES ONLY. At the end of Willow Street that ran from town and came to a T at Big Creek Road, a sign read NO LEFT TURN. It did not stop the flow of traffic completely, but most people did turn around, or turned right and went on back out to Claxton Boulevard.

*

Isaac and Lillian heard the news on the radio when it woke them Monday morning. "A third mysterious pit has been dug along Big Creek."

The announcer said, "The holes are about the same size, six feet deep and about six feet wide, actually, a six-foot cube. They're about a hundred feet off the river. Interesting that they're all on Wellsly property. Which raises some questions. What is it someone's looking for? And who is it doing that digging in the middle of the night? Is something fishy going on down that river we call Big Creek?"

Lillian turned the radio off and climbed out of bed. As she headed to the bathroom, she said, "We need to pray, Isaac. It sounds like real trouble ahead."

Isaac reached for his pants on the chair by his side of the bed. "Sounds like trouble's already here, Lillian. Somebody knows what they're looking for. We just don't know who it is yet."

"You have any idea what it is they're looking for?" Lillian found a green pair of pants and matching top she wanted in the closet.

"Yeah, I do." Isaac buttoned his plaid shirt. "But I don't think they're going to find it."

"What do you think it is?" Lillian slipped into her favorite loafers. "You think we ought to run down to the Landing and talk with Davie?"

"No, we'll talk with him later. Right now, we'd just be in the way. Besides I'm ready for some breakfast."

Lillian laughed. "I wondered what that rumbling was."

Chapter 5 Beauty Shop Talk

Monday morning, April 1

Jane's Beauty Shop and Pretty Woman Day Spa was bustling with activity. Mondays were never busy, and especially the day after Easter, but this year was different. Churches had made it "hat day" in honor of Mrs. Ida Fox's birthday. She turned 105 on Easter Sunday. She had never been seen without a hat, so almost every woman in town wore a hat to celebrate her this year.

On Monday they were back in the beauty shops preparing for the Spring Festival with new haircuts, perms, or color. This year's festival promised to be the best one ever with Mrs. Ida Fox, as Festival Queen, riding the Spring Hill Retirement Home float.

There would be carnival rides and activities for children. There would be art shows and concerts. There would be booths sporting the handcrafts and talents of area residents. Even Jane's top stylist, Nancy Wellsly, was planning a booth to show off her hobby, her crochet creations. Besides locals, numerous visiting artisans, clubs, and groups would be selling their wares or performing.

The Claxton news had been publishing articles every day about the upcoming events with applications for booths and registration forms for the many events. It was an annual festival that had grown over the past ten years and brought in thousands of visitors.

This morning's news was not in the paper yet. But word had spread like wildfire, so the topic in the beauty shop was not the upcoming festival. It was speculation about the three mysterious pits. The condition of Rebecca Willis was a concern. She was at Claxton Medical Center in a coma.

As stories spread, the holes got bigger. Because there were three of them, and they were about six feet deep, somebody got the idea that it was 666 and suggested it was the devil that did it. That created another spur of fear. Somebody thought they were bomb shelters like in the fifties.

Nancy Wellsly's imagination was not that wild, but she was disturbed. "Can you believe this?" Nancy said to Jane and the others. "Right down the road from my house, and I knew nothing about it! It sure rattled my nerves when Ray told me he heard it on the scanner."

Rachel Lee-Anders admitted, "It disturbed me, and I don't live on that road. What were they doing, digging up bodies? Or trying to bury some?"

"That's a morbid thought," Miss Rhoda, the head massage therapist, shuddered.

"It's big enough to bury a Volkswagen," noted Sharon Kramerton, whose husband ran a dealership.

"Or a baby grand piano," Deanie George, the town's premier music teacher imagined.

"Maybe it wasn't bodies. I hope!" Nancy threw up her hands.

Sharon wondered aloud, "Why did whoever dug the holes leave them empty? They must have had to leave in a hurry."

Rachel was intent on pursuing her theory, "Maybe they intended to bury something and were interrupted and left. Or maybe they're still planning to come back and bury it. Bodies probably."

Carol Evans, Jane's long-time receptionist said, "I got some pictures from my friend who works at the boat plant." She passed around her phone with pictures revealing a hole almost directly in front of WDGW Oars and Boat's blue steel building which housed the manufacture of a variety of boats. A dock on the Ingles Creek side of the plant held several boats in different stages of progress. In the background of some of the pictures was an elaborate yacht.

Chapter 6 Night Light

Monday evening, April 1

The boat plant operated only during the day since the completion of the yacht project. So everyone was gone by dark—except for Davie. He often worked late, developing his ideas, creating designs, and planning.

Occasionally, George Rutherford would work late with him. But not often. George ran Oarlocks and Bagels for Davie's grandfather. Since George had graduated with his Business Administration degree from the University of South Carolina at Claxton, Isaac had practically turned the store over to him. George managed it and worked closely with Davie's boatbuilding business. He sold many of the products Davie built.

The story on the radio was that employees were under suspicion. They were questioned even to the point of interrogation, but they all had solid alibis and the police finally determined that it was not done by any of the WDGW Oars and Boats employees. Davie was asked by a news reporter if it was a project of the company.

What the reporter said on the air was, "Davie Wellsly just said, 'We build boats. We don't bury them.' "

At the end of the day, when his employees left, Davie stayed around trying to tie up loose ends and trying to make some sense out of everything that was happening. When he turned on the nightlights to leave, it was dark outside. The security light on a telephone pole outside had not come on.

A slight breeze fluttered the crime tape in the quietness. Gulls squawked their last calls and settled down for the night. Davie called the electric company's emergency number. They promised to be there in about an hour.

"Okay, that gives me enough time to go home for dinner." He would come back because he wanted to be here when they came.

Jenny would be waiting for him now. He winced thinking of his lovely wife and the fright they had had the other night. He had not felt imminent danger afterward, but disturbing events today put him to thinking. The past few years bore on his mind now. Was his good life ending too soon?

He and Jenny met at the university eight years ago and quickly became an item. She was a classic beauty with blonde hair and blue-gray eyes, eyes that changed color with the weather and her temperament. When she was happy, they were pure blue, but he had noticed how anger or frustration turned them a lavender-gray. He hadn't seen that very often. But she had a dimple on one cheek that flashed when she smiled. He had seen that a lot.

She had met the Wellsly clan's approval at first sight. Davie's Grandma Lillian and Grandpa Isaac would have adopted her if she had been an orphan. But she wasn't. Her family had moved to Claxton after her father was hired as head of the new Claxton Heart Center.

Dr. Marcus Rosenberg was a heart surgeon and his wife Zoey was a psychiatrist with her own private practice in Nashville. She stayed behind a few months to close her practice and let the kids finish out the school year before coming to Claxton. Jenny was seventeen and her brother Patrick was fifteen when they moved into Country Club Hills off Phillips County Country Club Road. Their closest neighbors were Louis and Renee Renoir, but they were not friends.

The Rosenbergs were down to earth, compassionate people. That was one thing that attracted Lillian and Isaac. They felt a kinship. And of course, Davie's mom and dad had been of the same mind. Jessica and Jimmy quickly embraced Jenny and were thrilled when, after two years of dating, the couple announced their engagement.

Of course, Davie's sister Caroline made a beautiful and graceful bridesmaid. At eighteen, she almost upstaged the bride at the wedding in her pink satin and sheer gown. But she and Jenny had become fast friends, and Jenny had chosen everything in colors and styles that flattered them both.

It had been a blessing how the two families had meshed. They all went to New Covenant Church for All People in downtown Claxton, the church that Lillian and Isaac had founded back in the sixties. The pastor Rev. Daniel Rutherford officiated at Davie and Jenny's wedding.

The Rutherfords had been pastoring the church a dozen years now. Their adopted son, George, was Davie's best friend and was best man at the wedding. Davie in turn was best man for George. They had been best friends even before George, who was Giorgio back then, ran away and ultimately escaped the captivity of convicted human trafficker, Alana Rodriguez. A horrible story no one knew until it was over.

George's life was changed dramatically after that. Along with his brothers, who had also been abducted, he was taken in by the pastor and adopted. He graduated from high school, earned a college degree, and was hired by Isaac Wellsly to run the Oarlocks and Bagels Complex on the waterfront.

George Rutherford was well known for having a good business head and being a man of integrity. He had married Paulette Mills, always known as Lettie. She was voted the prettiest girl in their senior class, and George was voted the best looking boy.

Davie had been voted most likely to succeed. His total ambition was to develop his boatbuilding business, and everyone knew he would succeed.

After six years of marriage, Davie and Jenny had no children, but they had talked about it. His parents and grandparents tried discretely to broach the subject periodically. Especially his grandma. But he and Jenny had not felt ready to start a family yet.

Jenny's parents were more career-oriented and hadn't made an issue. But maybe in a year or so. In the meantime, he had his boatbuilding business going strong and Jenny enjoyed her Burgundy Blue Boutique, which was situated right next to Lillian's Riviera, that five-star classy restaurant his grandma owned on the waterfront.

These had been happy years. At only twenty-six, Davie felt very fortunate to have been able to choose the life he wanted. He had the girl of his dreams and a house on Big Creek Road across the street from his parents and grandparents.

This gaping hole mysteriously dug on his property now suddenly seemed foreboding. That on top of the incident the other night. For a moment he wondered if there was a connection. But he shook that off. Then he thought of Jeffry Smythe and felt sick in the pit of his stomach.

When he approached the black and white striped barrier, he pulled it back far enough to allow the Phillips Electric Company truck to pass. He would run back down here in an hour and wait inside if they hadn't shown up.

Jenny greeted him at the door with a big hug and a kiss. They still felt like newly-weds. She loved him and his family. Mrs. Lillian and Jessica were out-of-this-world cooks, and both had taken her under their wings, sharing their amazing artistry in the kitchen.

With the Wellsly Gristmill Restaurant & Resort, they had become famous for good food. The Bagel Diner inside the Oarlocks and Bagels Complex and Lillian's Riviera only added to their fame.

Jenny didn't want to break that tradition and had been a good student, cultivating impressive culinary skills of her own. She laughed aloud thinking about Caroline, her beautiful sister-in-law, and friend who had not followed the family tradition.

Everybody knew Caroline couldn't boil water without burning the pot. But she was a virtuoso pianist who could enrapture an audience. She had performed many concerts in Claxton and had performed in New York and Nashville.

It was in Nashville where she met and eventually married another musician, Paul Jason Jackson who was a country singer and guitarist. He was on the road a lot. Sometimes Caroline went with him. But she had her own career, and they were often traveling separately. They maintained a home here on Big Creek Road, but they were seldom home.

Jenny worried about them. "That could be a recipe for trouble," she had thought and always prayed for them.

As Davie sat down at her beautifully appointed table and began enjoying the dinner she had prepared, he slumped from the weight on his shoulders.

Jenny watched him. He was a strong dark-haired gentleman. When he wore a cowboy hat--which he sometimes did after Caroline brought him one from Nashville--he looked like he was right out of the movies. A young Sam Elliot, but without the mustache. He always told his grandpa, "You look just like Sam Elliot." His grandpa would say, "Look in the mirror, boy." It was a private joke.

Jenny reached over and patted Davie's hand. "You're looking pensive tonight. You're worried about that mysterious hole in the ground."

He winced. "Yes, I am. But there's something else. I tried to call Jeffry Smythe again today."

"Oh?"

"Today, I got an answer, but it was not Jeffry Smythe. The man on the phone said Jeffry passed away about a month ago."

"What? Oh, no!" Jenny picked up her napkin and held it over her mouth. Her heart sank.

"A month ago?"

Davie continued. "I told him I was so sorry. When I asked who I was speaking to, the man said 'a friend of the family.' I was so shocked, I didn't know what to say. I said, 'I have his yacht,' then I asked if Julie was there. And the man hung up."

"Really? Why? What in the world? A month ago and nobody ever let us know? Not even Julie. Poor thing. I know she's devastated. But why didn't somebody call us?"

"I called back, and there was no answer, not even voice mail."

"Did it sound like the same man who had answered before?"

"I couldn't tell."

"What are we going to do?" Jenny fretted. "This is awful. It's too weird. It's terrible."

Davie agreed. "And now that hole in the ground. I can't tell you how many phone calls I've had today asking me questions. I had no answers."

"Yeah," Jenny said. "Even at the boutique, I was asked about it."

Davie continued, "Some people think we're expanding again, and that hole is for a corner foundation. Two people came in asking to fill out applications today."

"Seriously?" Jenny asked.

"Seriously!

"People sure can jump to conclusions," she said. "Some people get their only exercise that way."

Davie grunted, "Yeah, jumping to conclusions."

Jenny groaned, "I can't get over that about Jeffry. What will we do?"

"I don't know. I've been depressed all day. That stupid hole didn't help."

"What do you suppose it is all about?" Jenny asked.

"I have no idea. I've speculated just like everybody else. Grandpa said he thinks it's related to that old Riddick mob from years ago. He suspects that somebody thinks there's a chest buried along there. Riddick's men were actually the pirates of Big Creek for years, you know."

Jenny shook her head. "No, I didn't know that. That was all before my time. I have heard some things, but mostly in the context of people being glad it's all over."

"Sometimes it's still fresh for Grandma and Grandpa, though.

Jenny's mind was going in a different direction and she laughed, "What if? Davie, have you thought about it? What if there is some buried treasure out there on the grounds?"

"What are you thinking?" He asked.

"Well, I was just wondering, if there is and we found it, would it be ours?"

Davie laughed. "That's a good question. I think it would be. Just like in a shipwreck. Depending on what it is, though. I mean, if it was gold from Fort Knox, we couldn't keep it."

Jenny laughed. "Well, you know there's no gold from Fort Knox buried out there."

Davie shook his head. "But I wouldn't put anything past that mob, based on what I've heard Grandpa say."

"You know," Jenny got serious. "If people get the idea that there is buried treasure out there, they're going to come flocking in from everywhere, digging holes, and searching for something. Have you thought of that?"

He nodded. "I sure have. That's one reason I asked the police to put up the barrier. But that only slowed it down a little. It didn't stop it. Having police cars out there helped—and armed policemen."

"But you know what?" Jenny stood and started clearing the dishes. "The police can't stay there forever, and if people have this idea, they'll be back."

Davie nodded. "Have you ever heard that if you break a mirror you'll have seven years of bad luck?"

Jenny sat back down. "I've heard all kinds of superstitions, Davie, but they're just superstitions. Don't get that in your head. Besides, you didn't break that mirror."

"I set it up after it was moved upstairs and I screwed the mirror to the chest. I just didn't do it well enough."

"Don't go thinking like that."

The clock on the wall in the foyer chimed eight o'clock. "It's time. The electric company should be down there by now. I have to run back down to the plant."

"Okay, be careful," she gave him a goodbye kiss as he hurried out the door.

As she stood at the door watching him leave, she shivered but couldn't shake off the eerie feeling.

Chapter 7 April Fools or Aliens

Monday evening, April 1

Davie had hardly been away more than an hour. He didn't notice anything at first. It was dark. The moon was still just a sliver behind a cloud, and, of course, the parking lot was dark. When he got down to the plant, the electric company's truck pulled in behind him.

He had gone to school with Carl. The name patch on the other man's shirt was John. They were both jovial and friendly. They wore yellow hard hats with an emblem that matched the one on the huge yellow truck they were driving. John climbed into the bucket with a basketball-sized bulb in a box, and Carl cranked it up to the top of the pole.

"Looks like it was hit by a rock," John yelled down to Davie.

Carl surmised, "Probably some prankster kids."

They watched as John took out the broken bulb and replaced it with the new one. After the bucket was lowered back down, John dialed a number and spoke into the phone that was attached to his belt. A second later the light came on.

Carl gestured. "Well, there you have it. That's always been something kids like to do, to show off in front of their friends. I can't tell you how many we have to replace."

Davie was frustrated. "But out here in the boondocks? Kids hang out where bars and other people are, not out here." He motioned around him. Only then did he notice that there was no crime tape.

There was no hole in the ground. Everything looked normal. That gave him the creeps even more than finding the gaping hole in the first place.

"Y'all didn't get here ahead of me, did you?" Davie asked.

Carl spoke up. "No, we pulled in right behind you."

"And you didn't see any other vehicles on the parking lot? Did you meet anybody down the road?"

Carl shook his head. "We didn't meet any cars, trucks, or anything. Looked like everybody was home, settled in for the evening."

Davie was visibly disturbed. "What do you make of this?" He asked. "When I left here, there was a hole in the ground, six feet across, with a bank of dunes on the other side. Crime tape was on sticks all around the perimeter. Who could have filled it in that quickly? I mean, you can't even tell it was ever disturbed."

John and Carl walked over to the plot of ground with him. The newly repaired nightlight gave ample light to see. But there was nothing to see. Davie shuddered. "This is really weird."

"The only thing that comes to my mind is an April fools' joke or more likely, aliens," Carl guessed. "I mean, you see stuff on television about aliens doing things like this. Maybe they swooped down and filled it up and took off. Maybe they're the ones who dug it in the first place."

"Maybe they buried something that could send messages back up to them," John said. "I mean, there had to be a reason for the hole to be dug."

"That makes sense," Davie said. "I don't want to believe that though. I wouldn't be as much afraid of pranksters and crooks as I would be aliens."

Carl walked over to the area. "On television when they show things about it, sometimes the ground is charred where something landed and took off. Maybe we need to search the ground for evidence of something like that."

"Yeah," Davie said. "But you sure can't tell anything tonight. As good as the light is, it's not showing anything like that."

"What are you gonna do?" Carl asked.

"What would you do?" Davie asked. He wanted to know their opinion. He was grasping for straws himself.

"To tell you the truth," John said, "I'd just get the heck outta here. It's giving me the creeps right now!"

Carl nodded his head. "I'm thinking like John. I don't know anything. Davie, I hope this gets resolved soon. Keep us informed. And call the electric company if the light goes out again."

"You might need a security guard on duty all night," John suggested.

"Yeah, and who would take that job if they heard what we're thinking?" Carl asked.

Davie grunted, "UGH. That's a good point. I feel like I'm in the Twilight Zone. Maybe we should just not say anything. I know the police will be back out here tomorrow, but there's nothing to guard now."

"I'll say a prayer for you," John stuck out his hand

"Me too," Carl extended his hand.

Davie shook their hands, "I need it. Thank you. I'll keep in touch, and thanks for the light!"

As he passed the barrier that had been set aside, Davie didn't bother to put it back. It seemed to be a futile effort. He was dealing with something bigger than curiosity seekers.

He pulled in the driveway and tooted the horn to alert Jenny. He met her at the door. "Come on, we need to go talk with Mom and Dad."

In the car, he told her what he had found at the river. They drove a hundred yards up to his parents' driveway. He was already on the phone with his Dad.

Jessica met them at the door. "What in the world's going on?"

Davie explained in detail. "There's not even any sign of the crime tape. They must have buried that, too. I'm not usually scared of anything, but I have to admit, this has got me."

Jenny snuggled up to him as they sat together in a wide armchair. "It's scaring me. I've never heard of anything like this."

Jimmy wondered, "You reckon we should call Jeb? Maybe we ought to have it dug back out and see if something was buried there."

"But not tonight. Everything we do has to be in broad daylight," Jessica declared.

"And with a lot of people around," Jenny chimed in. "Preferably armed policemen."

"Y'all want to spend the night here?" Jessica asked. "Davie's room is still available. I mean, not that I don't think you'd be safe at home, but I'd just like you to stay."

Jenny looked at Davie. "Let's stay here."

He shrugged. "Maybe it wouldn't hurt. But don't tell anybody we were scared to go home. I'd never live that down."

"Not with Caroline," Jimmy laughed. "She could hold that over your head forever."

"But I bet she wouldn't stay at her house alone if she were home right now," Davie looked at his mom. "When's she due back anyway?"

Jessica smiled happily. "Next week. She's supposed to perform at the Spring Festival. Maybe this will all be over by then."

Chapter 8 Vandalized

Tuesday morning, April 2

Jessica insisted that Davie and Jenny have breakfast before leaving, so it was almost eight o'clock Tuesday morning before they drove back into their driveway. They were in a hurry. Davie needed to be at the plant by eight o'clock and Jenny needed to open the boutique at nine. She ran on to the house, and he went to the mailbox to pick up the paper. He was almost to the mailbox when he heard Jenny scream.

His feet barely touch the ground as he dashed back up the driveway to the front door.

Ransacked!

Sofa cushions were on the floor. Drawers were open. Cabinets were open in the kitchen. Davie's desk in the den/office had been rifled. Papers were strewn. In a flash, he thanked God they had spent the night at his mom's.

Jenny dialed Jessica with fingers trembling. In five minutes, Jessica and Jimmy were there. Davie dialed the police department and spoke to Chief Jeb, and then called his grandparents. They arrived within minutes. Jenny refused to pick up a cushion or touch anything. She closed no cabinet doors nor drawers.

She defied her panic and took pictures, frantically. She zoomed in on handles and cabinet doors, daring to hope it would pick up fingerprints, even knowing that whoever did this would have worn gloves. She felt violated, as did the entire family.

Upstairs she checked her jewelry chest in the bedroom. Ironically, everything was in place. Even the things Davie's great grandmother had given her which she knew were valuable.

In the dining room, there was plenty of crystal, brass, and gold trinkets, candlesticks, a brass menorah, and statuettes, much of it also from Davie's great-grandmother. It all appeared to be in place which meant they were looking for something in particular.

Isaac observed the situation and wondered if his previous conclusion was right. "It must be the same ones who dug those pits. They are seriously looking for something, Davie, which they think you might have."

"They were interested in the file cabinet. But why?" Davie scratched his head as he looked around.

"Is all the damage inside? What about outside? Have you looked in the shelter where you keep your boats and all that gear?"

"No." Davie went out the back door with Isaac following. A table was turned over and cushions tossed out of the chairs. His boats were in the shelter. A fishing tackle box and a tool chest were open, but he couldn't tell if anything was missing.

Isaac looked around. "You've got so much stuff that it's hard to tell if anything's missing. You won't know till you need it and can't find it."

When Jeb arrived he questioned Davie, "Have you dealt with any unseemly characters in the business lately? Can you remember any incidents? Have you made anybody mad? Sorry, just looking for possible reasons someone might want to do this. What about that big yacht? Who did you build that big fancy yacht for? They haven't picked it up yet. Do you suppose there's a connection?"

Davie threw up his hands, "Whoa. Sounds like you think this is my fault."

"Oh, I'm sorry, Davie. Let's start over. I didn't mean to sound accusing. I'm grasping for a motive."

"Yeah, I'd like to know that, too." Davie sighed. "No. I can't think of any incident that would provoke this. As far as the yacht is concerned, I'm sure there is no connection to its owner. I've been trying to reach him for the past two months, but now they're telling me he died. I hope there's a mistake."

Jeb offered to check on that if Davie would give him the name and address.

"I can give you all the records. It's in the cabinet at the plant, though."

"Do you have a vault or safe deposit box anywhere in the house?" Jeb asked.

"Yeah, but it's not been touched. I guess they couldn't find it." He laughed at Jenny's cleverness at concealing it in plain view. She also had a desk in their den/office where she planned and designed for her boutique.

Jeb turned to Jenny. "Do you have clients who could possibly have done this?"

She thought for a minute shaking her head. "I deal with a lot of crazies, but I doubt any of my clients would have done this. I'll share my files with you."

The house phone rang. Davie answered, and looked at Jeb. "We need to go to the plant."

"What's going on now?" Jenny asked, afraid to hear Davie's answer. But he didn't explain, and Chief Jeb had not heard him. He was also receiving a call and heading toward the door.

Jimmy asked, "You need me?" Davie shook his head. "No, you go on to work. I've got this." But he grabbed Isaac's arm and said, "Come with me to the plant, Grandpa. We got another problem."

Chapter 9 At the Day Spa

Tuesday morning, April 2

A**cross town on the waterfront** at *Jane's Beauty Shop and Pretty Woman Day Spa*, before any patrons arrived, Jane, Carol, Nancy, Rachel, Sharon, and Miss Rhoda were in intense discussion, preparing for their day, and sharing their speculations about the strange events.

There was plenty in the newspaper about the holes being dug, though nothing about the one at Davie's Landing being refilled. Except that one of Nancy's clients was married to Carl, the electrician who had snapped a picture. She sent it to Nancy with the caption, "What if it was aliens?"

"This just disturbs me," Nancy shared the picture and caption with her coworkers.

Jane cautioned the others. "We probably should not talk about this. It could be just a prank. But it could cause a panic if it got out of hand. Whether it was a UFO or not, people would go crazy around here."

"I think you're right," Sharon said. "I don't think I'll even tell my husband. He watches that Roswell stuff on television and he believes it all. I'm sure he would think it was a UFO."

Rachel was still sticking to her original thought. "I think whoever it was, dug a hole and left, and then they came back with the bodies last night. Must be more than one body, big as that hole is. And I think it was humans. Somebody ruthless and wicked. If they had their strategy all worked out, they could have come in there, dumped the bodies, and raked that dirt in quickly. If there were enough of them, they could do it in no time."

"You've been watching too many horror movies, Rachel. Why would somebody pick that place anyway?" Carol was annoyed at the idea.

Rachel said, "I have to think on that."

"Well, that's probably what happened," Nancy said. "When I saw Davie's truck over at his mama's house, I knew something was wrong because I already knew about that hole being dug. I called Jessica, and she told me the hole had been filled back up. But she said don't tell it. Davie wants to talk with Jeb about it first. I told her my lips are sealed." She did a motion as though to lock her lips, and then said, "But now you all know, and I can't get it off my mind."

"Well, I like being in the know," Rachel said. "But I don't think it was aliens. There're too many other explanations."

"Yeah," Miss Rhoda looked at her watch and stood up. "But let's keep our ears open. You know we have a lot of different types coming through here. And some of them like to talk. We might hear something."

"Ears open and mouths shut," Nancy locked her lips again.

The bell jingled on the front door and everyone scurried to meet their guests for the day.

Carol greeted six women brightly and welcomed them to *Jane's Beauty Shop and Pretty Woman Day Spa.* Regular customers were arriving for appointments and three walk-ins came with them.

That's the way it was with boat people. Boats would dock at the waterfront, some staying a few hours, others a few days. A lot of people slept on their boats, from simple houseboats to luxurious yachts, but those people were mostly all alike—suntanned and shapely. Some were well-weathered but trying to maintain their youthful luster. That's what turned *Jane's Beauty Shop and Pretty Woman Day Spa* into the mega shop it was.

These today were still young and wore their beauty nonchalantly. They obviously worked out or got a lot of exercise somewhere. They didn't just "lay-out" on boat decks in the sun all day, though they were well-tanned.

As Day Planner, Carol set up each walk-in's day of activities. It was a Rubik's Cube of a task, working walk-ins around the standing appointments. The Spa offered a Jacuzzi, facials, massages, manicures, pedicures, and eyebrow shaping, as well as routine hair styling and treatment. Some things could only be done by appointment.

Each of the walk-ins signed in to begin her Pretty Woman Day with various routines. Patrons with appointments greeted them. Boat people were always a curiosity.

Walk-in, Jackie Summerlin, was friendly, a pretty redhead whose first activity would be a massage. Miss Rhoda welcomed her graciously and chatted a minute as she led her to a private room where assistant Sue Cox was ready with towels and a robe. Sue took over, explained the routine, and gave the patron a choice of music to be piped into her private cubby. The young lady seemed excited to choose Celine Dione. She said she had been in Vegas recently and attended Dione's concert.

Jamie Sampson from Boca Raton was guided to the pedicure chairs lining the wall in the Mani-Pedi room. There, she was welcomed and seated by pedicurist Kelly Minetti, who offered her a selection of magazines. Miss Sampson was shapely and toned, apparently a fitness fan. It was no surprise that she wanted to read Shape magazine. She asked if the Spa served wine. "I'm sorry, we don't," Kelly said. "I can get you a soda or water."

"Usually I have wine, but it is early," she admitted. "Water will be fine. Is there a shop around here that sells open-toed shoes or sandals with bling? I need some red ones."

Kelly answered, "Shoes Unlimited is on Claxton Boulevard. There's Walmart on the edge of town and there's Sears and a couple of places at the Blue Danube Mall. I'm sure one of them will have something fancy to show off those pretty toes," she smiled. "You going to a party?"

"I just like them," Sampson started thumbing through her magazine. As Kelly prepared the footbath, she tried to start a conversation, "Where are you from?"

"Chesapeake, Virginia," the lady said without thinking.

"Oh, I thought Carol said Boca Raton."

"Oh. Yes, I meant that." She spoke with a tone that implied *no more questions*. Kelly got the message and just continued with the pedicure quietly.

Sharon Krammerton who managed the Jacuzzi, led the third walk-in, Joliet Swan, to her area and introduced her to Lena Mills. Lena pointed out the display of essential oils and fragrances for her to choose among.

"O-o-o, I just love thiz jasmine," the lady said with a French accent. After sniffing a few others, she went back to the jasmine continuing to gush about the fragrance.

"Good choice Miss Swan," Lena amiably showed her some matching products.

"Just call me Jo," the lady suggested. "I'll see those before I leave. I just want to relax a little. I was up all night. Don't let me fall asleep and drown," she slipped into the jasmine-scented Jacuzzi, leaned her head back, and closed her eyes.

What pressure! Lena didn't dare leave the room now. She didn't want a drowning. And that woman didn't look too stable. After a few minutes, Lena turned the Jacuzzi to cold and spoke to her patron. "You awake?"

"Oooo," she shivered. "I am now. Thiz water is cold."

"Yeah, time to get out," Lena said. "Let's get your hair done. You got it wet."

"Well...I...okay. Hand me my robe."

"We'll get you set up with Nancy for your hair. While you wait, you can relax back here on the sofa."

"Oui, oui, c'est sympa, merci beaucoup. I mean, this is nice, thank you very much," Joliet Swan sank into the sofa and went to sleep.

Nancy was usually very confident and enjoyed her work, but today she was rattled by the strange things happening, so she wasn't her competent self when Carol told her Joliet Swan would be with her at eleven o'clock.

The shop was a beehive, but there was less talk than usual because everyone was afraid of divulging their secret. It would not be a secret long.

The radio playing softly on Carol's desk got her attention. She turned it up to hear better as the DJ said, "Strange things are happening in Claxton today. On Big Creek Road, in a neighborhood of upper-class homes, where no crime has ever been reported, there has been some strange activity in the past few days. Is it a prank or a crime? What's with that huge pit dug on the landing by WDGW Oars and Boats? Mr. Wellsly claims his company didn't do it. So now it's filled back up and no problem. What is Mr. Wellsly hiding? Is he the victim or the perpetrator? Is this a joke or just a six-foot deep misunderstanding? Stay tuned for further information after this." He played a jazzy country hit and then resumed his talk about the strange news.

"Well, now it seems that Mr. Wellsly's home has been ransacked. What's going on in the Big Creek Road community? If you have seen anything suspicious, call this station. There's a $1000 reward for information leading to the arrest of these vandals. Call us at this number and tell us what you know. Or just tell us what you think." He repeated the number.

Nancy said, "Turn that down please, Carol. I think he's just trying to stir up something. I hope nobody's listening."

"Well, they are," Rachel said. "And you can rest assured, he will get calls. People love a good mystery. He's just trying to build his ratings. I've known DJ Reeves a long time. Went to school with him. He's a creep!"

Jane said, "I think there's already been too much speculation. It concerns me that their house has been vandalized. And with this on the radio, there's no telling where it will lead. Are you next, Nancy? You live next door, don't you?"

Nancy shuddered. "Yes, I do, and I'm worried about Jenny and Davie. They don't deserve this."

Rachel spun her patron around so she could look in the mirror. "I wonder if it was just random or if they were targeted for some reason."

Her patron nodded, "I like that."

Nancy said, "They were targeted for sure. It was their place on the river and now their house. Somebody's looking for something. I just don't understand them filling that pit back up though. Unless they buried something."

"Well, they should have known the police would dig it up again. Criminals can be so stupid," Jane lowered her patron and walked her over to the dryers.

Carol said, "Unless it's all just a big prank."

Nancy was preparing her next patron for a new haircut. "It's not a prank when your house is ransacked. Somebody is looking for something. I think I need to go home."

Carol pointed out, "You've got four appointments today besides that walk-in at eleven. You'd need to have someone cover for you or let me call everybody. And I know one who won't be too happy. You know how Renee Renoir is, and you've got her at one o'clock."

Nancy sighed, "I know. But it's hard to get my mind on work."

Jane sympathized. "I'll take the walk-in for you at eleven. Why don't you leave then? Run check on things at home and be back here for your one o'clock."

Nancy snapped up that offer. "Thanks, Jane. I appreciate that. At least I can check on Ray. I called and he didn't answer, but I figured he was walking Trixie. He takes her out every day. I think it benefits Ray more than it does the dog."

"That's why God gave us dogs," Carol said. They all agreed and began talking about the value of having a dog and wishing they had time to walk one.

Nancy's attention was diverted to the dogs on Big Creek Road and how they had played such a big part in the lives of the family. She reminded them that Bruiser, the town's canine hero, was Isaac and Lillian's dog. Now a monument stood right outside in front of Lillian's Riviera just like the one at Bruiser's Park down at the Gristmill Resort.

"I remember," Rachel said. "And I remember that wreck about ten years ago. It was kind of mysterious. One of those women said a black dog caused it, and the other one said it was a black dog that dragged her out and saved their lives."

"And the boy that was missing. He saw that same dog, I think he credited that dog for saving his life," Carol said.

"You think there's anything to that?" A patron asked as she walked in on the discussion about the dogs.

"I do," Nancy said. "God can use anything. In the Bible, he used a donkey. Our pastor preached on that Sunday. That story in Numbers in the Old Testament."

The patron shook her head and rolled her eyes as she sat down in the chair Nancy had waiting for her. She didn't care to hear it.

Nancy shrugged and just turned her attention to shampooing the lady's hair. She looked at Jane and did the key turning motion at her mouth to indicate she was keeping her mouth shut.

Jane smiled and nodded then welcomed her next appointment coming in the door.

Chapter 10 Cleaning Up

Tuesday morning, April 2

Before Davie could get out of the house, Jenny grabbed his arm. "What is going on?" Davie stepped back and hugged her. "It'll be alright, it's that hole that was filled up last night. It's been dug out again and nobody knows how. I've got to get out there. Will you be alright? Mom and Grandma are here. And the deputy."

Jenny just blinked and nodded. It was all happening so fast.

Davie grabbed Isaac's arm. "Come with me, Grandpa. Maybe we can find a clue out there." Jenny noticed his hands trembling as he pulled out his keys.

"Hang on. I'll call you." But she followed him as he dashed out the door almost running into Nancy who had come through the opening in the hedges between their yards.

Nancy dodged him and rang the doorbell although the door was open. A board was partially ripped off the frame. Lillian beckoned her to come on in.

Nancy said, "It was on the radio at work. I wanted to come check on y'all."

"Can you believe this, Nan?" Lillian gave her a hug and said, "Jessica's cleaning up the kitchen. You can help her. Also, the police want to talk to you and Ray to see if you heard anything. It had to be after ten o'clock. I'm so glad they spent the night with Jimmy."

"Oh, my gosh! They could have been killed!" Nancy exclaimed.

Coming up behind her, Jenny said, "All this scares me to death, Aunt Nancy." She had followed Davie to the truck and brought back papers Isaac had picked up before Davie grabbed him.

"I'm glad you came." She said sadly as she hugged her and almost teared up. Her eyes had turned the dark blue-gray of storm clouds gathering. She blinked rapidly like she had done all morning to hold back tears.

"Davie just ran to the plant," she explained. "I don't know what's happening out there. He said the hole has been dug out again. Deputy Willis wants to talk with you and Uncle Ray."

While she was talking, Officer Willis came in from the den with an iPad and stylus. "Yes, to see if you heard anything last night," he said.

"You know what? We might have." Nancy greeted the deputy. "About four o'clock this morning Trixie had a barking fit and woke us up. We figured she had heard a raccoon or something."

"Did you look out the window and see anything or hear anything yourself--other than the dog barking?"

Nancy shook her head. "No, I didn't. Ray got up and looked around in our house. He didn't turn on any lights. Trixie sleeps in our bedroom, but she had gone downstairs, maybe because she heard something. Ray went down but didn't notice anything. Trixie came on back upstairs with him. After a while, she barked again, but Ray just quieted her down. Do you want to talk with Ray? He's over at the house now."

"Yes," Officer Willie nodded. "I'll step over there if you don't mind. I'd like to get that down for the record. In the meantime, if a reporter calls you, it'd be best not to divulge anything. It'll be safer if whoever did this does not know we know anything."

"Oh, my," Nancy clapped her hand over her mouth. "That is so scary. Ray's going to have his gun ready tonight."

Lillian shuddered. "I sure hope it won't come to that. Our only protection is God." Then she laughed. "Sorry God, I didn't mean it to sound that way."

Jessica came in with a dishtowel in her hand. Another policeman had come in the back way and dusted everything for fingerprints. She was wiping the cabinets down.

"I know, Mrs. Lillian," Jessica blew a sigh of relief. "It makes me weak to think what could have happened. They're staying with us again tonight."

"Has Davie learned anything more about the digging?" Nancy wanted to know.

Jessica looked at the deputy shaking his head, then turned toward the door as someone else came up the steps.

Without ringing the bell or knocking, the striking dark-haired professional woman in a beige suit and pink blouse came through the open door. Her pumps were the exact beige of her suit. A wide belt with a filigree design of pink and beige completed her sharp look. Jenny ran and fell into her arms.

Zoey Rosenberg consoled her daughter who finally let the tears flow and sobbed. "Somebody's going to pay for this," Zoey hugged Jenny and stroked her hair.

"We hope so," the deputy tipped his hat at Zoey.

Jenny pulled herself together, wiped her eyes, and introduced her mother to the officers. "Dr. Zoey Rosenberg, she's a psychiatrist at the hospital."

After they all greeted Zoey, the deputy taking fingerprints left. Jessica, Lillian, and Nancy went to the kitchen. Jenny sat down on the sofa with her mother and told her everything that had happened. Not that Dr. Rosenberg hadn't already heard, but Jenny needed to tell her. You couldn't look at the room and tell anything had happened now.

Everything was back in place and the living room was restored to Jenny's artistic charm. A blue velvet sofa and loveseat with a matching round ottoman were complimented by assorted pillows in shades of blue. Dark blue drapes framed huge windows and hung to the floor barely touching the sculptured white carpet. The blue walls were outlined by white woodwork.

One dark blue wall featured a white fireplace with assorted brass ships lining the mantel. Centered above the mantel was a mirror that looked like a ship's porthole. Paintings on the wall displayed nautical scenes that Jenny had selected from an art show to complete the theme of the room. Of course, Davie loved it. Blue was his favorite color and his livelihood was building boats.

Complimented with lamps and lush plants, Jenny's living room rivaled Mrs. Lillian's for elegance and style. A chandelier in the center could be adjusted from a soft romantic glow to daylight bright. The large windows gave ample lighting now.

After Jenny and her mother had talked a while, Jessica came in. "I have the table set, everybody come get some lunch." The Wellsly solution to most problems was good food. Right now, everyone needed something; she insisted they sit down and have tea or coffee or soda. A platter of assorted sandwiches and fruit made an inviting centerpiece in the dining room.

Nancy declined. "I ate a bite with Ray. But I'll have a glass of water with lemon. I can fix it."

Lillian helped herself and asked for coffee which Jessica poured into one of the blue Wedgwood china cups she had set on the table. The deputy accepted a sandwich and soda. He had been on the job for six hours and was ready for something. As soon as he finished, he excused himself. "I'll go next door and speak with Ray. I have to step back in the office and get my iPad." Nancy called Ray to let him know.

Neither Zoey nor Jenny would eat anything. Zoey was trying to convince Jenny to go home with her for the night. "Davie's not going to do that," Jenny told her. "He's going to stay close to everything here. And I need to stay with him. I'm worried about him. I wonder what's going on at the plant."

Her mother sighed. "I understand. I'm just thinking of your safety."

Lillian came into the room during that conversation. "I had even thought of us all going down to the resort. But I know the men won't agree to that. They'd rather stay here and guard the premises with their guns."

The deputy, coming out of the office with his iPad, offered a suggestion. "I'm pretty sure the chief will send a guard out here."

The phone rang. Jessica answered in the kitchen. It was Davie calling Jenny. "What's going on?" Jenny asked, then answered him, "Yes, I'm fine; we've got a lot done. Mom's here, Aunt Nan, your mom, and grandma. The deputy's going next door to talk with Uncle Ray. We've got the house back in order except for some things in the office. But what's going on there?"

"It's crazy, Jenny," Davie told her. "I don't know what's happening. When I got here and that hole was dug back out again, I about had a heart attack. I can't figure out why. But I'm glad Carl and John saw it last night. And Carl took a picture. So that proves it. Or I would have thought I was losing my mind."

"What in the world?" Jenny exclaimed. "I feel like I'm in the Twilight Zone."

"That's what I said," he told her.

"Did you know it was on the radio about our house being broken into?" she asked him.

"Oh, my Lord. No. I didn't know that! I didn't think anybody knew but the police and us."

"Well, everybody who listens to that morning show on RAT radio knows it. That's why Aunt Nancy came. She heard it at the beauty shop."

"I hate that show. They're always up to something." Davie clenched his jaw. "I'm sending Will Hasley up to the house now to fix the door. He's also gonna look at that hole I shot in the wall. I wanted you to know I'm sending him. I'm glad everybody's there helping you. I'll see if Jeb will keep the deputy there all day...hold on a minute." He paused a second then said, "Grandpa's going up there with Will. That's good."

"Okay, but what are you all doing?" She wanted to know.

"Sifting sand," he said. "The Chief is convinced there are clues in that dirt somewhere. We've got a crew operating a backhoe and a forklift. They're digging up huge buckets and dumping the dirt in tubs. Then sifting the dirt through screens. Looks like we're panning for gold or something. There's a dozen men out there working."

"Have you found anything?"

"One thing," he answered. "A jeweled cigarette lighter with the initials JS. That's not much to go on, but it sure doesn't belong to us. Tell Mama and Grandma. I'm sure they're praying about this already. Tell Grandma NOT to get a prayer chain going. Sometimes that leads to more talk. Right now, I'm leery of talking to anybody."

"Yeah, me too," she agreed. "I'll tell them that."

Jenny hung up the phone and talked with Jessica in the kitchen privately explaining everything Davie had told her.

"I think he's right," Jessica said. "We don't need to divulge anything we don't have to. You want to tell your mom, though? She's a psychiatrist. If anybody knows about keeping a confidence, it's her."

Jenny laughed. "You're right about that." She laid a ham and cheese sandwich on a plate and picked at it realizing she was hungrier than she thought. She went to the living room and offered her mom something again. Zoey gave in and went with her to the dining room. "What else do you have to do here?" Zoey asked as she layered a sandwich.

"I'm not through with the office yet," Jenny poured a glass of tea and said, "I'm the only one who knows what to do with those papers. But good company would be nice. How long can you stay?"

"I have a patient at two o'clock, so not too long, unless you need me. I'll call and cancel," she paused, but Jenny shook her head. "Well, I'll sit in your lovely office and watch while you restore it. This ham is delicious. Did you bake it?"

Jenny smiled. "I did. I'm learning from the pros."

"I'm impressed," her mom said. "Keep it up; maybe someday you can teach me." They laughed as they sat at the dining room table. The others had gravitated back to the living room.

Nancy stuck her head in to say goodbye, then on impulse came over and hugged Jenny. "I'm glad your mom's here. I'm going on over to the house and then back to work. We're here if there's anything we can do." She touched Zoey on the shoulder. "It's good to see you, Zoey. Hope next time it'll be under better circumstances."

"For sure!" Dr. Rosenberg agreed.

Nancy hugged Jessica and Lillian goodbye and again offered her help. "I'll certainly be praying about all this. And I'll keep my ears open and my mouth shut," she said and did that motion with locking her lips.

They laughed. Lillian said, "Yes, that's what we're all going to have to do. Thanks for coming, Nancy. I hope the information you're giving the police will be helpful."

"I hope so too," she said and headed back through the door just as Will Hasley, the carpenter, and Isaac came in. She hugged her cousin. Isaac said, "Thanks for coming, Nancy. We'll catch up with you later."

"Sure thing," she said and rushed on over to meet Ray and the deputy and then head back to work.

Dr. Rosenberg followed Jenny into her office. It was more than an office. A large den where she and Davie spent most of their time. They had matching mahogany desks where they spent creative hours designing their business ideas. Bookshelves reached almost to the ceiling. It was a corner room with double windows facing the street and one window facing the house next door where Nancy and Ray lived.

Natural wood slatted blinds remained partially closed between the gold drapes. Pictures, mirrors, and trinket-laden shelves left little of the deep burgundy walls showing. A burgundy leather sofa with matching wingback chair and a dark blue recliner provided ample comfort for Davie and Jenny to relax, or talk, or watch television.

A two-foot wide aquarium inset on one wall created a focal point between bookcases. It was mesmerizing to watch the scenic deep water with fish lazily swimming in and out of rock formations, green plants, and bubbles randomly drifting upward from the sandy bottom. It was always clean and clear.

Dr. Rosenberg sat in the blue recliner and gazed at the aquarium hypnotically. "I need one of these in my office. It could calm my patients down—and me too."

Jenny pulled a brochure from a desk drawer and handed it to her mother. "This is where we got it."

"Thanks," Zoey stuck it in her purse "I wish I could help you with all this." She gestured toward the pile of papers and books on the burgundy and gold patterned Oriental rug.

"It's okay," Jenny said. "It's just a matter of looking at everything and remembering where it goes. Some of it can be trashed, but I have to look at every piece to decide. That's the part I hate."

She picked up a stack of papers, spread them on her desk, and turned on the lamp. The mahogany file cabinet by her desk had been emptied on the floor. She would have to get Davie to go through the files from his desk which had also been emptied on the floor. A wave of sick nausea and anger engulfed her, and her voice cracked as she asked, "What were they looking for?"

Her mother got up and put her arm around her. "We'll find out," she comforted her. "We're putting this in God's hands. He knows."

"Thanks, Mom," Jenny grabbed a tissue from a box on her desk. "You go on to your appointment. Mrs. Lillian's here, and Mrs. Jessica. They'll keep me company and we'll call you if we learn anything."

Dr. Rosenberg looked at her watch and said, "I guess I should. It's one-thirty now. She kissed her daughter on the head and said, "Call me tonight. Your father's going to want to know how you are, too."

"Sure will, Mom." She followed her out and then stopped at the door and acknowledged the carpenter. Grandpa Isaac was lending a hand. "Good job, Mr. Hasley. It'll be good as new." She leaned in close to his ear. "Don't mention the bullet hole you're fixing. I don't think Davie wants them to know."

"Yeah, that's what he told me."

The deputy returned from his visit next door with information officially documenting the time of the break-in. Again, he cautioned, "We don't want this information out. Somebody was here at that time, and from the looks of it, there was more than one person. Probably good that you spent the night across the street."

"UGH!" Jenny shuddered, wondering if there had also been someone in the house when they heard that crash the other night.

Chapter 11 Renee Renoir

Tuesday afternoon, April 2

Nancy arrived back at the beauty shop at one o'clock just in time for her next appointment, Renee Renoir. Oh, *boy,* she thought when she saw her client already waiting, *Just what I needed today.* Aloud she spoke cheerily, "Hello, Renee. How are you doing?"

"Well, I was doing fine till now. I thought I'd come in a little early. I figured you'd be here and might go ahead and get started. I have a big evening and thought maybe I could finish here a little earlier, but you weren't here. Oh, well. I should have known."

Nancy's jaw clenched, but she tried not to let it show. She paused a second. "I'm sorry, Renee. My husband's not feeling well, and I ran home for lunch and checked on him."

"What's wrong with him?" Renee challenged.

Nancy looked at Jane, rolled her eyes, and shook her head. "Probably a twenty-four-hour virus. I think he'll be alright."

"Yeah, my husband had that. Lasted six days," Renee said. She leaned back and closed her eyes as Nancy tilted her chair back toward the shampoo sink and resisted the urge to dunk her.

"So you're having a party?" Nancy asked brightly, hoping to divert the conversation.

"Louis is having a party! He's got friends in town. He didn't even tell me about it until this morning! I'm so ticked at him. He went and bought that big red truck and he's been running around showing it off like a teenager!"

"Didn't he retire last year?" Nancy asked. "I've heard that when men reach that age, they just buy bigger toys."

"Yeah, he's getting another yacht. I think the one he has is big enough. But you know men. The bigger the better."

Nancy sat her client up and asked, "You want the same style, don't you?" Then she bit her tongue for asking.

"Well, I was thinking of a new style, but since you were late, I don't have time now. Just fix it like always. Next week though, I want you to fix it like this. She reached for her purse and handed Nancy a picture of Jennifer Lopez."

Nancy blew a deep breath to keep from exploding. "Okay. Let me keep that, and I'll try to make you look like that next week. You favor her a lot, but her hair is quite a bit longer."

"Couldn't you make mine longer? Don't you have those extensions?" Renee asked.

Nancy said, "I'd have to order them to match your hair texture and color exactly. Is that what you want me to do?"

"I'm sure you could dye them to match. Wait till next week and then I'll decide."

Nancy took another deep breath and continued to curl Renee's dark hair into the casual, wavy look she had worn for years. When she was under the dryer and out of hearing, Nancy said to Jane, "Can you believe her?"

Jane laughed. "Why'd you tell her she looks like Jennifer Lopez?"

Nancy said, "Because that's what she wanted to hear. But she looks more like James Farentino."

"Hush your mouth!" Jane laughed. "Why in the world would you say that?"

Nancy laughed. "I don't know. Ray and I watched an old movie last night that he was in, and it just popped in my mind. I'm sorry. She just makes me so mad."

Jane said, "You're having a bad day. You didn't need her on top of everything else. I'll say a prayer for you."

"Yeah, please do," Nancy said and went over to the dryer to get her patron back to the chair.

The shop was still full. All the departments were occupied and five more walk-ins were awaiting their turns. "It's going to get worse than this with the Spring Festival coming up," Carol said. More boats are docking every day and they're all bringing walk-ins; nobody wants to make an appointment. Jane, we need to develop some kind of policy about walk-ins, don't you think?"

"You may be right. It is getting out of hand. And it'll be worse this summer unless I can get some girls out of the college to come in, we do need to work out something."

Carol twirled her pen thoughtfully. "I've been thinking. Burgundy Blue Boutique has that extra room that's vacant right next door. I wondered if we should approach Jenny Wellsly about renting it, at least for the summer. We could cut a door in this wall," she motioned to her left. "Put my office in there and have a waiting room, and put a couple of other hairdressers in here."

"That would be nice," Jane chuckled. "But I don't think that's going to happen."

"Well, it was just a thought," Carol shrugged and answered the ringing phone.

Chapter 12 Davie's Dilemma

Tuesday afternoon, April 2

At the Landing, Davie was in his office, dealing with overwhelming issues. The hole had been partially dug out again, but whoever did it, stopped short of the previous digging. It was unbelievable how someone could get in and out without being seen. And what were they doing? Digging something up or burying something? But they weren't finding anything buried.

He rented a crew to come dig, expanding the hole's width and depth to try to expose whatever it was. What if there were bodies? He shuddered. Chief Jeb had stayed with him because of the highly suspicious event.

While everyone else was outside, once again, Davie called Jeffry Smythe's phone number. And once again, he got no answer, not even a voice mail. "This is so frustrating," Davie said and kicked the corner of his desk hard. "Ouch!" He yelped and sat back down to rub his foot and wait for the pain to subside.

Leaning forward, he caught a glimpse of something in his peripheral vision, a glint of gold. Reaching for it, he recognized the gold embossed edges of a book.

On the side of his desk, out of the way, was the Bible he had always kept at the office. Not that he ever read it, but he had grown up believing in God. He went to church most of his life—until the past couple of years. He and Jenny were good people, good Christians. They were kind to people. They provided jobs. Jenny often witnessed to people about God's love. Now he felt such a surge of self-pity, he reached for it, as though it could help.

"I don't even know what to read," he said aloud. "And I don't have time now." He pushed the Bible back across the desk out of the way. He didn't know what to do about Smythe and the yacht nor the chaos outside. He actually missed the Smythe's. He had some good times with them.

He was dumbfounded by this change of events. And dumbfounded at that infernal hole in the ground. He felt violated, angry, and frightened that his house had been ransacked. He thought about Rebecca Willis and Bud Littman and realized his whole family was under siege. *Were they all in trouble because of him?* He could almost hear his grandmother say "Don't be silly, Davie. God doesn't work that way." He hoped.

He reached for the Bible again and thumbed through it, but pushed it aside when he heard a knock on the door. Chief Jeb came in and pulled up a chair.

"Maybe you can give me some advice," Davie said to him. "I've got that yacht sitting out there. Now I can't get up with Mr. Smythe. I've been trying for a month. I was told yesterday that he was dead. The whole thing seems strange to me."

Jeb agreed. "Yes, that is strange. I told you I'd check on him. Give me his full name and address, whatever you have." Davie made a copy and handed it to him.

The chief said, "You might need to talk with John Frederick. It's good having a judge in the family."

"Almost family," Davie said. A sudden commotion and hollering outside snatched their attention and both he and Jeb jumped up. The crew had gone three bucket scoops down and struck something.

"Hold it. Hold it!" Davie yelled. "Don't break my drainage pipes!"

The operator stopped and backed off the hole. After eyeing it a few seconds, Davie announced, "Let's just refill it and quit this nonsense. I don't know what somebody was digging for but they didn't bury anything here. Let's quit this."

He had rented the equipment from Claxton Construction, a company that builds roads, parking lots, swimming pools, and such. "Fill it back up and let's get the equipment back," Davie ordered.

He told Jeb, "Sometimes you have to know when to hold'em, when to fold'em, and when to walk away. We're walking away. And I want that radio station to stop its mess. Tell that DJ there's nothing here."

Jeb said, "I think you've made a good decision." Then under his breath, "But I'll keep investigating this, Davie." Davie nodded agreement.

In an hour the hole was refilled, the ground was smooth, and the equipment was gone. "I'm gonna call the garden center and plant somethings out here. Maybe some azaleas." He motioned with his arm. "They'll look good all along the river bank."

With his decisiveness, everything almost felt normal again. The plant was back to work and he conducted business as usual. Jenny was okay. Will Hasley had finished and come back to work.

At five o'clock, though, Davie was ready to call it a day. He knew what he had to do now, and he didn't look forward to it. When he got home, the deputy was gone, his mom had gone back to her house. His dad was still at the Gristmill Restaurant. But his grandma and grandpa were still there with Jenny. She had completed the clean-up on her end of the office and was waiting to help him restore his files.

He got a Mountain Dew from the refrigerator and said, "Grandma, Grandpa, come with me and Jenny to the kitchen."

He motioned for them to sit at the bar with him and started telling them what had happened and how he had sent the construction crew home after they struck drainage pipes. He mentioned his idea about azaleas.

"I like that," Lillian said. "I love azaleas. They are gorgeous this year."

He looked solemn, as though trying to figure out what to say next. His grandpa did it for him.

"That's not drainage pipes, Davie."

"I know," he said. "But there were too many people standing around to let them go any farther. I had to get rid of them. Even Chief Jeb. I needed to talk to y'all and figure out how to handle this."

"Oh, my goodness," Jenny cried. "What is it? Do you know?"

Isaac started to say something, then looked around as though someone had walked into the room. He surprised them by saying, "It's a septic tank," and put his finger to his lips to shush them.

They were puzzled, but Isaac continued talking, all the while holding a finger near his lips so they would not say anything. "Jeb's going to send a deputy out here in a few minutes. It's a good guy, tough, very competent; he's taken down a few rough characters. Anyway, I want to take you out to the gristmill for dinner tonight. Jenny, call Jessica and tell her. Lillian, call Jimmy and tell him to just wait for us out there, okay?"

Confused but obedient, the two women scurried to their phones, and Isaac motioned for Davie to follow him out to the back yard. About thirty feet from the house by a patch of pink azaleas, he pretended to show Davie the bushes he thought would be good, then he talked softly. "I'm afraid somebody's bugged your house. You know it's not a septic tank."

"Yes, I do. It took me a minute to catch on, but, oh, Grandpa. What are we gonna do?"

Isaac said, "That part I said about the deputy, that was in case somebody was listening."

"I thought so," Davie said. "And the septic tank, too. Is there any way we can check for bugs?"

"Yeah, I'll take care of that. I'll call William. He's an expert. I also think we need to get surveillance cameras and security systems set up on our houses tomorrow. This might be bigger than you realize."

"William?" Davie asked.

Isaac clarified, "You know him, my cousin William. He's retired from Kingstown Surveillance Technologies. And he knows all about that stuff. He worked with the FBI ten years ago to catch Riddick. That box the men struck today might very well be something that was buried by Riddick's gang, maybe fifty years ago. You remember what you found in the fishing boat when George was rescued?"

"I sure do," Davie said. "Nazi relics, money, a gold bracelet, and a watch fob. I still have that watch fob."

"Remember when you restored that boat?"

"Yeah, about seven years now. We started on my building right after that."

"Remember that envelope you found in the compartment in the old boat?"

"Yeah, I remember, but you never told me what it was."

Isaac said, "I put it in a vault at the bank. It's a map of Big Creek drawn back in the fifties. There were also some pages torn from hymnals. After puzzling through them, I figured they held a message of some sort. I just thought I'd hang on to it until something came up that would help it make sense. I think this is it."

Davie said, "So what do we do now?"

Isaac said, "We think. We pray. We talk to your mama and daddy, and Lillian. We don't talk to anybody else. Not even the pastor. We need to handle this by ourselves. Well, us and God. God's never let me down yet. He will direct us."

"Oh, Grandpa. I don't think God has ever dealt with anything like this before."

Isaac laughed. "You need to read the Bible more, Davie. Of course, He has."

Davie couldn't imagine this ever being an issue in the Bible. They went back into the house. Lillian and Isaac got into her car and went home just a half-mile up the road. Jenny said, "I told your mom she could ride with us."

"Good," said Davie. "I'm gonna take a shower. I feel so grimy messing around that dirt all day. You say you've got your files all back in order? Was anything missing?"

"Yes, I have it all back in order. And no, I don't think anything is missing. I found everything. Even the files on…" he put his finger to his lips to stop her. She was puzzled. He took a pen and wrote down *Grandpa thinks the house is bugged.*

"Oh, my God," she said, then quickly played along. "Even the files on that dress I ordered that came in too small. Remember I had such a hard time getting my money back? They finally made it good, but you know how I save everything. Well, I trashed that. And a few other things that weren't any good."

"Good thinking," he said. And he wasn't just talking about the files. Jenny turned on the television to give camouflage noise. A game show with a lot of applause and music helped to put her at ease.

She thought back over the day's activities and tried to remember what had been said. She remembered the conversation between the deputy and Nancy and winced. She wrote it down on a piece of paper. Davie shrugged. "Maybe that will be alright. Give me that blue tie. You have such good taste. Thanks for buying that one for me."

"I'm hungry," she said. "I can't wait to get down there. Where is that deputy? He should be here by now."

While Davie hurriedly showered and dressed, she picked up papers and laid them in piles on the coffee table. At least she could help organize them a little.

He did not have any of the yacht records here, but in her files, she had all the records of her business with Mrs. Smythe. She was going to mention that, but he had stopped her. She wondered if he had been able to reach them today. She would ask him in the car.

Then she had a horrible thought. *What if the car's bugged too?* She thought *we have to drive the truck. It was at his mom and dad's last night. And he had had it today. No, maybe we should get Jessica to drive. No, maybe we should all ride together in Grandpa's truck. It's bigger.* She wanted to scream. *We can't live in fear like this. God help us, please!*

The doorbell rang and the deputy arrived. Suddenly, she had apprehensions of even leaving a deputy in their house. She opened the door just as Davie came downstairs wearing the blue tie he had pretended she was handing him. She smiled but went on out to the porch ahead of him. He and the deputy followed her.

"What will you be doing?" She asked. "I'll be sitting out here in your driveway, armed and ready if I see anything suspicious," he said.

"Oh. Well, that's good, I guess," she said.

Then as though he had read her mind, he said, "I recommend you all ride in Mr. Isaac's truck. I understand you've probably been bugged and that might include your vehicles."

Davie nodded and got in his truck. She followed and they drove across the street to pick up Jessica. Even in her house, they would not talk but wrote notes. She was ready, they left quickly and drove up to Isaac and Lillian's house.

Lillian opened the front door and said, "Come on in, kids. Get in the truck. It's in the garage. Jeb's got us up to date."

Finally, as they left the garage, and pulled out on the street, everyone started talking at once. "I can't live like this," Jenny said.

"We don't have to," Lillian proclaimed. "In the Name of Jesus, I rebuke this spirit of fear. I pray for God's protection for our family. Satan is trying to destroy us. We will not let him have his way. We will resist the devil and he has to flee from us. In the name of Jesus."

"Amen," they all said and began to relax a little. Except Davie.

Jessica said, "It's easier to fight your enemy if you know who it is. We don't know who these people are, but I know it is Satan behind all this. I'm claiming God's protection. Still, I don't want to do anything foolish."

They all agreed on that. They rode on to the restaurant in relative silence. Davie did tell them about reaching someone at the Smythe number earlier and being told that Mr. Smythe had passed away.

"Oh, how awful," Jessica said.

Jenny said, "I feel so sorry for her. She was always so cheerful. She wanted input on every detail of that yacht. She said she didn't know anything about decorating and insisted that I choose everything. She even said she was going to tell Jeffry to name the yacht Burgundy Blue after my boutique. I didn't want him to do that."

"Well, I don't guess he will now," Isaac said.

"If he's really dead," Lillian said.

"Why would you say that?" Isaac asked.

"I don't know," Lillian said. "It just came out. You spent a lot of time with those folks, didn't you Davie?"

Yeah," Davie acknowledged. "At first it was all business, but they liked us and started inviting us to things. We visited them in Chesapeake. They have a mansion on the beach."

"Sometimes I didn't like their crowd," Jenny said then bit her tongue as Davie elbowed her. He did not want the conversation going in that direction. He hadn't really done anything wrong. But he knew how his parents felt about some things and what they didn't know wouldn't hurt anybody.

They parked and joined Jimmy inside where he was already at a table waiting for them. After they ordered, they resumed their conversation. Davie told his dad about the Smythe call, and then Lillian mentioned that she had inadvertently questioned whether he was really dead.

Jimmy said, "Well, he wasn't dead last Friday. He ate lunch here, and he told me he was on his way to pick up his yacht. He didn't know it was my son that built it for him, and I didn't say anything. Of course, he had to recognize the Wellsly name outside. But then there are a lot of Wellsly's."

"Wait. What? Last Friday?" Davie asked. "The man on the phone said he passed away a month ago."

"Oh, Lord," Jenny said and put her elbows on the table and her hands to her head.

"There's a murder afoot," Lillian said.

"Shh," Isaac said. "Y'all need to stop talking. I remember back when I was little, I was about ten years old. World War II was going on, and there was a slogan everywhere 'Loose Lips Sink Ships' and Mama said it a lot."

"What did it mean?" asked Davie.

"Well, they didn't want people talking about things that might give away secrets. Even if what they talked about was true, they didn't want it talked about. Some of what was said was pure lies or just rumor. So there was a big push to keep your mouths shut. And I can see where it would be a good policy for us now. Loose lips sink ships, and that should be our motto until this mess is cleared up."

"We can't just go around without saying anything," Jenny said. "I found out how hard that was at the house just now."

"I think we should all condition ourselves to assume wherever we are, it's bugged," Isaac said.

"But Grandpa. How can we live like that?" Davie asked.

"You just have to be very judicious," Isaac said. "Just like you were today. You have to know when to hold'em. You used good judgment today."

Jimmy had not heard that part of the story until now. Davie and Isaac together explained. Lillian and Jessica sat in awe. The fact that on their property might actually be a pirate's treasure from more than fifty years ago blew their minds.

"Do you think there's any connection between Mr. Smythe and that buried chest or whatever it is?" Jenny asked.

Isaac said, "There's no telling. Jeb is doing a background search."

Davie added, "But it just seems mighty farfetched. He's from Chesapeake, Virginia. When he approached me three years ago about building the boat, I told him no, because my company is small, and we'd never even intended to build anything like that."

Jenny remembered and confirmed the conversation.

"He was very convincing though," Davie said. "He said he had retired from a corporate job in New York and moved to Chesapeake. He wanted a yacht to spend some time on the ocean. He didn't want to go to one of those corporate builders and hoped he could find a small company to do a custom job. He wanted to pay cash upfront."

Isaac said, "That's probably why he didn't go to a large corporate boat builder. They would not work on a cash basis."

"Maybe so," Davie said, "I couldn't do it that way either. I told him I couldn't. And besides, it would take two or three years to build it. Anyway, he finally agreed to that. And he just kept it paid as we went. He had to put out a half-million to get it started though. Didn't faze him a bit."

Jenny said, "It was a big boost to our business--both of us. They got what they wanted and we made money, too."

"Julie Smythe loved Jenny's work," Davie added.

"I liked her better than him," Jenny said. "We worked closely for more than two years. And then they just stopped coming. It's been a couple of months since we saw them. It sure makes me feel funny—well not funny—kind of hurt, and strange now that they say he died."

Isaac said, "It might be time to call in our family detectives."

Everyone looked at him. Lillian said, "You think Bernell is up to anything like this?"

Isaac said, "Bernell lives for something like this. She'll be up to it until the day she dies."

"Oh, don't put it that way," Lillian said. "I know Kit's probably sharp as ever, And Bree, she'll probably jump right on it. But they don't have any clues."

Isaac said, "Ain't that part of their job? To find clues?"

Jimmy said, "Might not hurt. They've got that big office up there on Claxton Boulevard, and I don't see much activity there."

"It's a detective agency, Dad. You're not supposed to see much activity. Most people don't even know what that office is."

"Unless they need an investigator," Jenny said. "And right now, we apparently do."

"So what are we gonna tell them?" Davie asked. "We've got a $2.4 million yacht we want the owner to pick up, and now we've been told the owner is dead, and we're stuck with it, but it's mostly paid for, so no problem. And we've got a possible treasure buried beside the parking lot a hundred yards from that $2.4 million yacht, but we don't think there's any connection. And we've had mysterious holes dug and refilled and dug up again. And we haven't found any bodies and no clues. Nothing but a jeweled cigarette lighter that says JS."

"Right," said Isaac. "That's all."

"JS?" asked Jenny. "Mrs. Smythe's name is Julie, and his name is James Jeffry Smythe."

"Well then that's not a clue at all," Davie said. "Jeffry may have smoked and she might have too, and I can't tell you how many times they were on the premises."

"But really, I never saw either of them smoking," Jenny countered.

Isaac said, "Well, so much for that big deal and all that sand sifting today. Wait till Chief Jeb hears this. He took it to the police department today to run fingerprints."

"Well," Davie said, "It just seemed good to find something tangible. Shoot! So we're back to square one now."

Jenny spoke up. "Even though I never saw Julie smoking, it could have been hers. Some people can hide things pretty well." She cut her eyes at Davie who looked away to avoid making contact.

She continued, "Maybe she quit or something. But does that mean we're not going to the agency? From what I've seen of Bree's work, she's pretty good. She's worked with the police department a lot and has done a few jobs with the FBI, you know."

"They've solved some heavy cases in the last few years, but they still keep a low profile," Lillian said. "That's actually a good thing, don't you think?"

Davie said, "We have to do something about that boat, and I don't know who to contact."

"Didn't they have any children?" Jessica asked.

"They never mentioned any," Davie said.

Julie added, "And don't forget about our house being ransacked, Davie. Even though the police are working on it, they don't know anything yet."

"Dang, you're right!" Davie said. "Dad, Grandpa, let's go up there tomorrow."

"Good idea," Lillian said. "And while y'all do that, it's my day at the soup kitchen. So I'll be going to the Manor."

"You're getting too old to do that," Isaac almost said before she whacked him on the shoulder.

Davie, said, "Grandpa, when are you gonna learn to never tell Grandma she's too old for anything?"

"Besides, I'm training a new volunteer tomorrow," Lillian said. "I only go once a week. Maybe after tomorrow, I'll cut back."

Her family just laughed.

Chapter 13 The Soup Kitchen

Wednesday morning, April 3

For years Lillian had volunteered at the Salvation Army's soup kitchen. *Isaac's probably right. It might be time to let someone else do it,* she thought as she got dressed to go. *It's been rewarding but it's getting tiring. I'm glad Susan's volunteered. She is so much younger and has a heart to help. Lord knows we need more people with a heart to help.*

"This used to be Magnolia Manor, the nicest restaurant in town," she told Susan as they dished out food in the breakfast serving line.

"But that crook, Riddick used it as a secret headquarters, and when he was taken down, it was donated to the Salvation Army and turned into a soup kitchen for the homeless."

"Do these people all stay here?" The new volunteer asked. "It doesn't seem that big?"

"No," Lillian answered her. "Many of them sleep on the streets, unfortunately. So sad. But there are four rooms upstairs providing sleeping quarters for those who want to sleep there. Sleeps about sixteen. It's only for men though. There's another women's shelter up near the hospital. We need more space in both places. There's so much need out there, it breaks my heart. I pray for God's help."

From month to month Lilian had come. There would be different people at the tables, so she usually didn't know many of them. Although a few were constant.

One veteran, Mr. Chad Harmon, who really was a veteran, had lost his home in a tornado years ago. He wound up here and never left. But he was a jovial fellow with words of wisdom for the younger ones he saw come and go.

"He's sort of the self-appointed caretaker of the place," Lillian told her friend. "I always enjoy talking with him."

"Maybe I will," Susan filled a bowl with grits and gravy and set it on a tray.

"I notice some of them could use a haircut," Susan was not fond of the unkempt look.

"Jane's Beauty Shop gives free haircuts once a month, Susan. But Mr. Harmon will never let them cut his hair or beard. He said, 'I need to know me when I look in the mirror. I can't lose my identity. It's all I have left.' So no one ever pressures him. I think he's a wise man."

"He looks clean," Susan liked that.

"Showers are free, and a washer and dryer are available in exchange for chores to keep the place clean. The Salvation Army manages it with limited staff and volunteers like you and me. I guess you could count Mr. Harmon a volunteer too, although he lives here."

Susan complimented Lillian on being so helpful to the institution over the years. "I know Lillian's Riviera and the Gristmill Restaurant are major contributors to the daily meals provided here. That's mighty nice of you."

"The least we can do," Lillian smiled at the young man with a tray in front of her. "And there are other restaurants that help, too."

When Lillian had arrived she noticed more young men than usual. Mr. Harmon said, "No telling. But that Spring Festival's coming up. Some of them may be getting drugs from somewhere, but they ain't getting it here. And they better not bring any here. I'll crack their heads if I find it out." He balled his fist and clenched his jaw.

Somehow, Mr. Harmon commanded respect in spite of the fact that he was living in a homeless shelter. "God works in mysterious ways," Lillian said.

But Mr. Harmon seemed depressed when Lillian arrived this morning. He was the last in line. Lillian could tell by the look on his face. "Something's on your mind," she said to him when he got his tray. He just smiled and went to his table.

"You got this? I'm going over there," she told Susan.

At first, he wouldn't say, but when she sat there and drank coffee with him while he ate, he finally said, "I just wish I could help some of these guys."

"People have to help themselves, Mr. Harmon. Some of these guys look able-bodied and could be working if they would accept employment."

"Yeah, but some of them's got problems in the head. They look good, but they're not good inside."

"I guess you may be right," Lillian said. "But most people don't see it that way."

"There's one upstairs, been here four days. Won't even eat. Slept about two days when he got here and now still sleeps all the time. I think something's wrong with him. He won't even talk."

"You think maybe we should call a doctor?" she wondered.

"You might could. Nobody will listen to me though."

"You're wrong about that Mr. Harmon. I've seen how they listen to you. What's the fellow's name?"

"He don't know."

"You don't know?"

"No, HE don't know."

"You mean he has amnesia?"

"Maybe. I've seen blood on his pillow, too. But he won't let me help him."

"You reckon I could go up there. I know that's the men's ward, but it sounds like he needs help."

"I wish you would. I'll go and make sure the coast is clear."

Lillian trudged up the stairs behind Mr. Harmon and waited at the door as he checked. All the cots were empty except one.

Mr. Harmon tried to talk to the man in the bed, but he didn't respond. A sheet was pulled up to his waist. He was wearing a long-sleeved, red shirt and lying still.

She was a little leery but approached the man when Mr. Harmon beckoned her over. "Sir, are you alright?" She could see that he wasn't. His face was bruised and his head had been bleeding.

She touched his shoulder. When he didn't respond she picked up his hand and checked his pulse. It was very low, and he felt hot. She pulled out her phone and called the ER.

To Mr. Harmon, she said, "They're on their way. Make way for them to get up here. This man's got to go to the hospital."

She called Isaac, "Can you come down here to the soup kitchen? I need help."

"You know where I am, and I don't like dishing out soup," he was honest.

"Oh," she winced. "I forgot. It's not that. We've got a man in trouble here. He needs help. I've called ER. I don't know what the hospital will do. You know how it is with insurance these days. But we have to get him some help. I don't know who he is, but from the looks of him, he does not belong here."

"Tell them to put him under Isaac Wellsly. We'll take care of it."

"Okay. I thought you might say that. Thanks, Babe."

She followed Mr. Harmon downstairs and waited at the front door. Mr. Harmon made sure no one got in the way.

"I'll meet you at the hospital and you can put this under Isaac Wellsly. We'll take care of it."

"Okay," the driver acknowledged her.

Susan joined Lillian as they waited with Mr. Harmon until the EMT's came back through, carrying the stretcher.

"Somebody just saved this man's life," the EMT said. "If we make it to the hospital in time."

"Is it an overdose?" Susan wondered.

Mr. Harmon shook his head. "No, I've seen them. He's not like that. He came in disoriented and had blood on his head and on his clothes. It was about midnight. He didn't know what happened. I felt like he was a war veteran and maybe going through PTS. I just gave him a bed and he went to sleep. I tried to keep an eye on him. He didn't wake up for two days. Then I got him up and helped him get to the bathroom. I tried to get him to eat something but he wouldn't. He was confused. He did drink some water and went back to sleep. I was afraid he was gonna die. I kept trying to wake him up. I'd talk to him and try to find out who he is, but he didn't talk. And he'd go back to sleep."

"Why didn't you talk to the Salvation Army Captain?" Susan asked.

"I thought about it. But they're all so busy with that Festival. And we're just homeless people taking handouts. I did say a prayer."

Lillian patted Mr. Harmon on the shoulder. "You saved his life. I'm going to the hospital and make sure they get him in treatment. Keep him in your prayers. I'll let you know how he is—and who he is if we find out."

He nodded. "Thanks, Ma'am."

Lillian hugged Susan and patted her on the back. "One more day at the homeless shelter. Always rewarding, but not always this eventful. I'm glad you're helping out. I'll be back in a little while. And I'm not quitting."

Chapter 14 The Agency

Wednesday morning, April 3

The front office of B.B. Jackson Private Investigating Agency was very inviting, and Isaac soon realized he had been wrong about his older sister. He had no idea the extent of Bernell's success. Her venture, founded in 2004, in one room of her house, was now a high-end detective agency and very impressive. She had a dream and was achieving it.

As Chief Investigative Administrator, her motivation had been inspired by her involvement in the capture of the mobster, Roger Riddick. After seeing the death and destruction he had left behind, she was intent on helping people who might still be suffering from his evil influence. And besides, she loved investigative work.

She was joined by sharpshooter Kit Griffiths, her cousin from Texas, and later Forensic Scientist Briana Beckford Ingles, otherwise known as Bree. Bree was the granddaughter of their cousin Ana Beckford Clark who had had a lot to do with the capture of Riddick.

When Bernell originally mentioned her plans to Isaac, he thought she was just dreaming.

"It's not like a doctor's office, where people will be waiting long," he said as Bernell shared her ideas.

"No," Bernell argued. "But it's a place that people might come to in trouble and under stress, and I want to create a pleasant atmosphere and a place where they can relax and talk."

"Like a psychiatrist's office?" Isaac had laughed at her.

"No, brother! Not a psychiatrist's office, but, hey, give me a call. You can be my first client." Even in their senior years they still carried on sibling banter. Of course, she had won. She was older and always won.

She had solved numerous cases during the past nine years with the help of her crew. She had started with only herself and Kit. Bree had joined them part-time while she was in the Forensic Science program at the university and then full time when she graduated.

Now the Agency had a full staff of six and Isaac was about to be a client. Isaac, Jimmy, and Davie came in together. Ironically, they had the pleasure of waiting in that lobby he had made fun of when she had described her dream a few years earlier.

Bernell had spared no expense, and Jenny had helped decorate. The artistry of the Burgundy Blue Boutique was evident with the deep red carpet and pale beige walls, the color of beach sand. Abstract paintings picked up the red tones from the carpet and green from the ficus trees and philodendron. An aquarium inset on the back wall was mesmerizing.

An older lady sat in a soft black leather chair gazing at the aquarium without looking up when Isaac, Jimmy, and Davie arrived. "Isn't that like yours?" Isaac asked, pointing at the aquarium.

"Looks like it," he said.

The receptionist was on the phone but beckoned them to come in and have a seat. She was cheerful and seemed to be taking notes with her right hand as she held the phone with her left. "Busier than I thought," said Jimmy.

An elegant dark cherry hutch at the other end of the room offered refreshments for those who waited. The awakening aroma of fresh brewing coffee came from the Keurig pot as Isaac made himself a cup. A basket of assorted snacks was free and a mini-fridge inside the cabinet held cold sodas and water for the choosing. Davie found a Mountain Dew, and Jimmy made himself a cup of cafe' caramel delight.

Half a dozen black leather chairs sat near a round table in the corner where a checkerboard was set up with a game in progress. Two gentlemen playing checkers were drinking coffee and arguing about something in the news that was on the television playing above their heads.

After a few minutes, the lady watching the aquarium got up to leave. She smiled at Isaac as he tipped his hat. "Lowers my blood pressure every morning," she said, as though this were a routine occurrence. She left, and he noticed through the window that she climbed on the City Bus that had pulled up to the curb.

"Heh-heh" he chuckled and shook his head. "She's really done it," thinking of Bernell.

Behind a dark cherry desk that matched the refreshment hutch, the red-haired, sparkling young lady jotted something on the desk pad and then answered the phone again. "B.B. Jackson Agency, Abby speaking, how may I help you?"

Isaac didn't listen but stood to stretch his legs. They had been waiting twenty minutes. "Good thing this wasn't an emergency," he whispered to Jimmy. Jimmy nodded.

Davie was becoming restless. "Wonder where 007 is?" He asked and pointed at the four doors across the back wall. Four white doors about twelve feet apart had brass nameplates with a number above each one. The first one, 001, was above the name Bernell Belinda Jackson, Chief Investigative Administrator. The second door had 002, above Abby Farrington, B.A. The third door number was 003 and said, Briana Beckford Ingles, B.S.F.S. The last door had 004 above a plate that said Kit Griffiths, Ph.D., F.G.W.

"Okay, F.S is Forensic Science, but what does F.G.W stand for?" Davie asked his dad. "Fastest Gun in the West, I imagine," laughed Jimmy. "I don't think it's an exaggeration though."

It was a pleasant atmosphere, just as Bernell had envisioned. The nameplate on the desk in the center of the room said Abby Farrington. "How've you been, Abby?" Isaac asked when she got off the phone. "I hope your grandma doesn't work you too hard."

Abby laughed. "She's cool."

Bernell's granddaughter had married a football player from Huntington, West Virginia. They had met while they were both attending Claxton University. When he graduated, they moved to Huntington, then he went pro for a while.

She had finished only three years of college but left to follow her husband. Things did not go well with them in West Virginia. She loved hiking, hunting, and fishing. He loved football and other women.

On a fateful day, when she learned of his affair, she went on a camping trip alone to renew her spirit. Unfortunately, she encountered a rabid bobcat who aggressively attacked.

Caught by surprise, but not unprepared, she struck back. He left her wounded for life. She left him dead. One thing she had learned growing up was how to shoot, and her left hand was fast as lightning. That's what saved her life.

She was in the hospital for weeks. Amid rabies shots and surgeries, she filed for divorce. In spite of multiple surgeries on her right hand, she never regained its full use. Her fingers remained in a position as though holding a pencil. Which she often did, just to make it look normal. But it wasn't. She could type on the computer, though, and adapted. She went back to college and finished her degree in Business Administration.

Fortunately, she was left-handed, and in spite of the appearance of being handicapped, it was not as bad as people thought. Like her grandmother, Bernell Jackson, Abby was blessed with a strong will and sense of humor. Her red hair and a sprinkling of freckles only complemented her cheery image. She conveyed exactly the atmosphere Bernell wanted for the Agency and was ready when Bernell invited her to take over the front office in her new building on Claxton Blvd.

Abby also had good ideas. A plaque on her desk that only she could read said *Loose Lips Sink Ships*. She knew what that meant from both sides of the desk.

She never divulged anything. If anyone asked her what time it was, she would direct their attention to the sunburst clock over the aquarium. And it was always right. But she listened. On any number of occasions, she had shared with her boss conversations that she had overhead as people waited, played games at the checker table, or muttered to each other at the refreshment hutch.

Her frontline position was an invaluable asset. People often confided in her like they do bartenders and hairdressers. The bus stop was directly in front of the office and often people waiting for the bus would sit inside out of the weather. It was the kind of friendly place Bernell had envisioned.

The staff worked closely with the police department, and once while Kit was investigating a homicide, two women waiting for the bus sat in the lobby and gossiped about their neighbor. It turned out that the neighbor was the one Kit was investigating. The women had both witnessed suspicious activity and discussed it.

Abby never said a word but later hinted to Kit that those women might have information the police needed. After their public chat, they were questioned separately by the police, and the case was brought to justice.

Isaac, Jimmy, and Davie did not make that mistake. They were already aware of the *loose lips sink ships* theory and did not give Abby a head-start on their case. They waited for Bernell. When she finally stuck her head out of door number 001, Isaac said, "It's about time. I was thinking of going somewhere else."

Bernell tossed her head and her silver hair shimmered as she winked at Abby. "Do these guys have an appointment?" She asked.

"No, they're walk-ins. That's why they had to wait so long," Abby said truthfully.

"Well, for crying out loud, Isaac. Next time call ahead." Bernell closed the door behind them and seated them in front of her desk in three leather chairs that matched those in the lobby.

She already knew everything that had been in the paper and on the radio. "We've got a mess, haven't we?" She started.

Isaac said, "Yeah, but there's more that's not been in the paper, and we hope it won't get there. That's why we wanted to come see you."

Davie proceeded to tell her everything about the hole at the landing, the equipment striking something, and his stopping them. He also told her about the yacht and the cigarette lighter. She stood up. "I know you don't want to tell all that again, but I need Bree and Kit to hear all this. Let's go to the conference room."

She opened a door to another room that stretched across the width of the building the size of the receptionist lobby. The same red carpet flowed through the rooms. Four doors along the wall obviously led into the other offices. Leather chairs sat around a long conference table, and a hutch like the one upfront stood at one end with the same refreshments offered.

On the other end was a bank of computers a printer and file cabinets, and on the back wall were three doors like the ones at the front. One had a label that said Maintenance, the other two had numbers 005 and 006 above nameplates. Bookcases stretched from the floor to the ceiling. On the far right was an exit door. "Wow," said Davie. "You use this room much?"

"All the time," she said. "If these walls could talk."

They laughed at her. She was lively and humorous and knew what she was doing. "Kit will be back in a few minutes. She'll join us, too. We work together on all our cases. We've found it to be more effective that way. Each of us has something to bring to the table."

"Hey, Buddy," Bree punched Davie on the shoulder as she entered from the third door. "How've y'all been? I haven't seen much of you lately. We're all so busy."

"I know. We need to get together and do something fun again."

"Oh, we always have fun here," she said laughing. She was a girl after Bernell's own heart. Ana Clark's granddaughter had moved to Claxton ten years ago and married Tony Ingles whose parents were best friends with Isaac and Lillian.

After a few minutes of small talk, they were joined by Kit Griffiths, the Annie Oakley type cousin from Texas who had also moved to the area ten years ago. She greeted them jovially.

After Davie went through his story, Bree asked for clarification. "The cigarette lighter, it's at the police department?"

Isaac answered, "Jeb said he would have it checked for fingerprints."

"I'll check with him on that," Bree said. "Do you have anything at all that might have the Smythes' fingerprints on it? Either one or both of them?"

"No," Davie said. "They used a pen to sign some papers, but no telling where that pen is now. We can ask Jenny though. Mrs. Smythe went to her shop a lot. She might have something."

"What about on the yacht?" Bree asked. "Were they ever on the yacht? Did he ever put his hand on the wheel or touch the dashboard or chairs?"

"Oh, well, yes. I'm sure he did. We were on the boat many times together." Davie remembered recently when Mr. Smythe seemed very pleased with the yacht and excited about its nearing completion.

"Okay, let's have it dusted," Bree made a note on her iPad. "I'll check with Jeb on that, too. Now about that septic tank, aka drain pipe, aka treasure chest. You know they use vaults in graves. Have you thought of that?"

Isaac sat up. "Dang. Never thought of that."

Jimmy said, "You're right. Davie, it might be a good thing you stopped that crew when you did."

"Eww," Davie uttered

Bernell tapped her long red nails on the table. "Well, we have to find out. Let us do a little research. There may have been a cemetery along there years ago. If so, there may be more of them that you don't know about."

"Hmm," Isaac shook his head slowly. "I thought I would have known, but there is one factor to think about. The river shifted its path around 1955 when that freak storm and flash flood came through. You remember it."

Bernell nodded. "I'll say I do. When Daddy was killed. It was a horrible time."

"Do you have a map of the old tract of the river?" Kit wanted to know, then she answered herself, "Never mind, I can find one."

Isaac wondered if he should tell them now about the map he suspected pointed to a treasure. He decided they should know and mentioned it.

"Yes, let's get that," Kit said, "And let me see what I can find, too. Fingerprints and old maps with the lay of the land--back around say 1930 to 1955?"

Isaac nodded.

Davie looked at Bernell. "We didn't mention fees yet. We need to get that information."

Bernell laid her hand on top of his and said, "This one's on me." Then she smiled and said, "On second thought, just in case it turns out you have a pirate's chest with some real treasure, I have dibs on a strand of pearls." They all laughed at that idea.

But Davie had another concern. "One of our big worries right now is that yacht sitting in our way."

Kit said, "You may be in for a lot of surprises. I'm thinking possible murder of its owner. You say Jeb's checking into that?"

Davie nodded. Kit scribbled some notes. "I'll do some checking, too. It's pretty simple to find an obit. If there's not one," she raised her eyebrows, "then we may have some work to do."

Jimmy said, "I think everybody on Big Creek Road is beginning to feel threatened, especially after Davie and Jenny's house was ransacked."

Bree agreed, "Yeah, we were over at Asher and Nana's last night, and Tony and John Frederick and their mom and dad all mentioned they didn't know how bad this could get. They're making sure their security systems are up to date."

"We're getting KST out there today," Davie said. "All of us. I should have already had it at the Landing but I..., well, there's never been any crime on that road that I know of."

Bernell nodded. "Not since our house burned was down back in 1955, a short while after Daddy got killed. Anyway, we'll start working on it. This is just for the record." She laid three forms down for Davie, Isaac, and Jimmy to sign.

"We'll keep in touch with you every day till this is resolved." Bernell shook their hands like it was a business arrangement among strangers. She was nothing if not business.

Isaac had to say, "I'm impressed, sister, you've really got it going."

"That would be Ms. Jackson to you, sir." She hugged him and laughed.

"What do we do now?" Davie needed to know.

"Get your KST security. Get rid of any bugs in that house. Do let me know if they find any. Other than that, just wait till we check on these things. It won't be long. Maybe as soon as tomorrow."

Bree said, "We'll check out Mr. Smythe, Davie. Should be pretty easy to find out if he has passed away or not."

"Yeah, I'm at a loss as to what to do about that yacht." Davie worried. "I can't move it, but right now, it's trespassing."

The back entrance opened, and two men dressed in dark suits came in carrying briefcases. Bernell motioned for them to sit. "Did you find anything?" she asked.

"Not much," said the darker one. They laid their briefcases on the conference table. "Take a look."

Inside both were cameras and stacks of photographs. Pictures of a warehouse and several cars. Some of the shots were from the outside of the warehouse and some were from inside. Close-ups revealed evidence of a chop shop. There were people in some of the pictures.

"How did you get these?" Bree asked.

The men laughed. "Don't ask," said the younger one.

"What you boys up to?" Isaac was curious.

Bernell answered for them. "Isaac you know better than to ask that. This is a detective agency. Our work is confidential."

"Good. You think Thomas and Adam will be working on our case?"

"Always a possibility," Bernell winked at Kit who said, "We let them do enough to earn their keep."

"I have a question." Davie said, "What's FGW?" He looked at Kit who grinned. "Federation of Graduate Women."

"Oh, Grandpa said Fastest Gun in the West."

She laughed. "Okay, that too."

"And Abby's got that big office up front."

Kit laughed. "And Abby's got the hallway. It goes to the restroom and breakroom—and back here."

Davie said, "Okay, then, one more question. Where's 007?" They all laughed with him. It was their private office joke. Bernell said, "We keep 007 in England. He only reports when he needs help." She pointed to a poster of 007's Shawn Connery on the back wall. He laughed. "Neat."

Thomas Madison 005, was a six-foot Denzel Washington look-alike with a gun holster under his jacket. His partner was 006, Adam Del Vecchio, Lillian's nephew, a little shorter than Thomas, not as dark but just as handsome with blue eyes and brownish hair. He also wore a gun holster under his jacket.

Davie laughed. "You guys need to wear sunglasses."

"Sometimes we do," answered Adam. Adam looked about eighteen but he was twenty-six. His youthful appearance was one of his assets when he was on a case undercover. Nobody suspected a young boy like him to be a certified private investigator. He had completed the Criminal Justice Program at the university and graduated about the time Bernell moved into the Claxton Boulevard building. She snapped him up.

She had anticipated having the best detective agency in the south and she picked her staff with precision. One requirement she had was that all the staff had to be related. Just a quirk maybe, but it was her agency and she could make the rules. Having served alongside her husband in the military for thirty years, she learned a lot about rules. Rules and regulations had ruled their lives. They didn't make them. They followed them.

Now she relished being the one who could make the rules. She had three main ones. Her staff had to be professionally qualified. They had to be courteous and friendly. And they had to be related to each other. Trust was essential and she didn't have to do background checks on family. But the staff all knew they were professionals, and they had her trust.

Kit was a given. Born and raised on a ranch in Texas, she was almost always described as a modern-day Annie Oakley. She was a cousin whose sharpshooter skills had saved lives and brought criminals to justice. She was one of the reasons Bernell decided to start the agency. Dr. Kit Griffiths was a retired psychology professor and author of several books. That was the way Bree's grandmother, Ana Beckford, had met her.

Ana had been an English professor and college administrator with a minor in psychology. The two never realized their paths had crossed until Ana did some genealogy research. That had brought them together and expanded the family from the foothills of South Carolina to the cattle ranches of Texas.

Kit had fallen in love with her eastern relatives and moved to South Carolina embracing her heritage. Her husband was FBI agent George Parnell who had also been assigned to the Riddick investigation. It was meant to be.

Bree Beckford Ingles got her degree in Forensic Science and married Tony Ingles, whose parents, Nana and Asher, were Lillian and Isaac's best friends. Tony's mother Nana Winthrop Ingles had a mixed heritage. Her father was an Italian immigrant and her mother was a descendant of slaves who had come from royalty on the Gold Coast of Africa in the eighteenth century. Thomas Madison was Nana's nephew. He had graduated from USCC at the same time as Adam. Adam Del Vecchio was the grandson of Lillian's brother Jacob Del Vecchio of Del Vecchio Jewelers.

Bernell took pride in her multi-national, multi-racial company. It would be hard to accuse her of nepotism with all that diversity. But she didn't care what anybody said anyway. She was almost eighty years old when she started the company. She didn't tell her age unless it was to her advantage. Most people thought she was about sixty.

Isaac had thought her venture was a whim. But it was a mission. She knew God was in it. She had rescued kidnapped children, foiled bank robbers, and solved a few mysterious deaths. Her team was a well-oiled machine.

She was now committed to solving the mystery her family was facing. She had a gut feeling it linked right back to Roger Riddick. *Would they never be rid of that monster?* She also had a sickening suspicion that Jeffry Smythe was somehow connected. But she did not tell Davie.

She did say, "Davie, you asked about 007 and we joked about the movie character, but our 007 is God. We have to call on Him a lot. We never know how He might work things out. But He's helped us more times than we can count."

"I am impressed," Isaac said as she showed them through door 002 which was a hallway that passed a closed restroom door and one other closed doors labeled Breakroom.

When they came out next to Abby's desk, Davie said, "I like it here."

"I like it, too." she said and picked up the ringing phone, "B.B. Jackson Agency. Abby speaking, how may I help you?"

Chapter 15 Loose Lips Sink Ships

Wednesday morning, April 3

Even good news travels fast when it is discussed on Claxton Radio's controversial morning show. People called and thanked them for announcing that Rebecca Willis was out of the coma and would be going home. She had a concussion, but no lasting damage and Bud's ankle was healing. So much for the good news from that show.

The DJ did what he could to encourage curiosity and speculation. So tension remained high as the radio station kept an ongoing conversation about the "holy ground" as he was calling it. Among advertisements about the Spring Festival, the DJ said "Come to Claxton's Tenth Annual Spring Festival. Bring your sand buckets and shovel and check out the holy ground on the riverside. You might dig up some buried Big Creek secrets."

He relished the calls he received reprimanding him for saying that as well as calls wanting more information on where to dig. His ratings went up as people argued back and forth through their phone calls which were aired as they spoke. Then one caller gave the audience chills. It was a deep voice with no identifiable accent. "Keep on talking and you'll lose that tongue."

The DJ laughed and started to say something, but the caller hung up. No one could mistake the ominous seriousness of that voice. The DJ laughed strangely and sounded nervous as he changed the focus.

"As Grand Marshall of the Parade, I'm so proud to be honoring my great-great-grandfather, Chief Flaming Cloud of the Cherokee Indian Nation I will be wearing his headdress and riding a white steed. My red and white feather headdress will be on display after the parade. Bring your cameras."

He invited people to pick up their Festival Guide from local businesses. He named a few. Wellsly Gristmill Restaurant was one of the sponsors. B.B Jackson Private Investigations Agency was another.

Abby Farrington's radio played at her desk. It was a typical morning. Isaac, Jimmy, and Davie Wellsly had been and left. Three retired gentlemen enjoyed a checker game near her desk.

Luke Finn, Willy Evans, and Mr. Roy Fields would gather almost daily. Sometimes others would pop in. Hearing the conversation and the strange caller, Luke Finn said, "Somebody's gonna knock him off one day. He's so stupid."

"You're right, Luke, that jerk's always stirring up trouble. They ain't nothing going on about them holes in the ground. I know what it was. Somebody thought they was some buried treasure out there and they didn't find it, so they quit. They ain't gonna go back out there now. They dun left town."

"Not so sure about that, Willy," Luke responded. "People don't give up that easy. Not if they really believe there's a buried treasure."

"They ain't no treasure," Luke said as his fingers click, click, clicked across the checkerboard, and picked up three of his opponent's men.

Mr. Roy, an older gentleman was standing with both hands on a cane watching the game and waiting to play the winner. "We always heard about that pirate, ol' Roger Riddick," he said.

"That crook buried a lot of people; he buried some stolen stuff, too. I guarantee it! There was a diamond heist in the fifties and the FBI never did find all that. They got some of it back when that fake Rabbi got arrested in the sixties, but he claimed his uncle had hid a lot more. He was Riddick's nephew. Served forty years in prison, but he's out now."

"Well, he's too old to worry about," Willy said, studying his next move.

"He's twenty years younger than me." The man standing said.

They laughed and Willy said, "Mr. Roy, you old buzzard, you know they ain't many like you," as he picked up the last of his opponent's men. "That's two outta three."

Abby didn't say anything but kept her ears open. The men switched positions. Luke, the loser, stood up and Mr. Roy took his chair. As they shuffled positions, they changed the subject.

"You know about that old yeller house on Chattanooga Road, don't you? Luke asked, eager to tell what he knew.

"I know it's been vacant ten years and everybody says it's haunted," Willy said.

"Yeah, but now somebody's moved in it," Mr. Roy said, stealing Luke's news.

Abby was not familiar with the haunted house story but figured if she listened, she'd learn something. She had ridden by the two-story yellow house at the beginning of Chattanooga Road many times. She knew the Drug Enforcement Administration had seized the property when Alana Rodriguez was convicted of drugs and human trafficking. That woman had kept three children that people thought were hers until it all came out. Davie's friend George Rutherford was one of them.

There was talk that that woman's father was a Nazi and that she was, too. She was also convicted of killing two people who were Jews. She was finally sent to a woman's maximum-security prison in New York.

Luke picked up his story. "My daughter works in the register of deeds office and about a month ago, a woman came down from New York and bought that house. She claimed she wanted to bring her invalid sister south to get her out of that northern snow and the house was cheap."

"Can't blame nobody for that." Willy said, "But that house has an evil spirit. Some people say it's haunted. I've heard some strange stories."

"Yeah, me too," Luke said. "Like screams coming from the house and babies crying."

Mr. Roy said, "The police have investigated, but they ain't never found nothing. It gives me the creeps just looking at it. Them tall skinny cypress trees, they just make it spookier."

"Not to speak of that woods around that electric power station right next door," Willy said, and then noted, "Well, there's that canal between them."

"There's a big red danger sign, but in the summertime, you can't even see it." Luke said, "Can't even see the power station, but you can hear noises."

Mr. Roy agreed, "Yeah but in the winter, all them leaves are on the ground and you see the power station but you can't see what's making all them crunching noises. May be animals scurrying around. Sometimes, I think they act scared, too. You can hear the wind whistling through them trees and it is creepy. I been living in sight of that place for forty years. Sometimes it scares me."

"Where you live?" Asked Willy. "I thought you were in a nursing home."

"You better quit making fun of an old man, boy. You might not make it that old." Luke kicked Willy, but Willy laughed. "Aw, he knows I love him. He reminds me of my grandpa."

Mr. Roy just chuckled and answered Willy. "Been living at the end of Claxton Boulevard for forty years, right where Chattanooga Road begins. It's like we got a front-row seat. They need to move that red caution sign out by the road. Tiffany would never let our boys play out there. And they always wanted to go down to that canal, but she'd have a fit when they did. And that was even before the Rodriguez's moved in it. It's always been a creepy place."

"How's Mrs. Tiffany doing?" Luke asked. He knew Mr. Roy's wife was thirty-some years younger, and it had raised a few eyebrows back when the beautiful twenty-five-year-old model married the old well-to-do widower.

"She keeps me young," Mr. Roy said, nonchalantly.

Luke said, "So you been watching that house all these years?"

"I remember when the old cypress trees were planted. At first, they just made a nice little line along both sides of the property. They helped separate this side from the canal. But now they're so big we can't even see the house, hardly, unless we go upstairs. And with that big old Magnolia tree out back by their garage, you can't even see the river anymore."

"You spy on 'em much?" Luke asked.

They all three laughed. Abby pretended to be doing some work on the computer. The phone wasn't ringing much, so she just listened.

Mr. Roy said, "Used to be better'n television. In the last ten years, though, they ain't been nothing going on. Then about a month ago, stuff started happenin' again. Construction crews have been poppin' in and out, making repairs and remodelin'."

"Yeah," Luke said. "I've noticed the broken windows have been replaced, the shingles straightened and painted white. We go to the church down there, and we drive past that house every Sunday real slow, just checking it out. There's been a handicap ramp built from that front porch to the driveway. Guess that's for the invalid sister. And there's a big van that sits in the driveway with one of them wheelchair things on the back."

"Yeah," Mr. Roy said, "But at first you could see another handicap ramp at the back, then they built over it."

"What do you mean, built over it?" Willy asked.

Without looking up, Mr. Roy said, "The garage behind the house. They added to it from the front and now it comes up past the back porch so it's attached to the house now. That back handicap ramp goes right into the garage now. I remember when that driveway didn't go past the front porch. Now it goes up to the new garage front. It's a big paved surface now. My boys would've loved that. If it'd had a basketball goal, they would've stayed over there all the time."

"They're all married now, ain't they?" Luke asked.

"Yeah. The twins, Elwood runs Claxton Pharmacy, Charlie's a dentist. And the young one, Shawn, he's a contractor. He's the one been telling me what's happenin' over there. He had a crew buildin' the handicap ramps and that garage. It's weird what they're doing."

"Weird! I think the whole place is weird, but what did you mean?" Willy asked.

Mr. Roy didn't answer for a few seconds, he was studying the checkerboard. Then with a few jumps across from one corner to another he cleaned out his opponent and laughed. "Gotcha!"

Willy slapped the table and said, "You were just distracting me with all that talk. Okay. Two outta three." He set the board back up.

Luke opened the mini-fridge and asked, "What y'all want to drink?"

"Mountain Dew," Willy said.

"Make it two," Mr. Roy said. Luke pulled out three and passed them around. "Want one, Miss Abby?" He asked.

"No. Thank you, I'm good," she said and pointed at a coke sitting on her desk. He pulled a chair closer to the table to watch the next competition.

The front door opened and a pleasingly plump lady came in with a picnic basket and set it on Abby's desk.

"Made these and thought of you," she said as she opened the basket to show Abby the pile of cookies inside.

"Oh-h, still warm," Abby said and took one. "You guys want a cookie. There's a bunch here."

"Yeah, go ahead, try 'em," the lady said. "I'm entering this recipe in the Cookie Contest at the Festival. Be good to get a preview opinion."

"You do know I'm one of the judges, don't you?" Mr. Roy asked her.

The lady laughed. "I didn't, but I do now. Go ahead. It won't make you biased. I happen to know that Emma Jane Jones has been passing hers around town all week. But hers don't hold a candle to mine."

"Thank you, Mrs. Friar," Abby said. "You waiting for the bus?"

"Yeah. Got to watch those fishes a little, though." She took the chair near the aquarium and sat back to relax.

As the men crunched on cookies, Willy brought the subject back around to the yellow house. "What did you mean, it's weird what they've been doing?"

"Oh," Mr. Roy said as he made his first move on the new game. "It's like they didn't have enough of them cypress trees. They set a couple more full-grown trees beside the house."

"Full-grown?" Willy asked. "What's that all about?"

Mr. Roy said, "Well, almost; they're about twelve feet high. They got some equipment in there and dug big holes between the driveway and the side of the house, and set them twelve-foot trees down with a crane, and fixed it up. But I didn't see where they needed any more trees."

"Besides I bet it blocks your view," Luke said and laughed.

Mr. Roy laughed, too. "Yeah, I watched from my bedroom upstairs as they pulled old carpet out and brought new carpet in. Then one of them Trinity trucks brought in furniture. They put a big birdbath in the middle of the front yard. They laid sod and got a lawn already green, a little early, I think. Must be a special kind of grass. But now all the equipment's gone, the planters, and pavers, and equipment's all gone."

Luke said, "Well, to me, in spite of all that fresh yellow paint and white trim, the paved driveway, and the big new garage, that house is still just as eerie as it was. I think it's always gonna be a haunted house to me."

The city bus pulled up at the curb and Mrs. Friar jumped up. "There's my bus, y'all enjoy the cookies. Abby, I'll get my basket back next week." And she was gone.

The men became more engrossed in the moves on the checkerboard as those first few moves are critical. Abby answered the phone and then said to Luke who was seated watching the game, "Y'all take some more cookies, then I'll go share some with Grandma. I feel like Little Red Riding Hood," she said as she picked up the basket.

"You look like her," Luke said, and she laughed. He grabbed a handful of cookies on a napkin and laid them on the table by the checker game.

Abby took the basket through the hallway and around to Bernell's back entrance. In a low voice, she said, "I think I've heard some things you might be interested in."

She quickly conveyed the conversation and Bernell hit a button on her desk phone. "Adam, Thomas, Kit, Bree, conference room, pronto!"

Abby returned to her desk in time to hear Luke congratulating Roy on beating Willy again. Another gentleman entered the front door and greeted Abby and the others.

"Hey, Joe. You can take my place, and let Mr. Roy skin you. Well, after Luke's turn I mean." Willy got up from the table. "Evie's gonna kill me for staying out here so long today. He looked at the other guys. "Same time tomorrow?" They nodded.

He tipped his hat at Abby. "See you tomorrow, kid." She smiled and nodded. "Tell Mrs. Evie I said, hey."

Bernell met her crew in the conference room and shared the speculation about the yellow house. Bree shuddered. "I remember that creepy place. I haven't been by there in a long time. There's a secret staircase from the back door to the upstairs hallway. I'm sure it was used to get all those drugs up there and no telling what else. That's the way we came out that night when we got Sammie and Rodney out. We thought it was a closet but the boys told us it was stairs."

"Hmm," Bernell said. "I didn't know that. But it sounds like somebody's gone to great lengths to create a hideout there. Those cypress trees. That magnolia tree at the rear of the garage that blocks sight of the river."

Kit said, "You know what Bernell? Remember when we escaped the old sawmill through that boat garage? What if that yellow house has a boat garage like that and boats can go in there?"

Bernell leaned forward with interest. "That would certainly give them a concealed access point wide open to the river." She leaned back. "Well, we know what we have to do. Tell me what you think. Should we tell Mr. Roy what we're doing or just keep it quiet? I know the old man, and he's a good guy. But he might talk too much."

"Yeah, you know what Abby says, loose lips sink ships."

"We better just keep it undercover." Bree agreed.

Thomas spoke up. "I have an idea."

Adam said, "Does it have anything to do with me working on a roof?" They laughed, knowing where that was going.

Bernell said "Or doing a visitation to the new people on Chattanooga Road. You know, sharing some tracts or something."

Adam frowned. "I'd rather be on the rooftop. Send the women to the mission field."

Thomas said, "I'll call Mr. Roy and offer a free roof inspection. I think I can convince him that we need to check it out. It's an old house. The roof has probably not been replaced in many years."

"What if you find that it needs a new roof?" Bree asked.

"Gimme a minute," Thomas said. "Okay, we don't do the roof work, we just inspect and recommend someone."

Bernell gave him a high five. "You'll have to wait until he gets home or just deal with Tiffany. She's okay though. We need a good vantage point for effective surveillance."

Kit remembered the river angle, and said, "Yeah, a fishing trip might be in order."

Bree said, "We don't know if anything unlawful is going on there. The woman says she has an invalid sister and all the things he mentioned just point to her being a good care-taker looking after her invalid sister."

They laughed at Bree's naiveté. Adam said, "I have some beachfront property in Death Valley I want to sell you." They laughed at that.

Bree said, "Okay, I was just trying that out. The giveaway is those trees planted by the house. That digging equipment could dig some holes down the river, too. But Mr. Roy said that it's all gone now."

Bernell went to her office and buzzed Abby's desk. "Can you come here a minute?"

Abby came to her grandmother's office. "Get on your computer out there and look up construction rental equipment."

"Got it! Check your printer." Abby said and returned to her desk taking the empty cookie basket with her.

When Bernell returned to the conference room, Thomas and Adam were still there. "What's the holdup?" she asked.

"Oh, we're on it!" They both fled to Adam's office to tackle their first job at the yellow house.

Kit said, "Bernell, I got the records on cemeteries around here. There is nothing; not even an old slave cemetery or Indian burial ground on that side of town. So that property is clear. Davie can do what he wants. You want me to call him, or you want to handle that?"

Bernell said, "You can do it. But let's look at that map."

Kit rolled out two maps she had brought in with her. One was drawn in 1950 and one was drawn in 1995. Bernell got out her glasses and studied the maps. "Wow, I didn't know it shifted that much," she said. She pointed to a mark along the edge of the river in 1995. "It's about a hundred feet in from where it was in 1950."

"You mean the river is wider there?" Bree asked. "How can you tell?"

Kit said, "If you read these numbers," she pointed to the markings on each map.

"Oh, yeah," Bree said. "Cool."

"It's deeper along there too," Bernell said, "Otherwise, Davie couldn't dock all those big boats. I used to walk down there when I was a kid. It was three miles from our house growing up. It was shallow along there fifty years ago. I guess that flash flood washed out a chunk of land. It certainly looks like it. Good job on the topography research, Kit. I didn't know the river had shifted that much. I do remember that after the hurricane, Spring Hill was an island. They had to use boats for a while until they got the bridge built to get to Spring Hill Nursing Home and Retirement Village. I lived there a few years ago."

"Whose land is this?" Kit asked pointing to the marshland across the road from WDGW Oars and Boats.

Bernell said, "That belongs to our cousin William Michaels. It was Uncle Hinson's property and after he got killed, Ma sold it to

Jay and he's left it to William. You know what? I have an idea. William's got no use for that land. I bet if I approached him, he might develop a park there. Maybe a memorial to his dad." She got more excited as she talked, walking around the table gesturing with her arms.

"Some equipment could be brought in and cut some channels and make a canal running through there, and flower gardens, and picnic areas, and a playground. It would make a great park. In the meantime, it would give us a chance to do some digging around there."

Kit picked up on Bernell's enthusiasm. "And if he doesn't, some developer is going to approach William about putting a hotel or apartment building there. The town doesn't even have a park. It'd be great to have that land along the river, wouldn't it?

"This is exciting," Bree caught the enthusiasm. "I want to help!"

Deciding to strike while the iron was hot, Bernell buzzed Abby. "Get me an appointment with William Michaels at his earliest convenience."

"Should I tell him what it's about?" Abby asked.

"Yeah, developing a park."

Bernell turned to Bree and Kit again. "Okay, we'll contact Davie. I think he needs to dig up that chest. I believe I can get him and William working together and that will help."

"What about that digging at the Gristmill Restaurant and the Pine Ridge Landing?" Bree asked. "Is that a dead issue?"

"I believe it is," Bernell said.

Abby came through door 002 and handed Bernell a note. "Is two o'clock tomorrow okay?"

"Better than okay. Perfect. So the guys are checking out the yellow house. We've got Davie cleared to dig, and a possible city park on the horizon. Now let's get that fingerprint report."

"On it," Bree and Kit gathered up their folders and headed to their offices.

Bernell said, "I love it when a plan comes together!"

Chapter 16 Man in the White Suit

Wednesday evening, April 3

"Oh that is creepy!" Jenny shuddered when Davie told her that night what had been suggested at the Agency. "Eww, a vault? What could that mean to us? If they determine that it is a grave and there're more out there. You can't build anything over a cemetery. Not even a parking lot."

Davie said, "I know. This whole thing is just going crazy. Besides that, we got this mess going on about the yacht and Jeffry Smythe's disappearance. They're gonna get fingerprints tomorrow. Did Julie handle anything in the boutique that you know of where she could have left fingerprints?"

"Most likely. I'm glad KST finished their work here today. It feels good to be home. And by the way, they found three bugs. One in our office, one in the kitchen and one in our bedroom. Can you believe it? I just about died when they told me. I was so mad, I wanted to scream. When did they do that? And who did it?"

"Did they scan everywhere to make sure there aren't anymore?" Davie asked her.

"Oh, yes. They were very thorough with some sort of device. It was embarrassing, but I followed them around and I could tell when it detected one. Your Grandma was here the whole time, too."

Davie closed his file cabinet drawer on the last of the papers he had to refile. They were almost done restoring their study to normal. "I can't help but believe Grandpa is right," Davie said. "It's the only thing that makes any sense."

"You mean they're looking for a pirate treasure? And looking for a map or something here? But who?"

"That's the question," Davie said. "I think digging up whatever it was they struck yesterday will tell us more than anything else."

"Well, you better wait for Bernell's report. In the meantime, tomorrow I'm going to be furnishing my consultation room at the boutique. The stuff I ordered finally came in today. I'm also thinking of hiring another seamstress. We get a lot of sewing projects. I never realized I'd get so much work from boat people."

"Me either, but you've become quite the designer, Miss Burgundy Blue."

Jenny laughed. "Who'd have thought it? I just like focusing on things that are pretty."

Davie scooped up some papers for the trash and took them out. When he returned, Jenny had plopped down on the sofa and turned up the television. The lead story on the ten o'clock news was shocking.

"An unidentified body was found near the Claxton Waterfront about eight o'clock this evening. A male about fifty, wearing a white suit. Police are investigating. There have been no missing persons reported in the area. Please call the police if you have any knowledge of a missing person. Stay tuned to this station for updates as we learn more."

"Oh, no," Davie said. He went to the phone and dialed his dad's number. "I know it's late, Dad, but did you see the news?"

"Yes, Jessica and I were just talking about it. The man I saw Friday who said he was James Smythe was wearing a white suit. I thought it was a little odd, but then he wasn't from around here. You reckon it was Jeffry Smythe?"

Davie said, "He wore a white suit sometimes. But Dad, I don't believe it was him. He didn't act like that. And he would have contacted me. You say that was last Friday? I don't think we've told Jeb about that."

"I'll call him first thing in the morning," Jimmy said. "He might want you to come down and identify the body."

"Oh, shoot. I'm not doing that," Davie said. "I hope it's not him. But where is he? I don't believe he's passed away. I just don't believe it." As he hung up, he plopped back down on the sofa muttering, "I can't believe all this is happening. I wish I'd never built that yacht!"

The phone startled him. "Oh, no. They're calling already. I'm not answering." Davie got up and went to the kitchen. Jenny said, "It's probably not them. But it's usually bad when the phone rings so late." She picked up the receiver.

It was Lillian. "I know it is late Jenny. But we just saw the news."

"Yeah," Jenny answered, "Davie doesn't think that's him. You want to talk to him?"

"It's your grandma," she handed the phone to Davie as he returned with a Mountain Due in his hand.

He frowned but took the phone. "Hello."

Lillian had another idea. "Davie, we saw the news about the man in the river. But I wanted to tell you about something else."

When she finished the story about the man at the homeless shelter, Davie said, "Well you saw that man, so we could clear that up now. We've got a picture of Jeffry Smythe; you would be able to identify him from that. Can we run it up there now?"

When he hung up and explained to Jenny, she found a good picture of Jeffry and Julie Smythe. "I'll go with you. If that's him, then it proves he's alive. But what about Julie?"

She asked the question again when Davie handed the picture to his grandmother.

Isaac speculated, "They could have been attacked, and he escaped, but she was killed or abducted."

Jenny shuddered. "How horrible, don't even think that."

Davie told Isaac, "I've already been through all that in my mind, too."

Lillian studied the picture. "That's not the man in the homeless shelter. They're not alike at all. I don't have a picture of him, but he's darker, his hair is darker. The man in this picture is very fair and his hair is almost blonde. He also looks taller. I didn't see the man standing up, but that is definitely not him. His hair is darker."

Davie said, "Well, that settles that. But it doesn't clear up anything. He's still missing and I am getting ticked about all this!" Jenny could understand his reaction. She felt the same way.

Chapter 17 Identifying a Body

Wednesday evening, April 3

J**enny was on the phone in the den** when Davie arrived home. Bree had called with her progress report. They were done dusting for fingerprints on the yacht. "We'll know something soon." When Jenny hung up, she kissed Davie hello and flopped down on the sofa with him.

"That was Bree. They're moving right along with things. And listen to this." Bree had told her about the yellow house, the maps of the river, and Bernell's idea about a park.

"Wow," Davie said. "For a ninety-year-old woman, she's got the tiger by the tail, hasn't she?"

Jenny laughed at his imagery. "Not quite ninety, but absolutely! I'll say she does. What do you think about all that?"

Davie said, "I'm glad we went there yesterday. I didn't believe her when she said she might even have something today. I'm curious about that house. You've heard about the time George ran away, and mom and I got involved in looking for him. Bree and Niki came from California for a visit at that same time, and they got involved."

Jenny nodded. "I've heard a little bit. I think y'all went over there to babysit and the woman got arrested, and y'all rescued the boys because there was a room full of drugs and marijuana. And you took the boys to your grandma's house, and everything started coming out about Alana Rodriguez kidnapping them."

"Yeah. And the good part was Pastor Rutherford took the boys and changed their lives. That was ten years ago. Nobody's lived in that house since then. Isn't it ironic that that same house is coming into the picture again?

"Maybe," Jenny said. "Oh, did you hear about the threat to that stupid DJ this morning?"

"No, I don't listen to that station."

"Well, I don't listen to him either, but Carol at Jane's Beauty Shop does, and she came in the Boutique for a few minutes today. I think she came in just to tell me stuff about him and ask me what I thought. It sounds like a threat that would be coming from you or your dad or grandpa. It was a man's voice and she said it was deep and ominous. Anyway, somebody told him if he didn't shut up, he was going to lose his tongue. What do you make of that?"

"You know what, Jenny? He probably put somebody up to that just for the effect. He's just that kind of a jerk."

"You think? Well, he does keep an ongoing rant about something. He's promoting the Spring Festival now. I don't know why in the world they chose him to be the Grand Marshall, but it must have gone to his head. Carol told me today that he's thinking of running for mayor. And some people will be stupid enough to vote for him. Especially if he 'exposes the buried secrets of Big Creek' like he's saying he's going to do."

Jenny got up from the sofa and pulled him up. "Let's get some supper. I've got a beef stew simmering in the crockpot. Might not be as good as your mom's, but I had to work today."

"I'm sure it is," he said and followed her into the kitchen. She already had the table set with her everyday china and a salad in the fridge. As she dished out the stew, she asked, "What do you think? Now that we know that box they struck is not a vault for a grave, what will you do?"

"Ugh! It may not be an official cemetery, but what if it's still a grave? I want to find out, but I don't want to do it."

"Eww. I hadn't thought of that," Jenny shuddered.

"I'm just gonna leave it covered up for a while and maybe the news will die down. If that radio jerk will stop carrying on about it."

"Don't say anything, Davie. Somebody will think it was you that made that threat."

"That's what he wants people to think. Well, it wasn't. Didn't even know about it till you just told me. And I bet Daddy and Grandpa don't know about it either. I wonder what kind of following he's got. Must be a lot of them for the station to keep him going like that."

Jenny and Davie bowed their heads, he asked the blessing, then asked, "Did you take the frame to the shop today?"

"No. I decided we could just fix it here. I'll measure it and find a mirror that fits. Probably have to have one custom cut."

"Well, I'll fix it when you get the mirror."

"Okay, I guess that's the least of our concerns right now," she sighed.

"Yeah," Davie agreed. "Did Bree mention Smythe?"

"Oh, you know what? She didn't. Let me call her back." Jenny jumped up from the table, but Davie grabbed her hand. "No, don't worry about it. It's six o'clock. If she had anything she wouldn't have left that out."

"Okay," Jenny said. "But how long does it take to look up an obituary?"

"About five minutes," he said. "We did that looking for George's real parents."

"So you know how to do it then," Jenny observed.

"Sure, and I can't just sit here and relax. Maybe we could do something on our own." As they ate, they discussed the possibility of going to the library, or to the college. They decided to go to the library. Whoever was there would help. Everett, the computer technician, was still there and now had an assistant. Lisa the librarian was, but she was married now, so she had a life outside the library. She also had a larger staff than she used to have, so there would definitely be someone there to help. While they were mulling that thought, the phone rang.

Bree said, "Davie, I've got nothing on Jeffry Smythe. You think he could possibly have given you a fake name?

"No way," Davie said. "I saw his driver's license, he had the number on his checks from VCU bank in Chesapeake, Virginia."

"Well," Bree said. "I have contacted that bank and, of course, they won't give me any information. But something's just not kosher. I'll get back on this tomorrow, but I just wanted to touch base about it."

"We were just about to go to the library. Remember when we did all that stuff, looking for George? Well, he was Giorgio back then."

"I remember it well," she said. "But his parents were dead and there were obituaries. There is no obituary for Jeffry Smythe."

"Well, he ain't dead then!" Davie blurted.

"I'm inclined to agree with you. We may have to send somebody to Chesapeake and look for him. We got the fingerprints. They don't match anything in the database. He obviously never had a record. I think that is a good thing. At least you're not dealing with a criminal."

Davie sighed, banged his head against the wall, and kicked the baseboard a couple of times. "I don't know what to do about all this stuff. I just wanted to build boats. I didn't want to deal with break-ins, treasure hunts, and missing persons."

"Okay, then. Don't try to deal with it. Just let us do it. You and Jenny go to a movie or something and get your mind off it. Let me talk to Jenny for a minute."

He handed the phone to Jenny and heard her say "Run over to the Boutique tomorrow. I'll help you find something pretty. You can take some swatches home and see how they work."

"Good idea," Bree said. "I'll run over about noon?"

"Perfect!" Jenny said. As she hung up, she put her arms around Davie and said, "It'll get better. We've got a lot of support." She wanted to believe that herself.

The phone rang again. "We're popular tonight," Jenny said as Davie answered. He recognized the police department number. "Oh, no," he said. He knew this was the phone call he had dreaded.

When he hung up, he said to Jenny, "I don't want to do this."

"They want you to identify that body," she guessed.

"Chief Jeb said they have not been able to find out anything about him and that it might be Jeffry Smythe."

"It's not. I just know it's not him," Jenny said.

"Want to go down there to the morgue with me?" He asked her.

Jenny closed her eyes; "I couldn't wait for you to ask me that." Then she looked up at him and shook her head. "No, I do not want to go, and I am NOT going to look at him, but I will go with you and sit in the lobby or somewhere and wait for you."

"I appreciate it," he said and ran upstairs to get a different jacket. Jenny quickly dialed his mother's number.

"We got a call, too. Jimmy has to tell them if it was the same man who was at the restaurant. We can ride down there together."

"Or you and I could stay here," Jenny said.

"We should go and show support though," Jessica suggested.

By the time Davie got back downstairs, his parents were at the door. Jimmy said, "I'm looking forward to this as much as you are, son."

"Yeah, I can tell," Davie closed the door behind them. "I'm glad you're going though. I don't like dead people."

At the hospital, Jessica and Jenny waited in the lobby while Jimmy and Davie were escorted to the basement. Jessica nervously flipped through a magazine. Jenny scrolled through pictures on her phone. She paused at one and showed her mother-in-law. "This was Julie Smythe at the shop one day. She wanted me to take a picture of that tapestry and email it to her. I did."

"That means you have her email address," Jessica said.

"Oh, you are right!" Jenny quickly scrolled to her email contacts and found the address. She typed in a quick note. "Hey, Julie. Been trying to contact you about the yacht. Where are you? Please call." She entered her cell phone number as well as Davie's and also the plant number "That should cover it," she said and hit send. "Why hadn't I thought of this before?"

A minute later her phone dinged notification of an incoming email. "Yes!" She said and excitedly scrolled to the appropriate app.

"Oh, no" she groaned.

"What? Bad news?" Asked Jessica. "Is he really dead?"

Jenny handed her the phone. The email had bounced back. "No recipient of this address."

"What has happened to these people?" Jenny slapped the arm of her chair.

Jessica shook her head. "It certainly is weird. Maybe Bernell can find out something."

"Bree called tonight and said they hadn't found anything yet. They've looked for an obituary but there is no obituary. In a way that's good news, but what in the world has happened to them?"

When Jimmy and Davie stepped off the elevator at the other end of the lobby, Jenny and Jessica stood up. They could not tell by the men's demeanor what they had determined. When Jimmy came closer, though, he started shaking his head. "Not either one of them."

Davie said, "It was not Jeffry Smythe for sure!"

"And I did not think it looked like the man who was in the restaurant." Jimmy said, "So we're back to square one. Or worse. We don't have any idea who the man was at the restaurant, but I didn't think this was him."

Jessica said, "Can you find out how he paid that day?"

Jimmy raised his eyebrows. "If he paid by credit card or check, yes, that is a good idea. I will check on that tomorrow. Of course, if he paid with cash, we won't have anything to go on."

"In the meantime," Davie said, "The doctor downstairs said he would let the Police Department know that we could not identify that man."

"Did he drown? Or was there some other cause of death?" Jessica asked.

Davie shuddered.

"He wouldn't tell us," Jimmy said. "I don't know why that mattered, but he just wouldn't tell us anything. Jeb probably will if we want to know."

"Or that stupid jerk on the morning show. He probably already knows," Jenny said.

"It would be interesting if he does," Davie said. "Maybe we need to listen to his show tomorrow."

Jessica shook her head. "That is exactly what he wants. He's doing all this for ratings, don't y'all know that?"

"Well, I think he's playing a dangerous game," Jimmy said.

They all agreed. "On second thought, we won't be listening to him at the plant," Davie said.

Since Jimmy was driving, he said to Davie, "Call your Grandpa and get him up to date."

Isaac was not surprised. He brought up something else, though. "I think it's time to take a hard look at those papers that you gave me from that rescue boat, Davie. Can you and your Dad meet me at the bank tomorrow?"

"Hold on and I'll ask, "Davie said, "Daddy, Grandpa wants to know if we can meet him at the bank tomorrow?"

"I guess so," Jimmy said. "What time?"

"What time?" Davie asked Isaac. "Okay, we'll pick you up at ten-thirty."

After he hung up, Jessica scoffed. "Really? Why does he want y'all to go with him to the bank? Why doesn't he just get it and y'all meet him at the house?"

"I don't know. Daddy's getting old. He can be weird sometimes, too," Jimmy said.

In an understanding tone rare for Davie, he said, "He must have a reason."

Chapter 18 Breakfast at Tiffany's

Thursday morning, April 4

"What took you so long?" Mr. Roy asked as he opened his door to Thomas and Adam Roof Inspectors at eight o'clock Thursday morning. Thomas handed him their business card and said, "Eight o'clock is what we said. We didn't want to get here too early."

"Yeah, I know that's what you said. I'd of thought Bernell would send you out here yesterday. Come on in. Tiffany's got your breakfast ready."

Jaws dropped as Thomas and Adam both looked at him in shock. *Who told him?* They wondered if Abby had slipped up. But that was not like her. And Bernell wouldn't have said anything. *Who else knew?*

"Oh, don't act so surprised, boys. You think I was born yesterday? Why you think I made such a point of talking in front of your little girl up there. I know she's the front office spy. Abby's a cute little thing and she does her job well. I appreciate that."

Dumbfounded, the two detectives followed the old man back to the kitchen where his still beautiful wife was smiling knowingly. In the dining nook, four places were set on the maple table by double windows with ruffled blue and white curtains. It was very inviting. Orange juice was poured. A platter of bacon and sausage was in the center of the table beside a bowl of scrambled eggs and a basket of warm toast. They sat down dutifully.

"How you like your coffee?" Mr. Roy asked. Tiffany set a hot bowl of grits beside the eggs and then sat down as Mr. Roy poured four cups of coffee. He handed one to her and she passed it across to Thomas and then to Adam.

When he finally got his voice, Thomas said, "This beat's all I've ever seen. So much for the roof inspecting business, Adam."

Adam laughed. "This is one for the books. Who's hoodooing who?"

Tiffany spoke for the first time. "How else could we get you guys out here? We've been suspecting something weird going on over there, and we knew it would have been foolish to go to the police. I mean, what could we say? We've been spying on our neighbors, and we suspect they're up to no good? They'd have laughed us outta the park. Now y'all can do it for us."

Mr. Roy went to the pantry and brought out a basket of assorted jellies. Tiffany said, "Thanks, I forgot that."

Adam said, "I just want to go ahead and make a reservation for once a week. This is better than the Pancake House."

"Oh, pancakes. We have them on Tuesdays," Mr. Roy said. They all laughed and joked for a few minutes. The detectives finally reconciled themselves to the situation. "Well, you have to admit we dressed the part," Thomas said pointing to the uniforms they were wearing and their name tags that said, Roof Inspector.

Mr. Roy laughed and said, "You got that truck and ladders and everything. Y'all did great. After you eat, I'll show you the best place to go up if you want to."

Adam said, "Okay, but maybe you could fill us in on what you've found so far. What's made you suspicious?"

"Well, there's been several things," Mr. Roy said. "For one, they ain't no invalid living there. All that's a front for something."

"How can you know there is no invalid there?" Thomas asked.

Tiffany spoke up. "You have to understand. We get bored with television and we can see all down Chattanooga Road. You'd be surprised what we see. The church parking lot is an ongoing drama. A lot of people hook up there. I could have told you about some divorces before they ever hit the paper. But that's another story."

She got up and refilled her coffee and offered others. Mr. Roy said, "From the day that van first drove in the driveway with that wheelchair lift on the back, there's never been no invalid, not even a person who was crippled or handicapped. When the woman gets out of the van, she always looks around to see if anybody's watching. She's even looked over at our house but she's never been able to see us. We keep those rooms dark on the front."

Tiffany picked up the story. "We sleep in the bedroom on the backside where the sun comes up. Our garage is facing the back driveway and we're never in the front. The rooms on the front were the boys' rooms. I doubt she could have any suspicion about us. We go to the church down there, and the visitation committee has tried to visit that house. Nobody ever comes to the door, even if the van is home. Some of the ladies in my class have talked about it. I've never said anything. I just watch." She winked at Mr. Roy. And he patted her hand.

"Well, it doesn't sound like much to go on yet," Adam said.

Mr. Roy said, "Oh but I've got pictures. They're on my phone. She never parks inside the garage. She's got that van that she always leaves in front. Why'd she build all that big garage? She sure ain't using it to park a car in."

Thomas and Adam looked at each other. "That's an astute observation," Adam said.

"So what do you think we'll see from on top of the roof that you can't see from that bedroom window?" Thomas asked.

"Probably nothing," Tiffany said. "And it'd be safer inside. We just wanted to get you over here to talk about it. He knew you'd come." They all laughed at that.

Mr. Roy said, "I've known Bernell all her life. She's almost as old as I am, you know."

"We don't know nothing 'bout that!" Adam said. And they laughed again.

Mr. Roy said, "Well, she always was the prettiest thing in Claxton, and from the day Roger Riddick came down from New York, he wanted to get that girl. But she would have nothing to do with him. He hated her family for it. He figured they thought he was not good enough for her. And trust me, they were right."

Mrs. Tiffany said, "That was before my time, but I am sure he's right. I heard about it. All that stuff about Roger Riddick and then Alana Rodriguez's connection when she was living in that house is what's made us suspicious of everything over there. We watched the traffic in and out way back when the Rodriguez's lived there. We knew it was a drug house. We were so glad when all that was over. We were hoping the city would condemn the property and tear it down, but then that woman bought it."

"Zelda Midget," Mr. Roy said. "Our son told us her name. He did a lot of work over there. He says she is a creepy person. She ordered his crew around like she owned them. Wouldn't listen to reason. Seemed to have a motive for everything that didn't make any sense. Like those trees for instance. They are in such a stupid place. It is obvious they were intended to conceal the back entrance from view."

"I thought the back entrance went into the garage," Thomas said.

"There's two," Mr. Roy said. "We watched as they built it. The handicap ramp runs into the garage. But there's another door that just comes out the side."

Adam said thoughtfully, "Well, you know, Mr. Roy and Mrs. Tiffany, it could all be perfectly innocent."

"It ain't," Mr. Roy said without any hesitation. "There's something crooked going on there. I'd stake my life on it. I been around too long not to recognize evil in action."

"Well, I think Bernell has a lot of respect for you," Thomas said. "That's why she wanted us to check this out."

Adam said, "Maybe Thomas and Adam Roof Inspectors ought to visit the yellow house and see if they need a roofing job."

"You can try, but she won't let you in," Tiffany said.

Thomas remembered what Kit had said about the boat garage and asked, "Mr. Roy, you think maybe the garage backs up to the river and a boat can go in and out that way?"

"I'm sure of it," he said. "They're either packing drugs in there or something else is going on. You just got to get in that garage to find out."

"How?" Both Thomas and Adam asked.

"You any good at scuba diving?" He asked.

"Oh, you mean?

"Yep. It's the only way. Get off your boat out there on the river where it's not suspicious, come over to that canal and you'll see the water runs right up into that garage.

"How do you know all this?"

"You got to keep his name out of it, but our son is a contractor. He built the boat garage."

"Well, that's not illegal, you know," Thomas said.

"Weird thing is the river didn't come up that far. Then we could hear noises at night for a while. Like machinery running. Probably digging with a backhoe or something. I figure she started inside the garage and dug till she got to the river."

"Well, there's nothing illegal about that if the property goes up to the river," Adam said.

Mr. Roy said, "Well, I guarantee something illegal's going on. I just don't know what."

"Is it possible that you have such suspicions because you have memories of other illegal stuff going on there?" Thomas posed.

"Maybe. Don't think so, though. You add all this up and see what you come up with. You got our house to work from. Just don't involve us, and don't mention our son's name."

Thomas stood up. "Thank you for this delicious breakfast and the good company and all this information. I think Adam and I need to go talk with the boss and see what she wants us to do next."

Mr. Roy nodded. "Good idea. She'll birddog it. Here, take my phone. I'll pick it up tomorrow."

Adam said, "You going down to play checkers today?"

"No," Mrs. Tiffany answered for him. "He's got to go shopping with me. We're picking up some new curtains for those front bedroom windows. They're kind of frayed."

They all laughed. "Well, if we can be of any help in replacing them, let us know," Thomas said as he handed them a couple of business cards and thanked them again for such a lovely breakfast.

"One more thing," Mr. Roy said. "If you want to set up surveillance in the bedrooms upstairs, just let us know. We'll be here."

"And for going and coming, you can use our back entrance," Mrs. Tiffany added.

Thomas and Adam laughed. "You got this all worked out. Well, Mrs. Jackson will let you know. But I have a feeling we'll be back. And thanks again for that wonderful breakfast."

"One more thing," Adam said. "Did you say Pancake Day is Tuesdays?"

Thomas punched him on the arm. "Get outta here," he grinned, shaking his head.

"Oh, wait, I have an idea," Adam held up his hand. He looked at Thomas. "Let's leave that telescope here to give Mr. Roy a better look."

"Great idea," He looked at Tiffany. "Be right back." They both ran to the truck and each brought back something with his jacket wrapped around it."

They pulled their pieces out, connected them, and Mr. Roy whistled. "That a beaut!"

Tiffany laughed. "He's going to have a ball with that."

"I'll set it up at that middle window. It has the best view." They followed him upstairs.

"Feels like Christmas," Mr. Roy said.

Mrs. Tiffany laughed. "I'm not going to be able to drag him shopping now. Boys, you've made an old man's day."

Thomas chuckled. "Good! Thanks for this." He held up the phone. "We'll get back with you. Kit can download your pictures and you can get your phone back later today or tomorrow. It will be safe."

Back at the agency, there was a little excitement stirring. When Thomas and Adam entered the back door, Bree, Kit, and Bernell had some papers spread out on the conference table.

Bernell said, "What are y'all doing back so soon? You haven't had time to do much surveillance."

"No," Thomas said. "But we sure learned a lot." They proceeded to explain.

Kit said, "Wow, I think we've found our diggers. But it's going to take some doing to get proof."

"Yeah," Thomas said. "But we've got a lot right here." He handed Kit the phone. "Mr. Roy says to get his pictures and use them however we want to."

Kit took the phone to her office, connected the phone to her computer with a cable and a hundred pictures flooded her screen. She laughed "Gee Whiz! Bernell you got to see this." She started printing out pages.

Bernell tapped on the table with her nails as though tapping out a Morse code. Nobody said anything. They had seen that process before. She was waiting for the answer that usually came after a minute or so. She tapped again a little more urgently. Then after a pause, she said.

"Go back to Mr. Roy's. Get a fishing boat, your cameras with a high powered telescopic lens. Go fishing across the river. Keep a twenty-four-hour surveillance on that garage. If they dug that dirt out to the river, they certainly could have dug those holes at the landings. Right now they might be planning to go back out and dig some more. If they do, follow them. They've not found what they're after yet, and they're not going to give up this soon. They've got the equipment, we need to see it though."

"Sounds like you believe Mr. Roy," Adam said.

"Every word," Bernell said. "He always was a smart man. And he's always been discrete. He's not shooting you any bull. Yes. I am taking him very seriously."

"Okay, we're on it!" Thomas said and they headed out to their next mission.

"Back to this classified ad," Bernell said. "Abby, you've done it again. Kit, what do you think of applying for one of these jobs?

Didn't you serve as the chef on the Queen Mary or something? And you got the Julie Child award that time, didn't you?"

Kit laughed. "Well, yes ma'am, I believe I did. It's about time for me to get my sea legs again."

"I never knew that," Bree said. Then slapped her forehead in a V-8 gesture, and started laughing. "Okay. Stupid me. I'm a little slow this morning. You go ahead on with your sea legs and be yacht Chef. That's out of my field. I can't take a skiff without getting sick."

"Well, she figured they wouldn't buy me as a Crew Captain," Kit explained.

Abby had printed a classified ad from the internet version of The Morning Sun in Chesapeake, Virginia, a detailed ad to hire a six-member yacht crew. Applicants had to contact the newspaper between March 1 and April 30.

Bernell said, "It's a long shot, but we have to take the long shots. This Jeffry Smythe has dropped off the face of the earth." She folded the pages and gave them to Kit just as Abby came back with some more printouts.

"What've you got there?" Bernell asked.

Abby laid one sheet down, "This is a list of rental agencies that rent out heavy equipment, backhoes, forklifts, and such. They rent by the day, by the week or the month."

"Find out if Zelda Midget still has any digging equipment and when they expect it back."

"I can do that," Abby said. "Right now, Luke and Willy are out there playing checkers and Miss Waylon and Georgia Franks are sitting in front of the aquarium chattering away. I think they're talking about that stupid DJ. He made another comment this morning that's got people stirred up."

"Did it have anything to do with the holes that were dug out there by the river?"

"Nope. He's talking about his Indian heritage and what he's going to do at the Festival. The Wellsly's are getting a rest today."

Chapter 19 Clues from the Hymnbook

Thursday morning, April 4

When the three Wellsly men entered the Bank of Claxton early Thursday morning, Isaac signed in, and the teller led him to the vault. Davie and Jimmy just waited for him in the lobby. When Isaac returned, he was carrying a small briefcase. "Let's go over to the Agency. I think it would be good to get some other eyes on this."

"Oh, so that's why you wanted us to come too," Davie said. B.B Jackson Private Investigating Agency was two doors down from the bank. They walked over, without an appointment.

Davie remembered. "Oh, you know what she said? Call ahead the next time."

"Oh, dang. I forgot that." Isaac pulled out his cellphone and punched in her number.

"Grandpa, we're right here at the door," Davie said.

"I know, but we're calling ahead. Hello, Abby, I need to see your Grandma this morning. She busy?"

"As a beaver," Abby said. "What's happening?"

"Well, I don't want to say out here," he said.

She saw them at the door, hung up her phone, and motioned for them to come on in. Luke and Willy were engrossed in their usual game but looked up when Isaac, Davie, and Jimmy walked in.

"Hey Jimmy," Luke said. "I'm glad to hear that Rebecca Willis is better."

"You got that right," Jimmy said. "Who's winning?"

"It's back and forth. I think Willy's ahead four outta six right now. I gotta leave soon. So he'll be the winner today."

"Maybe tomorrow will be your day," Jimmy said.

"No, can't come tomorrow. Gotta get some plowing done. It's that time of year, you know."

"Yeah, you gonna have some cucumbers and squash for the restaurant again this year?"

"Oh, yeah. Already planted. Molly's got some sting beans yesterday that she said you'd like. Kentucky Wonders. We got corn coming up already. Got to feed the good citizens of Phillips County and Claxton."

"Right, we depend on you farmers," Jimmy said. "Don't know what we'd do without you."

Isaac and Davie had already sat down, and Jimmy was about to when Abby said, "Mrs. Jackson will see you now."

Isaac said, "Well, that was quick."

Abby winked. "It always pays to call ahead."

They laughed and entered the door where 001 was beckoning them. Her white teeth flashed that signature smile and her silver hair shimmered. She winked at Davie, and he noticed a youthful sparkle in her amber eyes. "You're alright, Aunt Bernie," he said.

"Well, let's hope we can solve some mysteries around here," she said. "First let me tell you what we've learned." She shared the speculation about the yellow house and the boat garage.

Davie said, "We've got three bays like that at the plant so we can work on boats in the water. I never knew that yellow house was that close to the water though."

Jimmy said, "That's a pretty elaborate scheme, don't you think?"

Bernell nodded. "Yes, but when millions of dollars are at stake, people will go to great lengths. Besides, that's our only lead right now, so we'll play it out."

Bree held up her hand. "Ah, there is one more lead. I just got back from the Police Department looking at fingerprints. Like I told you, there is nothing on Jeffry Smythe, but fingerprints on that cigarette lighter match a woman wrestler who got in trouble with the law about ten years ago in New York. Her name was Jamie Sampson. She served a few months in prison."

"So how did her cigarette lighter wind up on Davie's parking lot?" Bernell started tapping her nails on the table. "I wonder how long it's been there. Did you see the cigarette lighter? Does it show age or rust like it's been out there for a long time? There's nothing conclusive about this yet."

Bree said, "And where is that woman now? You're right. All we have is a cigarette lighter. It's in perfect condition. Since it has initials on it, it could have come from a jewelry store. I'll check that out."

Bernell looked at Isaac and went straight to the point. "You came here with something on your mind. What is it?"

"Maybe nothing," Isaac said, as he opened his briefcase. "This is what I told you Davie found in a compartment of that boat."

He laid out a brown envelope. Inside it was an older envelope, fat with contents.

"This is nothing but songs ripped out of an old church hymnal," she said. "Roger Riddick was not a religious man. Everything he did had an ulterior purpose. So maybe these are clues to those holes being dug. Somebody must have known what these songs meant."

Kit said, "I know what this song means. 'At the Cross,' Jesus died on the cross for the sins of everyone. And the writer is thankful that Christ died for him even though he didn't deserve it. It's a pretty song. We used to sing it at church."

"And this one," Isaac laid out the song, "Rock of Ages."

"Same thing," Kit said, "Jesus Christ is the 'Rock of Ages.' And the writer is wanting to hide in the cleft of the rock."

They all pored through the lyrics, looking for a clue. "It mentions water and blood, but that's not talking about a river," Davie said.

"This one is," Isaac said and laid out "Down by the Riverside."

"Oh, yeah, now we're getting somewhere," said Davie. "But what does it mean laying down burdens and study war no more?"

"You know what that means," Jimmy said. "Giving it all to the Lord. Maybe it's talking about when he dies he won't have to worry anymore."

"Yeah, but I'm thinking the clue in this is just the riverside," Isaac said.

"This one is pretty clear. 'At the End of the Road.' It's sung at funerals, but I'm pretty sure he's just meaning the end of a road that goes down to the river."

"That's pretty clear," Bernell said. "But what about this one, 'Old Hundredth.' It's torn from a hymnal, but I don't remember that song."

Jimmy picked it up. "It was written in the fifteenth century, but it's still in the back of the old hymnals at church. We talked about this song at church one Sunday because it seems like such an odd title."

"It's in those old books that were left there by Claxton First Church when y'all bought the building in the '60s." He looked at Isaac as he spoke. "Some people think it's talking about Psalm 100."

Bree interjected, "The 'Old Hundred' is mentioned in Mark Twain's 'Adventures of Tom Sawyer.' I had to read that in college. I remember the scene was at the funeral service being held for the boys after people thought they were dead--Tom Sawyer and Huck Finn—then they found out that they were still alive, and it was a praise song. Mark Twain called it 'Old Hundred' in that book."

"I doubt if Roger Riddick ever read Tom Sawyer any more than he read the Bible," Bernell said.

"Well, the point is, it was in the hymn book, and somebody ripped out pages and connected them to create a set of clues."

"So maybe something is buried a hundred yards or a hundred feet from the river," suggested Kit.

"Probably a hundred feet," Jimmy said. "People can visualize that better, don't you think?"

"I don't know," Davie said. "A hundred yards would be like a hundred steps. That's pretty easy to measure."

"That's a very good point," Isaac said. "But I guess the other things would have to add up to know whether it's feet or yards. What about the other two songs. How do they fit?"

"Rock of Ages," Bree said, "Is there a big rock down by the riverside?"

"Hmm, there are lots of big rocks down by the riverside. We have tons at the Gristmill Restaurant."

"There's a few at Pine Ridge Landing," Isaac said. "But not many."

"There are some near the boat plant," Davie said.

"Wonder if any of them have any markings on them?" Kit asked. "I bet that's the key."

Davie spoke up. "We can all do some searching around. Do you think that is what Riddick was referring to, Grandpa? Do you think he buried a treasure chest and this was his record to remember where it was?"

"That's what I wondered," Isaac said.

Jimmy said, "But if we go digging a hole by every rock out there, well, that's just impossible. Besides, there's been so much digging on the property around the mill, looks like we would have run into something by now."

"Good point, Jimmy," Isaac said. "But stuff tends to sink further in the ground, I mean from 1955 to now, that's almost sixty years. He could have dug only three feet then and it'd be deeper than that now. But I think it's futile to search for anything."

"But somebody's doing it, Isaac," Bernell suggested. "Somebody is searching, and they're not done."

Kit raised her hand. "Did you notice that they dug a hundred feet from the river's edge in each of those three places?"

"They must have these same clues then."

"But the map of the river now shows it much wider at Davie's plant than it is now. So 100 feet 60 years ago, that could be like 10 feet now." Kit had laid out an old map and a current one.

Isaac said, "Yep."

Jimmy said, "We're still back to the point I was making. You're just stabbing in the dark to keep digging holes here and there. There's got to be a better way."

"Will a Geiger counter help?" Bree asked.

Davie spoke up, "That only detects gaseous material. What you mean is a metal detector, but that won't detect anything more than about a foot. And it has to be metal. I doubt one of those would do a bit of good."

Everybody sat thoughtful but dumbfounded. "As I said, this is all futile," Isaac repeated.

"Well, let's look at it this way," Bernell suggested. "If we read these like a sentence, it would go like this. There's a treasure at the end of the road, down by the riverside, a hundred feet, by the rock of ages at the cross."

"Wait a minute," Kit raised her voice. "What about the backsides? Is there a message in them too?"

Isaac said, "No, I went through all that. That's why I placed them in this order. See the bottom of every page there's a number penciled in. When I saw that, I knew he meant that side. And Bernell, you got it right. I'm sure that's what it means."

Bernell was a little solemn when she said, "I can vouch for one thing. Roger Riddick did not love hymns. He just wanted an obscure way of remembering where he buried it, something that wouldn't look like a map. He used to go to church once in a while to be seen. I guess this is what he was doing. You want to take this back with you, or you want me to put them in the vault here?"

"You keep them," Isaac said. "Just help us figure out what to do."

"Okay," Bernell said. "It doesn't prove anything. But you can be sure he was not saving these because he wanted to worship the Lord."

Chapter 20 More Radio Talk

Thursday morning, April 4

Back in the car, Davie turned the radio on. Just out of curiosity, he twisted the dial to the station he said he would never listen to. And of course, DJ Reeves was taking calls. The topic of the day was the upcoming Spring Festival. He had been talking about his role as Grand Marshall. He would be leading the parade, riding a white horse, and wearing full regalia and headdress as an Indian Chief.

Not everyone appreciated that. "I am not mocking," he defended himself to a caller. "It is perfectly appropriate for me to dress as a Cherokee Indian Chief. My great-great-grandfather was Chief Flaming Cloud, and this is to honor him—not mock him."

The caller started to say something, but he cut her off. "We have a group of Cherokee natives performing ceremonial dances and giving talks about Indian culture. It will be educational and entertaining. Don't tell me this is wrong. You're the one with the problem, madam. If you are offended stay home!" He sounded a bit agitated and pulled the plug on the caller.

"Well, that's a switch," said Isaac. "From what I've heard of him, he is the one attacking and being critical all the time. I've never heard him on the defensive before."

"It's about time," Davie said.

Jimmy agreed. "I don't see anything wrong with him wearing the headdress, but I do question the Festival Committee making him the Grand Marshall."

Another caller said, "Hey, I'm looking forward to this Mr. Reeves. My kids are all excited and we're planning on shopping from that Indian booth. The kids have been playing cowboys and Indians all week."

Isaac winced. "I never did like the way they made the Indians the villains."

Davie shrugged. "It was just the movies, Grandpa."

"You know your great-grandma was full Cherokee," Isaac said to Jimmy.

"Yeah, I always heard that, but I never looked into it." Jimmy acknowledged.

Isaac continued, "Yeah, your great-grandma was a Cherokee princess named Joleah Lightfoot. Callahan Jones was a Daniel Boone type out there on the frontier. And he got along good with the Indians. He married that beautiful Indian princess. Then they had a little girl they named Ramey Laughingwater."

"Laughingwater!" Davie laughed heartily. "What a name!"

Isaac shook his head. "You needn't laugh, boy. Indian names are sacred. They always tell a story. Your great-grandma was a happy baby and that's how she got that name. Daddy told me the story a long time ago. He said they didn't talk about her Indian background much because everybody didn't approve. Her daddy was Callahan Jones and that was all that mattered."

Jimmy, in the back seat, joined the conversation. "That's an interesting tidbit, Daddy. I never heard that before."

"Yeah, I reckon what's happening in the present always overshadows the past, and there's not much need to talk about it. I kind of agree with that caller who's mad about the DJ riding in full regalia though. For one thing, his own reputation ruins the image."

"I can see that," Davie said. "Hey, I bet I'm more Cherokee than he is!"

"Good chance of it." Isaac agreed. "But don't go getting a headdress. Y'all got your floats about ready for the parade?"

"My committee's about done," Jimmy said. "Nothing fancy. They're doing a thing on a flatbed truck to represent the Gristmill Restaurant's three themes. Got people lined up to sit at three tables.

The table on one end will have the Jewish look, with a menorah and satiny tablecloths and flowers. At the other end, a table will have the southern look with some baskets of collards, tomatoes, corn, and stuff. In the middle, they've got a counter with the red checkered hamburger theme. They've been having a lot of fun coming up with ideas. Rebecca was supposed to be on the float, but I don't know if she will now. They're gonna have food cooking so you can smell it. Then they'll serve it after the parade."

"What you doing, Davie?" Isaac wanted to know.

Davie sighed. "Nothing so elaborate. My committee's got a fishing boat on a flatbed and about five or six of them are gonna be pretending to be fishing. They'll have their kids in the boat with them and the kids will throw out little packets of goldfish crackers."

"That sounds pretty clever," Isaac said. "Course, you could have pulled a yacht. You gonna be driving the truck?"

"I might," Davie said. "But Jenny wants me to help with her float, too. Now she's got some fancy ideas. But she's been distracted from it in the past few days."

The radio regained their attention as raised voices argued with the DJ about the Indian theme. Suddenly, deflecting the conversation from himself, Reeves said, "Don't forget to bring your shovels. I'm sure Davie Wellsly wants some more digging done down there by the river. No telling what he's got buried there. Maybe some skeletons from the Wellsly closet?"

Davie turned red with anger, jerked the steering wheel, accelerated his speed, and then slammed on the brakes as he almost hit the car ahead of him.

Jimmy shouted from the back seat "Watch out!"

Isaac turned the radio off. "Gonna be an interesting Spring Festival this year."

Chapter 21 Who Goes There?

Thursday morning, April 4

The Wellsly men had barely left the agency when the back door opened and Thomas and Adam came in laughing and sat down at the conference table where Bree, Kit, and Bernell were talking about their latest discovery.

"Hello, boys. What'd you find out?" Bernell greeted them. "We went shopping. Got set up for surveillance. Did you print those pictures out yet?"

Kit opened the folder lying on the conference table. "Printed out these," she said. "There's more but these are the best."

The pictures showed the yellow house dark at night. Then there were pictures of different windows with lights on. All the pictures were time-stamped. In one picture, zoomed in through a sliver of light between Venetian blind slats, were two blondes, a brunette, and a redhead sitting at a dining room table. The time was 1:15 a.m.

"Mr. Roy took that picture last night. It verifies his theory," Thomas said. "That gray van sits in the driveway all the time. And the house stays dark until after midnight. Then he said lights come on and he takes pictures."

"They come in through the boat garage," Kit said.

"I'm pretty sure Mr. Roy was right." Thomas chuckled. "He'll be holding the fort upstairs today. He likes that telescope. It does better than his phone did. Although these are pretty good." They all agreed and laughed. "Good job, Mr. Roy!"

Bernell shook her head. "But he can't see behind the garage. You got scuba diving gear?"

"Got it," both Thomas and Adam said.

"Oh, Mr. Roy and Mrs. Tiffany said to tell you 'Hey.' They appreciate what you're doing."

Bernell smiled. "Old coot. I don't know what Tiffany Weaver ever saw in him. But they're a happy couple."

Thomas tapped the picture with four heads in it.

Bernell said, "What have we got that connects these four women to the digging?"

Thomas said, "The only thing concrete we have is one fingerprint on a cigarette lighter. And nobody's seen her. We don't know if she is one of them or not."

"I have another idea. But we need somebody good with disguises. I might be able to pull it off. Or maybe Adam would be better."

He looked at Bernell, then said, "On second thought, let me think about that some more, it may be illegal." He did not explain.

"Okay, it's getting late," Bernell stood up. "Go on and let's see what else you can dig up. This was excellent! A very good start."

"Thanks," Thomas beckoned Adam into his office. He couldn't let go of his idea and finally decided to try it out on Adam.

Demonstrating his idea, he doodled on a sheet of paper. After a little deliberation about legalities, they decided to go for it. He found a small cardboard box and they headed out.

They drove fifteen miles to the Merryville Post Office, bought brown wrapping paper there, and then mailed a registered package to Jamie Sampson, 1001 Chattanooga Road, Claxton, SC.

The receipt indicated expected delivery the next day at 3 P.M and the recipient had to sign for it. They had to work fast.

From an enlargement of the picture taken through the Venetian blinds, they created their ruse. A blonde wig that looked much like one of the women in the picture was their first item. A woman's turtleneck sweater from Walmart and padding in the right places transformed Adam into a believable young lady.

He opted for slacks and tennis shoes because he could not master the heels. He laid out his clothes for the next day. Thomas cautioned him that he had to be at the post office before 8:00 A.M the next day to intercept the package.

Adam crossed his fingers.

The box had no return address and was empty, so the worst it could cause would be a little angst on the part of the recipient and could not be linked back to him and Thomas. They even managed to avoid leaving fingerprints which was no easy task.

After their excursion to Merryville, the two wily detectives put out their boat at Pine Ridge Landing, posing as two fishermen enjoying their sport they motored on up past Claxton Waterfront and on around the bend. Phones with zoom cameras would be very useful in catching the prize they were after.

As they pulled around the bend where the river widened, Thomas said, "We could pretend to be River Keepers cleaning the bank of the canal from that barge over there."

Adam noted. "That would bring us closer," he shook his head though. "That's been done already. Looks like brush has been cut along there recently. Their equipment's still on the barge."

Thomas cut the motor and they settled down to do some fishing. After a few minutes, Adam shed his fishermen clothes and slipped into scuba diving gear.

Thomas cast his line out and noticed a nice yacht just drifting lazily on the river not far away. A couple of blondes and a dark-haired girl were sunning on the upper deck. A redhead was standing at the bow of the boat with her arms outstretched like Kate Winslet in Titanic. He couldn't resist taking pictures.

"Are they suspects or do you just like the view?" Adam asked as he fastened his flippers.

Thomas laughed. "Both. Everybody is a suspect. Not my fault some of them are so pleasing to look at."

"Be on the lookout for me too," Adam said. He tightened the oxygen tank and tumbled overboard. Thomas panned the area with his camera. The barge that sat at the mouth of the canal was idle.

An excavator, two barrels, and tools of the cleanup operation sat waiting for the next workday.

Obviously, no one is working today but us. Thomas wondered if it was a holiday. *But the Post Office was open.* He checked his phone: April 4. "Okay."

Thomas settled back for some fishing and photo snapping. *A beautiful day for this job* he thought and waved back when one of the women on the yacht waved at him.

About twenty minutes later Adam bobbed up on the opposite side of the boat. "What'd you find?" Thomas asked as he pulled him aboard.

"Nothing."

"Well, I can see plenty from here," laughed Thomas. "I got pictures of the back of that garage, too. They've got the door down. Did you get up close?"

"All the way inside," Adam said as he shed his scuba gear.

"Well?" Thomas asked.

"Nothing." Adam pulled on a dry shirt. "Mr. Roy's gonna be disappointed."

"Not to speak of Bernell," Thomas added. "When you say 'nothing' what do you mean? Was it empty? Was the water deep in there?"

"Oh, yeah. It was deep on one side. There was a fishing boat with a motor and oars. There was a skiff. The mast and sails were laying on the deck floor. Several oars and lifesavers were mounted on the wall. The back porch of the house is enclosed in the garage as Mr. Roy said. I listened for noises in the house but it was quiet. I couldn't take a chance on going in with this scuba gear. I need to get in another way. That handicap ramp Mr. Roy talked about does go down to the edge of the water. I guess she takes her invalid sister for a boat ride sometimes. I took some pictures."

"Okay, you were pulling my leg when you said 'nothing' weren't you?" Thomas whacked Adam with the flipper he had removed.

"Ouch! I just don't see how any of that is going to prove anything," Adam continued to dress. "It's a nice boat garage.

Nothing incriminating." He pulled on his jeans. "Now if they were hiding a barge in there with excavating equip...."

They looked at each other then looked back at the barge plain as day sitting at the end of the canal.

"You don't suppose...?" Adam said and snapped some more pictures.

Chapter 22 Current Resident

Friday morning, April 5

Friday morning by 7:30 A.M. the two investigators were ready to conclude operation Post Office. Thomas, disguised as a priest was already in the post office when Adam arrived. The priest was studying the greeting card section in the lobby. Intent on finding a birthday card for a nephew he told another person shopping.

Adam, looking like a demur but athletic young woman, got in line with four people already ahead of him. His heart pounded as he anxiously waited his turn. He crossed his fingers again, hoping he was not too late. The clock ticked on the wall. A calendar said 267 days till Christmas. Finally, he stepped up to the counter when the postal clerk looked at him and said "Next."

"I wonder if you could help me." He said softly. "I was expecting a package in the mail today and I'm going out of town. Could I go ahead and pick up my mail now?"

"I'll check," the mail clerk answered. "If it's not been put on the truck yet. I need to see an ID."

Adam opened the handbag he was carrying and produced a driver's license which appeared to be issued from the state of New York with a picture quite like one of the heads on the photograph through the Venetian blind.

The postal worker glanced at the picture, then looked more closely and eyed Adam for a minute. Then she handed it back to him and said, "Wait right here."

Well the jig is up, thought Adam. *She knows I'm not Jamie Sampson.* He considered ducking out before she got back. Two or three people were in line behind him. He turned to leave and noticed at the front of the line was a priest with a greeting card in his hand. Thomas winked at Adam and said, "Good morning."

Adam nodded. "Morning," then turned back to the counter and took a deep breath. He'd play it out. The mail clerk returned shortly with a box in hand and a couple of letters atop the box.

"Sign here," she said and pushed a slip of paper toward him. He took the pen and scratched Jamie Sampson in an almost illegible scrawl. He shoved the mail in his purse, picked up the box, and turned to go.

"Next!" the mail clerk said. The priest paid for stamps and the birthday card as Adam headed to the door with his bounty. Outside, he blew a sigh of relief and hurried down the street to his parked car.

His heart was pounding, and he expected any minute to be apprehended. Reaching his car, he looked around. Apparently, no one was following him. He tossed the box in the back seat and sat behind the wheel patting the letters in his purse.

What luck he thought. *Letters addressed to Jamie Sampson, 1001 Chattanooga Road.* Thomas did not send the letters. This was just what they had hoped for. He gulped down the twinge in his throat that said *this is a Federal offense.*

He had to get out of these clothes. He was elated and still nervous as he drove home and managed to get into his apartment unnoticed. He tossed the turtleneck sweater on the bed and changed into his suit slipping the letters into his pocket.

This had worked way better than they had envisioned. He didn't even have to ask for any other mail. Though he intended to if she had brought out only the package. They knew it was a long shot. But it worked!

He headed for the office to meet Thomas and open their prize.

"The clerk just assumed I wanted it all. I was going to ask, but I didn't have to," he excitedly told Thomas when he laid it on the desk.

Thomas grinned. "I didn't know it would work. You did great. Now let's read some mail."

"We can mail it to her after we see what it says." Adam leaned over Thomas's shoulder as he very carefully opened the letter so it could be resealed without damage.

"Oh, crap!" Thomas muttered and tossed the letter on the desk.

"What?" Adam asked, "What is it?" He picked it up and read aloud, "Congratulations! You are one of the top winners of Publisher's Clearing House Sweepstakes. Return the stub below with your corrected address and bank account number and your $25000 will be promptly deposited into your account."

He did not read further. He picked up the other envelope and read the addressee's name.

Current Resident*****

1001 Chattanooga Road

Claxton, SC 26999-1001

"Shoot! Doggone it! What a bust!" He flounced around and sat down in the chair opposite Thomas. "All that for nothing. We could have just asked for her mail instead of going to all the trouble of mailing a box."

"No. It was the box that had her name. They probably wouldn't have brought out current resident letters otherwise. But we're not telling Bernell about this." Thomas stood up. "We better go in there."

Bernell was hyped for action all morning. The Agency had been working on this case for several days now and she was ready for results. By 9:00 A.M. she had everybody at the conference table with their heads together for reports on the progress they were making.

Abby said, "I finally reached Claxton Equipment Rentals. The girl was helpful. They have been very busy lately she said. They rented equipment to WDGW Boats and Oars. They have rented to a Zelda Midget. Apparently, not all equipment is back at the site. But she said it was rented for a month and the month is not up yet"

Bernell scribbled some notes and looked at Thomas. "How did the Postal Caper go?"

Thomas shuffled in his chair and Adam started coughing. "What do you mean?" Thomas asked.

"Oh, come on Thomas. You know what I mean. I found this in your trash last night."

Thomas's mouth flew open. "What! You're going through my trash? But why? Isn't that..." He was about to lose his cool, but she started laughing.

"Oh, don't get your panties in a wad. When you mentioned an idea, and then said 'never mind, it might be illegal,' my mind started ticking. I just wandered by your office, the door was open, the trash basket was right there inviting my attention, so I pulled out an interesting piece of paper. Oh, and it wasn't April Fools' Day."

Thomas and Adam looked at each other. Was this her late April Fools' joke? This seemed like an invasion of privacy to Thomas. "We are investigators. We have to do things outside the norm sometimes."

"Yes," she agreed. "We do have to go beyond the norm. I want us to stay clean, though. Frankly, I wish you had found something. I take it you didn't."

Thomas went to his desk and brought back the Publishers Clearing House letter and handed it to her. "It was a bust. The women living at 1001 Chattanooga Road are all named Current Resident."

She laughed. "I just wanted to caution you to be careful."

The detectives agreed and said "Yes. Ma'am."

Their boss was sixty years their senior; they had to respect her. But Adam said, "There's a lot we do that could get us in trouble if we were caught."

"I am well aware of that. Don't get caught," Bernell said. "Be judicious. I just have to play mama sometimes." Adam saluted.

Bernell winked at Thomas. "Now what did you find on your fishing expedition?"

They both opened their briefcases. Thomas had a stack of pictures of a yacht with sunbathers. Bernell's first reaction was "What's this? Couldn't resist the cheesecake?"

Neither Thomas nor Adam said anything. They were determined to let the pictures speak for themselves. Bree and Kit leaned closer to view the snapshots. Bernell shuffled through two or three.

Kit made a connection and pulled out one of Mr. Roy's pictures. Bernell leaned forward. "Well, dang boys! That's them. That's our yellow-house gang. They were on a yacht out behind the house. I still think one of them might be Jamie Sampson. And one of them is probably Zelda Midget. We have no name on the other two."

"Current Resident," Thomas couldn't resist. They all laughed.

"But, hey!" She did a high-five with him and said, "Good job!"

He beamed. "Keep looking."

"Okay, a barge, the city's cleaning the canal, I suppose."

"I don't think it's cleaning the canal," Adam said. "That excavator could dig a mean hole in the ground."

Kit and Bernell did a double-take and studied the picture.

Bernell started tapping the table with her nails. "We've got them! That's the crew who's been doing the digging. Now we have to figure out who they are and how to prove it."

Adam pointed out, "Here are some pictures of the inside of the boat garage. No big deal there, but I bet there'd be fingerprints on that handrail."

Bernell smiled. "If it comes to it, you can go back. But that would be risky."

Bree spoke up. "Fingerprints are undeniable proof."

Bernell said, "Yes, but where are you going to get them? Other than Adam's idea, I mean."

"Unless it was these women who vandalized Davie's house. We have prints from that. If there is a single one that matches the cigarette lighter, we've got them nailed."

"You know they would have worn gloves, don't you?" Adam offered.

"Probably, I know whose prints we do have," Bernell said. "Wouldn't it be something if we found them in Davie's house, or on that rail?"

They all looked at her and laughed. Bree said, "You wish!"

"Well, what about the machinery on that barge?" Thomas pointed at the picture.

"Still," Bree noted, "you've got to get their official prints. You'd have to arrest them on suspicion of something. You could fingerprint them then."

Kit punched Thomas on the arm. "You know, from the way you said they acted, waving at you and all, you might have gotten an invitation on that yacht if you played it right."

Thomas snapped his fingers. "Should have thought of that."

"I'm curious," Bree said. "Who owns that yacht the women are on? Have you got any pictures of the yacht name and permit numbers or anything?"

"*Sea Breeze* is the name of the boat," Thomas said. Bernell used a magnifying glass. "And there's a series of numbers but too little."

Kit said, "I'll check that out."

"I love to see a team at work," Bernell said. "These pictures will go a long way. I'm pretty sure we know who's been digging now. I'm going to pass this along to Jeb and see what ideas he might have."

She switched gears "We do have another issue. What have we got on Smythe's disappearance?"

"Working on that too," Bree said. "But nothing concrete yet. I don't think he's dead though."

Bernell said, "Thomas, Adam, how would you like to go up to Chesapeake, Virginia? I hear it's beautiful up there now. And there are some crew jobs needing applicants." She handed them the Chesapeake newspaper ad.

"Was waiting for you to ask," Thomas said and grinned at Adam.

Adam chuckled. "I'm not gonna be a woman again."

"Heh-heh-heh. You never know," Thomas said.

Chapter 23 Burgundy Blues

Friday morning, April 5

Burgundy Blue Boutique shared a parking lot with the B.B. Jackson Agency and Pretty Woman Day Spa. Jenny arrived just before nine when she was to open. As she weaved through the parked cars, the hairs on the back of her neck bristled and shivers ran down her spine. She hastened her pace and rapped on the back door of the beauty shop instead of going on to the boutique.

Miss Rhoda let her in. "What in the world's the matter, Jenny? You look like you've seen a ghost."

Jenny shuddered. "No. I didn't see anything. I could just feel somebody watching me." Miss Rhoda stepped outside and scanned the parking lot, but saw nothing suspicious. "Come on in, get a cup of coffee before opening up. You got a few minutes?"

'Thanks," Jenny shook her head. "I'll skip the coffee, but it feels safer here. I need to open up for Ruby and Violet, though. I'm going in through the front. They'll be showing up any minute."

Hearing the conversation, Nancy said, "You're probably a bit rattled from all that's been going on. Ray and I've been taking more precautions. I don't know what's happening on Big Creek Road."

"It's scary. Thanks, Aunt Nancy, for helping keep an eye out. Now I just wish that creep on the radio would stop harassing us," Jenny said.

"I think all you can do is ignore him," Nancy said. "But I'm sure praying that God will stop him."

"Yeah, me too," Jenny said. "I better get next door, you have a good day."

"Tell you the truth, I'm dreading this day," Nancy said, "Renee Renoir's coming in and she's always so condescending. I wish she'd find a new hairdresser."

"She's not going to do that. You're too good," Jenny said. "I'll say a prayer for you."

"Thanks, I need it." She went to her station and Jenny almost bumped into Renee Renoir on her way out the door.

Entering her shop next door, Jenny breathed in relief. She loved the smell of the candles and potpourri. She loved the art, the fabrics, and soothing colors. Through the large front window, her eyes savored the blue river and the mountains in the distance. It was calming. It was only a few minutes before her assistant Ruby arrived scowling and fuming. Ruby stashed her purse under the counter, then went to their coffee nook and made a fresh pot of coffee.

"What's wrong?" Jenny had not seen Ruby in this state before.

"That stupid jerk on the radio!" She said as she set two mugs down hard on the table.

"What now?" Jenny asked.

"He is seriously trying to stir people up against the Wellsly's, I think. He got that same call again today too, about if he didn't stop talking, he was going to lose his tongue. Only thing, this time he answered the caller back by saying, 'Is that you Mr. Wellsly? I'm not afraid of you.' Then the phone rang again and it was the same deep, scary voice saying 'Keep on talking, and you'll lose that tongue,' and it just made me so mad because I knew it was not Mr. Wellsly. Not either one of them."

Jenny took the cup of coffee she handed her. "You're right, Ruby. It's not either one of them. Davie thinks it's a recording that the DJ is using just to stir up interest and raise his ratings."

"Can't he be stopped? Can you call the police?"

"Chief Jeb knows about it," Jenny said. "I don't know if they can do anything or not."

"Maybe they could just call the show and say it's not them," Ruby suggested.

"Davie says he's trying to provoke something like that. He refuses to listen to him because he gets so angry. Maybe we should just ignore it, too."

Ruby set her cup on the counter and climbed up on the high stool by the register. Peering out over the river, she said, "I don't know how y'all can ignore it. It's getting on my nerves." She jumped as the phone rang. "See?" She said, and then into the phone, "Good Morning, Burgundy Blue Boutique."

Jenny waited to see if it was anything she needed to know about, then Ruby handed her the phone. "It's somebody named Joliet Swan. She wants to apply for the job you're advertising."

Jenny frowned listening to the voice on the other end and then said, "I'm sorry, I have not advertised a position."

The voice on the other end insisted. "I heard you are hiring and I'm looking for a part-time job. I love the art and beautiful things in your shop, and I thought about how much I would love to work there. Could I come in and talk with you about it?"

Jenny looked at Ruby puzzled and said into the phone, "You're welcome to visit the shop, Miss Swan. But I'm not hiring right now."

"I'll just come in anyway," the lady said and hung up.

"What do you make of that?" Ruby asked.

"I don't know," Jenny answered as she dialed Davie's number. "Do you think our house is still bugged?" She asked him and explained. "I just got a call that makes me wonder. Have I said something at home about needing help in here? I can't imagine someone just making that up."

"Let me tell Aunt Bernell," he said. "KST might have missed one, but I don't remember you talking about that. We've talked about your float and how busy you are, but still."

Jenny got her purse. "Hold the fort, Ruby. I'm going over and talk with Aunt Bernell." She stopped. "If that woman is coming out here, she's up to something. I'm afraid I may have mentioned to Davie that we needed help. And our house might still be bugged. I know we're getting more sewing projects than Violet can handle. Can you help her in the sewing room today and let's just leave the front locked?"

Ruby said, "Sure, but ..."

"Oh, shoot," Jenny sighed. "You're right. I hate this!"

The bell buzzing from the back door of the boutique made her jump. She hurried back to open the door to a pleasingly plump middle-aged lady. "Come on in Violet," she said. "Sorry I had you locked out. I'm in a funk today. We're going to have to keep our doors locked from now on. Things aren't like they used to be. Come on upfront and let's talk a minute."

She pulled a couple of chairs up to the table in the coffee nook and said, "Ruby, leave the front door locked and the closed sign up for now; come back here and let's talk."

As the three of them sat at the table, Jenny began. "We are under attack. I don't know who it is, or what they're after, but somebody wants something. You know about the holes by the river, and our house being ransacked, and the talk on the radio, and now somebody wants a job I've not advertised. Although, I know we do need help."

Violet added cream to her coffee and said, "Yeah, I've been following all that. Makes me nervous. I didn't know about that last part."

"Please don't take this wrong." Jenny said, "But have either of you mentioned that you need help here?"

Both women shook their heads. "I'm overloaded right now," Violet said. "But I love my work, and I've never complained. You think Breck or Opal might have said something?" She looked at Ruby.

Breck was Ruby's nephew, a college student who worked four afternoons a week keeping the shelves stocked and everything orderly. He was handy with heavy stuff and did a good job. He was due to come in this afternoon. Opal ran a local housekeeping service and came in once a week for cleaning.

Ruby, a very pretty brunette said, "I seriously doubt that, Jenny. You reckon you may be overreacting because of everything that's happening?"

Jenny chewed on her lip. "I don't know. On the way in here, just crossing the parking lot, I knew somebody was watching me. Maybe I'm getting paranoid."

Ruby and Violet both tried to console her. "You have a very beautiful place." Ruby said, "Who wouldn't want to work here?"

Violet added, "Maybe it was just a ploy. And she did say part-time, right?"

Jenny nodded. "Okay." She put her elbows on the table and her chin in her hands and thought a minute. "You may be right. But I just have this weird feeling. I may be paranoid, but still." She paused, then said, "Okay. But I think I'll call Bree and see if she'll come by. She wants to look at some fabric anyway."

Bree was ready. She loved Burgundy Blue, and a break from paperwork seemed good. She needed to return Jenny's catalog anyway and order that material she wanted.

Jenny smiled. "Okay." Then she turned to Ruby. "Go open up. And Violet, you have a stack of cushions waiting. We'll get you some help soon, but I'm not hiring anybody right now."

Ruby followed Violet back to the sewing room to assist her. Jenny climbed onto the stool at the counter and adjusted the volume on the classical radio station she played every day. As she looked out across the beautiful blue river, she said a prayer. She did need help, but she didn't want to be forced into it this way. And she did not trust anybody now.

Chapter 24 Jo Swan

Friday morning, April 5

Several yachts were docked along the waterfront. Some people were stretched out on their decks getting an early start on today's sunbathing—obviously, one of the requirements for the yacht life. As Jenny watched, she noticed a slim, light-skinned nymph in white shorts and a green tank top standing on one of the decks. She appeared to check her watch, pulled her long, blonde hair up in a ponytail, and disappeared from the deck. She reappeared at the gangplank connected to the dock.

The phone ringing diverted Jenny's attention. "Good morning, Burgundy Blue Boutique," she said.

"Be a few more minutes," Bree said. "I ran to the house to get that catalog you loaned me, but I'm on my way."

"Okay," Jenny answered. "I probably overreacted, but I'm glad you're coming."

As she hung up the phone, the bells jingled over the front door and the boat lady she had been watching entered. Unlike most people who came in to browse around, the lady stuck out her hand. "Hi, I'm Joliet Swan. I called earlier. You can call me Jo." The woman said with a slight accent Jenny could not identify. It wasn't the southern twang she had heard from the Smythes, it wasn't the northern accent she'd heard from many tourists, but it certainly was not from around here.

Jenny smiled warily and shook the lady's hand. "I didn't know you were so close by," she said, without acknowledging that she had seen the lady on the yacht.

"Yes, I live right around the corner," Jo Swan said. Jenny was quite familiar with the neighborhood and knew there was no place just around the corner this lady could be living.

"Are you interested in anything in particular?" Jenny asked, treating her as she would any customer.

"No. I just want to browse around." The lady said, cocking her head and smiling in an attempt to be friendly. "These are so beautiful," she said referring to a basket of artificial daisies.

Jenny eyed her suspiciously. Even though she was wearing shorts and a tank top, she was carrying a very expensive Coach purse with an open top. Very convenient for dropping things into.

Jenny shook her head to shake off her suspicions and said silently to herself, *you need to get a grip*. Still, she followed the lady, smiling, being friendly, and offering to help her find things until she heard the bells over the door jingle again. She was glad Bree was here!

It was not Bree.

Two ladies came in together and chattered away as they browsed toward the side room where Jenny had several impressive paintings on the wall. The ladies paused, inspecting each carefully, and talking almost inaudibly.

"May I help you?" Jenny asked in as friendly a tone as she could muster. "Is this a real van Gogh?" One of the ladies asked.

"No." Jenny laughed. "It would be a hundred-thousand dollars instead of just a couple of hundred, wouldn't it? My husband's uncle fancies himself an artist and he does a lot of van Gogh imitations. He is quite good, isn't he?" She pointed to the JDV initials in the right-hand corner.

"Wow. It certainly could have fooled me. I've been to museums all over the world, and I'd say this is pretty good. It could pass for the real thing. I was wondering why you had such an expensive painting hanging here. You can see it from outside."

They were admiring Jacob Del Vecchio's rendition of *Fishing Boats on the Beach at Les Saintes-Maries-de-la-Mer.*

Jenny pointed out a couple of others Jacob had painted. Then she directed their attention to several sunrise and sunset pictures that Asher Ingles had painted. Something he had gotten into after he retired from his veterinarian practice.

The bells over the door jingled again and Bree came in carrying the catalog. As she laid it down on the counter, she observed the women admiring the paintings and joined them.

"Hey, Bree," Jenny said with a tinge of relief in her voice.

Bree hugged her and then said to the women, "We have a talented family, don't we? My father-in-law painted these." She pointed at one and said, "That's my favorite. Sunrise on Big Creek. It's at the boat plant at Davie's Landing."

Jenny noticed the look that passed between the two women as Bree pointed out the painting. They admired it briefly then decided they had to be somewhere else and left abruptly. Jenny raised her eyebrows; Bree shook her head at their rudeness. Obviously boat people. The locals were always friendly.

In the meantime, Jo Swan was wandering around as though she were casing the place. Or that was Jenny's conclusion, but she had hesitated to stay on the woman's heels. Ruby and Violet were in the back also, maybe their presence would be a deterrent.

Bree pulled up a chair at the catalog counter and asked Jenny to sit with her a minute and help pick out some suitable colors to go with her sofa. But when they put their heads together over the catalog, Bree whispered, "Stay calm, Jenny. I understand you're nervous, but it's alright." Then in a louder voice, she said, "Have you got this?" pointing to a tapestry design.

"Oh, yeah, it's in aisle three. I'll bring that out and let you look at it."

When Jenny turned the corner to aisle three, Jo Swan met her carrying a bolt of material designed for deck chairs and umbrellas. It was a unique burgundy and blue geometric design that had not sold well. The roll was still uncut.

"Oh, let me help you with that," Jenny said. "How much of it do you want? We'll lay it on the cutting table."

"No. I want it all." Swan said and wouldn't let it go.

Jenny shrugged. "Well, certainly. It's twenty yards, in case you don't need that much."

"I'm sure," Miss Swan said and held on to it. As she reached up to lay it on the counter, she dropped it, her purse slid off her shoulder, and items spewed out.

"Oh, zut! I mean drat! Clumsy me!" she said.

Jenny came from behind the counter to help.

Bree rushed over to help as the bolt of cloth came rolling off the counter. Swan frantically grabbed things up. From Jenny's vantage point, nothing appeared to have come from the boutique shelves.

Bending over to help, Bree picked up a yellow slip of paper and in a flash, the words on it burned in her brain.

End of the Road

By the Riverside

A Hundred feet

Rock of Ages

At the Cross.

Swan snatched it, and said, "That's my grocery list."

"Sorry," said Bree. "I like your purse, but this is why I can't use an open top. I'm always spilling it."

Bree calmly pretended not to have recognized anything, but her thoughts were running rampant. Back at the catalog counter, she pulled her phone from her purse and said, "Hello," as though receiving a call. Discretely she snapped shots of the woman paying for the roll of cloth and zoomed in on the purse. She couldn't get a picture of the lady's face but noticed the beveled security mirror in the corner above the counter reflecting everything.

She hit record and continued to pretend to talk on the phone. Jenny rang up the purchase, accepted cash, and started to wrap the bolt of cloth. Swan said, "That's alright. I'll carry it like this. Just give me the receipt."

Jenny's sense of pride in her products took over. "No, I don't want it to get dirty. That's a very nice material. I'll wrap it."

Swan relinquished the bolt and Jenny rolled it in brown paper and taped it securely. Then she handed it back to Swan along with the receipt.

"Thank you," Jo Swan said and left struggling with her awkward, heavy package. She did not go back to the yacht, but short of following her out, Jenny could not tell where she went.

"That was weird," Jenny said when the woman was out of sight.

"You don't know how weird," Bree said.

"What do you mean?" Jenny asked.

"You know about that envelope Mr. Isaac has with the hymns in it?" Bree asked.

"Yeah, why?"

"That woman knows about that. When I helped pick up her stuff, it was written on a note. She grabbed it from me like it was top secret, and said it was a grocery list. That was not a grocery list!"

"Oh, no, Oh, no, Oh, no," Jenny said. "I knew it! I knew something wasn't right!"

"We've got to let Bernell know about this," Bree said. "You going to be alright here while I run over there to the office?"

"Yeah, I guess," Jenny said, although inside she knew she was not.

Bree had hardly left before the phone rang and the bells jingled over the door at the same time. Jenny answered the phone. Davie was checking on her. She turned her back to the door for a moment to assure him that she was alright. She did not mention her fear in the parking lot nor this morning's customers. As she hung up, the bells jingled and she came face to face with Jo Swan again.

"What wrong?" Jenny blurted instinctively.

The lady laughed. "Oh, nothing's wrong. I just thought I'd find out if I could have some cushions made today from this material. I need them desperately tonight."

Jenny was taken aback. Torn between her fear of this strange woman and her professional ethics. She took the bolt of material

143

the woman handed her and looked at her carefully. She would remember that face if she saw it again. Pale, slightly pretty, blonde with green eyes; she looked French, Jenny concluded. *So that's what that accent was.*

"Ma'am you're asking the impossible. You'll have to buy some cushions already made. We have plenty. But we have a backlog of sewing right now. It would be two weeks before we could even get to this. We have other cushions already. Please take a look at them."

"No!" The woman stomped her foot and raised her voice. Then she seemed to catch herself, and said, "I'm sorry. It's just that I have to have this today. And this is the design I want."

Jenny sighed. *Who is this woman?*

The woman pulled money from her Coach purse and said, "Here, I'll pay for the trouble." She laid five one-hundred-dollar bills on the counter; all the while Jenny was shaking her head.

"You must!" demanded the woman emphatically. Jenny's insides churned. She hated confrontation. She also hated to be forced. Without taking her eyes off Jo Swan, Jenny called out, "Ruby, Violet, can you come here a minute?"

Joliet Swan smiled at Jenny as a child would who has just won a tantrum. But Jenny was determined not to lose. She spoke again without taking her eyes off Swan's face. "Ruby, Violet, I know you're busy, but Miss Swan wants a favor and she's willing to pay for it. If you can make these cushions for her today, there's a $400 bonus for each of you. Are you interested?"

Ruby and Violet looked at each other and grinned. "I think we can do that." They agreed.

The woman said, "That's only $500."

Jenny said, "Yes, but you need the cushions today. That will be $800."

Swan bit her lip, looked defeated momentarily, then said "Alright! Thank you!" and laid three more hundred-dollar-bills on the counter. Jenny picked them up and stuffed them in the cash register drawer. "Tell them what you want," she said coldly and watched as Swan pulled some pictures from her purse.

"Wait," Jenny said, "Ruby, figure up the cost of materials."

"I already paid for the material," Swan said.

"You want cushions?" Jenny asked.

"Yes! Cushions, like these!" Swan pointed at the pictures.

Ruby said soothingly to Miss Swan, "We have materials to make the cushions, you only have the outer material. We still have to get the insides, foam rubber padding, piping or welt cord, thread, zippers..."

"Okay, okay!" Swan said. "How much?"

Ruby took the pictures, went behind the counter, and began punching in numbers on the register. "Six seat cushions and six back cushions. This will be a beautiful set," she said pleasantly.

In the meantime, Jenny was seething and wondering if she would continue running the shop if she had to deal with people like this again. Nothing like anyone she had dealt with before. But she was making this woman pay. "Hah!" she chuckled to herself.

Ruby printed out the receipt and Swan plunked down another three hundred-dollar-bills and some change. "I will be here at five o'clock to pick them up." She said victoriously.

As the door jingled behind Swan, Jenny asked, "Are y'all sure you can do this?"

Violet said, "If we push the Evans order back a day and don't take a lunch break."

Ruby nodded. "She's the expert. I'll do what she says."

"I'll add the four-hundred to your paychecks this week," Jenny said.

"I hope this will be the last we see of her."

Joliet Swan was back at the shop promptly at 4:45 P.M. Breck was helping Ruby and Violet clean up the scraps from their daunting project. Jenny had helped them in between routine customers. Bree's discovery had been shattering. And Jenny's nerves had been on a razor's edge all day. Bernell called and assured her this was setting into motion a whole new avenue of investigation and for her to not worry. That did not make her feel less nervous.

When the last stitch was done, Ruby and Violet did a high-five and laughed at their feat. Their fingers were sore but they were proud of their accomplishment. They also thanked Jenny for bringing them some lunch and helping the little that she could.

Jenny printed a pick-up receipt and made Swan sign it. The total cost, over $2000 had been paid in cash for custom cushions for outdoor chairs. Breck helped Swan carry her purchases out the back door and loaded them into a gray van in the parking lot behind the store.

As they all left the shop at about five-thirty, Jenny remembered how she had arrived in fear this morning and then all that had transpired. She wanted to go back through the beauty shop and speak to Nancy. Now she wondered if her fear was just a premonition of the days' events. But what if someone had been watching her? She could not discount that.

Nancy seemed equally frazzled from her day. "This has been some day!" she said.

"Tell me about it!" Jenny said, then regretted the expression because Nancy proceeded to tell her about Renee Renoir.

"I wonder if she has a sister named Jo Swan." Jenny laughed aloud.

"I wonder what was so urgent about those cushions," Nancy said.

"What was so urgent about Renoir looking like Jennifer Lopez?" Jenny asked, and they both laughed. It's amazing how much relief laughter can bring.

"I worked with that woman four hours," Nancy said. "And listened to her go on and on about her aggravating husband and his new friends. They're having another party tonight. He's got a new yacht and they're having a christening party at the Claxton Country Club Marina."

"My parents live out there, but they don't participate in much. It's a snobby neighborhood."

"I can understand that," agreed Nancy.

Chapter 25 The Letter

Friday evening, April 5

Jenny sank into her sofa in the den to relax a minute. She had arrived home a little before Davie and even though she could smell their crockpot dinner, she wanted a minute before setting the table. What a harrowing day. One good thing, though, she had received a mirror she hoped would match the frame upstairs. Maybe repairing that would help her and Davie both. She decided that would be a good omen if it worked.

She didn't have long to ponder. Davie came in tired and depressed. He had heard about Jo Swan and the yellow note from Bree. He knew about the cushions. Although nothing new had happened at the Landing today, this was getting worse. This Jo Swan had some kind of connection to the digging. He was sure of it.

"Hey! JS could be Jo Swan. Jenny. That might be her lighter that we found."

Jenny shook her head. "She is not a smoker. I would have smelled it on her. That certainly could implicate her, considering everything else. But she's so petite, I don't think she could lift a shovel. She struggled with that bolt of material. And Breck had to load the cushions in that van for her. But she's got a connection with somebody on that yacht on the waterfront. I saw her on it before she came into the shop."

"Did you tell Bree about that?" Davie asked.

"Yes, we talked later after she met with Bernell. They're researching that. For some reason, I didn't feel so scared after I found somebody to pin things on and she's so...so...well, I don't know the word. I wanted to say stupid, but maybe flaky is better." She thought about that a minute then nodded her head. "Flaky. And speaking of flaky, I have some flaky rolls to heat up. Give me five minutes and we can eat. Are you hungry?"

"Starving," Davie said. "And something smells so good." Jenny was mastering the crockpot dinners. Her chicken cacciatore almost met the five-star standard of her mother-in-law.

"One good thing happened today," Jenny said as they enjoyed their dinner. You might not want to do anything on it tonight because I know you're tired. But that mirror came in."

"Good, let's fix it tonight. All this bad mess started with that mirror breaking. Maybe if I fix it, the other stuff will stop."

Jenny smiled. "Still superstitious aren't you?"

Davie shook his head. "Noooo. I just know what they say about breaking a mirror bringing bad luck."

"But you didn't break it."

"Well, it had to be my fault anyway. So, yeah, let's fix it tonight."

An hour later, sitting on the floor in the craft room, Davie tried to match the new mirror Jenny had brought home to the old frame. Something was not letting it fit. Examining the edges he discovered the obstruction.

A folded piece of paper was stuck to the bottom edge of the frame like it had been slid down between the frame and the mirror. Maybe not intended to be hidden, but discretely stuck there to be found later. Over the years it had slipped down and had not been visible until the mirror broke.

Davie opened it carefully so as not to tear it. Laying it out flat on the dresser top, he turned on a lamp to give more light. Even though smudges blotted out words and some words were illegible he could figure out the most of it and read aloud slowly.

9/10/55

Dear Ramey. I am writin this in case sumthin happens to me. Roger Riddick sent Frizelle and Winton -------- mill again. When I said no again, they tried to get me to join Riddick's people --------- after they tried three times they-------mill and showed me --------- They took me on Riddick's boat and ------- jewelry and diamonds. They said it's a drop in the bucket. I could make millions ---------I pretended to be interested. They wanted to celebrate ------moonshine ----- drunk, I got a flour sack crammed the stuff in it. I hid it in my boat -------fish box. When they left, I ------here to the landing and buried my fish box just a hundred feet from------edge at the end of our road ------ big rock- ---- chiseled cross -----bushes ----- I'm giving that stuff back to its rightful owners. The men or----------- ---- garage sale. I wanted you to ------ Love, Antry.

"You know what?" Davie said. "This matches up with what Grandpa said about those song pages."

"You think we should call Aunt Bernell, or maybe your grandpa?"

Davie had his phone in his hand already dialing Isaac's number. "I got something to show you. Can we come over now?" He asked without even saying hello. "Okay, we'll be right there."

He hung up, grabbed Jenny's hand, and said, "Come on."

"You want me to call your mom and dad?" She asked.

"Not now. They're both at the gristmill tonight. Some big event, I don't know what."

In five minutes, Lillian opened the door and pointed to the dining room table where Isaac was waiting. "What have you got?"

Davie and Jenny sat down and Davie stretched out the paper. "We found this tucked in the edge of a mirror. It was on the dresser Great-Grandma Ramey gave us. Remember it?"

"Yeah," Isaac remembered. "It was in their bedroom."

Davie spoke hurriedly, "Remember that night the pits got dug? We heard a howling like a wolf. And the mirror on that dresser crashed on the floor. All about the same time. It was weird and scared us to death."

Isaac nodded his head remembering. "It was a weird night. We heard that howling, too. Reminded us of Bruiser. He sensed things and he'd howl like he was telling us something."

Jenny listened with interest as they spoke of Bruiser. She had heard about the dog Lillian's dad had given her just before he died. Bruiser seemed to have a supernatural sense and lived almost twenty years. Jimmy was about sixteen when Bruiser died. Then they got Bolt, who was a grandson of Bruiser. Then there was Buddy, his grandma and grandpa's dog, and Buster who had grown up with him.

They were all gone now and Davie said, "It just hurts too much when they die. I'm never getting another dog."

Jenny hadn't minded. She grew up with a longhaired white cat and she remembered how it felt when Snowball died.

"Well, back to this letter," Isaac tapped it with his fingers.

Davie answered, "Jenny ordered a mirror, and we were fixing it tonight and found this stuck to the inside of the frame."

"Can you read it?" Lillian reached for her glasses.

Davie read it aloud pausing at the smudged words he had to skip. Isaac and Lillian listened thoughtfully. Then Lillian said, "I've been singing those songs all week. I think you ought to take this to Bernell."

Jenny speculated, "I wonder if anybody else heard about it, and maybe that's what they were looking for in our house."

"How could anybody else hear about it?" Davie asked.

Isaac spoke up, "You never know. Daddy might have told it. Mama might have read it and talked to someone. I wish she was here now."

Then he said, "I wish Daddy was. But they're both gone. Still, somebody knew something and this must be it. This is what all that digging's about," Isaac said. "We'll see Bernell tomorrow."

Chapter 26 Deciphering the Letter

Saturday morning, April 6

By eight o'clock, Isaac, Lillian, Davie, and Jenny were entering the front door of B.B. Jackson Agency. Perky as always, even though it was Saturday and she was normally closed on the weekend, Bernell greeted them, cheerily. "Hey, y'all. You're out kind of early today. Must be important."

Davie lugged a big tote bag with the Burgundy Blue Boutique emblem. Isaac said, "Let's go back there, pointing to the conference room."

"You brought me a gift?" Bernell grinned.

"Sort of." Isaac handed her the letter as Davie laid the package on the table.

"What's this?" Bernell read the letter aloud. "Oh, my goodness. Where did this come from?"

"It was in this," Davie explained as Jenny helped him pull the mirror from the large tote bag.

"That was Mama's mirror on their dresser. I remember that." Bernell took it from his hands.

Davie showed her exactly how they found the letter.

Bernell caressed the frame, remembering the old days when she was growing up with her parents on Big Creek Road.

"What are you thinking?" Isaac asked.

Bernell didn't answer. She clicked her nails on the conference table and sat in deep thought. She would stop and then start clicking her nails again.

Isaac said, "That's annoying."

"What?"

"You clicking your nails on the table like that."

"Oh, I was? I didn't even realize I was doing that. I'm thinking and listening."

"Listening? To what? Voices in your head?" Isaac chided.

"Well, sort of," she said, ignoring his needling. "Things are beginning to make sense now."

"What do you mean?"

"We had it all wrong. Roger Riddick did not put those songs in that envelope. He didn't care about God. He went to church sometimes for show. He went to the Catholic Church, too. And the Jewish Synagogue. He had to cover all the bases."

"Well, where did the songs come from then?" Davie asked.

"Daddy did it," Bernell said. "It makes sense now. I think when Riddick figured out Daddy stole his stash, he confronted him," she paused. "And you're gonna think this is weird, but I know my Daddy. And he could do some weird things. He was in church all his life. And even though he had a temper and was rebellious, he was familiar with every song in that book. Mama would play them on the piano. We had a couple of those hymnals at the house. And I remember one of them had pages torn out."

She paused, looked at the letter again, and started, "All we have now is speculation. It was 58 years ago, but here's what I think."

She spoke thoughtfully. "Riddick thought he could draw Daddy in and use him. I think Daddy would not be bullied; and in a way Daddy outsmarted him."

"But it cost him his life. So how smart is that?" Isaac interrupted.

"Yes, I'm pretty sure now that's why Daddy was killed." Bernell reiterated. "Nothing else really made sense. Daddy stole that stash worth millions. Riddick wasn't about to let him get away with that." She laughed at the thought.

"But I believe Daddy wanted to give it back to the owners," Isaac said.

"Yeah," Bernell said. "I do. He always thought he could fix things his way. And it got him killed."

Isaac remembered that day they had found Antry in the boat, bloody from a gunshot wound in the chest, and the coroner had called it a suicide.

"You know," Bernell was pensive. "I don't think Mama ever read this letter. If she had, she would not have insisted it was an accident."

"But why'd they kill him without finding out where he hid the stuff?" Davie wondered.

"Maybe they thought they did. I believe he gave them those clues with the songs. I don't know why he did it that way. He could be challenging. I bet with those clues, though, Frizelle figured he could find it. They knew my family was religious and just figured Daddy used it for his clues and knuckled under and gave it to them."

Isaac nodded. "I can see Daddy doing that."

She propped her elbow on the table, resting her chin on her fists, and thought a minute. "And here's another thing." She spoke slowly as though testing the theory. "Frizelle was under Riddick's thumb. Maybe he thought he could find that stuff and not tell Riddick. You know what they say about no honor among thieves."

"Isn't that a little farfetched?" Davie was skeptical.

Bernell laid her hands on the table, and leaned back, more sure of that idea. "That envelope with the songs in it was in Frizelle's boat, wasn't it?"

Isaac and Davie nodded. "We're pretty sure it was Frizelle that killed Daddy," Isaac said.

"But still, why didn't he find the jewels?" Davie asked.

Bernell studied the letter again and then smiled. "God works in mysterious ways. And sometimes he has a sense of humor."

"What are you talking about?" Davie asked.

Bernell stood up and walked around the room as she talked. "When Daddy was shot, he was left there in his boat, but it drifted to shore."

She stopped and looked at Jenny and Davie. "That's how we found him."

She went to a file cabinet, pulled a file, and laid it on the table. "We know now that somehow Winton got killed, either deliberately, or perhaps by a stray bullet from the same gun. Frizelle got that boat down the river and abandoned it near the Wellsly Sawmill. The storm hit causing a flash flood and Winton's body washed down to Georgetown where it was found several days later. His name was engraved on his money belt. That's how we found out who he was. He was listed as a victim of that hurricane until they found he was killed by a bullet. We learned this ten years ago when we were helping Ana."

She tapped the manila folder. "It's all in this file."

Isaac said, "You keep records of everything, don't you?

"Yep." She sat back down at the table. "When we found Daddy that day, we got him to the hospital and he died the next day, but during that night we had the worst storm ever and it tore up the river. When it was all over, the river never did go back like it was. It had widened in places and made islands in others."

"And that's important because...?" Davie asked.

Bernell smiled at him. "That is important because it changed the map. Whatever clues Frizelle had didn't work anymore."

"Oh," said Davie. "Then it won't work for us either."

"Well, let's think through that," Isaac said.

"Right," Bernell said looking at Davie. "Frizelle's boat is the one your buddy George was rescued in."

"Yeah, I know all about that," Davie said.

Bree had come in quietly and sat down beside Jenny. She remembered that well. "In that boat, we also found a bracelet with Alana's name on it and learned Alana Rodriguez was Fritz Frizelle's daughter. So he could have told her about that envelope."

"Exactly!" Bernell looked at Jenny. "You know about all that?"

"I know a little," Jenny said. "Alana was the one who lived in the yellow house. Everybody thought she was George's mother, but she wasn't. And now she is in prison."

"Okay," Davie asked, "Why didn't Alana find it back then?"

Bernell said, "Well I think she was busy doing something else. Besides, finding a hidden treasure on somebody else's property is not that easy--as you now know. She was into human trafficking and drugs. She got caught, thanks to you kids—and the Lord. Bless little George's heart for running away, and bless you, kids, for figuring things out and exposing her."

Bree smiled, acknowledging Bernell's compliment. "It was an awesome experience. It's what got me here."

"Yes, it is."

Bernell studied the letter again. "If I may continue to speculate, I'd bet Alana Frizelle is orchestrating this search right now from a gray tower somewhere in New York State. She's had time to think and plan. All that digging is part of that search for something she knew about."

She leaned back, finished with her hypothesis. "She's been creative before. She is no doubt conniving to get out somehow."

Nodding his head, Isaac said, "I agree with you one-hundred percent." He balled his fist and clenched his jaw. "I still get mad when I think about how they killed Daddy. I just don't feel like justice has been done!"

Lillian reached over and patted Isaac's hand. "God's taken care of it, Isaac. Remember that scripture? 'Vengeance is mine, I will repay.' God's got this. We just have to trust Him."

Davie watched his grandparents and wished he had his grandma's assurance. "But what does this mean to us? What do we do now?" he asked.

Bernell tapped the letter. "I am glad you found this. This means so much to me, just knowing more about what happened. This is in Daddy's own writing. Let me make a copy of it for our files. You can keep the original."

When she handed the original back to Davie, he pointed out, "I wonder what's under the smudges. Reckon it was tears?"

"Or a leaky pen," Bernell said. "But we've got enough to figure some things out."

Lillian wanted to read the letter again. "That garage sale is bugging me," she said. "I remember a strange garage sale one time. It was like God sent me a suitcase that was just right to ship a painting to England."

Bernell laughed. "I remember it well. I still have that old suitcase."

Lillian laughed, too. "I had a crazy thought like your daddy putting that stuff in a suitcase."

Isaac shook his head. "No, he said he used his fish box. I remember that fish box. It was a metal cooler, about like a trunk."

Davie got excited. "That thing they struck the other day?"

Isaac shook his head. "Couldn't have been that. It's in the wrong place. But we do need to find out what that is."

Kit had come in and was listening. "I think you're on the right track about Alana," she observed. "I suspect the woman who bought that house knows Alana, might have even been sent by her."

Bree sat up straight. "Wait a minute." She went to her office and came back with a paper in her hand. "A fingerprint on that JS cigarette lighter matched a former woman wrestler who was arrested about ten years ago in New York—drugs, I think."

Davie slapped the table. "They knew each other. But then what about this Jo Swan? I had her pegged for it."

"Kit, see if you can find a connection between Joliet Swan and Jamie Sampson and Alana Frizelle Rodriquez."

"Will do!" Kit scribbled some notes.

Bernell buzzed Abby. "Where is Zelda Midget from?"

"New York," Abby was quick to respond.

"Add Zelda Midget to your list Kit. Now that's four women. We have four women in that house. See where I'm going?"

"You're putting Alana in the house," Kit said.

"Find out if she is still locked up," Bernell said. "We don't know for sure."

Chapter 27 Man in the White Suit

Monday morning, April 8

Abby made the calls early asking Davie, Isaac, and Jimmy to be back at the Agency at 9:00 A.M. Monday. Lillian said, "If it's that important, I'm going, too." When Davie told Jenny what was up, she joined him as well. Jessica had an early morning appointment at the resort and could not go, but Jimmy assured her that he would call her as soon as he knew anything.

The aroma of coffee and doughnuts greeted the Wellsly clan when they entered the Agency. Davie noted that no one was at the checkerboard table nor the aquarium yet. "But they will be soon," Abby said.

"Glad you all came," Bernell said as she invited them all back into the conference room. Bree was already there with a portfolio spread out. "We have a report from the coroner's office on the man in the white suit," Bree announced.

"Oh, wow!"

"Great."

"Alright!" They were all eager to know more. And the fact that they were called implied there was a link to their case.

"The Man in the White Suit," Bree started. "Coroner Jones says he was whacked on the back of the head with a blunt object."

She held up a picture. "This is a picture of the wallet which was turned in to the police station anonymously. From all we can determine, it belonged to the man in the white suit."

"The name on the driver's license is Martin Morgan Montegue, and he went by 'Monty' according to other papers in the wallet. His money was gone."

"Sounds like robbery then," Davie said.

"We don't know that. Whoever turned the wallet in could have considered that their reward, and took it. But at least we do have something to go on now."

"The address on the driver's license is Chesapeake, Virginia, so there is a possibility he was connected with your yacht friends, Davie. And Jimmy, we think he might be the man you saw at the Gristmill Restaurant even though you did not recognize him when you and Davie were called to identify the body."

Davie shuddered.

Bree handed Jimmy a copy of the license. He studied it a few seconds, then nodded. "Yes, I think that does look a little more like that man. Nothing like the corpse though."

Jenny shuddered as though she were cold, and Lillian put her arm around her shoulders.

"So, what does this mean to us now?" Davie asked. "If he's from Chesapeake, do you think this might lead us to Jeffry Smythe?"

"Exactly!" Bree said. "That's what we are exploring."

Jimmy said, "He did say he was here to pick up his yacht. Was he pretending to be Smythe?"

"We don't know," Bree answered. "We do know that Smythe is not dead. There has been no obituary. Adam and Thomas have been there since Friday. They have been able to locate some people who say they know Smythe. No one has heard anything about him being dead. One of them was a cousin, so we put a lot of stock in that."

She looked at Davie. "The cousin said he had not seen him in a while, but he had not heard of him being dead. We figured that news of his death would certainly travel through the family, so we are pretty sure that Jeffry Smythe is alive and kicking--somewhere.

However, he is not at the address you gave us, Davie. And no one else is either. The house appears vacant."

"What? Wow! Drat! Dang his hide! What in the world is he doing?" Davie was angry now instead of worried.

Bernell watched as Bree continued. "We have not ruled out foul play, though. There are many possibilities we are pursuing."

Bree looked at Davie apologetically. "Now, maybe I should not have said he isn't dead. We don't know that for certain. We just know he is not dead of natural causes and reported through the system. There is no trace of his wife either. So my imagination is running rampant. I think you and Jenny might be able to help us. You did spend quite a bit of time with them."

Davie slumped. Jenny cut her eyes at him. "Oh, no," she said under her breath.

Bree continued, "Here's what we are doing first though. We've given Thomas and Adam this information about Martin Montegue, and they are investigating him. They will find out what connection there is between him and Smythe if any. Just keep your fingers crossed. But what I want you to do, Davie is to think back on your experiences with the Smythes and whatever contacts you may have encountered. I know you went up to Chesapeake a couple of times, maybe for a weekend or something? You might have run into some people."

She looked at Jenny. "You're good with the camera. Maybe you took some pictures or something. I know the scenery there is spectacular. Did you go out on the beach? Go to a party? Take a ride on a boat? Were there other people along? Everything you can come up with might help, no matter how small and insignificant, it might be a clue."

Davie was disturbed but just said, "Okay. Are we done here now? Because I have to get to work."

Jenny tried to cover so no one would wonder at his agitation. "I'll go home and start looking right now. I'm sure I have pictures."

They all arose to leave. "I have to go to work too," Jimmy said.

Lillian laughed. "What about you Isaac? You have to go to work?"

He stood up and said, "Ha-ha, Lillian. But, you know what? Let's run over to the store and see George. I haven't been in there in a while. We can pick up something for lunch while we're in there. What do you think?"

"Sounds good," she said.

The bell jingled over the door when Lillian and Isaac entered Oarlocks and Bagels.

The sporting goods store was well stocked. The aroma of fresh baking bread drifted from the Bagels nook in the corner. Lillian took a seat at a bistro table while Isaac ambled through aisles of hunting and fishing gear to find George.

The handsome young man came out of his office grinning. He could see Isaac through his one-way window. He loved that man and his whole family. They had become family to him.

He tried not to think of those old days much. Before they rescued him, he had been captive in the yellow house on Chattanooga Road. Running away to the woods, with a plan to make a place for his two little brothers and himself, turned out better than he ever dreamed. His brothers were not blood kin but they felt like brothers. They were two other captives. They were all too young to understand what was wrong in their life but it turned out well, thanks to his only friend Davie Wellsly and Davie's wonderful family. Now George was managing Oarlocks and Bagels and had a good life with his beautiful Lettie and their own two little boys.

Isaac didn't shake George's extended hand but put both arms around him and gave him a manly hug. "It's been a while, good to see you, boy," Isaac said.

"Yeah, and what brings you out today? Want to pick up something?"

"Oh, no. Just wanted to come by and visit a bit. Catch you up with what's going on. I guess you've heard about it."

"Unfortunately." George acknowledged. "Have you learned anything yet? I mean the truth of it. That jerk on the radio keeps rumors flying. If he had any sense he'd be fearing for his life."

"Yeah, I wish he'd stop that, but there's nothing we can do. We don't listen, but other people do."

"I'm glad you came. I wanted to mention something to you." George changed the subject. "I've been getting a lot of cash sales lately. I mean the boat people, a lot of them always use cash, but some have traveler's checks and credit cards. Usually, anything as big as a thousand dollars is not paid for with cash. But we've had a couple of really large purchases in the past week with cash. It just struck me as odd."

"A sale is a sale and money is money. You're doing so good here, I'm proud of you. Was it odd what they bought?"

"Well, not really. WDGW oars, Davie's top of the line. A boat motor and a skiff. A mast, sails, and lifesavers. No fishing gear. I reckon I noticed because the woman had red hair and, well, you know, my real mother had red hair, and ever since I learned that I always notice."

Isaac's heart was touched. "I know. But Martha has been a good mother hasn't she? You and Rodney and Sammie have had a good home, haven't you?"

"Oh, yes. We could not have asked for better. And the boys act like they never even remember."

"Well, they were younger than you. Is it hard for you to talk about it?"

"Not really. I don't, though. But I can talk to you."

"Any time you feel like talking, I'm here, son."

"I know and I appreciate it. Do you think there's a problem accepting so much cash for a sale? You know, I'm always leery of drug money after--well, you know."

"As long as you're not the one in the drugs. You're not responsible for finding out where people got their money. I've had my suspicions over the years, but there's nothing you can do. You've done enough for a lifetime."

"Thanks, Mr. Isaac. Hey, Miss Lillian." George hugged her as she approached them.

"Come on over and have a bagel with us," she laughed.

He laughed, too. "You know I'm never eating another bagel."

She laughed again. "Yeah, saved your life, though, didn't they?"

"Speaking of enough for a lifetime," he looked at Isaac, and Isaac understood.

"I know what you mean. And speaking of lifesavers." He patted Lillian on the back.

George grinned. It was a moment of mutual understanding.

Chapter 28 Counterfeit

Monday morning, April 8

Good morning, Burgundy Blue Boutique," Jenny forced herself to say cheerfully. She had left the Agency and come to the boutique and Davie had gone to the plant. They would go through those pictures tonight. She was not feeling her best self. It was Mr. Yelverton, the bank president. She knew him, but her business was always conducted with others. So why would he be calling?

"Good morning, Mrs. Wellsly. I need you to come in this morning if you can." He sounded very pleasant, but Jenny's heart sank. *What can be going on now? There's been so much lately. This can't be good.*

Mustering up her cheerfulness again, she said, "Sure, what do you have in mind?"

Rather than explain, he said, "Is 11:30 good for you?"

She looked at the clock, already 11:15. "Well, I guess so, that means right now." Her voice almost faltered. *This can't be good.*

Ruby noticed Jenny's demeanor and asked, "What's wrong?"

Jenny shook her head. "I don't have a clue, but this is weird. Although so many weird things have happened lately, I should not be surprised. Can you hold the fort? Mr. Yelverton, the bank president, wants to see me at 11:30."

"Of course," Ruby looked at her watch. "That's now. Go on over there."

"Hopefully, I'll be back soon," Jenny said as she got her purse and pulled on a light jacket. It was windy with March winds lingering into April.

She went out the back door and crossed the parking lot she had become so leery of lately.

A mile across town, she parked in the bank's parking lot and wondered why she saw Jimmy's car among the others parked there. Maybe it was another car like his.

She entered the bank and told the security guard she had an appointment with the president. He pointed her toward the appropriate door. All appeared normal.

She spoke to tellers and loan officers as she walked through. She was not a stranger in town. Everyone knew the distinguished owner of Burgundy Blue Boutique.

Mr. Yelverton's door was open, but he closed it after she entered. She swallowed and butterflies weakened her stomach. *This can't be good.*

Mr. Yelverton seemed to be attempting to be nicer than he wanted to be. She accepted the coffee he offered just to be polite, but after one sip, she set it on the coaster on the edge of his desk.

She listened to his take on the recent weather and his interest in the upcoming Spring Festival. She wanted to shout *get on with it*. But she just smiled and responded with small talk. He apparently was trying to put her at ease before the kill.

Finally, he pulled a folder from his desk drawer and laid out some hundred dollar bills. She blinked at them wondering if he wanted to pay her off about something. The butterflies were going wild.

He smiled at her obvious misery, then said, "I don't suppose you recognize these?"

She blinked and shook her head. "Looks like you got some hundred dollar bills, but this IS a bank," she chuckled nervously.

"Yes, I have quite a few hundred dollar bills. And your fingerprints are on them."

Now she was about to get angry. *What is this game he is playing? He is toying with me!*

Jenny's back straightened. "Well Mr. Yelverton, I run a business that deals with a lot of cash. I would imagine my fingerprints have been on thousands of dollars in this bank."

"Yes," he agreed. "But these are the first counterfeit bills I've seen in a long time. And your fingerprints are on them. Do you think you could shed any light on this?"

Jenny's jaw dropped. Her brow furrowed. Her fingers trembled. Then she stiffened. *I have done nothing wrong!*

"Mr. Yelverton, are you accusing me of something?"

He surprised her by laughing. "Not yet, Mrs. Wellsly. Technically I could, and you would have to prove your innocence. You have passed a couple of thousand dollars in counterfeit to my bank, but I suspect you are completely unaware. We do need to trace it down though, and I needed to see if you could remember any particular cash-paying customers in the past week. This was in your deposit Friday evening."

Jenny sat stunned then muttered, "That dreadful woman! She got me."

"Ma'am?" Yelverton asked because he did not understand what she said.

The butterflies turned into scorpions, and Jenny was ready to fight. "Mr. Yelverton, may I use your phone?"

He pushed it toward her.

"Oh, never mind. I've got this." She pulled her cell phone and called Bree. Her number was programmed in.

While Jenny was waiting for Bree to answer, she said to Yelverton, "I think we can trace this. I just need to get my cousin here. Could I ask her to come here now?"

He nodded as Bree answered. "Bree I think we can nail Jo Swan, can you come to Mr. Yelverton's office at the bank now? And bring your cell phone!"

Jenny sounded so authoritative that Bree said. "Yes. Be right there."

While they waited for Bree, Jenny explained about the lady named Jo Swan from the yacht, visiting her store and how she had demanded cushions be made immediately, and how she had plunked down several hundred-dollar bills because Jenny made her pay extra for the special service.

"Smart move," Yelverton said.

Jenny shrugged. "I didn't know it was a smart move. She made me mad and I made her pay."

"Well, it may have turned out to be a smart move anyway."

He looked up. "Come in," responding to the knock on his door.

Bree bustled in and sat down in the chair next to Jenny. "What's going on?" She asked and did a double-take when she saw all the money on the desk.

Mr. Yelverton said, "These are counterfeit. And they have Mrs. Wellsly's fingerprints on them."

"How do you know that? Why do you have Jenny's fingerprints?" Bree asked defensively and before he could answer she said, "Oh, I know."

She looked at Jenny. "You had to be fingerprinted last week after your house was vandalized so they could separate your prints from any strange ones. And now they are in a universal database. UGH."

Jenny nodded in recollection and blew a long sigh.

Yelverton surprised her. "I've been hearing about all that. I guess you feel like you're under attack from all sides."

"You've got that right!" Jenny said. "And when you called, I had no idea what next. I think Bree has some pictures that will clear this up though."

Bree scrolled furiously through her phone, then showed Yelverton the snapshots and the video she took of Jo Swan buying the bolt of material.

"Yes, that would work. You don't have pictures of the money though. She could have used a card or written a check."

"No, look at her motions, look at the reflection in the security mirror."

Jenny said, "This was when she purchased the material. And she paid for that with cash, too. Her fingerprints will be on that money."

Bree asked the president, "Does Chief Jeb know about this?"

Yelverton shook his head. "I contacted the U.S. Secret Service, but he might know about it by now if they've told him."

Bree was already dialing the Chief of Police. "Edna, can you put me through to Chief? This is Bree Ingles." She stood up and walked across the room.

Yelverton looked at her suspiciously. Jenny smiled and said, "They're working on a case that this might be connected to."

"Oh," Yelverton said.

He pulled another document from his drawer and said, "Well, of course, you do know that your bank account will be minus this amount, so you have to make those adjustments in your records. That could be an issue, I suppose, but there's nothing I can do about that."

"I'm sure. I would not expect you to," she responded matter-of-factly.

After a minute she asked, "Is there such thing as repossessing the merchandise bought with counterfeit money?"

"Well, I've never had to deal with that, but there are repossession laws. You might want to check that out."

"You can count on it!" Jenny said. "I don't think Jo Swan knows who she's dealing with. In the meantime, am I free to go? Are you going to file any charges against me? And besides, could you even do that anyway?"

Another door opened and two men in black entered the room.

"He can't, but we could," one of them said.

"But for now, Mrs. Wellsly, just don't leave town."

"So you were listening all the time?" she accused.

"It's our job ma'am."

Jenny took a deep breath. Most any time now she could fall apart.

Chapter 29 Regrouping

Monday afternoon, April 8

Jenny went back to the Agency with Bree. Jeb had said he would meet with them there and he was already in Bernell's office when they arrived. Jenny wanted to just fall in somebody's arms and cry. Maybe she should call her mother. She had spoken with her a few times since that day at the house, but she had not seen her since then. She mentally made plans to go see her.

Jeb was very friendly. "You poor thing," he said to Jenny. "You're catching it from all sides, aren't you?"

"That's the same thing Yelverton said. I know he wasn't attacking me, but it felt like it. Well, actually, he was. He said I would have to prove my innocence."

"Don't you worry about it," Jeb assured her. "I'm a little miffed that he didn't call me, but he might have thought I was too close to the Wellsly's and he was about to accuse one of them of dealing with counterfeit money."

They chuckled. Bernell said, "Jeb, looks like we got a tiger by the tail."

"Yeah, but you've got a super team working on that tiger. What's your latest?"

Bree said, "Well, you know about Morgan Montegue. That opened some doors for us. Thank goodness somebody turned that wallet in."

Bernell said, "That has been a boost. I sent Thomas and Adam to Chesapeake to investigate the missing Mr. Smythe and now they've added the murdered Montegue to their investigation."

Jeb nodded. "Unfortunately, it's a criminal investigation now. I consider myself and Claxton lucky to have your agency working undercover for the police department like you are. Y'all sure have made a difference."

Bernell beamed. Bree said, "It's what we're all about! But now we do have a possible murder with Montegue being hit on the head like that. Do you guys have a clue as to what happened? Where was he? What was he hit with?"

"The Sanitation department found an oar with blood on it in the parking lot behind Lee Fish Market on South Waterfront. They called me," Jeb said. "It was an oar with WDGW on the end. One of Davie's oars."

"Oh, God, no," Jenny cried out and put her head down on the table.

Jeb shook his head. "No. Don't go there, Jenny. Davie makes those oars. It could have belonged to anybody in Phillips County or anywhere in the world for that matter. He sells them over here at Oarlocks and Bagels. You can order them online. So just because it's his brand does not implicate Davie."

"Tell Davie that!" Jenny raised her head. "Just look at it. It's closing in around him. He built the yacht for Smythe. Smythe has disappeared. Montegue claimed to be picking up the yacht. He was murdered. He was from Chesapeake. Smythe was from Chesapeake. And on top of that, somebody is digging for an imaginary treasure on his parking lot. Davie is in the middle of all this no matter how you look at it. And our house was vandalized. You think all that is connected? How can it be? And how can it not be? And that DJ on the radio. Oh, God, what's he going to say next?"

Bernell said, "Jenny, you got the shop covered this afternoon?"

Jenny said, "Ruby's there, and Violet."

"Call her and tell her you won't be back in today. Your mama's off today. I think you need to go out there and see her."

Jenny smiled at Bernell. "So you think I need to see a psychiatrist?"

Bernell smiled. "Your mama. I was talking to her earlier and she told me how worried she is. She needs to see you. Think you could do that? It will do you good being out there in the country."

"I've been thinking of it. I'm concerned about Davie, too. He doesn't even know about this latest thing."

Bernell said, "I think he might. Jimmy called me. He had to go down to the bank this morning, too. And so did Davie and George Rutherford. That counterfeit money is being pushed through the Wellsly businesses for some reason. Jimmy deposited $3,200 that went through the Restaurant and the Riverside Hotel and Marina. George deposited several thousand that went through Oarlocks and Bagels."

"What? Why? How?" Jenny moaned.

Jeb said, "It's interesting. A counterfeit ring usually wants to get the money out of their hands and in the public. Sometimes they'll buy something cheap, for instance, fishing tackle for $10, and pay for it with a $100 bill. Then they get back $90 in clean money."

Bernell argued, "But these people have passed out large bills with, seemingly, no attempt to get smaller change back. George has accepted cash for some big purchases, boats, oars, and lifesavers. And Jimmy's resort has been hit. Some people have evidently spent nights at the resort and paid cash. They've eaten at the Gristmill Restaurant and paid cash."

Bree wondered, "It seems like they're targeting the Wellsly businesses. You reckon that's deliberate or just a coincidence?"

Jeb answered, "We're investigating that very thing. That's why I wanted to get Bernell and her crew in on it. It's more than a Secret Service issue like Yelverton thinks. I'm beginning to think it's a personal vendetta. And Yelverton doesn't know as much about the whole thing as I do. Heh-heh."

Kit had come in while Jeb was talking. She asked, "Do you think it's possible that Alana Frizelle is behind this too?"

Jeb was all too familiar with the Alana Frizelle Rodriguez he had arrested, who had turned out to be the daughter of Nazi connected

Fritz Frizelle, who had killed Antry Wellsly. So this could, indeed, be one more attempt at revenge against the Wellsly's. And she couldn't be caught because she was in prison. *But what minions might she have?*

"Seriously?" Jenny said when Jeb explained his thinking.

"I need to call Davie." Jenny pulled out her phone and walked across the conference room.

Davie answered quickly, "Yeah, I had to go to the bank today, too. I didn't know they called you. I had no way of knowing where the money came from. It didn't have my fingerprints on it, though, which was good. Alex is the one who took the money for a dinghy somebody bought. He put it in the safe deposit box and then he made the deposit for me because I was tied up with that dang hole in the ground. And he couldn't remember anything except that it was a young, redheaded woman, and she paid cash. She didn't even have a vehicle to pull it. She just put the boat in the water at the landing and rowed away."

"Really? Wasn't that weird?" Jenny asked.

"Yeah. But everybody just laughed about it. It was last week. Then when all that mess started, I forgot to tell you about it."

"Davie, Mama wants to see me. You got any problem with me going over there this afternoon? I might be late getting back for dinner."

"No. Go ahead. You need to see her. I'll be alright. I'll eat supper with Mama and Daddy and see you later, okay?"

"Okay. I didn't put anything in the crockpot this morning anyway, so that'll be good. We'll talk about Chesapeake after I get home, alright?"

"We have to sooner or later, I guess," he answered. "I love you, baby, no matter what happens. I will always love you."

"I know. Me too," she said and hung up.

Jenny walked back over to the conference table where the group was discussing the events of the mysterious case they were dealing with.

Jeb asked, "You feel better after talking with him?"

"Yes and no," she said. "He told me about having to go to the bank." Then she explained about the dinghy the woman had bought and put in the river at the landing.

Bernell sat up straight. "Wait. Say that again." Jenny retold what Davie had said.

Bernell smiled. "You know who that was? This is all coming together. That's the yellow-house-gang, Jeb. I think you are right on target. I think this is being orchestrated from a prison cell in New York State. Those prison walls are hiding some secrets."

Kit asked, "Do we have the pictures Thomas and Adam took?"

Bernell pulled them from a portfolio she had in front of her and handed them to Jeb.

He studied the pictures, nodding and smiling all the time. "You got'em nailed. Now we just have to figure out how to catch them. I may have to pay a visit to the princess of evil."

Chapter 30 Country Club Hills

Monday afternoon, April 8

The ride to the **Country Club Hills** estate of Doctors Marcus and Zoey Rosenberg was pleasant. Even though Jenny was depressed, the blue sky, the sunshine, the dogwoods blooming in the edge of woods, and the azaleas along the road, were uplifting.

As she drove, she processed the past few weeks and events leading up to this fiasco they were living in now. She wondered how much she should tell her mom about their experience with the Smythes. Probably nothing.

Davie did not want anybody to know. His mom and dad would be so disappointed. His grandma and grandpa would be hurt. But it was over now. Or was all this mess a result of it? Davie had alluded to that. That and the broken mirror. But the mirror was all fixed now. And the letter had given them some valuable clues to solve the mysterious diggings and probably the reason their house was ransacked.

When she pulled into the driveway of the elegant two-story house, her mother was on the portico. It was a beautiful April day, a little windy but warm enough the breezes were more like caresses than blusters. It was the kind of day she loved.

Zoey met her in the driveway. "You waiting for me outside?" Jenny hugged her mother.

Zoey laughed. "In a way. I bought some nice geraniums at the nursery, and I was setting them on the portico. See?" She pointed at the white Chippendale pots by the steps.

"They're beautiful, Mom." Jenny admired the rich, peach and coral geraniums that matched the brick of the house.

Zoey hugged her again. "I have missed you and worried about you this past week. Your dad's worried, too."

"Is he here?"

"No," Zoey shook her head. "He's in surgery today. There are a lot of heart problems in Claxton."

"Yes," Jenny said, and thought, but didn't say aloud, *some of them can't be fixed with surgery.*

Zoey pulled Jenny's hair back off her neck and faced her, "I know all this mess is getting to you. It's showing in your pretty face. You shouldn't have to be burdened with all this."

Tears pooled in Jenny's blue-grey eyes, but she wiped them away. Her mother could always bring out what she was trying to suppress. Maybe that was good.

Arm in arm they entered the majestic foyer and Zoey led her daughter to the den. As they plopped down in a huge plush armchair together. "Like old times," Zoey said.

"Like when I was ten," Jenny laughed.

"Well, you will always be my baby, you know that."

"Is Patrick enjoying his new school?" Jenny asked of her brother.

"Yes, he says he loves Richmond, and the law school there is one of the best in the country."

"More power to him, "Jenny said. "He should come home more often."

Zoey laughed. "Girl after my own heart. I'm glad you stayed here in Claxton. The Wellsly's are good people."

"I think so," Jenny agreed. "But some people don't." And then she poured out her heart. Everything that had happened in the past week, but nothing that had happened in Chesapeake. After a half-hour of unburdening herself, Jenny said, "I'm hungry."

Zoey jumped to her feet. "Come on. I've already got the table set on the balcony. Let's carry it up there."

When they entered the sunny white and blue kitchen, Zoey said "Rosie was here yesterday and prepared a banquet dinner for your dad and me. I told her it was way too much. So we've got roast beef and all the trimmings for some super sandwiches. Good timing, huh?"

"I need to borrow Rosie, Mom. Or find somebody. My house needs some good cleaning. I just don't have time to do it." She put together ingredients for her sandwich.

"You know what? She comes here twice a week. She might take you on. I'll ask her. What do you think you would need? One day? Two?"

"One day a week would probably be good, especially since I've been getting by with no help at all," she laughed. "She might need a whole week to start with though. I'm way behind in cleaning. In other words, we live in filth!" She laughed as she arranged a plate and silverware on her tray.

"No, you do not live in filth!" Zoey exclaimed.

"I was there last week, remember? Ketchup?"

Jenny shook her head. "You didn't look under the bed."

Zoey laughed and spoke above the refrigerator's ice crusher. "Of course not. I would never do that."

She filled their glasses from the pitcher of lemonade. "Rosie will be back here Thursday. I'll talk to her then."

Carrying their trays loaded with sandwiches and drinks, Zoey and Jenny climbed the stairs from the kitchen up to the balcony where Zoey had already set the table with placemats and a decorative pot of those peach and coral geraniums.

Looking out over the river, Jenny commented, "It's so peaceful here, Mom. I'm glad I came."

"I'm glad Bernell called me. She's been worried about you and Davie."

"I know. It's a very close-knit family."

It was rejuvenating to Jenny, relaxing and enjoying the pleasant spring day in such peaceful surroundings. Bernell was a wise old lady. But nobody would ever call her old.

The neighboring house was visible but too far away to even holler at people. Not like on Big Creek Road where in some cases only a driveway separated yards. There had been a lot of development over the past ten years.

Mother and daughter chatted about pleasant memories and enjoyed an hour of solace before Jenny noticed a yacht out on the river, and it reminded her of the whole horrible mess with Jo Swan. She had already shared the story with her mother, so Zoey understood the wince on Jenny's face when she noticed the yacht.

"Fly in the ointment," she said as she watched Jenny's expression change.

"Mom, are you familiar with that yacht?" she asked.

"They all look alike to me," laughed Zoey.

"I'll be right back," Jenny said and ran down the stairs to get her phone. Bree had sent her the pictures she had taken in the shop.

The yacht was moving slowly and was closer when Jenny got back to the table. Jenny scrolled to the pictures Bree had taken of Jo Swan.

"Well, this doesn't tell you anything, I know. But this is the woman that we think might be involved in that diggings and maybe vandalizing our house, and also passing the counterfeit money. Thomas and Adam, detectives for Bernell, saw her on a yacht on the river out behind that yellow house on Chattanooga Road."

Zoey motioned toward the yacht, "And this is the same river a few miles up. But there are thousands of yachts."

"I know," Jenny said. "I hate them all."

Zoey laughed. "I understand, including the one Davie built."

"Especially the one Davie built," Jenny proclaimed. It felt like all their problems had started with that boat.

She held her phone up to focus on the yacht in the distance. As she zoomed in, she blurted, "Oh, no" and jumped up to get closer.

She started snapping, zooming in, and getting every angle she could. She could see people but couldn't make them out yet.

"What's the matter?" Zoey asked.

"Wonder where that yacht is going?" she asked her mother.

Zoey shrugged, "The Claxton Country Club Marina is not far up there, and then another mile up is the Phillips County Country Club Marina. It could be headed for either one. Or it could be just out for a cruise and will turn around and go back the other way. Why? What are you thinking?"

"I don't know. It's just that everything means something lately." As the yacht moved closer, she zoomed in and snapped more pictures.

She tapped Bree's number and sent her a picture with the comment. "Does this look familiar?"

A minute later she got a text back. "Yes, it does. Where are you?"

"On mom's balcony. Show Bernell."

Bernell looked at the yacht and verified, "Looks like the same one Thomas got pictures of. Send Jenny a picture of that."

When the phone pinged and Jenny saw the picture, she showed it to her mother.

Zoey confirmed, "Yes. It does look like the same one. But then I told you they all look alike to me."

"No, they're not all alike, Mom. The one Davie built for the Smythes is not like this one. Look, this one has a third upper deck where those girls are in those chairs." Then it was close enough.

She recognized the cushions, burgundy and blue. In crisp detail, the colors stood out. She flipped to the picture Bree had sent. "Look, Mom. Can you see the cushions? They're mine!"

"Now look at this one." She zoomed in and snapped another picture of the yacht in front of them. Jenny's fingers flew across the screen as she sent the picture to Bree.

Bree sent back a text. "If this was on the highway, I would say follow that car! LOL. But it's pretty hard to do that from where you are and it's not a car."

Zoey's house phone in the kitchen rang. "Let's answer that, Mom," Jenny said.

It was Bernell. Zoey told her what she had told Jenny, she never noticed the differences in yachts, but she knew there were many of them at both marinas around Country Club Hills.

When she got back on the balcony, Zoey said, "Bernell wants us to see if we can find out where the yacht goes. I feel like a detective now," she grinned.

"I'm not sure we can, but I can drive around down there. We've got a sticker on the car that lets us in through all the gates. Want to go for a ride?"

"I came out here to get away from all that," Jenny said. "But if it will help, sure."

Bernell called back. "Hold on. Don't go anywhere yet, I'm getting Jeb on the phone. Here's the deal. He could arrest Jo Swan on suspicion of counterfeiting. That would give us a break. We've got her fingerprints on the money and in Jenny's shop, and who knows? She might talk. But Jeb or a deputy has to be there. What I need you and Jenny to do is keep the yacht in sight, find out where it docks. Think y'all could do that?"

"But you don't even know if she is on the boat," Zoey said.

"Not yet," Bernell said. "But I have a hunch, and this is too good to pass up; can you play detective for us for a while?"

"My pleasure. We'll wait for further orders." Zoey laughed and hung up.

"Mom you're too excited about this. They may have guns."

"Oh," Zoey said. "I hadn't thought of that. Maybe we better just stay here and leave the hard stuff to the police."

"All this makes me nervous," Jenny said. They moved over to the far edge of the balcony where they could see down the road leading to the house. From that vantage point, they could see both the yacht and the driveway.

In thirty minutes a black unmarked car pulled into the Rosenberg's driveway. Zoey went downstairs and opened the door to a deputy dressed in plain clothes bringing Kit and Bree. They joined Jenny still on the balcony watching the yacht like a cat watching a mouse.

The yacht appeared to be stalled directly behind the house. "That might be bad news," the deputy said.

Zoey brought more glasses of crushed ice up to the balcony and Jenny poured lemonade. "We have plenty for sandwiches," Zoey said.

They all declined until she set down a tray. It was too tempting. "Well, just a little," Kit said and made a small sandwich.

The deputy made an observation. "You know they can see us. We shouldn't appear to be watching them." He made a sandwich and sat down with his back to the river. Bree pulled up a chair and joined him.

"Maybe we should have some music and pretend it's a party," Zoey said.

"Not a bad idea." The deputy agreed as she went to the door, flipped a switch, and turned a few knobs. Classical music wafted on the air and they continued with their pretend party. Moving around talking, they took pictures of each other, many with the yacht in the background.

"Oh, look!" Jenny said. "I mean, don't look. But look! They're letting a dinghy over the side!"

Zoey said, "They're going to row that boat up to the Renoir house. They can't pull the yacht in there. They could go to the Marina about a mile up, but this is closer. The Renoir waterfront is not deep enough for the yacht. There's a sandbar."

"Mom! How do you know that?" Jenny exclaimed.

Zoey just smiled. "I know things."

She refilled lemonade glasses as she explained. "When we first moved here, Louis Renoir tried to get Marcus to build a pier so he could dock his yacht there. He wanted to build a boardwalk to it from his property. For some reason, the environmental people would not let him dredge and remove the sandbar so he had to dock at the marina. Marcus would not do that, and they have not spoken to us since."

"So that's what it was," Jenny said.

"Well, that and the fact that we're Jewish and they don't want us in the club," Zoey exclaimed. "As I said, we don't talk."

"They cannot legally exclude you from the club," the deputy noted.

"Legally," Zoey said. "But we don't care to go where we're not wanted."

"They have to keep their yacht at the Marina. I heard he just bought a new one even bigger."

"You think that might be it?" the deputy asked.

"I don't know." Zoey shook her head. "Jenny thinks so."

Bree and Kit put their heads together chattering away in a low voice. Jenny knew they were into their sleuthing.

Leaning on the balcony rail and pretending to be taking pictures of flowers, Jenny snapped here and there. She got a few strategic shots of two ladies climbing down into the lifeboat. One had red hair, the other was blonde with a ponytail. Zooming in, she almost squealed. "Look, look, look. That's Jo Swan."

Kit and Bree jumped up. "Just as we figured." They leaned on the balcony rail. "Take our picture."

Jenny took their picture, but she kept zooming past them to the little boat being rowed to the big house just up the river.

Kit said, "I've been looking for who owned that yacht, *Sea Breeze*. I'm going to the Marina. I can talk to someone."

The deputy said, "I don't think I can go up to that house and arrest her without getting shot. This is good to know, but I'm not going over there right now. I'll drive you and Bree over to the Marina, Kit, if you want to go in and snoop around."

"Let's go. We'll check things out," Kit said. "We'll get back with you, Jenny and Mrs. Rosenberg. This has been very productive. Thank you for the delicious lunch."

Jenny said, "Wait a minute. I know somebody else you can talk to who may know more than she thinks she does, but be careful about it."

"Who?" Bree asked.

"Aunt Nancy," Jenny said. "She is Renee Renoir's hairdresser, and the woman drives her crazy. She talks all the time. Aunt Nancy wishes she would go somewhere else, but she's been with her so long. There's no telling what she might have heard that could be useful now."

"Wow! Thanks, Jenny. I'll mention that to Bernell."

In a matter of minutes, they were gone. All the excitement died down, the yacht sat idle, and Jenny helped her mom clean up the table.

"I don't want you to go home yet," Zoey said.

"I'm not. Davie's eating supper with his mom and dad. I'm staying till Daddy gets home. I haven't had dinner with y'all in a long time."

"Oh, good, that's what I was hoping for." Zoey gave her a hug and their mother and daughter time continued for a few hours. It was sweet.

***

Bree and Kit wasted no time getting up with Nancy Wellsly. Bree called the beauty shop on their way back to town and asked if she could come to the Agency and discuss something about the case. Like Jenny said they wanted to be careful and not frighten her off. Nobody wants to be a pigeon and rat on friends.

Even though Renee Renoir was far from being a friend, Nancy would be loyal to her patron. It's one thing to spout about how someone ticks you off; it's another to tell things they have told you which might have been shared in confidence. Hairdressers are like bartenders who hear the darkest secrets from their clients.

Discussing the ramifications of questioning Nancy, Bree and Kit decided to be open and forthright about everything. She could be a key in cracking this whole case and not yet know it, but it would be her choice.

Nancy was a Wellsly. Still, they knew it was tricky to ask her to reveal possible secrets her patron had shared. They need not have worried. When Bree called Nancy, she was about to leave the Beauty Shop but eager to help. She could come first thing in the morning, she said.

"Wonderful," Bree exclaimed. "I don't think you will regret this Aunt Nancy."

That was what Jenny and Davie called her, though she was not their aunt. She was Isaac and Bernell's first cousin, but they had not grown up together. Her father was Jacob, Antry's older brother, who had left the plantation home when his father left around 1902.

He moved to Virginia where he settled and raised his family. When Nancy was grown, she moved to South Carolina where her grandfather was from.

When she married Raymond Drew, she did not change her name which was becoming a more common practice during that time.

She was not a feminist, but she said she did not want to be called Nancy Drew. Ironically, now she was inadvertently becoming a sleuth.

Chapter 31 Nancy Drew, the Accidental Sleuth

Tuesday, April 9

When she entered the Agency first thing Tuesday morning, Nancy was greeted with the usual friendly, sparkling smile of Abby and then her cousin Bernell. Nancy admired the décor and was as impressed as Isaac had been. "This is the first time I've been inside. You have a fantastic place here," she complimented Bernell. "I bet people love to come in the lobby and just hang out."

Bernell laughed. "Yes, as a matter of fact, they do. And Abby is always a good hostess."

They waited in Bernell's office while Kit and Bree readied their positions in the conference room. "Do you think we should record this?" Bree asked Kit.

"Hmm, under normal circumstances, I would say yes, but, I don't know. She's family, and I don't want her to feel offended."

Kit and Bree were also Nancy's cousins. When William Doran Greene Wellsly left the plantation in 1809, he went to Texas and became a cattle rancher. He remarried there, and Kit Griffiths was his great-granddaughter, the same relation as Ana, Bree's grandmother. It was certainly a family affair. The Wellsly clan revered their ancestor WDGW.

The most notable thing about him was that he was the son of an abolitionist and instrumental in freeing his wife's plantation slaves. A tycoon, he amassed wealth in South Carolina and Texas. His boatbuilding business was known for the quality of his oars and boats. It was the mobster Roger Riddick who infiltrated and destroyed it in the forties after having Hinson Wellsly and his family murdered. It was all documented in court records now, sixty years later.

Davie Wellsly's ambition had been to restore the WDGW name and build the quality of boats and oars his grandfather's grandfather had a reputation for. But things were going awry. And from all indications, the adversity was coming from the same source. That suspicion charged Bernell's Agency to fight with passion.

"If you think about it," Kit told Bree, "Davie is repeating what the original WDGW did without even knowing it. Have you thought of that? Davie was responsible for freeing slaves in Alana's human trafficking operation. Of course, she was just continuing what Riddick had started."

Bree sighed. "There's a lot of evil in this world."

Kit said, "Yeah, and we fight it every day."

Bernell entered on that note. "But one day, God's going to put us out of a job. Satan's days are numbered."

Bree was not as much into the scriptures as Kit and Bernell, but she was glad she was on the right side.

Nancy entered, cheerful, and eager to be of help. Bernell explained the situation: "Nancy, we want to get you up to date about what we know so far and see if there is anything you can add to it. We have evidence that the vandals who ransacked Davie's house might be the same ones who did the digging. We think they are looking for something Riddick's people may have stolen and that Daddy might have got a hold of and buried."

"Oh, wow. That sounds intriguing and scary. You think there's a map somewhere they're looking for? Or maybe the actual stuff that was stolen?"

"Well, both," Bernell said. "They want the treasure, and a map would help them find it. An age-old game, isn't it?"

Nancy laughed. "Yeah, I've read the books. But this is for real. And it's our family, so I am taking it personally."

"We're all taking it personally," Bernell said.

For the next hour, Bree, Kit, and Bernell shared everything they had learned including their suspicions about the women in the yellow house, about how Jo Swan had acted over the cushions, and about the counterfeit money.

"Wait a minute." Nancy interrupted. "Jane had a meeting with the staff yesterday and told us the bank president called her in. She had deposited $500 in counterfeit bills. We had to go through a training session on how to spot counterfeit. We'd never paid attention before, but we have to be on the alert now. She can't get the money back and she doesn't know which one of us might have received it. Of course, Carol handles all the payments, but we get separate tips, so she cautioned us. Very interesting."

"I wonder if Jo Swan went to the Spa last week," Bree said.

"I don't recognize that name. Could she be one of the boat people?" Nancy asked. "We get a lot of them. And they all look alike. We don't keep records on walk-ins unless they become recurring patrons. Carol's got all that. We probably had twenty last week."

Bernell said, "Bree, Kit, tell Nancy about your visit yesterday."

"Well, we didn't learn anything at the Country Club Marina because they threw us out," Kit laughed. "That's one exclusive, snooty place."

"Yeah, but at Jenny's mom's house we had a good time and learned a lot." She proceeded to tell about the yacht being discovered by Jenny and how they had gone out there, too and pretended to have a party on the balcony so they could watch and then how they had seen two women let down a boat from the yacht and row it up to the neighbor's house.

"Does Zoey know the neighbors?" Nancy asked. "Maybe she and Jenny could pay a neighborly visit and kind of snoop around." She laughed at her idea.

"They've been there ten years and they don't speak," Kit said. She explained about the pier idea that the neighbor wanted.

"Well, I don't blame Marcus for that one bit," Nancy said. "Some people are so presumptuous. They think the world revolves around them and they can get whatever they want. Who are they?"

"Louis and Renee Renoir," Bree said and watched as Nancy's demeanor changed.

Nancy clenched her teeth. "Well, that explains a lot. So those women on the yacht--you think they're involved in the digging and vandalizing? And somehow they're connected to the Renoirs?"

Bernell said, "Apparently there is a connection. Why else would they be going to their house?"

Nancy closed her eyes as though trying to remember. Finally, she said, "Ten years. Ten years I've put up with that woman. Ten years I've heard her babble about that horrible man she is married to. Ten years I have heard how he treats her. Ten years I have heard how much better she is than her neighbors or anybody else. Ten years I have put up with her putdowns and slurs, but for the life of me..."

"And you never heard anything like..."

Nancy interrupted Bree. "I try not to pay attention to what she says. Now I wish I had. I've wanted to dump her for so long, but frankly, I was afraid to make her mad. Her husband is into a lot of stuff. I was afraid he was connected with the mob."

"Really?" Bernell asked. "I had no idea, Nancy. You never said anything."

"Well, I was scared to. Sometimes I think, she could have me whacked and nobody would be the wiser."

"Seriously?" Bernell asked. "I didn't know it was that bad."

Nancy said, "She was in there Friday morning, annoyed about something."

"Do you remember what it was?" Kit asked.

"A little," Nancy said as she thought back. "Louis has a daughter she calls Julet."

"Joliet?" Bree jumped on that.

"It might be Joliet, but Renee says Julet. She is from a previous marriage and was raised in France. Louis divorced her mother and came to the United States about twenty years ago. But he's kept up with her. She's probably twenty-five now and she's been in and out of trouble."

"What kind of trouble?" Bree asked.

"I don't know. She said Julet was a wild teenager and had been in trouble and her daddy always bailed her out. She was married about a year and then divorced. She bounces back and forth between the United States and France."

"That's her," Bree said.

Nancy continued her story. "Yesterday Renee told me she had dreaded Julet coming this time more than ever. They hate each other. But Louis's birthday was last week. And he had bought himself a new yacht."

"The *Sea Breeze*?" Kit asked.

"She didn't tell me its name." Nancy shrugged. "Just that he was going to have a christening party and Julet would be there. She told him she was involved in a game some people are playing and it was going be in Claxton just before the Spring Festival. And she was coming to see him."

"A game?" Bernell asked.

"I don't know what kind of game. She just said some people are playing a game and she joined it and she could get a lot of money out of it."

Bernell asked, "Did she describe the game?"

"Renee didn't, not to me, or else I didn't hear that part. But I would have picked up on it if it mentioned digging, or looking for a treasure. But you know what? That could be it, couldn't it?"

"So could she be one of them that broke into Davie's house?" Kit suggested.

"If so, we've got her fingerprints," Bree said. "If she touched anything I mean."

Bernell cautioned, "Nancy, do you think you could not breathe a word of our suspicion? Heaven forbid that we accuse Renee Renoir's stepdaughter."

"It's been a one-way conversation for ten years. I can't see it changing now. She talks. I listen, even if she gets on my nerves especially with the slurs and putdowns." Nancy laughed wryly. "Sometimes I want to slap her. But you can't do that. The Bible says to turn the other cheek."

"You think you could put up with her a while longer? It might not be a good time to dump her." Bernell suggested.

Nancy sighed. "Yeah, I know what you mean. And I was so looking forward to it."

They all laughed, then she said, "Well, I can play this game, too. I can be a spy. I doubt that Renee is involved in anything except being a snob. And she's 'eat-up' with that."

Chapter 32 Gray Tower

Tuesday, April 9

True to his word, Jeb Stanton, Claxton Chief of Police, contacted Maximum Security Allegheny State Prison in New York. He had a hunch he couldn't shake. He told Bernell, if he could confront Alana, he might be able to get to the bottom of all this. In his heart, he agreed that she was behind it.

He remembered his own experience with the woman when she was in Claxton jail. He felt sure he could read her if he could see her face. He knew she still hated him and hated the Wellsly family for ruining her life. "Why wouldn't she be behind this current series of events?" He asked.

Bernell agreed with him. "I cannot go to that prison and see Alana, but as Chief of Police, you can."

When Jeb contacted Warden C. F. Riggs at the prison, he didn't know how hard it would be. He told the warden he had another case that Alana could clear up if he could talk with her. He did not expect to be alone with the woman.

The Warden listened to Jeb's explanation, then finally said, "Chief Stanton, I'm afraid it will be impossible for you to see Alana Frizelle."

"Well, even if I don't see her, if you get her on the phone with me--it wouldn't be as good as seeing her in person--but better than nothing."

"I cannot put her on the phone with you," Warden Riggs continued.

"I could request a lie detector test then, and have her questioned, but I wanted to see her if possible."

"I'm sorry Chief Stanton. I cannot arrange a lie detector for Miss Frizelle."

"But, I think it is within the law for me to make this request and I believe you have to comply," the Chief argued.

"Perfectly within the law," answered the warden. "But Alana Frizelle is dead."

"What? Seriously? I thought...when? Was it suicide? Or did someone else get to her? She had thirty years. But her crimes were heinous and sometimes other prisoners..."

"Nothing like that," the Warden interrupted Jeb. "She apparently died of a heart attack."

"A heart attack?" Jeb was incredulous. He rubbed his forehead and asked, "When?"

"A couple of months ago, in January."

"Who claimed the body? Can you tell me that?"

"A cousin in Octavia, New York," the warden answered.

Jeb was taken aback, and at a loss for words. "Well, thank you," he said and hung up. Immediately he dialed the Jackson Agency. "I need to come over a minute," he told Abby.

"Come on. I'll tell Mrs. Jackson."

"Good," Bernell said. "I want to share some things with him, too." Nancy had just left them with information that she wanted Jeb to know.

Bernell's reaction to Jeb's news was sheer shock and defeat. "Well, God bless her soul," she said.

They sat there looking at each other in a state of despair. All their suspicions and speculations now squashed. Finally, Bernell said, "Jeb, I still feel like she orchestrated this before she died. She had ten years in prison to plan things out. She had to have a contact on the outside."

"Or on the inside," Jeb agreed.

"We have to get those women off that yacht and question them. They must have heard from her. Somehow we have to get to them."

Jeb agreed. "Jenny says she is certain that one of the women on the yacht was Jo Swan. Deputy Mills told me that."

"Yeah, I know. We have pictures. And Bree can vouch for it. She has seen her in person, too, at the time she passed hundreds of dollars in counterfeit to Jenny in the shop. Can't you arrest her under suspicion for that?"

"Yes, but we have to be able to get to her. What about the other one?" He looked at the pictures Bernell showed him.

"This one with red hair, she must be the one that George sold a boat to. And also the boat from Davie's place. Might be it right here in this picture. They must have had a well-devised plan. Sure wish we knew what it is."

"Why can't you just go to the yellow house and arrest them?" Bernell asked.

"I can't go break the door down. And no one is ever there, even when that van is in the driveway. I sent a deputy this morning. He said no one was at the house. He did say the van was gone this time though, which was unusual. But you can't arrest someone you can't find."

"You can swear out a warrant, can't you?"

"Have done so. The deputy had it this morning. You can't leave it nailed to the door. The warrant is only for Jo Swan because she's the only one we have evidence on. The redheaded one is a little trickier. Alex at Davie's plant says a redheaded woman bought a dinghy there. And she paid cash, but he can't prove it. The problem is neither Alex nor George at Oarlocks and Bagels reported it at the time. Obviously, because they didn't know it was counterfeit. Jenny didn't either, but we do have pictures. And no doubt Swan's fingerprints. It's just a matter of time before we arrest her. But in the meantime, she has disappeared."

"Well, she climbed down from that yacht and rowed up to Louis Renoir's house. She's probably hiding there. We now know what her connection is to them."

"Oh, yeah?" Jeb perked up.

"Jo Swan is Louis Renoir's daughter."

"Oh, my God!" Jeb looked up at the ceiling and shook his head.

Through Bernell's open door to the conference room, she could see Kit and Bree discussing some documents.

"Come on back here, Jeb," she motioned. "Let's see what they've got. And tell them what you just told me. That sure adds a kink in things."

Kit spoke first. "I have a dossier on Jamie Sampson," she said.

"Well, let's see it," Bernell said as she and Jeb pulled up a chair.

Kit looked at Jeb. "I've found that the jeweled cigarette lighter with Jamie Sampson's fingerprint was purchased from a jewelry store in Chesapeake, Virginia."

"No kidding. That's becoming quite the hotspot, isn't it?" Bernell exclaimed.

"Did she know the Smythes?" Bree asked.

Kit said, "I doubt it. Yachts pull into waterfronts and marinas all up and down the coast. So it could be purely circumstantial."

Jeb argued, "But when they were both in Chesapeake and then both show up hundreds of miles off the beaten path here in Claxton, that's a bit more than a circumstance. I'd say it's highly suspicious."

Bernell agreed. "So what does this mean then? What is the connection between Smythe and the women we think are digging up Davie's parking lot? If he knew them, HOW did he know them, and why is he missing?"

"Oh, Lord, and that man in the white suit. We're never gonna figure this one out, Bernell. This might be the first case we can't solve," Kit fretted.

"Well, I'm not giving up," Bree said. "There's a key somewhere that will start opening things up."

"Do you think it might be Jo Swan?" Jeb asked. "If so, I'll flush her out if I have to arrest Louis Renoir."

"What could you arrest him for?"

"I'll think of something. Trespassing, disorderly conduct, jaywalking. I'll find something."

"From the sound of it, his wife could give you lots of reasons. But I doubt any of that would hold water."

"Maybe we need to just focus on Jo Swan. We do have the counterfeit money. Although for the life of me, I can't figure why they're passing counterfeit money. The Renoirs are filthy rich."

"Is it possible she did not know it was counterfeit?"

"Where would she get counterfeit money anyway?"

Kit said, "Wait a minute. Let me think. Roger Riddick had a counterfeiting operation, Bernell. Remember ten years ago when you and I went with Ana to the old sawmill?"

"I'll never forget it," Bernell said.

"Remember that room with all that equipment that looked like machinery for printing counterfeit money?"

Bernell tapped her nails on the table and thought a minute. "Yes, I do."

She stopped tapping. "But I also remember the warehouse burned that day. They set it on fire. What are you thinking?"

Kit nodded. "There was counterfeit money hidden somewhere else, and it's just now being circulated. And the only one that I know who could get their hands on it would have been Alana Frizelle. But she's been in prison ten years, and now..."

Bernell interrupted her. "Oh, you didn't hear yet." She looked at Jeb.

Jeb took the cue. "I just learned that Alana Frizelle died a couple of months ago."

"No way. Seriously?" Bree had to sit down.

Kit's jaw dropped. "How bizarre is this case going to get? She was our main suspect." She paused, frowned, and then looked at Bernell. "Maybe it was just too easy to accuse her because we knew her and what she was capable of. She was a 'known' among all this other 'unknown.' We may have to adjust our thinking."

"You're a smart lady, Miss Griffiths," Bernell said to her cousin. Then regrouping thoughtfully, she said, "Okay, then, Jo Swan is our only concrete link. We have to get her."

Bree sat up straight. "Hold on," she said. "Just give me a minute."

She tapped her phone until she found the number she wanted and then punched it in. She held up her finger for the others to be quiet and spoke in French. Apparently, the one on the other end did not understand French so she had to repeat everything in English, but she maintained the French as her disguise.

"Bonjour, madame, puis-je parler à Joliet?"

With bated breath, they stared at her and waited.

"Une amie Briana. Oui, her friend, Briana."

"Sleeping late? Pourrais-je venir? Could I come by? j'adore la voir, ah, love to see her. Oui, oui merci madame, thank you."

She looked at Jeb. "You want her? The maid said she's sleeping late. She'll probably be up in an hour."

Kit hit her a high five. "I can't believe you did that. I didn't know you could speak French."

"Thanks to USCC foreign language requirements," Bree said.

"This is it," Jeb said as he stood up. "I'll get Deputy Mills and we'll pay a visit to the Renoir house."

*

An hour later Jeb called Bernell. "The eagle has landed."

"Woohoo!" The ladies at the Agency had not been able to do a thing after he left, but were anxiously awaiting his call. Now she was in the back seat, sitting quietly. There had been no incident.

Joliet Swan had been arrested before and seemed to take it in stride. As it turned out Louis Renoir was not at home and Renee was glad to see her arrested. She told Jeb it was not the first time. She didn't know what Julet had done, but she was not surprised.

"It's just for questioning right now, Mrs. Renoir," Jeb explained.

All Joliet said was, "My father will take care of this."

"Like he always does," Renee said.

The maid said, "I reckon she won't be here when her friend arrives," and shook her head.

Chapter 33 Through the Looking Glass

Tuesday, April 9

J**oliet Swan could not have been more cooperative.** She produced a picture ID with her street address in Paris, France. The department obtained fingerprints and created a file including a headshot. Chief Jeb then set her up in the interrogation room so Bernell, Kit, and Bree could watch through the one-way window.

After establishing her name and address again, Jeb said, "We merely need to question you right now, Miss Swan. So relax and just tell us what you know."

"Of course," she smiled which was off-putting to Jeb. *Is this going to be a cat and mouse game?* He wondered.

"Do you understand why you are here?" Jeb asked.

"No."

"Do you remember shopping at Burgundy Blue Boutique on Thursday last week?" Jeb asked.

Jo looked down a minute then said, "Oui.

"You made a purchase and then requested cushions be custom made."

"Oui. It was my father's birthday and I gave him the cushions for his new yacht. What is wrong with that?"

"Nothing at all," Jeb said. "But there is something wrong with passing counterfeit money. And you dropped $2,000 on Jenny Wellsly, right?"

Swan looked puzzled. "Counterfeit money?"

"You know what I mean," Jeb grew impatient.

"I'm sorry, Monsieur. You are wrong. I know nothing of counterfeit money."

Kit, Bree, and Bernell looked at each other with raised eyebrows. Bree shrugged.

Bernell said "Hmm."

Kit said, "Don't buy that. She's acting."

Jeb said, "Then please explain why you were carrying so much. I know you might not be used to American money, but where did you get that amount of cash? If you cashed a traveler's check and someone gave you counterfeit money, then they are liable. But right now, ma'am, the buck stops with you—so to speak." He leaned back and waited for her answer.

"I know nothing of counterfeit money," she reiterated.

"Well, what DO you know?" Jeb raised his voice a little. "What have you been doing in the past few months?"

She frowned, looked around the room. Stared at the window as though she knew what it was. Finally, she said, "I was at Boca Raton on vacation and I met some nice people on the beach. We hung out together for a while. Then one day my friend said she was playing a treasure hunt game and wondered if I would like to participate. I said 'sure, sounds like fun.' When she told me where it was, I told her my father lives there. Then she said 'sorry,' I could not play. I said 'why.' She said it is a secret game. I said I won't tell him. She made me promise and said I would be in big trouble if I told him. I might even get killed. So I said, I'll never tell him. So you cannot tell him either."

The chief rocked back in his chair. She had said a mouthful. And now suddenly he was in the position of having to protect her while getting information about this secret game.

"Excuse me," he said and left the room for a minute. "You getting this?" He asked Bernell and her agents.

"Wow!" said Bree. "She knows a lot. You have to work with her."

"Yeah, I know. I just had to come out and digest that." He rubbed the back of his head. He went back into the interrogation room with a paper cup of water and handed it to Swan.

"Oui," she said and took the cup.

He scratched his head again, glanced at the deputy operating the recorder, and sat back down across from her. He put his elbows on the table clasped his fingers together under his chin and said, "Miss Swan, I think you have accidentally fallen in with a bad gang. You have a right to be afraid. I will provide police protection for you, but you need to cooperate with us and help us catch the bad guys."

"My friends do not appear to be bad guys."

"I am sure of that. But this secret game is illegal. So if they are breaking the law, and if you continue with them, you are breaking the law. I can arrest you now for passing counterfeit money because your fingerprints are on it. You would have to get a lawyer and prove your innocence. Passing counterfeit money is not an 'innocent until proven guilty' offense. It's the other way around."

She squirmed. She was a pretty woman, looking younger than her twenty-five years. He had found a record of drug possession in her teens, but she had never been convicted of anything. He suspected that she was truly unaware that the money was counterfeit. But she had been a spoiled brat. This might be her wake-up call to grow up. He had seen glimpses of maturity which in his mind was to her credit. He wanted to help her. He kicked himself mentally remembering when he actually wanted to help Alana. On impulse, he asked, "Have you heard the name Alana recently? Alana Frizelle? Alana Rodriguez? Or just Alana?"

"I had a friend in school in France named Alana."

"In school? Like college?"

"No, first grade."

"Oh, so she would be about twenty-five now?"

"Oui."

If she was telling the truth, he could rule out that connection. "Do you know Jamie Sampson?" he asked.

"Jamie Sampson is in the game."

"Ah! Is she the one you met on the beach in Florida?"

"No."

"Can you give me that person's name?"

Swan sighed. "Jackie Summerlin. Please don't tell her I told you. She will be mad at me."

"Miss Swan, in this game do you have to dig holes to look for the treasure?"

"Oui."

"How did you know where to look?"

"We have clues."

"Who gave you the clues?"

"Zelda."

"Who is Zelda?"

"Is this really important?" Swan asked.

Jeb's patience was wearing thin. "Miss Swan, do you want me to protect you and get you out of this illegal group?"

She hung her head. "I guess."

"No!" He snapped. "You cannot guess. You either want help or not!"

"Well, since I didn't think I did anything wrong I didn't think I needed help!" she raised her voice.

"Where did you get the money?" He asked.

"It was in the house."

"Which house?"

"On Chattanooga Road."

"Where in the house?"

"This is very annoying!" Swan answered.

"Where was it in the house? I have been in that house. I never saw a stash of money."

"It was buried in the garage."

"Buried in the garage?"

"Yes!"

"Did Zelda know it was there?"

"Yes!"

"So you were given a bunch of money from that stash buried in the garage."

"Yes."

"And you did not wonder whether it was counterfeit or not?"

"Why should I?"

"Excuse me," Jeb said and went back out. He shook his head and said to Bernell. "I can't hold her. She is ignorant. She did not know it was counterfeit."

"You can't let her go. She's our key right now," Bree said.

"What if she tells them what you have asked her?" Kit asked.

Bernell tapped her nails on the table. "She can't tell them. She's supposed to be keeping this secret. They trust her, but she might be in danger if they find out. We don't know a thing about the other two – or three. They might not be as naïve as she is. They might be as ruthless as Alana."

"The one that is now dead," Kit said.

Bree said, "You know?"

They looked at her, waiting for her to finish. She continued, "You know, Louis Renoir might be the biggest jerk in the world, but he probably would be protective of his daughter. What do you think of bringing him in on this and having him protect his daughter? He could conceivably be an asset."

They all thought that might be worth considering. But they had no idea how to go about that. Jeb said, "I'll ask a few more questions, then think of something."

He reentered the room and said, "Sorry, let's continue."

Swan sighed. "I don't know what else you need. I've told you everything I know."

"Oh, no you haven't. Where did you dig a hole last?"

"By the boat place."

"How many times did you dig a hole there?"

"Two. It was filled back up and we weren't done. So we had to dig it up again."

"What were you looking for?"

"The treasure!"

"What did it look like?"

"I don't know. We didn't find it."

"What did you think it would look like?"

"A trunk like a pirate's chest, of course."

"What is supposed to be in it?"

"Diamonds."

"A trunk full?"

"Well," she laughed. "That would be a lot of diamonds, wouldn't it? No, I think it has other stuff in it, too. But the diamonds are the main thing. There's a lot of them and they are priceless. That's why I agreed to play. I love diamonds."

"And you would get to keep them?"

"Some of them."

"What are your clues to the treasure?"

She looked at him and sighed like she hated to tell him. "If I tell you and you find it, then you will get the diamonds, and I won't get any."

"Miss Swan, you are not twelve years old. This is not Treasure Island. Did you have to go to a doctor before playing this game?"

"How did you know?"

"Just a guess."

"They had to make sure we were fit and trustworthy."

"Have you been hypnotized?"

On the other side of the window, Bree's eyes grew wide and Kit's jaw dropped. Bernell whispered, "Oh, my God."

Swan said, "Noooo." But of course, that was not a knowledgeable answer.

"Miss Swan, do you know someone named Martin Morgan Montegue?"

"No."

"Do you know someone named Jeffry Smythe?"

"No."

"Have you ever been to Chesapeake, Virginia?"

"Yes."

"Whoa! Back up," Jeb said. "Who did you visit in Chesapeake, Virginia?"

"I don't know. It was a party. We all went."

"By 'we all,' you mean, you, Jackie Summerlin, Jamie Sampson, and Zelda?"

"Zelda didn't go. We didn't know Zelda then."

"Was that before you came to Claxton?"

"I've been to Claxton a hundred times before then. My father lives here."

"Let me rephrase that. Was that before you went to the house on Chattanooga Road?"

"Oh. Yes. Just before. It was cold. January."

"You think that is where you saw a doctor?"

Swan laughed. "There were lots of people there. Davie Wellsly was there."

Jaws dropped again in the other room. Jeb had trouble controlling his own demeanor. "How did you know Davie Wellsly?"

"He was the life of the party."

"What do you mean?"

"You know what the life of the party is. He makes people laugh. He has a good time. Are we going to be much longer? I am tired and I am hungry. And I am sure my dinner will be getting cold."

"Do you plan to spend the night at your father's house?"

"Yes."

"Is anyone else there?"

"Well, of course. My father is there. Rotten Renee is there. Sassy, the maid, is there. She's very nice. I like her."

The women on the other side of the glass were laughing. Jeb wished he could see through it. He could imagine their reactions. But he didn't want to get up again. He got out his phone, "Miss Swan, I'm going to call your father to come get you."

"Thank you," she said.

Jeb knew now what he had to do. As much as he hated to rely on Louis Renoir, Jeb needed to trust him to take care of his daughter. She did not need to go back to the group. He felt sure that she had been under some hypnotic control, and that needed to be broken. But Lord knows he did not know how to handle that.

"May I speak to Mr. Renoir?" He asked the maid. "This is Chief Jeb Stanton calling."

After a pause, Renoir answered and Jeb said into the phone, "Mr. Renoir, could you come down to the police station? Your daughter is here. She's alright. And she is not in any real trouble, but she might be in danger. I'll explain when you get here. Right, okay, thirty minutes. Thanks."

"Oui, monsieur," Jo Swan said.

"While we wait, I'd like to ask you a couple more questions," Jeb said.

"Sure."

"Do you know what your plans are next, now that you have already dug and did not find the treasure?"

"No. We were supposed to get orders tonight. We dug in several places, but no treasure. And that was hard work when we had to use shovels. Mr. X worked the machine and that looked easy. I think it is a fake game now though. I don't think there are any diamonds at all."

"Who's was Mr. X?"

"Just a man."

"Does he live at 1001 Chattanooga Road?"

"No."

"Was the machine on a barge?" Jeb asked.

"How did you know?" She asked.

"Just a guess. Did you dig up at the Gristmill Restaurant?"

"Yes. And that dog was vicious. He was on a pedestal. He didn't jump. But I heard him howling."

"Really?"

"Yes! Scared me to death."

"Did you dig at Pine Ridge Landing?"

"With the woods all around?"

"Yes, that would be it."

"Yeah, I don't know why. There's nothing there."

"What were your clues?"

"You asked me that before. I don't know. It's on a piece of yellow paper. I was not in charge. I was a digger."

"Do you think the group will continue digging?"

"Yes. We haven't found it yet. But Zelda says she knows it's there. Her father told her where to look. He said three places, though, and we have looked at all three. So I don't think they'll find it. I'm ready to quit."

"I think you're going to be sick tonight and not be able to go back out, don't you?"

"Oui."

"Your father will take care of you. I appreciate all you have told me. And your secret is safe. We won't tell anyone you have been here. Our secret." The deputy nodded also.

"Okay? We might talk again tomorrow."

"I guess." She shrugged.

When Louis Renoir arrived, Jeb decided to lay the cards on the table and tell him everything. He took him into his private office to talk. He was taking a big chance, but somehow he felt it was the right thing to do. He prayed he would not regret it.

Chapter 34 Second Thoughts

Tuesday, April 9

Bernell, Kit, and Bree couldn't wait to get out of the jail so they could talk. They wanted to talk with Jeb, also, but had to wait until he was through with Louis Renoir and Jo Swan. They left a message with Edna for him to call the Agency as soon as he could.

Back in their office, they met in the conference room. "I'm reeling," Bree said. "I can't believe all I've just heard. We *have* to talk with Jenny and Davie now."

"Our case is almost wrapped up. I don't know what else Zelda and her girls can do. And we now know who they are. We have all their names," Kit said.

"Their NAMES, but do we know who they are?" Bree asked,

"What do we actually have?" Bernell asked.

"I'll tell you soon." Kit pointed to her office. "I have some queries printing now. We know Sampson was a wrestler. She spent a little time in jail for drugs ten years ago. She lost a cigarette lighter at the landing that she bought in Chesapeake, Virginia."

"Or someone else bought in Chesapeake, Virginia, and gave to her," Bree said. "The jewelry store could not identify the purchaser."

"True," agreed Kit. "It's really out of character for a person in sports to be a smoker. From the pictures, she's in pretty good shape. So I've wondered about that."

"And they all went to that party in Chesapeake where Davie was the life of the party," Bree added. "I'm not sure I believe that part. I've never seen Davie the life of any party and we've been close for ten years. She may be mistaking somebody else for him. Maybe she's seen him, or a picture of him, here and thought it was the same person. I really would not put too much stock in that. And besides, she didn't even know who the host was."

"That's true," Kit said.

"Bottom line," Bernell concluded, "is that we aren't a hundred percent sold on Jo Swan's story. Kit said to begin with that she was acting."

"If she was acting, she was good," Bree declared. "But I think Jeb swallowed it hook line and sinker."

Kit said, "Well if she was honest, have they exhausted their search since they have found nothing? So what do they do now? And if the treasure does include diamonds, it could be worth a lot of trouble for them to continue searching for it."

"But where else are they going to look?" Bree wondered.

"They may not be through digging near Davie's parking lot," Bernell said. "It certainly is pinpointed by the clues. Those songs Daddy put together. And where did they get those clues if not from Alana, as we figured in the first place?"

"As you said, she had ten years to plan it." Bree reminded her. "And speaking of ten years, that counterfeit could have been buried in the garage when Alana lived there."

"Well, it's obvious, now, we're a long way from being done with this. The only way for this to come to a head is for that buried stuff--those diamonds, specifically--to be found," Kit said.

"So maybe Davie needs to start digging, too. He *does* have an advantage. It's his property and he can dig in broad daylight. And by the way, we have to catch him and Jenny up to date." Bernell buzzed Abby. "Get up with Jenny and Davie and see how soon they can come down here. It's very important."

"On it!" Abby cheerily replied.

Bree fretted. "The only thing we have accomplished is that we have exposed the ones doing the digging."

Bernell agreed. "But that's a big step."

Abby buzzed Bernell. "Is eight o'clock tomorrow morning okay? They couldn't either one come today but both said first thing in the morning."

"Fine. I want to get Isaac and Jimmy back in here too, but I'm not calling them until I have cleared up some things with Davie. He told us he'd been up there. Honestly, I was shocked by what Swan said, though. That's troubling."

A ding in Kit's office told her the print job was done. "Hold on while I get that," she said to the others.

"I hope this will tell us something," Bernell said.

Bree got them both a drink while they waited. Kit came back in grinning. She gave them each a copy and directed their attention to segments of the document.

Jamie Sampson had been married to a doctor for six years before divorcing him two years ago. He was a psychiatrist who promoted hypnotism as a means to change unhealthy behaviors like overeating, drinking, and smoking.

"Wow. I bet she learned the tricks of the trade from him," Bree guessed. "She probably went to him to quit smoking herself and they got together."

"I'd buy that," Bernell said.

"So you think maybe she used that technique on Jo Swan?" Bree asked. "Why would she need to do that? Why pick somebody like her. She seems so, I don't know, flighty. I think Jenny called her flaky."

Kit said, "Remember what Swan told Jeb, that when they found out her father was in Claxton, they told her she couldn't play? I bet they chose her BECAUSE her father was in Claxton. But I don't see why. Not yet. You think he has a closer connection to them than we know?"

Bernell tapped her nails. "Nancy told us that Renee complained about Louis's new friends. Are these the new friends?"

"I'd lay odds," Kit said.

"Oh, my goodness," Bernell uttered. "What has Jeb done? If Renoir is one of them, then Jeb has revealed his hand--and ours. What's going to become of this now?"

"I left word with Edna for him to call us." She buzzed Abby. "Jeb hasn't called, has he?"

"No. You want me to buzz him?"

"Yes, I've got something he needs to see."

When Edna buzzed Jeb, he dropped what he was doing. He had been sidetracked by other emergencies when Renoir and Swan left but he wanted to share this with her anyway. In ten minutes he entered the Agency door in a huff.

"Hey, guys. Wish I had time to join you," he said to the old men playing checkers."

"Well, you got work to do," Mr. Roy chortled. He was pleased with the efforts he had seen about that yellow house. He felt partly responsible. He saluted and motioned Jeb to go on to Bernell's office.

Bernell ushered him into the conference room. "Sorry ladies, I got waylaid by an emergency." He had a folder in his hand. "This is the car that was rented to Martin Montegue. There was a receipt in his wallet that matched the stub in this SUV that was found near Pine Ridge Road. There was blood on the door handle and the steering wheel. Forensics is checking that out now," he looked at Bree.

"Also, I checked with the car rental agency, Acme. He had paid with a credit card. I ran a check on that card and found that he used it to pay for a registration at River Woods Motel by the airport. That was the last time the card was used. I called the motel. He had paid for three nights. He checked in but he never checked out."

"I don't know what to say," Bernell spoke first. "It's getting thick, isn't it? But that could open up some things. I wonder what enemies he had, or who he crossed."

Bree remembered. "He was at the Gristmill Restaurant talking about picking up his yacht. Maybe he had a lot of money on him. If he was--just bear with me a minute."

She went to her desk and picked up the file she had on the man in the white suit. "If Jeffry Smythe actually SENT Montegue to pick up the yacht, and he still owed Davie $10,000, he might have had cash on him. There's a lot of people who would kill for $10,000."

"You may be on to something," Jeb said. "We have established that Montegue was from Chesapeake, Virginia."

"But Davie declares that he knows nothing of Montegue," Bernell reminded them.

Kit added, "And the oar that you said had blood on it was found in that parking lot across the street. I wonder if he was hit and robbed there, and didn't die but drove down to Pine Ridge Road."

"No. It didn't happen that way," Bree said. "He didn't know anything about Pine Ridge Landing."

"Well, maybe he thought that was the road where Davie's plant was, where the yacht is," Jeb suggested.

"That could be an explanation, I guess," Bree said. "But I don't think so. Would he get out of the car, walk to the river, fall in, and float back up to the waterfront?"

"No," Jeb said. "That doesn't make any sense."

Kit suggested, "Maybe the killer dragged him to the water at the waterfront, and then the killer drove the car down to Pine Ridge and left it."

"That would make more sense," Bernell said. "But whose blood is it on the steering wheel?"

"That's what we're trying to find out," Jeb said.

"Back to the motive, your premise that he was carrying $10,000 in cash. Why did he think Davie would take cash?" Kit asked.

Bernell said, "Smythe wanted to pay Davie with cash, to begin with, remember?"

"Yeah, but Davie told him he didn't want to do it that way and the man wrote him a check for a half-million dollars as a down payment."

"And who has three million dollars in cash lying around?" Kit asked. "You know, I think there's been something fishy about that yacht all along. Why did somebody like that come to little, old Claxton to get a yacht built?"

"He told Davie he had heard of the quality of his boats, and he wanted the best," Bernell said.

"Yeah, right," Bree said. "I mean, I do not doubt that Davie builds the best boats around. But how did Jeffry Smythe learn that? Did he know someone in Claxton already?"

They were all silent a moment thinking through that question, then both Bernell and Kit said, "Louis Renoir."

"Man!" Bree said. "You reckon?"

Bernell slapped the table. "And that brings us back to Jo Swan and her father."

Kit handed Jeb her copy of the report she printed and went to the computer to print another one for herself. After rehashing what they had learned, or guessed, from the information, Bernell asked, "What do you think, Jeb? Have we got the fox guarding the chicken coop?"

Jeb shuffled and thought a minute. He remembered how he felt listening to Jo Swan. Could he never trust his feelings? Or his instincts? If he was wrong now, he might as well turn in his badge.

Bernell said, "Jeb, let me ask you something. All these diamonds these people are searching for. What if they find them? What then? Do they think they can use them, or sell them?"

"Small ones, maybe they could have mounted in jewelry with no problem. But to get the money they think, they would have to sell them on the black market. Maybe in Europe. But there's a black market out there that you ladies know nothing about."

Kit said, "Well you forget my husband is with the FBI. I've heard a little."

"I learned a little, too, working with him," Bree said.

"You think we need to get the FBI in on this?" Bernell asked.

Jeb was quick to respond. "If those diamonds are found, by us anyway, the FBI will be in on it. Remember Isaac and Lillian's experience in 1963? I don't know that there's anything the FBI could do right now though. I don't want anybody else involved."

"I know what you mean," Bernell said. "From what I gather, these diamonds daddy mentioned in his letter might be the ones from that diamond heist in Michigan in 1955. The FBI only recovered a few of them in 1963. Isaac and Lillian turned them over when they found them. I was not home at the time, but I know the story well."

"So, what now?" Kit asked.

"I'm tired. It's been a long day," Bernell wiped her brow. "Tomorrow we'll talk with Davie and Jenny."

"I'll talk with Louis Renoir," Jeb said. "I think it's time to find out what he knows about Jeffry Smythe. My deputy Mike Riley is working on the Montegue case. I've told him to keep you apprised, Bree, and he might call on you."

Bree nodded. "Okay."

Kit said, "I'm finishing up with the yellow house gang. Zelda Midget was a nurse at Alleghany State Prison. She quit her job in January. She has an invalid sister in a nursing home in--guess where?"

"Not Chesapeake, Virginia," Bree uttered.

"Chesapeake, Virginia." Kit nodded. "It does not say which one, but, despite what Mr. Roy said, and what we all thought, she brought her sister to Claxton. That is what the report says."

"What is the source of that report? Bernell asked.

"That's a fair question," Kit said and laughed. "I googled it. But what I found was a small article in a society column in a Chesapeake newspaper on what's happening this week. It said that the Jeffry Smythes were hosting another one of their famous parties. That could be the one Davie and Jenny went to. And then below that, it said Zelda Midget is taking her invalid sister south to get some sunshine. I wondered why it didn't mention her sister's name."

"Well, she sure has kept her hidden," Bree said. "But we know about the other three. We have these pictures, and we have Jo Swan's testimony."

Kit continued, "Zelda has money from somewhere. Do state prisons have a big pension plan?"

"That's actually funny." Jeb chuckled.

Kit pointed to the document. "Zelda has a bank account with half a million dollars. Money transferred from a Swiss bank account in February. And don't ask me how I got that. Just suffice it to say I have friends." They laughed.

Bernell said, "It always pays to have friends in high places."

"Whew. Her sister must be wealthy," Bree speculated. "So why would she go to all this trouble to find a buried treasure?"

"Beats me," Bernell said and looked at Kit. "What have you got on the Summerlin girl?"

"Wait! Go back!" Bree insisted. "Zelda left her job at Allegheny State Prison around the same time Alana Frizelle died? Let that sink in."

They all sat there processing Bree's insinuation.

Jeb shuffled in his seat. "We've got some work to do. I'll ask Warden Riggs what he knows about Zelda. He didn't sound too cooperative, but I've got to chase that down."

Bernell tapped her nails on the table. Everyone looked at her and waited. They knew she had something on her mind. "I've been thinking all along that Alana escaped from the prison. And she would certainly need an accomplice. Who better than a nurse who could help her fake her death? She could have promised her millions because she knew where to find those diamonds."

"That's crossed my mind too," Bree said. "But that's awfully complicated. She had to have a fake burial and everything."

"Wouldn't be the first time," Kit said. "That's an old trick in the criminal element."

"It's still complicated, though. You know what might be easier?" Bree continued.

"What are you thinking?" Bernell leaned in.

"Wouldn't a nurse know how to induce a heart attack?"

Kit raised her eyebrows. "Oh, I see where you're going. Zelda, the nurse, could have agreed to Alana's idea and learned about the treasure, the house, and everything. I think after ten years, she had plenty of time to get cozy. Alana had all the details worked out for the 'game' and I'm betting Zelda double-crossed her. She could have induced a heart attack. Then with Alana out of the way, she just walked out and did exactly what Alana had planned to do."

"Pretty clever." Jeb absorbed that thought and jotted some notes on a pad.

Bernell looked at Kit. "That's a believable theory. And a lot easier than faking the death scenario. I wonder if there is any way to prove that."

"Not until they're caught, for sure," Bree said.

"Actually, you can have the body exhumed and do a DNA test now," Kit said.

"Unless they were cremated, and I believe that's what the warden told me," Jeb remembered.

"UGH!" Bernell shook her head.

"Yeah, ugh!" Jeb agreed.

Kit sighed. "Well, back to Summerlin." She referred to her printout. "Born in Nevada, went to college, got married, divorced in Vegas two years later, came east, went to Yacht Crew Training in Fort Lauderdale. Worked on a Cruise Liner for three years. Lives on the beach at Boca Raton."

"Pretty cut and dried. Except for that yacht training. And I suppose she was befriended by Jamie Sampson to join the game, too." Jeb asked.

"Apparently," Kit said. "That's all I have right now. But that sure would qualify her for a participant in the game, wouldn't it?"

Jeb stood up. "I'm with Bernell. It's been a long day. But it's not over for me. Call me if you guys run into anything else I need to know. I'll get back with you on whatever we find about the car."

On the way out he paused at the checker game. "You know, that looks very tempting, fellows. Think I'll put in for retirement and join you."

"Now you're talking," one of the guys said.

Mr. Roy said, "Nope, not yet, Chief. We need you around here. Best police we've had in fifty years." Jeb smiled. It always felt good to hear that. He wondered if they could say that tomorrow.

Chapter 35 Pictures and Proof

Tuesday evening, April 9

Jenny and Davie arrived home at the same time. They had both been working hard to catch up. Davie had hired a professional landscaping company to do the grounds work. He had consulted with Jimmy and Isaac and the three of them had agreed that it would be better to have a professional landscaper handle the project. Ed and Jake were trusted landscapers who had worked for the family many times.

They signed a contract that included confidentiality. Isaac met them in Davie's office and explained the issue they faced. The men had heard the radio talk and had seen articles in the paper. They sympathized with Davie for the hard time the DJ was giving him and were glad to be able to help.

Isaac said, "We want to clear this up once and for all. There may be something buried here my daddy hid sixty years ago."

Davie said, "I want every inch of that lot dug up like a swimming pool, but fill up sections as you go. We'll get the azaleas down and sod it all when it's done."

The finished design would be a scenic landing from the river to the boat plant, with a drive-way to the paved customer parking area in front, and a new employee parking lot in the back. In the meantime, people would have to park along Big Creek Road and behind the plant.

All routine business to the unsuspecting eye. But to Davie and his family, it was the treasure hunt of a lifetime.

"Do people have heart attacks at twenty-six?" Davie asked Jenny when he got home.

"I'm sure they can," Jenny said. "Another bad day, huh?"

Davie said, "To be honest, it was a very productive day. But the whole idea is so stressful, sometimes I think I'm gonna have a heart attack." He explained the plan they had developed and had started working on already. "And all that's costing me a pretty penny. But it's got to be done."

"It sounds good to me." Jenny consoled him. "It's going to be beautiful, and you will solve that issue once and for all. But those people have to be caught."

As Davie and Jenny ate her usual, incredible, crock-pot dinner, they caught up with all they had missed in the past couple of days. She had stayed so late at her mother's, and they had rushed around to get out the next day, they had hardly spoken except in passing.

Now, she told him all about her visit with her mother and seeing the yacht, her cushions, and Jo Swan and the red-headed woman going to the Renoir's house. She told him how Bree had confirmed that these were the people that Thomas and Adam had seen at the yellow house, and how Bernell had concluded these were the people doing the digging.

"Wow!" Davie said. "Unbelievable. Well, that will put an end to that secret digging anyway. They're gonna go to jail. But they've started something I've got to finish."

He helped himself to more of her London broil and creamed potatoes. "I guess all that's what we'll be talking about in the morning."

"I guess so," Jenny agreed. "But there's another thing. You know they're working on that case about the man in the white suit."

"Yeah, have they learned anything else?"

"I'm not sure about that," Jenny said. "But there's something up. And you know Bree told us she wants pictures of everything we saw in Chesapeake when we were there."

"Oh, God." Davie groaned. "I just might go ahead and have that heart attack and get it over with."

"Don't talk like that. It turned out okay. You learned a lesson. I learned a lesson. It won't ever happen again."

"No, it won't, especially at the home of Jeffry Smythe."

"Nor anywhere else," Jenny said.

"Yes." He looked at her. "Nor anywhere else."

"We'll look through the pictures after dinner and print them out," Jenny said. "They're on my computer now."

"All of them?" He asked.

"I just inserted the chip and, yes, all of them went to the computer. There's none on my phone anymore."

"Have I seen them all?" He asked.

"I'm not sure. You can take a look."

"We were there four nights. Did you take a lot?"

"Yes, I'm afraid so."

"Ugh," he groaned.

Positioned in their den/office after dinner, they took on the task of printing pictures. Jenny clicked on the album and said "UGH!" There are almost a thousand pictures. I don't want to print out all these."

"You'll run out of ink," Davie said. "We'll just have to pick the ones we think might help."

"Not this one," Jenny said, pointing to one with Davie standing fully dressed on a diving board over a pool with a crowd of people standing around. Everyone had wine glasses in their hands, obviously a party. Davie was holding up a wine glass."

Jenny clicked the arrow to play a video and could hear the crowd cheering, "Jump, Davie, Jump!"

"Turn that off!" He snapped.

She clicked it off, but there were several more pictures of the same scene.

"I can't believe you took all those," Davie said accusingly.

She sighed. "I couldn't believe you were doing that. And I don't remember taking so many either. I definitely won't print them."

She scanned the pictures, printed out some ocean scenes, a marina with several yachts, and some sailboats in full sail. The pictures were stunning, and there were some people in them.

She scrolled to pictures of people sitting at tables by an Olympic sized swimming pool. Brightly colored umbrellas shaded some people while tanned model types lay on chaise lounges in bikinis and sunglasses. Some were in the pool. It looked like a party at the Playboy Mansion. "I guess I'll print some of these," she said.

"Am I in any of them?" Davie asked.

"I don't see you. You were probably sitting beside me at that time."

Some pictures were at night; women in evening dresses, men in white suits, some in black. It appeared to be a formal event. In some pictures, people were dancing.

"Why did you take so many?" Davie asked.

"I don't know. I was bored. I didn't know anybody there except Julie and Jeffry. And they were occupied with other people. I don't know why they even invited us."

"We should have left before..." Davie's voice trailed off.

"I wish we had," she said. She printed out a dozen more pictures of people in groups chatting and drinking, people in formal attire at a banquet table, people holding up their glasses in a toast.

There was one picture of Davie and Jenny together, smiling with their faces side by side, apparently having a good time. Someone else had taken it for them.

Chapter 36 Davie's Secret

Wednesday, April 10

"I was not having as much fun as that looks like." Jenny told Bernell and Bree the next day at the Agency as they reviewed the stack of prints that she and Davie had brought. "Me neither," Davie said.

Kit brought in a magnifying glass. "You know, some of these people look familiar," she said. She pulled the pictures, Thomas had taken of the women on the yacht.

"Look at that redheaded one," she said. "Now look at this one."

They did appear to be the same person. "Who, Jackie Summerlin?" Bernell asked. Then said "Hmm," as she studied the pictures.

"Look at this one," Bree said. "If that's not Jo Swan, I'll eat my hat."

"Do you see Jamie Sampson in any of them?" Bernell asked.

"Yep. I think so. Green evening dress, dancing with some man in a white suit. Wait. It's hard to tell, but that man could be Martin Montegue. I guess he liked wearing white suits."

Jenny looked at Davie. "You're kidding. Is that him? I did not know."

"Me neither," Davie said.

Bernell and Kit studied the picture and compared it to the ones Thomas had taken.

"So the party Jo Swan went to in Chesapeake was at Jeffry Smythe's house. And they were all there. Interesting she didn't even know whose house it was, isn't it?"

Davie's stomach churned and he went pale. Jenny reached for his hand under the table and squeezed it. She spoke up. "So you're saying those people digging up our parking lot, were at the Smythe's when we were there?"

She looked at Davie. "We were there in September and in January. Those pictures of the ocean, and the marina, and some of those at the pool. That was last September. Were they there then?"

"I don't recognize them in any of those pictures. Only the ones at the night party. So that was in January, right? January is when she said it was. I guess that verifies what she said then."

Bernell chuckled. "Davie, she remembered you. She said you were the life of the party."

Before he could speak, Jenny said, "Crazy woman. Davie's never been the life of any party."

Bree nodded. "That's what I said."

"I'm dull." Davie's chest ached and he wondered *is this a heart attack?*

Jenny diverted the focus. "Do you think they learned something at that party? Maybe something Jeffry Smythe said about his yacht and where it was, something that made them think there was something buried here? I mean how else could they have known about it? Why would they come here soon after that? We never knew those women. We didn't know anybody there. We were definitely out of place. I couldn't wait to leave. And we have not seen the Smythes since then." She looked at Davie for verification.

Davie said, "And he still owes me $10,000. But..." he looked at Bernell. "How does this fit in with the report that Jeffry Smythe is dead?"

"That is a very good question, Davie. I don't know."

"We don't think he's dead," Kit said.

Bree added, "Unless there's been some foul play. He's not been reported missing though."

"Except by me!" Davie said raising his voice, a little angry at the whole story unfolding.

Abby buzzed Bernell's office. "Excuse me," Bernell got up. "This must be important."

When she came back from her desk, Officer Mike Riley was behind her. He walked around the table to Davie, and said "Davie Wellsly, I'm afraid I have to arrest you on suspicion of murder."

"What!?" Bree and Jenny both screeched. Bernell glared at him. "You said you needed to SPEAK to Davie. You didn't say you were here to arrest him. What the heck is going on?"

Davie was pale and looking like he might pass out. All he could think of was Chesapeake, Virginia. Jenny jumped to his side to keep the officer from taking him away. "No! Davie has done nothing wrong! Take those off!" She said as the officer handcuffed Davie.

Bernell grabbed her phone and called Isaac. "Get down here, the police are arresting Davie."

"Kit, get Jimmy," she ordered while she was dialing the police department. "Edna put me through to Jeb! Emergency!"

As soon as Jeb picked up the phone, she barked, "Jeb Stanton, what the heck is going on? Why have you sent an officer down here to arrest Davie?"

"I haven't sent anybody. What's going on?" He asked.

"You tell me," she ordered.

Jeb answered, "Calm down. I'll be right there. Tell Mike to wait for me."

She hung up and said, "How'd he know it was Mike if he didn't send him?" Then she spoke to Officer Riley, "Chief Jeb said for you to wait. He's on his way."

"Just doing my job, Ms. Jackson," the officer assured her.

"I'm sure," Bernell said, "But nobody's on fire, so sit down and tell us what this is all about."

They all sat down except the officer. "You know this guy Martin Montegue that we pulled out of the river?"

"Yes, we know all about that," Bernell said. "Davie doesn't know him, though."

"Ms. Jackson, that doesn't matter. What I'm going on is the fingerprints on the oar along with the blood of the man who was killed. Plus, blood on his car and fingerprints we found there."

For the first time, Davie spoke, sitting down at the table with his hands cuffed behind his back. "Wait just a dang minute! I have never met that man. I've never seen his car, and I sure as heck didn't kill him!"

"Your fingerprints are on the murder weapon, though," the officer argued.

Bree walked around to the officer. She spoke calmly, "Officer Riley, you know that Davie builds those oars. He sells them. His grandfather sells them. There are a number of reasons his fingerprints could be on that oar. I think you have to have a little more proof than that before you can arrest him. Were there any other prints on that oar?"

"Some," the officer said. "But his were plain. And on the car, too."

Davie shook his head. "That's impossible. I don't even know what car you're talking about."

Commotion in the front lobby told them that Jeb had arrived. Abby escorted him through Bernell's office.

"What's going on?" He looked at his officer.

The officer explained again. "You put me on this case, Sir, and I assumed you wanted me to see it through. We've got the prints back. Mr. Wellsly's fingerprints are on the weapon and also on the car with the blood on it."

Jeb pulled a note pad from his pocket and flipped through some pages, "What about the time frame? Do you have a time when Montegue was killed?"

"No, sir. That has not been pinpointed. But fingerprints are usually considered proof of one's presence."

Commotion again in the lobby got their attention, then Isaac and Lillian were ushered in by Abby.

"What's going on?" Isaac asked as he and Lillian sat down at the table.

Jeb gestured toward his officer giving him the floor. Once again Mike Riley explained how Davie's fingerprints were on the oar with blood on it, which had been determined to be the weapon that killed Montegue. And that his fingerprints were on the car with the man's blood on it.

Isaac looked at Jeb. "What's the bail? You set anything yet?"

Jeb shook his head. "Don't get ahead of me. I'm as shocked at this as you are. I totally get that Davie's fingerprints could be on any oar in this town. But now he's saying they're on the car. We've got to pursue that."

"Didn't you say it was a rental car?" Bernell asked.

"Yes, we found a receipt in his wallet and a stub behind the visor in the car. The car has been impounded for now and the Acme Agency contacted. I don't think this is the time to get too deep into questioning, but Davie, I will ask you this. Have you rented a car from Acme in the last week or so?"

Davie shook his head. Jenny's mind went rampant. She opened her mouth but couldn't say anything.

Bernell's office door opened again and Abby showed Jimmy and Jessica in. Jessica went straight to Davie and put her arms around him. "What's going on? What are they saying you have done? You didn't do it. I know you didn't do it." Jimmy stood between the officer and Davie.

"It's okay, Mom. I don't know what's happening either. You might need to call John Fredrick."

Jessica put one arm around Jenny and drew her in. "I don't care what it is, God's got this."

Jenny nodded, her blue-gray eyes pooled with tears she wouldn't let fall.

Jeb said, "Officer Riley, just book him for questioning. We'll get to the bottom of it. There has to be some explanation. Davie hasn't killed anybody, I think I can vouch for that. We just have to figure out how his fingerprints got there."

Jessica asked, "Can somebody get your fingerprints and transfer them to something else?"

Bree answered, "That would be pretty hard to do. People have tried to forge fingerprints, but there are always microscopic differences." She looked at Jeb. "Can we hold off on the arrest until we do some testing?"

Jimmy took the floor. "Have you got a coroner's report as to the actual time of Montegue's death? Wouldn't you have to place Davie at the scene of the crime? Don't you need more information before you go arresting my son?"

Officer Riley blew a deep breath and pulled the keys to the handcuffs from his pocket. "You want me to let him go?" He looked at Jeb.

The Chief said, "If it was anybody else, I'd say book him for questioning. I commend you, Office Riley, on your diligence. We do have a murder. But for the life of me, I cannot accept that it is this boy. There's got to be some explanation for the fingerprints. We have to check that out. In the meantime, we also have to look for a motive, and any other lead that could implicate someone."

Bree said, "We've already discussed the possibility of robbery. He may have been carrying a lot of cash."

Jeb nodded. "We'll check into that." He looked at each of the family sitting around the table. Friends for many years. His most ardent supporters. "This is a pickle, isn't it?"

He turned to Bernell. "There's no better agency in town to pursue this. Y'all know what to do. Looks like your nephew's life is at stake. Can you be objective and fair?"

"Absolutely, leave him in my custody for twenty-four hours," she said.

Jeb looked at the officer and said, "Give him twenty-four hours, Mike."

Unlocking the cuffs, Officer Riley said, "Don't leave town, Mr. Wellsly."

Then he looked at Jeb and said, "I have to say that."

"I know." Jeb smiled. "In the meantime, get out there and question everybody you can about Montegue's activities in the days before he died. Comb this town. Get something concrete from the coroner. As Jimmy said, he hasn't even pinpointed the time of death. Why has Jones been so slack? You all need to remember this in the next election. Somebody knows something. Find it."

"We'll be searching too," Bernell said. "And for the record, this is not the first time we've had a slack coroner."

Isaac nodded. "You'd think with the program at the university now, they would hire a coroner with a forensic science degree, or at least person with a concern for real investigating. But it's always been just a political position. I think it's time for a change."

Jeb didn't want to say much in front of Riley because he knew it would go straight to the coroner, but as he got up, he reached over and shook Isaacs's hand and nodded agreement. Then he and his officer left.

Bernell looked at her family sitting around the table in desperation.

"That was close," she said. Davie sat with his elbows on the table and both hands shading his forehead as he looked down at the table. His parents stood behind him.

Jenny spoke up. "Could Davie and I go home for a while? I promise you we will not leave town." She half-smiled. "I'm in such a panic right now, I can't think. Let us go home and see what we can figure out. I have more pictures that might help. Is that alright?"

Bernell nodded. "Go home. Go back through those pictures. See if Montegue is in any of them. See if he is talking to someone. Maybe one of those women in the yellow house. We may have some suspects that Mike Riley is not aware of."

Jenny and Davie hugged everyone goodbye and promised to call Bernell back in a couple of hours.

After they left, the others decided to stop at Lillian's Riviera for lunch. It was on the waterfront just around the corner.

As they left through the back door, Abby came in from the front with a tidbit of news she felt pertinent.

"What you got?" Bernell asked because she could read her granddaughter's face.

"May not be important," Abby said, "But after Officer Mike Riley left, I heard Luke and Willy talking about him and how he was best friends with that DJ on the radio that's such a jerk. I thought you might like to take that into account."

"Ugh!" Bernell grunted. "Yes, indeed. I suspect there's a little negative influence going on. That could explain why the DJ always knows what's happening before it's in the news. I need to speak to Jeb about that. He ought to take Riley off this case. You going to lunch with the others?"

Abby shook her head. "Brought me something."

"Yea, I did too," Bernell said. "We'll eat in the breakroom together. Is anybody up front now?"

"No, everybody just left."

"Lock the door and put a sign up, 'Back at 1:00.' We need to shut out the world for a few minutes. This has been a rough morning."

Through the hallway door number 002, the first door on the right was the breakroom which provided a little respite. No work was allowed in the breakroom. A fully stocked kitchenette provided convenience for meals. A small pantry held supplies.

The back wall was a twelve-foot mural of Big Creek at the end of Big Creek Road. With the mountains in the distance, it was very relaxing. The other walls were creamy white. A deep blue sofa sat along the left wall.

A round maple table with matching chairs was in the far right corner. A stereo system in one of the cabinets allowed them to play CDs. They all had their favorites. Today, Bernell wanted to hear Beethoven. So as "Moonlight Sonata" played softly she and Abby enjoyed a reprieve.

Abby shared things that she rarely talked about. In spite of their divorce, her ex had called her recently. Not that he wanted to get back together. He seemed bent on harassing her because she caught him and ended the charade. But he was with another woman. And there was no way she was interested in going back to him anyway. It had been five years since the divorce was final and they had been good years.

"I get lonely," she said. But it's better than being miserable."

"You won't always be lonely, Sweetie. There's someone out there waiting for you. He might not know it yet. But I pray for him every day."

Abby laughed. "I pray for him, too. I hope we're praying for the same person."

"Any ideas who it might be?" Bernell asked, fishing for a hint if she was interested in anyone.

"Not a clue."

"Well, he'll come along at just the right time. I'm sure of it." Bernell told her. And somehow, it was convincing. The room was relaxing, the music was soothing, and the conversation nourishing.

"We need to do this more often," Bernell said and her granddaughter agreed.

When everyone left the office for lunch at Lillian's Riviera, Bree suggested they take a slight detour across the street and walk through the parking lot behind Lee Fish Market.

She reminded them, "The bloody oar was found there. If there was a struggle, it's possible something was dropped. Let's all look for anything suspicious. I don't think that's been done."

The six of them kicked gravel and picked up trash. In all, they saved a couple of odd buttons, some loose change, a penknife, a woman's red shoe, and a jogger's headband.

"We still might have missed something," Bree said, "But it's a lot more than has been found. I'm fingerprinting all this. There's DNA on this sweatband. And I'm testing it." Her nose twitched as she pushed it all into a plastic bag she had brought for that purpose.

The next stop was the restroom at Lillian's Riviera to wash their hands.

Before they ate lunch in the quiet serene restaurant, they joined hands and Isaac prayed. Not just for the food, but for the truth to come out, and for Davie to be exonerated. "I pray for this family's safety in the days ahead as we work to resolve this crazy dilemma, in Jesus' Name."

And they all said, "Amen."

Chapter 37 Reckoning

Wednesday, April 10

On the way to the house, Davie said, "I want to see that car, let's go by the police department." He turned around. Jenny called and asked Edna if she could speak to Jeb. He had just come in the door.

"Chief Jeb, can you arrange for us to come by and look at that car that Davie's fingerprints are supposed to be on?"

"Now?" He asked.

"Yes, we're right outside."

"Come on in. Edna can take you back there. I've got a meeting in ten minutes." He handed the phone back to Edna.

"Ok, thank you. We'll be right there." Jenny said and told Davie.

Edna greeted them with her always friendly smile and said, "Chief said for me to take you back there to the impound area."

"Yes, where the cars are," Davie said.

Edna didn't ask questions but led them through an exit door and walked around with them.

"Don't touch anything," Davie cautioned Jenny. "You don't want your fingerprints on anything out here."

"You got that right," Edna said.

Jenny pulled out her phone and snapped a few pictures.

"Y'all sell these?" Davie asked.

"Yes, eventually. Well, except for that green one. It goes back to Acme after we're done with the investigation."

Jenny snapped pictures of it. "Like anything you see?" Edna asked.

"No, not a thing," Davie said. "Okay, we're done. Thanks, Miss Edna."

As soon as they closed the door behind them, Davie said to Jenny, "My fingerprints are on that car. And yours are too, on the passenger side."

"What? How do you know?"

"That's the rental we used in Chesapeake. How could you forget it?"

"Oh, my God. That ugly green car. Yes. I remember it. Didn't expect to see it here." She walked on a bit, then said, "Oh, no. Davie. That is it!"

"Yeah, I know," he said. "The only way I can clear my name of one crime is to admit to another. I don't know which would be worse."

Jenny sighed. "Yes, you do. You know what the Bible says, 'Be sure your sins will find you out.' God must love you an awful lot. He's gone to a lot of trouble to get to you."

"Aw, come on. It's more like the devil's been tracking me down. And it all started with that mirror breaking."

"No," Jenny said. "I think it all started with the seal on that wine bottle breaking."

When they were back in Davie's truck, he asked, "You think we can tell them about that car without telling everything?"

She sighed. "I don't know, Davie. It's not going to be the end of the world for your parents to find out you spent the night in jail. They're not going to disown you. And your grandparents won't either."

He was silent the rest of the way home. He was silent while she prepared their lunch. He remained silent while they ate. His life was on the line.

"I think I'll have that heart attack," he said finally.

"Oh, Davie, stop it! Let's go through those pictures and see what we can find."

"Only about 900 more to go," he said. "You didn't take any at the jail did you?"

"Don't be silly. I didn't take any while I was crying in that car all night either. You can thank your lucky stars that Jeffry Smythe sent his lawyer to get you out and they did not file any charges."

"I do every day," Davie said. "Only now, it might not matter. I'm gonna be hung for a sheep as a lamb."

"You're not going to be hung. They know you didn't kill Montegue. They'll prove it. And be thankful you didn't have to spend more time in jail for that DUI. You could have. I prayed so hard for you all night long--in that stupid ugly car."

"Then we had to drive it home because we missed our flight. We should have waited for another flight the next day."

"I wanted to get out of that town."

"I did, too."

They didn't say anything for a few minutes as Jenny clicked the computer and found the tell-tale pictures.

Noticing the date, Davie said, "That's been over two months. I'm surprised my fingerprints are still on that car. You'd think they would have rented it out since then."

Jenny laughed. "No. It's so ugly, that's why. If anybody saw it first, they wouldn't rent it."

"Evidently, Montegue rented it when he flew in."

Jenny said, "That's what killed him. That ugly car." Then she laughed at her joke.

Davie didn't laugh. "Have a little respect, Jenny. A man is dead. And I'm accused of murder."

"Right, all because of that stupid ugly car," she said giggling and then bursting into tears.

Davie put his arms around her. "No, it's not the car's fault. It's mine. I've never been drunk in my life. Never even tried any liquor until we hooked up with them. I couldn't hold it. Went crazy that night."

She nodded, "And then when that brawl broke out, and somebody called the police, you were afraid of going to jail and your parents finding out, so we ran."

"Straight into more trouble. I didn't know that car was going 95."

"You were too drunk. I was scared to death. I thought we were going to die. When that cop chased us and you finally pulled over, I was so relieved. I just thanked the Lord we didn't crash and kill ourselves and maybe kill somebody else, too."

Davie couldn't let it go but continued to rehash the horrible night. It was a catharsis to talk about it.

"They locked me up and that's the last I know till noon the next day."

"And I cried all night in that car. When I went inside, they wouldn't let me see you. I called Julie Smythe and couldn't get her until 8:00 A.M. I begged forgiveness for running out on the party. She said no problem and wanted to know where we were. When I told her, she got Jeffry to send his lawyer out there to the police station. I don't know how he did it, but by the time you woke up, they let you go."

"And by then we had missed our flight so we just extended the rental on that ugly car and drove it home."

She said, "When we took it to Acme at the airport I thought that would be the last of that ugly thing."

"And the whole sordid ordeal," Davie muttered. "But it's haunting me now. It's gonna make me pay."

Jenny didn't know what to say next. She could see the remorse on Davie's face and felt so sorry for him. This had cost him many sleepless nights. That was what made not hearing from Smythe so bad. He blamed himself.

"But Smythe had put more than two million dollars in that yacht you built. The $10,000 left was chicken feed. And, surely, considering the crowd who was at that party, there were others who were not saints. Even Smythe himself." Jenny tried to console

Davie. "At least, the brawl that caused the police to come had nothing to do with us."

"Yeah, I was up on the diving board acting like a fool. When I saw the blue lights, though, I panicked and jumped in the pool. Thank goodness you were there to help pull me out."

She stroked his arm. "I was glad I had seen the back gate and we could run around that side of the house."

Davie frowned, "I thought I was gonna fall down that slope. I could hardly stand up on level ground."

Jenny said, "And that ugly green car was sitting right there by the curb, like a chariot waiting for us."

"I thought that was lucky."

"I don't know, Davie. Maybe it was God. And he protected us."

"Till the police took me to the station and locked me up. Why didn't he protect me then?"

"Davie, maybe he did. Maybe he saved our lives. I sure thought so. But people have to take responsibility for their own actions. I have a feeling God answered a lot of prayers that night."

She had rehashed that event many times in her mind. But they had an unspoken agreement not to talk about it. Now it was apparent that they were going to have to confess.

Finally, she said, "You know Davie, in light of everything, I think your parents will be more forgiving than you know. You certainly have a reason for your fingerprints being on that car. Nobody would make up such a story. And you have an alibi for every hour of every day."

"Not Sunday morning between ten and twelve. You went to church. I didn't. And Friday night. Remember I worked late? And you fussed at me for it. I have not worked till eleven o'clock in a long time, but I was trying to figure out how to work around that yacht so we can use that bay. Alex was with me till nine remember?"

"Yes, I remember, when he left, you called and said you'd be home soon. But you didn't get here until eleven and I went to bed. And, yes, I was upset." Her heart froze.

"But you didn't do it. Maybe it was some other time anyway. They can't blame you for this."

She sat down beside him and put her arm across his shoulder. "We'll get through this, Davie. You feel like looking at those pictures and see if there's any more we need to show Bernell? We might have to show the ones you hate, so we can prove our story about the car."

"Sure. Who knows who else might show up in those pictures? On second thought, why don't we just give all of them to Aunt Bernell and let them do it."

"Oh, that's a good idea. So much simpler. And they've got all that equipment. I'll just give them the chip. They can look at them all, print the ones they want, and everything. We can't hide now. Want to go on back out there? Get it over with?"

"Yeah. At least Mom and Dad and Grandma and Grandpa aren't there. They went out to eat and then they were going back to work."

A quick phone call confirmed that Bernell was there, Kit and Bree were back and the others had left.

Chapter 38 Confession

Wednesday, April 10

"It is my fingerprints on the car." Davie said after they settled in at the conference table. "Here's the proof." Jenny handed Bernell an envelope with the chip containing all the pictures. "Wait, what?" Bree was puzzled.

"Kit, set up a laptop here at the table," Bernell said and handed her the chip.

"It's a long and sordid story," Jenny began. "You all know we went to Chesapeake a couple of times. We had a good time in September. They invited us back in January for a long weekend. So we flew up there and they had a rental car waiting for us."

Davie picked up the story, "We booked a hotel but we spent most of our time with them at their house on the beach. There was a ton of people there. It was Jeffry's birthday, and he celebrated it in style. Several parties. A lot of the people knew each other, but there were also a lot, like us, that didn't know many. We didn't know anybody but Jeffry and Julie, so it was kind of awkward."

"Boring," said Jenny. "So I just took pictures to occupy myself. But by Sunday night, Davie had loosened up. He had made a few acquaintances. Everybody was a drinker but us. Well, everybody except me, as it turned out."

Bernell cut her eyes at Davie--the look he expected.

"Some of the pictures are self-explanatory," Davie said.

Bernell walked around and she and Bree watched over Kit's shoulder as she scrolled, enlarging a picture every now and then.

"My word!" said Bree. "I never would have believed it, Davie."

He put his head under his arms on the table. "Don't say it."

The last picture was of blue lights flashing in the driveway. "When Davie climbed out of the pool, he grabbed my hand and we ran for it. Our rental car was by the curb and we took off."

Davie barely remembered the next part, so Jenny did most of the talking. She concluded with the return of the ugly green car to Acme Rentals at the airport in Claxton.

"You poor thing," Bernell said. "What an awful experience. And on top of that, trying to keep it from everybody. Well, your folks are forgiving. We've all done things we'd like to hide. I remember when...well... never mind."

Kit and Bree laughed, which helped break the intensity of the moment for Davie.

"I could go ahead and call Jeb and get this cleared up," Bernell suggested.

"Good," Davie said. "Because I have a lot of work to do at the plant."

"And I need to go to the shop too," Jenny said.

Jeb took the call, and after listening to Bernell's shortened version of the story, agreed this was good. He would have to get confirmation from the police department in Chesapeake and verification from Acme Rentals and that would be over.

"Shouldn't take but about thirty minutes to get this all cleared up," he said.

"Whew, what a relief!" Bernell wiped her brow. She had been as worried as anybody about this accusation.

Bree and Kit were getting surprises from the pictures and had printed out several suspicious ones. They asked if Jenny and Davie could identify certain people, but they couldn't.

The phone rang. Bernell listened, "No. What? You're kidding. Hold on." She looked at Davie and said, "There is no record at Chesapeake Police Department of Davie Wellsly ever being there. No

DUI. No arrest. Nothing. The police department does not even have a record of going to the Jeffry Smythe house that night nor any other time."

"But the pictures. You can see for yourself," Jenny said. "Were we in the twilight zone?"

"Oh, no," Kit said. "You can't even identify the people in the pictures. Except for Jeffry and Julie Smythe."

"Well, they could verify it," Jenny said.

"How?" Bree asked. "They're missing. Remember?"

"Dang!" Davie stood up, put his fingers to his temple, and paced. "Okay, Acme Rentals we can check there. That's where the car came from."

"Jeb, what about the car?" Bernell punched the speaker button so they could hear what he said.

"Acme Rentals keeps records of those they rent from here. It was not rented from here in January. If Davie rented it in Chesapeake the record would be there. But someone else rented it on that date. They do have a record of this car being dropped off and confirmation sent back to Chesapeake, but they don't know who left it here. They have a record of it being rented last week to Martin Morgan Montegue though. And you know the rest of the story."

"What?" Davie sat down and whacked the table with his fist. "You think I made this up!"

Jenny fought back tears and said pitifully. "Aunt Bernell. Jeffry had the car rented for us and waiting at the airport when our plane arrived because it was late. I don't even know whose name it was in. We just took the car when a man asked us who we were and said the car was ready for us. We didn't make this up."

Bernell's heart went out to the young couple. "I know you didn't," she said. "We'll prove it."

She picked the phone back up. Jeb was still waiting. "Jeb. We will find proof. Don't do anything yet, please."

She hung up when he agreed to their initial plan.

"Oh, I have an idea," Kit said. "The hotel. When you checked in you had to identify your vehicle. I always do."

"That's right," Jenny said. "I remember saying, I hope they don't think this ugly green car is ours."

Bernell rubbed her fingers together. "Gimme the name of the hotel."

"Oh, my goodness. Where did we stay Davie? It was a local place, not a chain."

Kit had Chesapeake hotels online. "Hyatt Regency?"

"No, not a chain."

"Aloft?"

"No."

"Oak Square?"

"No."

"Oceana?"

"That's it. Oceana."

"Let me do this," Bree said. She dialed the hotel's number and used her French which she had found to be effective more often than not. For some reason, people think the French are sophisticated and important.

In the same French and English, as she had talked to the Renoir maid, she explained that she had lost something at the hotel. She gave the date when she stayed, explained that they were driving a rental, and described the "moche vulture verte" they were driving. As luck, or God's mercy, would have it, the desk clerk snickered. She remembered the ugly green car.

Bree was elated and thanked her. "Can you please fax a copy of our registration that day? I have to prove I was there and this would do it." The desk clerk laughed.

"Thank you for remembering that ugly car," Bree said.

"How could I forget it?" The lady said, "I saw it when you checked in," and snickered again.

In five minutes, a fax came in from the Oceana Hotel in Chesapeake. The registration form identified Jenny and Davie Wellsly, showed his driver's license number, king suite, January 24-28. The vehicle was a green Acme Rental, license plate number UV33234X.

"Hallelujah!" Bernell said. She called the police department back. "Jeb, I've got the registration form from the hotel where the kids stayed. I'll fax it to you now."

"Or Kit will," she said after she hung up.

The phone rang in two minutes. "That might work," Jeb said. "Riley's going to be a stickler, though, so be on the alert."

"Yeah, well, we're going to be sticklers too, Jeb. And we've already got some things from the parking lot the girls found and are examining. You might want to know about that. The thing I think is the most suspicious is a woman's red shoe."

She listened a minute, then said "Yeah. You bet. She was planning to. Thanks, Jeb."

She looked at Bree, and Bree nodded. She knew he wanted her to bring in the shoe.

"You know," Bree posed, "If Mike Riley would work with me, instead of thinking he has to do everything by himself, we could be more effective. But whatever, I'll do it anyway."

Bernell smiled. "Jenny, Davie. Get out of here. You've got work to do."

"I just want to go home and curl up," Jenny said.

Davie agreed, "Yeah. We might do that. Alex is at the plant. He'll be closing up soon. I've got security cameras working and a security guard out there all night. Let's go home. I feel like I could sleep a week."

"Me too," she said. "But we can't. Tomorrow's another day."

When the door closed behind them, Kit smiled and said, "Fiddle de dee."

Bree laughed, "But that's not the same. I'm going back over to that parking lot."

"Wait, I'm going with you," Kit said and looked at Bernell for approval.

"Go ahead. Let me know what else you find."

"Right boss." They saluted.

Chapter 39 Isaac, Lillian and Old Times

Wednesday, April 10

When the others returned to work, Lillian and Isaac lingered at the restaurant a while. She was proud of her restaurant and always enjoyed being there. Lillian's Riviera had been her retirement hobby and had become just as famous as the Gristmill Restaurant. For ten years it had flourished. One of its greatest appeals had been its romantic setting.

The navy blue ceiling with twinkling lights gave the ambiance of eating under the stars. Classical music set the mood. Lillian couldn't count the proposals that had been done there. Reservations were required if you didn't want to wait two hours.

Lunchtime was different. It was the 'go-to' place for daily business lunches. Local civic groups held their monthly luncheon meetings there. Tourists flocked in during the summer and holidays.

Lillian noticed many tourists today. The Spring Festival was already drawing them in. It was good having lunch with Jimmy and Jessica, Bree, and Kit. She wished Bernell had come but understood.

After they all left and she had relaxed a little, Lillian said, "Isaac, you know what I want to do?"

"No telling," he said. He was used to her impulsiveness. She would never grow old, although she complained a lot about it. But when an idea struck her, she was sixteen again.

"We haven't been to the library in a long time."

"No, we haven't," he said. "I haven't needed to."

"Well, I don't need to now, but I have an urge to. I mean really, I feel like going to the library. We might run into Lisa. She's done such a good job. Especially since the town council gave her enough money to operate on. Remember when she didn't even have the resources when the kids were there looking for something to help them find Giorgio?"

"Of course, I remember. It's only been ten years. I can even remember fifty years ago. And you look just like you did then."

"Silly," she smiled, even though she knew better. "Thank God you can't see as good as you can remember."

They drove around to the library and made their way inside. It looked the same as always. "What did you want to do?" Isaac asked. "You gonna check out a book?"

"Well," Lillian said, "I've been thinking how everybody else can get on the computer and look up things. I know they've got good help here now. The computer section used to be right next to the newspaper section. You could sit there and read the paper and I can get somebody to help me figure out how to go online. I want to Google something."

"Google, google," Isaac said. "Is that baby talk? Or is that a google of geese?"

"Both," she said. He would never outgrow his silliness.

"Okay, I'm okay with that. They have newspapers we don't get. I can read the comics while you google. Google one for me. I hope Lisa is here. I'd love to see that kid again."

Rex Richards watched the older couple coming into the library and felt the anger rise to his throat. He remembered them. They were the two who had recognized him fifty years ago. If it hadn't been for them, he might never have gone to prison. He watched them banter and smile, friendly with each other and everyone who spoke to them.

What are they doing here? He wondered. *Well, they won't catch me doing anything wrong now. All that is behind me.*

He wondered what his life would have been like if the diamonds he hid had not been discovered. And that dog. It was the dog that recognized him. Some strange dog. And they had made him a hero with statues now at the Gristmill and even on the waterfront. As he watched them and remembered his life, he grew angrier.

Why are these people so happy? What is it that makes them act like all's right with the world when it's not? What do they have that I've never had? They've had trouble. Isaac lived with a limp for forty years. His father was murdered. His uncle's family was murdered. But they still keep coming up happy. What is it with those people?

As he watched, he thought back over his own life. Not what he had planned nor expected. Then a thought struck him.

I would be dead if they hadn't stopped me.

Why do you say that?

His other voice argued. Being in prison for so many years, he had spent a lot of time alone and learned to be a conversationalist. There were two sides to everything. So he argued both sides until he figured out the best thing. He had always been smart and could remember what he heard and what he read.

If you just hadn't let your uncle control you.

What choice did I have?

You were just stupid sometimes. You couldn't outsmart him. He had control over so many people. You were smart, but you couldn't outsmart your evil uncle. The almighty powerful Roger Riddick. Remember that painting?

Don't remind me. I would have won that time if those two old people right there hadn't figured out a way to get rid of it.

So your efforts to steal it were thwarted.

Thwarted. That's a good word.

My whole life has been thwarted.

What are you going to do about it?

What do you mean?

You heard those preachers at the prison.

I didn't see much of God at the prison.

Look at those two people.

Why? They sent me to prison.

Why? Have you ever thought about it? That was the only place you would be forced to listen to God's Word?

God's word is everywhere.

You know that now.

Remember when I was a Rabbi?

You were never a Rabbi.

They thought I was.

You knew you weren't. It was a mockery. You're lucky God didn't strike you down.

Maybe he did.

Oh, now you think so. So, that was why you went to prison.

Feels good to be out.

Feels good to be out.

Got a nice normal life, haven't you?

Yes.

Why don't you go to church?

Are you kidding? I'm a fake. They would not accept me as myself. I have to do this.

I dare you to try it.

You're crazy.

I'm okay.

Are you going to help Zelda? You could get millions. All those diamonds will finally be yours.

Zelda is worse than my uncle.

And you're falling right into that trap again.

I don't want to go back to prison.

You're not going to prison.

Go talk to the Wellsly's.

Are you crazy?

You owe them an apology.

I served my time. And more.

More! That's because you escaped and had to redo the time.
I'm never going back.
You better stay away from Zelda then. Go talk to the Wellsly's.
Why?
Why not? You work here. It's your job.
I'm afraid of them.
Why?
They have power.
They don't look like they have power.
Something is protecting them.
Maybe it's God.

Sometimes Rex would forget which side he was on. But it always helped to argue it out. For some reason, as though he were being propelled, he walked over to Lillian and asked, "May I help you, Miss Lillian?"

"Oh, yes. Well, maybe. I wanted to learn how to Google."

"Okay, I think I can help you with that. You need an ID. Can you remember your library card number?"

"Heaven's no. But I have it in my purse." She turned to look at Isaac. "*PSST*, Isaac."

Isaac looked her way and frowned. "Bring my library card, it's in my purse," she whispered.

Isaac came over smiling, "How're you, Mr. Richards? Are you sure you can teach this old lady anything?"

"I think we're the same age," Richards responded. "So, yes, I'm sure I can."

"Touché," Isaac grinned and handed Lillian her purse.

He returned to his newspaper and ten minutes later, Lillian said "*PSST.*"

Isaac turned. She was beckoning him to come over. Mr. Richards was smiling behind her.

"Look! I found you on Google."

She handed him a print out with his name, age, occupation, and a blurb about his businesses on Big Creek. A footnote said he had had surgery in 2003 that had restored his leg after forty-two years. The surgeon was named in blue and the name of the hospital was in blue. She told Isaac if she clicked on the blue words, she could read all about the hospital he was in.

"Well, that's neat," Isaac said. "Now do YOU."

"No. I'm done. I just wanted to learn how to do that."

"Thank you so much, Mr. Richards. I know this must be a very rewarding job."

Richards smiled at her and said, "As a matter of fact it is. I think I'll keep it."

"I hope so," she said. "God needs people like you around to help people like me."

He smiled and said, "Thank you."

As they went out, his little voice said, *so you liked that. What are you going to do now?*

"Aww, shut up," he said aloud. Fortunately, there's was no one close enough to hear.

Chapter 40 The Parking Lot

Wednesday, April 10

Lee Fish Market on South Claxton Waterfront bought fish from local fishermen who pulled their boats up to a dock beside the building. A bulkhead of rough rocks separated the water from the parking lot. Steps about midway the parking lot led down to the small pier. Kids would sometimes climb down the rocky bulkhead but it was treacherous.

Seagulls soared and squawked in the air as Kit and Bree scrutinized the parking lot. A few cars of customers and employees of the market waited for their owners.

The curious detectives stood at the steps and observed the lay of the land. The scenic beauty of the river and the distant mountains were a distraction, but they turned their focus to the ground, and the jagged rocks down the slope to the river.

"You know, this would be a good place for somebody to get hurt," Bree said.

"That's what I'm thinking," Kit agreed.

"The sanitation department found that oar in the parking lot. I bet that was not unusual, seeing those boats out there with oars in them. I imagine there are oars out there all the time," Kit observed.

"But not with blood on them," Bree said. "That's why they called the police."

Kit mused, "I wonder if they checked what kind of blood it was. Fish have blood, too."

"You know they weren't that careless," Bree scoffed. "Surely, Riley has checked that out thoroughly."

"Just saying," Kit shrugged.

Being brave and daring, Bree climbed across the one rail between the parking lot and the embankment. A curb at the edge of the pavement would prevent a car from rolling past but people would climb across the rail as a shortcut to the pier, even though a sign said do not cross the rail. Bree quickly learned why. A rock slipped, causing her to lose balance, and her feet shot out from under her. She screamed as her butt hit the rocks, and her elbows bled as she tried to scramble up.

Kit didn't know whether to laugh, or scold, or try to help her. "Are you alright?" was her lame reaction.

"I'm alright, I'm alright!" Bree screeched, "Ow, ow, ow," as she turned to crawl back up to the parking lot. But she suddenly stopped and called, "Kit?"

"Yeah! Can I help you up? I can't reach you. I need something." She looked around. "Something like an oar. You could hang on to it while I pull."

"No," Bree said. "Look!" She was clinging to the rocks with both hands and jerked her head to the right. "Over there. Under the edge of the building. Right near the water. Can you see it?"

Kit leaned over the rail as far as she could without falling. "What am I looking for? OOPS." She backed off when the rail moved a little. "This thing is not secure at all!" she yelled.

"Go to the steps. You might be able to see it from there," Bree ordered.

"Okay, but see what? What am I looking for?" Bree didn't say anything. She was hanging on to keep from slipping into the river.

Kit scurried on down the steps which were secure and walked along the boardwalk behind Bree so she could help her down.

"Look over there," Bree cried again and jerked her head toward the building again.

"Okay. But I think I need to help you down first. It's not a snake, is it? Or alligator?"

"No." Bree was exasperated that Kit could not see what she had seen. It was not within her view from this angle. She hoped it didn't wash away. "Okay, help me. But don't drag us both in the river."

"UGH!" With Kit grabbing her clothes, Bree wrenched herself around and tumbled down to the pier. It shook a little. "Is nothing solid around here?" she cried.

She clung to Kit as she pulled herself up and then pointed. "There!"

"Oh," Kit squinted. "It looks like a little suitcase. Maybe a briefcase?"

"Yes. That's it. Can you reach it? Your arms are longer than mine. I'll hold on to you while you crawl over there and reach it."

"Okay, let's do it." Kit got down on her knees at the edge of the pier and reached as far as she could until she struck the brown object. "Oh, it's wedged. It's not going anywhere."

"We've got to get it," Bree said.

"Okay, how?" Kit asked.

"Look! Get the oar in that boat. Could you poke it with that and dislodge it?"

"I'll try, but I don't want it to float away." Kit climbed into the boat holding onto a pylon. Grasping the oar, she pushed it toward Bree.

"Got it," Bree said.

Kit climbed back out of the boat and stood behind Bree as she punched and tried to position the oar blade under the briefcase.

"It moved," Bree said.

"We can't climb on the rocks," Kit declared. "We could slide into the river and it is deep here."

"What can we do?" Bree asked.

"We could leave it and find a man to reach it. I bet Davie could get it."

"No," Bree said. "We're going to do this. Pry it again with the oar."

Kit said, "You hold the oar and pry it, and I'll reach for it. I'm almost as tall as Davie. We can do this."

For a moment Bree was dizzy. The water was murky and lapping against the bulkhead, *like a hungry lion*, Bree thought. She was still afraid of this river. In a pool, she could swim like a fish, but the river was something else. Maybe it was psychological. She never got over that day on the river in the rain with Davie, Caroline, and Niki when they pulled in that boat that turned out to be Fritz Frizelle's.

"The secrets Big Creek harbors," she said aloud.

"What?" Kit asked.

"Nothing. I was just thinking."

Working together for balance and reach, the two finally worked the briefcase from between the rocks and Kit grabbed it just as the river tried to pull it away.

"YAY!" Bree said and held the oar up in victory. It was kind of heavy. She laid the blade against the bow of the boat and slid it back into place. "Did you notice this?" she asked Kit.

"Notice what?"

"That boat is missing an oar. This was the only one in there."

"I bet the other one is down at the police station," Kit said.

"I bet so too," Bree agreed. "Whew! That was an ordeal. Now let's get this thing up those steps and see what it is."

"You've got blood all over your clothes," Kit said. "And your hands."

"Oh, shoot," Bree complained. "I need to get myself cleaned up. But I want to see what this is."

They didn't dare lean on the rail but sat down on the steps to open the briefcase. It was locked. But they couldn't miss the gold embossed letters, MMM.

"What do you reckon that stands for?" Kit asked.

"Martin Morgan Montegue, of course," Bree said resolutely.

"Yes!" Kit said. "You know what this means?"

"I think it means Montegue died trying to get his briefcase out of these rocks."

"Why was it there?" Kit wondered. "And why was there blood on the oar?"

"I bet I left blood on the other one," Bree said.

"So he got his own blood on the oar and then on his car? And drove the car away?"

"No, he fell in the river," Bree said. "I almost did."

"Let's take this to Bernell and figure out what next."

When they entered the back door of the office, Bernell was about to lock up. Abby had left and the front lobby was locked.

"What have you done? You're a bloody mess!"

"But look what we got!" Bree held up the briefcase grinning from ear to ear.

Bernell took it and laid it on the table. "MMM. That could only be one thing."

"Right!" They both said.

"So how are we going to open it?" Kit asked. "Is there a can opener, a corkscrew, or anything in the refreshment hutch?"

"If Thomas and Adam were here, they'd have a pocket knife or something."

"Maybe there's one in their desk," Bree suggested.

Bernell wiped the briefcase down. It was still wet. She studied the lock.

"Magnum would do this with a hairpin," she said and pulled one from her hair. It didn't work so well for her. "Okay, think, girls," she said.

The three stared at the lock as though it would provide an answer.

"It's a combination lock," Bree noted. "Hold on." She went to her office and came back with a sheet of paper.

"Copy of Montegue's license," she said. "Okay, locks have a pattern. Left, right, left. Kit, turn the dial like I say. Spin it a couple of times to the right, clockwise, then stop on one."

"Done."

"One time to the left, all the way around and stop on one again."

Kit followed her direction. Bree continued, "Okay now turn it clockwise, all the way past the one and stop on zero."

"Done."

"Now counter-clockwise, a complete turn, then slowly to stop on seven."

"Done."

Bernell watched Bree, wondering if this was going to work. Kit was poised, waiting for the next instruction.

"Okay, now clockwise one full turn and on to the seven."

"Done."

"One more time, counterclockwise, a full turn, and stop on seven again."

As soon as Kit stopped on seven, the lock clicked open.

"Oh, my, gosh! How did you know?" Kit gushed.

"In school, we had to practice many patterns. We could get a lot of them. Montegue's birthday is 11/07/77. What better code?"

"I guess that proves it's his," Kit raised the lid on the briefcase.

"Aha!" Bernell exclaimed. "There's your $10,000, Bree. You were right on target when you guessed that he might be bringing cash for that yacht. Smythe did send him. Kit, didn't you do a background check on Montegue?"

"No, Bree did. It's in her folder."

Bree opened her folder titled *The Man in the White Suit*.

"He got a law degree in Richmond, Virginia, in 2001 when he was twenty-four. Twelve years ago. I expect he has been Smythe's lawyer for several years. I bet he's the one that got Davie out of jail."

"Smythe claimed he had just retired from a corporate job when he started talking to Davie about building that yacht. And that was just two or three years ago."

"Wonder where he got all his money?"

"CEO's of large corporations make enormous salaries."

"What corporation did he retire from?"

"Google him." Bernell pointed at the laptop.

She and Bree waited patiently as Kit clicked away. James Jeffery Smythe, she typed in. That's a philosophy professor in Vancouver, Canada.

"Take the second 'e' out of Jeffery," Bree said.

A string of items popped up.

James Jeffry Smythe. CEO of ALANAKIN ASSOCIATES, Inc. New York, New York. $6-8 Mil 1999. Supplier of marketing and advertising promotional products, cigarette lighters, key chains, pens, flashlights etc. Logo shirts available in variety of styles, sizes and colors. Capabilities include screen printing. Personalization services available.

"What does that tell us?" Kit asked.

Bernell's heart sank to the pit of her stomach. "Read it again. Read the name of the company."

"ALANAKIN ASSOCIATES. Oh, no." Bree winced. "You don't think. Please, no. Not her."

"ALANA," Bernell said.

"Okay, let's sort this out," Bree said. "When Alana was arrested, it put an end to her human trafficking. But the home base was in New York--she had lawyers there. I don't know what happened to them. I know some were caught. If this corporation was part of her conglomerate, then Jeffry Smythe worked for her. He could have made millions. But it was not in cigarette lighters. Which by the way could explain the cigarette lighter with JS on it that was purchased in Chesapeake."

"In those pictures," Bree said, "I am almost sure that one of the couples dancing is Jamie Sampson and Martin Montegue."

"I'm getting a headache," Bernell said. "And it makes me sick to think that this man that Davie trusted--and liked--could have been an associate of Alana Frizelle all those years. It just makes me sick to my stomach."

"Knowing what I know about her now," Kit said, "she could have had Smythe and his wife killed. Nobody would ever know what happened to them."

"This is depressing," Bree said. "And overwhelming. How can we do anything? I think we need to be very careful."

"I'm afraid so," Bernell said. "I think we need to get Jeb in here and don't let this go any further—just to him. He's dealt with her before."

"But he found out that she was dead. The prison warden told him that," Kit reminded them.

Bernell said, "I have trouble believing that. I don't know how she did it. But I'd lay odds that she got out of prison somehow. Maybe faked her death. Maybe killed a cellmate, and traded places."

"But then the other prisoner would be missing too, wouldn't she?"

"I don't know. I'm having trouble processing this."

"I thought you had a criminal mind," Bree said.

Bernell laughed wryly, "Alana should have been executed."

Kit nodded, "This country is getting so liberal, people fight the death penalty, and let criminals go free. I know once in a while an innocent person is convicted, but that's not nearly as frequent as criminals going free. But we still have to do what we can to get them off the street."

Bree said, "Let's keep trying. Every little drop in the bucket counts."

"Yeah," Bernell said. "We'll keep trying. As Lillian likes to say, 'God's got this.' If she is out, maybe this time He'll help us get Alana for good. I cringe when I think Jesus died for the likes of her."

Kit said, "It's not the size of the sin, but the depth of God's love. Remember Saul on the road to Damascus? Remember the thief on the cross?"

"I'm reminded of it often," Bernell said. "And God chastises me for resenting it. I have to ask him to forgive me."

"And he does," Bree said.

Chapter 41 Gray Tower Revisited

Thursday, April 11

With indication that **Zelda Midget** had been a nurse at Allegheny State Prison, Chief Jeb Stanton was compelled to speak with Warden Riggs at the prison again. When he called, he learned from the Administrative Assistant that the Riggs was on vacation.

"I wonder if you could help me then," he asked. "I'm trying to reach Zelda Midget and I understand she works there? Would it be possible to leave a message for her to contact me?"

"Ordinarily, yes, but she doesn't work here anymore."

"Did she retire?"

"No, she wasn't old enough to retire."

"Oh, she just resigned then. I guess it's kind of stressful working in a prison."

The Administrative Assistant laughed. "It can be. But she didn't resign. She just quit. She didn't show up for work one day and we haven't heard anything from her since."

"Well, that's odd. Do you know if she had any problems with any of the staff or the prisoners?"

"Not that I know of. She was friendly and everybody liked her."

"That's nice. Do you have any idea where she might have gone? I'd like to get up with her about a relative of hers."

"No, like I said, we haven't heard from her. I guess I could check her file if it's important."

"I shouldn't tell you this, but you sound trustworthy. She may be coming into some money. This is Chief Jeb Stanton at Claxton..."

"I see the caller ID," she interrupted him. "Let me look it up."

After a few minutes, she returned to the phone. "I'm sorry, I haven't been able to locate her file. The warden might remember, but he won't be back for a couple of weeks."

"Hmm. I'm sorry to hear that. Oh, one more thing, do you remember when she quit?"

"Sometime in January. Oh, I remember. She didn't come in after the Martin Luther King holiday."

"Okay, well, thank you for your trouble. I'm sorry to bother you. You have a good day."

"No problem. You, too."

The chief studied his notes. Alana died. Zelda quit. Where did he say Alana was buried? Octavia, NY, he had written in his notes.

After contacting four funeral homes in Octavia, New York, Jeb found one that said they had conducted a ceremony for Alana Frizelle on January 21.

Jeb asked, "Can you possibly tell me the name of the cemetery the family used?"

"Just a minute," The voice said. Jeb heard some pages turning, and then the voice said, "It was a cremation, and we only conducted a short ceremony here in the chapel. We don't have any way of knowing where they took the remains."

"Oh, I didn't know you did cremations there," Jeb said.

"We don't. That has to be arranged somewhere else."

Jeb decided not to pursue this further. He had heard enough. Maybe Bernell's Agency could pursue it. As far as he was concerned it was a dead issue--no pun intended.

It looks like Alana is really gone. He didn't know how to feel. Zelda Midget must have been one smart cookie to take Alana's place and pull this off. Someone as evil as she was.

Chapter 42 Game Plan

Thursday evening, April 11

Arriving home early for a change, Davie sat in his recliner in the den, watching the mesmerizing aquarium. "I could get lost in there," he said. "It's so peaceful. Something I haven't experienced in a while. You were smart to get this. I notice Aunt Bernell has one at the Agency, too."

"Yeah, and Mom's getting one. It's hypnotic."

"Speaking of being hypnotic, it was a surprise to learn that Jo Swan was hypnotized. I never knew hypnotism could work like that. I mean, I thought when people were hypnotized, they were like zombies instead of acting normal."

"Well, running around on a barge in the middle of the night and digging holes in the ground on other people's property is not exactly normal, is it?" Jenny asked.

"No. They were all crazy. Thank God your mom is such a good psychiatrist."

"I know. Jo Swan is lucky, too. At least she's out of the gang. Wonder what will happen now?" Jenny asked.

"I don't know what they'll do, but I can tell you what we're doing. Jeb called me today. He's been working on this. He has come up with a plan that I think will work. It's a shame to have to go to such lengths to protect your property, but I'm glad he offered."

"What's he doing?"

"Jeb's got help from the Merryville Police and the Phillips County Sheriff's Department. They are all on the alert for the three other women. Those pictures Thomas and Adam took are being circulated. The only problem is they don't have any pictures of Zelda Midget, just Sampson and Summerlin. But Chief Jeb says they're together somewhere. He's afraid they've left the yellow house. The van is still there, but he thinks that's just staged to make it look normal."

"There's that normal again," Jenny noted. "What's the plan you have now?"

"The chief's got three officers in police cars guarding the plant all night. Two security cameras are recording every movement. And we've installed an additional nightlight. It will be almost like daylight around there."

"Sounds like Fort Knox." Jenny laughed.

"Yeah. Jake and Ed have been digging up the lot. They've already planted azaleas and laid sod over most of it. It's beginning to look nice. They're not doing anything more until Sunday morning at ten o'clock though. The police will be guarding until then--then I'm letting them go."

"Why not tomorrow? Why wait until Sunday morning?" Jenny asked.

"That was Chief Jeb's idea. For one thing, the Spring Festival starts tomorrow. Another thing is. Chief says most people around here will be gone to church between ten and twelve on Sunday and the Festival doesn't have any activities until one. Based on our calculations, I figure Jake will hit that chest at ten-thirty. I know exactly where it is now. Right where the clue said. Except it's only ten feet from the river. We didn't realize the river had shifted like that."

"I'm going to church Sunday; I wish you would."

"I know I should probably go to church, but this one last time, I can't go. I'll be at the plant so when they dig up the chest, I can take it inside. Then the guys will set the last of the azaleas and finish the sod. They'll be done by noon and it will all be over."

"You sure sound positive about this," Jenny noticed. "Why no police Sunday morning? Are you really not going to have any out there then?"

"Nope. Won't need them. Besides, there's a limit to what you can expect."

"And you're sure about all this?" Jenny asked. "I don't know how you can be so positive."

"Scientific calculations," Davie said. "We have been over every inch of that property. Besides I found the rock."

"With the cross on it?"

"Yes, it was hidden by bushes. Like Kit said, "sixty years is a long time."

"I'm just worried about you," Jenny said.

"Don't be. Chief Jeb thinks the women will be picked up before then anyway. I mean everybody's looking for them now. It's almost like it was when everybody was looking for Giorgio. Kind of ironic, isn't it?"

"Well, I wasn't here then, but from what I've heard, yes, it is," she agreed.

"We've got that parade at three o'clock tomorrow. Everybody's been finishing their floats today. Tomorrow they'll be setting up tents for the Festival. The guys are pulling our trailer out about noon. I'm not too thrilled about the Spring Festival this year," Davie picked up the Festival brochure and thumbed through it.

"It's sure been spoiled for us. I turned it all over to Ruby and Violet. And Breck's going to drive the float. They're also setting up a booth on Claxton Boulevard with items from the store. There'll be some fun things going on. Caroline's concert tomorrow night will be the highlight for me. It was so good having her home today. I've missed your sister."

Davie laughed. "Yeah, I have, too. And Mom's on cloud nine."

"We're going to hang out some Saturday a little. Oh, and she's going to church with us Sunday. Well, with the rest of us. You know, when this is over, you have to get back in church."

Davie hung his head. "I know."

Chapter 43 At the Yellow House

Thursday evening, April 11

As they sat around the table, Zelda spoke to Jamie Sampson and Jackie Summerlin about the change in plans. "We've lost Jo Swan as you know. She called and said she is sick and is staying at her father's house."

"I don't think she's sick," Jackie said.

"I know. I told her if she gets out of the game now, she cannot come back. She begged me to let her back in when she gets well. I told her no. It's now or never. She said she was not able, so we're writing her off. I'm not worried about anything she might say. She's so ditzy, nobody will believe her anyway."

Jamie and Jackie laughed and looked at each other wondering. "Well then, does that mean we get more since she's out?" Jamie asked.

"No. You still get what we agreed on. Fifty thousand dollars, whether we find it or not. But we'll find it. Then you get a million dollars apiece. How's that for a week's work?"

"It's been longer than a week with all that training. And we've taken a lot of risks," Jamie said.

Zelda didn't like being disputed. "It's a game!" She said briskly. "There are rules you've known all along. You play by the rules or you don't play."

"I don't want to question you," Jackie said nervously. "But we've dug all those places, one of them twice. Are you sure those diamonds are buried there?"

"It's alright to question. I wouldn't have taken you on if I didn't respect your thoughts. But, yes, I am sure. I have the clues burned in my brain. Now Davie Wellsly has become my best player without even knowing it. He has figured out why they weren't where we thought. And he's doing the work for us."

Zelda opened a box and handed each of them a gun. "You will need these."

"I was hoping it wouldn't come to this," Jackie said.

"But you went through the training, and you can shoot," Zelda reminded her.

"Yes, I was just hoping it wouldn't come to it."

"Well, to be honest, so was I," Zelda told her. "But it didn't turn out that way. And this is why you were trained--just in case."

"Well, how do you expect it to play out?" Jamie asked.

"It's all going down Sunday," Zelda told them with a tinge of excitement. "Davie's going to get the chest then. He knows exactly where it is. He's planning to have it dug up at ten-thirty Sunday."

"Really how can you know that?"

"Trust me, I know. I've been listening. It's closer to the river than I thought. We didn't account for the river shift over time."

"The bugs you planted must still be working," Jackie said.

Zelda laughed. "Like a charm. That aquarium was the best spot, and it's the only one they didn't find. It's all I needed though."

"Well, if he knows exactly where the treasure is, why doesn't he get it now? He'll probably do that, and then we won't get any of it."

"No. He knows it's safe where it is, and he has too many armed guards there. It's like Fort Knox." She laughed.

"But he's letting all the guards go Sunday morning because he does not want them there when he gets it. He's got it figured down to the minute. Sunday morning at ten-thirty. I've been watching—and listening."

Jackie kicked Jamie under the table and said, "Zelda, want let's go for a swim? I've been cooped up here for two days. I'd love to stretch my legs."

"No. You two go ahead," Zelda said. "I've got some things to do. Stay near the garage."

"Sure. We won't be seen," Jackie said.

"Be right there, Jackie. Let me get a suit," Jamie headed upstairs.

"It's a little chilly for a swim, isn't it?" Zelda asked Jackie.

"It's invigorating," Jackie smiled. Then she surprised Zelda, "I'm glad Jo Swan is gone. She got on my nerves."

"Hahaha," Zelda laughed. "I thought I was the only one."

Jamie came in wearing a black swimsuit and carrying a white terry cover-up. "Don't be long," Zelda admonished like a mother.

"No, ma'am," they both said.

They went out through the kitchen door that led into the garage and climbed into the small boat. They rowed out to the end of the canal before speaking. Finally, Jackie asked, "Are you thinking what I'm thinking?"

"I'm afraid so," Jamie said. "We are expendable now. At first, it was fun. She was fun and it was a game. But her colors have changed."

"Jo's not sick. She's broken out. Guess I'm not as good at hypnotizing as I thought I was. She came out too soon."

"Maybe she was faking. Why did Zelda want her hypnotized anyway?" Jackie asked.

"To control her. She didn't want her. She wanted her father."

"Oh. So she was just a pawn?"

"Yeah. I think so. I think she actually used us to get her."

"Did she think he'd participate in the game? You think she promised him a cut too?"

"I doubt it. I overheard some things though. I think she knew him already and wanted to renew something."

"I wonder what went on between them."

"At the yacht christening party, I saw them huddled in conversation for a long time."

"I saw that."

"After a while, she flounced away, and she was different after that. I guess she couldn't get him back."

"So that's why she changed. And that's why she doesn't want Jo back. Jo didn't have the influence Zelda thought, did she?

"He let us use his yacht. But that was only for Jo, not her."

"Evidently."

"I've been thinking."

"I know. Me too."

"She won't need us after she gets the chest, will she?"

"No."

"She's going to kill us, isn't she?"

"That's what I'm afraid of."

"We have to think of something. We could leave right now."

"She'd find us. She has spies everywhere. We better go back in."

When they entered the kitchen, Zelda said, "You're not wet."

"You were right. It was too cold. When we got out there, we changed our mind and came back. Feels nice in here, though. I love the spicy potpourri." Jamie added to divert the subject and avoid further questions.

"Me too," Zelda smiled. "You girls should turn in early tonight. You only have tomorrow and Saturday. That will be your last day here and you have a lot of packing to do. I want you fresh on Sunday morning."

"Oh?" Jamie asked. "Can you tell us the plan?" She looked at Jackie who sat down to hear also.

Zelda sighed. She was losing patience. "You won't go anywhere tomorrow nor Saturday. The whole city is on the lookout for you since you've managed to have your pictures taken. As soon as I get in the helicopter Sunday, you'll come back here and drive the van to meet me in New York. You have the address."

"That's only if we get the stuff, right?" Jackie said.

Zelda was undaunted. "I'll get it. I'll be watching Sunday morning." She proceeded with the details which she had explained before. "Ten-thirty Sunday, it will all be over. Trust me!"

"Why couldn't we get on the helicopter with you?" Jamie asked.

"You know why. Just do as we planned."

"Yes ma'am." They responded together.

Jackie said, "I'm excited."

Jamie didn't say anything. It was not excitement they felt. It was fear.

Chapter 44 Reflections and Plan B

Thursday evening, April 11

Enrico "Ricky" Riddick had been released from prison in 2003. For the next ten years, he kept a low profile. Before his arrest in 1963, he had been a student at the University of Michigan. But his life took a bad turn, and he wound up in prison.

When he learned that a big part of prison reform is education, he took advantage of it. During the next few years, he studied diligently and earned two degrees, a Bachelor's and then a Masters' in English and a Master's in Library Science which earned him a job in the library at the prison.

Ironically, when he was released, he was sixty-two years old, an age when most people would be retiring. But he had unfinished business and it kept him motivated. He knew the diamonds he had stolen in 1955 for his mobster uncle Roger Riddick, were never found.

He had kept a small part of that heist for himself. He deserved them and knew Uncle Roger would never give him anything for what he had done. So he kept a handful and thought he had hidden them well in the Garden of Eden, an arboretum which was built in memory of popular physician, Dr. Alexander Eden. Unfortunately, he was outsmarted when Lillian Wellsly's father found them.

Disowned by his uncle, he served time in prison while his uncle went free. And his uncle had hidden the bulk of those diamonds along with other contraband his men had stolen. That bounty had never been recovered. He was certain of it because something that big would have been in the news.

When Enrico Riddick was released, he changed his name to Rex Richards, and under the guise of having retired from a job in Chicago, applied for a part-time job at the Claxton City Library. He altered his name on his degree documents, and it was never questioned. The university was legitimate, but Enrico Riddick became E. Rex Richards with a little artistry.

Alana Rodriguez had just been convicted and sent to prison. The town of Claxton was rejoicing that such a heinous criminal had been removed and children were safer on the streets.

In spite of being understaffed and underfunded, the Claxton City Library had been instrumental in exposing Alana. The library had been ground zero for the Wellsly teenagers' efforts to find the missing Giorgio Rodriquez, one of Alana's captives.

Afterward, increased funding enabled the library to update equipment and add much-needed staff.

Rex Richards was hired under the library's Computer Technical Services Supervisor, Jim Everett. With that job, Richards was in the catbird seat, watching, waiting, and planning.

He had always known Alana. She also worked for his uncle. After she was arrested, he hid in the yellow house for a while until he found an apartment near the library and lived a quiet and unnoticed life for the next ten years.

But he was haunted by the fact that those diamonds were still waiting to be discovered. When Alana contacted him with news that she was about the get them, and he could have half, he couldn't resist. It was more than he could have gotten otherwise.

But he feared. "When they see you, you'll be caught and it will all be over." All she said was, "They won't. Trust me."

Now that same library was ground zero for a game she had devised.

Rex assisted Zelda Midget often at the library. Sometimes he thought, *neither of us needs those diamonds. A sizeable sum from Alana's Swiss account is in the Claxton Bank in Zelda's name. She is set for life. And this library job is sufficient for me.* Something about aging.

He loved his work. But then the memory of those diamonds was sweet. And Zelda had caught the fever.

The lure of those elusive diamonds drew them in like the sirens of Greek mythology luring sailors to their destruction. Neither Rex nor Zelda could resist.

Zelda drafted her crew and gave them clues under the guise of a game that would net them all a fortune. The girls stayed with Zelda and he only met them on the barge at night. He operated the machinery, and they called him Mr. X. *Silly, greedy girls. Could they be trusted?*

It was Zelda's decision to use girls instead of men. They would be more easily manipulated and would settle for less in the long run. They would also be easier to get rid of when the time came. Jo Swan was the weakest link--but for some reason, she was the most critical to Zelda.

On Thursday evening, after the girls went to bed, Zelda slipped out to the library. She sat at a computer in the Communications Section. "Time for a change in plans," she said in a low voice.

"You're giving up the game?" Rex asked.

"No. Changing. It didn't work the way I planned." She pointed at her screen as though commenting on it, but she squinted at him through dead-brown eyes.

"It didn't work. Swan's gone to her father. Sampson's gone soft and Summerlin is getting restless. We moving to plan B."

"That's too dangerous."

There were very few people in the library, but he spoke under his breath. She was slim with dark hair and medium brown eyes. Could have been a beauty. She wore black slacks and a nondescript gray top. She never wore jewelry or dressed attractively. She didn't want to bring attention to herself.

They had agreed that she would never go to his apartment and he would never go to the yellow house. She was leery of telephone communication and relied on their personal contact at the library. The river and darkness had been their ally. He used a rowboat from a small pier behind the fish market to maneuver around the bend to the barge.

They did not talk much on the barge. Everyone had a task to do and only he and Zelda knew the whole plan. It had been harder than he thought. Zelda had gotten discouraged and angry, but now she was excited again.

"Here's what's happened," she told him. "Davie Wellsly has started digging. He's found it. I've studied the area. I know the clues. I've watched what they're doing. I've been jogging by there every day. And tonight, I learned from the horse's mouth."

"You mean the bug you planted?"

"Shh, yes. They won't work tomorrow nor Saturday. It's that stupid Festival and the parade. They're shutting down operations at the landing. The plant is closed so there won't be any people there."

"So that will make it easier for us tomorrow night."

"No. They've got police cars and cameras up the yin yang. There's no way we can get it ourselves. So we'll let Davie do the work for us."

She printed out a page and pretended to ask him something. "Tonight, in that cozy setting of his, he told his wife that they will find the box on Sunday. He knows exactly where it is. They're starting at ten o'clock Sunday morning. To keep it secret, he's letting the police go then, so there will be nobody at the landing except him and those two men digging."

"That will be better," he pointed at the computer screen.

She looked at him smiling. "When he finds it, we'll take it."

"But how?"

"I have scheduled a FedEx helicopter to pick up a package from the boat plant at ten-thirty Sunday."

"They don't usually pick up like that."

"I paid him well enough. His name is Dirk. He'll work with me. You and the girls will be armed on the river to cover me. They'll be on the sailboat close to shore, and you'll be in the fishing boat. You love to hunt and fish, don't you?" She laughed a hollow laugh.

"Never have." He was honest.

"You will use the rifle. Wellsly won't be armed. We'll take them unexpectedly and we'll get the chest in the helicopter. Monday night, we'll meet in New York where I said, and you can leave Claxton and this stinking library forever."

"What do you mean take them?"

"You know what I mean."

"No. Zelda, I'll have no part in murder. I spent a long time in prison. I'm not going back. I heard too much religious talk while I was there. I never committed to murder in this game of yours."

"You'll rethink that Mr. X. It's the only way. The diamonds are priceless. Remember how you felt with them shimmering in your hand? You could see infinity. You told me so. Now they'll soon be yours. You've paid for them behind four walls. We're two of a kind, Ricky. And we're about to get that happiness we always deserved."

He didn't say anything. A soft voice over the intercom announced that the library would be closing in five minutes.

She got up from the computer. "Sunday morning," she whispered.

Her fingers brushed his cheek. "Trust me."

He watched her leave and wondered if he could trust himself.

He could not understand the heaviness in his heart as he said goodnight to Everett and started home. It wasn't far, just a few short blocks. As he walked, he shivered in the April night air.

He could smell the flowers in the huge pots along the curb. The town had dressed up for the Spring Festival. Were they white roses?

Easter lilies. He breathed their fragrance as he brushed past them.

A cross in the spotlight on a distant church seemed to glow like he'd never noticed before.

Why were his eyes blurring? *Allergies?*

As he approached the police station, he noticed the chief coming out, his shoulders slumped like the weight of the world was on him.

The *chief must have had a long day,* he thought, and couldn't understand why he suddenly felt such compassion for a man whose job was to put people behind bars.

People like me, he thought. *People like Zelda.*

He remembered Lillian and Isaac Wellsly just a day or so ago. "God needs people like you around to help people like me," she had said.

His heart ached for the happiness they had.

You'll have that with the diamonds.

Why do I have such dread?

You should be happy. This is what you want. You're about to grasp your lifelong dream with those diamonds. Your diamonds.

But...

But what?

He increased his pace as he neared the Chief. He couldn't understand what he felt nor why.

He could see Zelda's face.

He could hear Lillian's voice.

His heart raced as he caught up to the chief.

"Evening, Sir."

Chapter 45 Spring Festival Begins

Friday morning, April 12

Traffic was atrocious. **Claxton Boulevard** was closed for through traffic and people had to detour around town. Colorful tents marked booths. Stores had merchandise on tables out front. Spaces were marked for several competitions: flower arranging, homemade pickles, vegetable canning, and a cookie bake-off.

Chief Jeb had to deputize several people to serve as patrol officers for the festival. Too many of his men were on duty guarding Davie's Landing. The newly deputized crew were hardly more than crossing guards, but uniforms made them look good. And they provided ample information to serve as festival guides.

On the porch of New Covenant Church for All People was a podium, amplifiers, and a microphone for the directors of the Festival to speak. The lawn beside the church was filled with folding chairs.

Floats lined up half a mile down Big Creek Road preparing to travel the length of Claxton Boulevard and end at the First Baptist Church parking lot on Chattanooga Road. A field between the church parking lot and Claxton Boulevard was set up with a Ferris wheel and kiddie rides.

As Jimmy had described to his dad and Davie, the Gristmill Restaurant's long float featured the restaurant's three themes. The Jewish Cuisine was depicted by a table with a white tablecloth and a menorah. The smell of freshly baked bread was mouthwatering.

Baskets of wrapped bagels were ready to be handed out by the couples at the table.

In the middle of the float was a bistro table with a red-checkered cloth where Rebecca Wilson and Bud Littman enjoyed their hamburgers. Bud's foot was in a cast, but he and Rebecca were a big hit throwing out sealed packets of French fries from the grill.

At the front end, a table was laden with southern cooking, with a family sitting around the table. Terra cotta pots held fake green corn stalks. Three pigs inside a pen squealed and entertained kids.

The Grand Marshall in full regalia rode a white steed bareback. He was taunted by some but applauded by most of the crowd. He sat proudly and spoke to people as he passed. The brochures of the festival had pictures of him which he autographed for people who asked. A schedule of activities encouraged attendees to enjoy authentic Native American food and arts and crafts. "Tribal elders" would be there to share words of wisdom about their proud culture.

A blurb on the program said, "The Spring Festival offers an opportunity to enrich your knowledge and appreciation for native tribal customs and culture." Shows included singing and dance demonstrations featuring some Native American dancers and a drum brigade. An area was designated "Cherokee Reservation" for activities that the DJ had promoted on the radio. That's where he would dismount as Grand Marshall and pose for pictures. His teepee had been set up all week to promote the Festival.

Ironically, the yellow house residents had a front-row view from a window on the second floor, but Summerlin and Sampson were warned not to be seen at the window. The house was locked, and even though the gray van sat in the driveway, there was no sign of life. A fact that did not deter the residents of Claxton and visitors from miles around from enjoying the festivities.

Caroline's concert Friday night at the high school auditorium was sold out well in advance. She performed "A Tribute to Spring," featuring Mendelson, Grieg, Chopin, and Vivaldi.

The standing ovations inspired her and thrilled the hearts of her family. Lillian Wellsly's cheers might have been heard above all others, though she would not admit it.

Chapter 46 Chesapeake Horses

Friday morning, April 12

Adam and Thomas would miss the Spring Festival in Claxton. But they would have a festival of their own. They had work to do, but there would also be time to play. And the beach was close by. Their snooping and investigating around Chesapeake had turned up things they had not anticipated. The roadside scenery was beautiful. Horse farms surrounded by white rail fences enhanced the countryside.

"I always wanted a horse," Thomas told his partner.

Adam shook his head. "I was never into that. I was a nerd."

"Well, in a way, I was, too. I couldn't have a horse, but I could read about them. Mama got me started on that. She made me read *The Black Stallion* because she liked it growing up. I sort of got hooked on it, which made her happy because there were a lot more books about it. Then I read about Secretariat. You know about Secretariat?"

"Sure. I saw the movie."

"The movie was good, too."

"Hey, let's stop here," Adam pointed at the roadside stand.

Thomas slowed, pulled over, and stopped the car at a roadside stand near a sign that said Seashore Farms. For a minute they watched horses in a green pasture that seemed to stretch for miles.

Adam got out and spoke to the ladies running the stand. Besides an assortment of fruits, spring vegetables, and eggs they had fresh-baked breads and sweets.

Thomas bought a coke from an ice-filled cooler. When he paid, a stack of colorful brochures by the register caught his eye.

"Hey, Adam. Let's go there for lunch." He pointed to the colorful pictures of Triple M Bar and Grill. A wall lined with television screens showed Horse Races from all over the country. He read aloud: *"Pick up your free card. Odds and Horse Betting Analysis for all Saturday horse races this season from some of the best US racetracks."*

"You know we can't do that."

"Yes, we can. It's a grill. We can eat lunch and watch."

The lady running the stand said, "It's a nice place. It's legal. We go there a lot just to eat. My husband picked up $600 last week, though. He put a little money on a horse he liked, and it won."

"We don't gamble," Adam said.

She shrugged. "It's just entertainment."

"You work for the horse farm here?" Adam asked her.

"Yes, well, my husband does. He is the stables keeper. They have riding lessons, and people pay to go horseback riding here."

"Hey, you could do that," Adam punched Thomas.

Thomas grinned. "No. I'd break my neck."

"Nobody's ever done that here," the lady smiled.

"Are these racehorses?" Adam asked.

"Not yet. We breed horses. We also offer breaking and training services and riding lessons. We have skilled trainers and instructors. People who've trained here have received awards even on a professional level. You should go up to the main office and check it out."

"Sounds fascinating," Thomas said. "But I don't live around here. I sure do love your place though."

She thanked him. "We love it, too. Hey, you could still check out the grill. Best food in the area."

"We might do that," Thomas said as he and Adam returned to their car.

"You're crazy. Bernell would kill us."

"No, she wouldn't. Look at the name of that grill."

"Triple M. What does that mean?"

"I don't know, but aren't we supposed to be looking for Martin Morgan Montegue?"

Chapter 47 Spring Festival in Full Swing

Saturday, April 13

S everal flatbed trucks served as stages for bands on Saturday. They were strategically placed around corners off Claxton Boulevard, far enough apart to keep their music from clashing. Bluegrass, Rock & Roll, Country, Jazz, and Gospel groups all drew crowds of their own. Those who had them sold their CDs.

The smells of hotdogs and funnel cakes permeated the air. The boat rides launched from the Waterfront by Oarlocks and Bagels were popular. The restaurants and diners were open but the beauty shops and other offices were closed. Burgundy Blue Boutique had a sign indicating directions to their booth on Claxton Boulevard.

For once, B.B. Jackson Agency was dark. Bernell entered from the back but never turned lights on except in her office. She had too much going on to take a day off. Thomas and Adam were on the job and needed to report. Bree and Kit joined Bernell for a few hours without anybody knowing they were there.

Yachts drifted along the channel down Big Creek. Red, yellow, blue, and green sails decorated the river. The air was warming and people celebrated it.

At four o'clock, on the porch of the New Covenant Church for All People, the Festival Director, Mrs. Tiffany Fields, former beauty queen herself, rapped on the microphone to make an announcement. Most people milling around got quiet to hear what she had to say. Three people sat in chairs behind her.

"I am happy to introduce a speaker today that some of you will know. Especially if you're as old as I am." People laughed; she wasn't nearly as old as her husband, Mr. Roy Fields.

William Michaels got up from one of the chairs and was welcomed to the podium. In his hand was a legal length document.

Then Director Fields turned to another gentleman in a chair behind her. "Mr. Mayor, will you please come to the mic?"

Mayor Mills took the mic and said, "Hi. Whatever it was, I didn't do it. If you don't believe me, ask my mama."

Everybody laughed.

The director said, "Thank you, Mr. Mills. We know you didn't do it. But we want you to do it now. I think everybody is going to like what you're about to do."

The Mayor looked puzzled. He had not been apprised of this part of the Festival but played along.

"Okay, what am I about to do?"

Tiffany Fields said, "We want you to take what Mr. Michaels is holding in his hand."

"Is he gonna hit me?"

Everybody laughed.

"No," she said.

"No," William shook his head. "I'm not gonna hit you. I'm afraid you could whoop me good fashioned. Seeing as how you're about half my age and twice my strength."

Everyone laughed again. Only a handful had any idea what was going on. Bernell did. She sat with Kit and Bree in the front row of the chairs on the lawn.

The director said, "Well I think we've had enough fun at the Mayor's expense. Actually, the City Council knows about this, but we decided to keep it a secret until today."

Mayor Mills took the document and studied it as everybody waited to hear what he would say. In the far distance, the native drums were going BOOM, boom, boom, boom, BOOM, boom, boom, boom, for a dance at the Indian culture show. Kids were screaming on the Ferris wheel. A dog was barking.

After a minute or two, Mayor Mills held the document up, "This is the deed to that land from Willow Street to the river. That's a seven-mile stretch."

"And seven miles wide," William said into the mic. "From Hickory Street to Big Creek Road. Right at 5000 acres. If you'll notice the bottom line," he pointed to the document, "everything has been done except getting the mayor's signature."

"Sign it!" Somebody yelled, and the crowd picked it up the chant. "Sign it! Sign it! Sign it!"

The mayor started feeling around for a pen. William handed him one and turned around so he could use his back. The other lady, everyone recognized as a teller at the bank, stood up with a notary seal, and signed and stamped it.

The Mayor was speechless. He took the mic and said, "Well, I'm speechless. I mean literally. I wish I had a speech to say what a wonderful gift this is to the city of Claxton."

The crowd applauded, whistled, and cheered. Director Fields held up her hand. "We're not quite done," she said and handed the mic to William.

He took the microphone with his left hand, and with his right hand, pulled something from his breast pocket. "When my cousin Bernell here," he gestured toward where she was sitting, "approached me with her idea, it struck me right here." He put his fist to his heart. "I didn't even have to think twice."

He turned to the Mayor and said, "I think nothing would have pleased my Daddy more than to turn that piece of land into a park for the children and all the citizens of Claxton. Bernell has already sketched out playgrounds, baseball diamonds and softball fields, gardens, hiking trails, bicycle trails, and boating canals that connect with the river."

People cheered, but he held his hand up indicating he was not finished. "Now it's going to cost you something to get all that developed. You'll need a planning committee, Bernell has already volunteered to head that up, but she'll want some help."

The mayor nodded, already envisioning the new project about to begin. William continued. "So take this check for development of

Jayson Wellsly Michaels Park, a place that all the citizens of Claxton and Phillips County can enjoy and be proud of."

He handed the Mayor a check. "If you run into a problem, give me a call, or tell Bernell and she'll handle it."

The Mayor read the check and put the back of his hand to his forehead. "If I was the kind to faint, now would be the time to do it."

People laughed.

He shook William's hand. "Thank you, William Michaels. This is a wonderful tribute to your dad. I am honored to accept this deed on behalf of the City of Claxton. And this check for FIVE- HUNDRED THOUSAND DOLLARS."

He emphasized the amount so people could hear. "What a thoughtful and wonderful gesture. This will go a long way toward giving the wonderful citizens of Claxton the most beautiful park in the state."

The high school band, who had been seated behind Bernell, broke out with "Take Me Out to the Ball Game," written by Jack Norworth, lyricist, and Albert Von Tilzer, composer. The crowd cheered.

The director took the microphone at the end of the band's piece and said, "Thank you Claxton High School Band. Thank you Mayor Mills, and thank you, Mr. Michaels. I am sure the citizens of Claxton and Phillips County and people all around are going to love Jay Michaels Park. Roy and I remember Jay Michaels, a fine man, and I agree with William. He would be proud."

The audience applauded. To the audience, she said, "Enjoy the rest of your day and don't forget to pick up your raffle tickets for this beautiful sailboat," she pointed to the blue and yellow sailboat mounted on a stage beside the church. "This sailboat and nine other prizes have been donated by WDGW Oars and Boats and Oarlocks and Bagels. Ten prizes to commemorate our tenth year," she said and everybody applauded.

"Proceeds will go to the children's ward at the Heart Center. Drawings will be right here at three o'clock tomorrow."

People cheered, then the crowd, which had grown larger during the presentation, started breaking up and milling around. Some booth attendants called out, "Get your tickets for the sailboat here."

It had been an exhausting two days. One more to go. Davie stayed busy and tried not to think about the knot in his chest. Tomorrow would be the last day.

Chapter 48 Game!

Sunday morning, April 14

It was one of those beautiful **Sunday morning sunrises**. The sky was a painting with pink and orange between the blue sky and the blue river. All appeared normal as Jake and Ed prepared to complete Davie's landscaping project.

They would have the parking lot to themselves. Davie had made it clear, there was one more place to dig. They expected to hit the chest at ten-thirty.

An unmarked police car was in the employee parking lot. Empty. All law enforcement had been sent home. Davie was in his office. His truck and Jake's were sitting at the side entrance of the plant.

At ten o'clock Jake climbed on the excavator and Ed marked a spot with his shovel. A helicopter occasionally crossed overhead as though looking for a place to land.

A fisherman sat on the river discreetly watching the shore. A sailboat floated in the middle of the river with two shapely models, one red-haired and the other one blonde, obviously enjoying a morning sail. They guided the sailboat closer to shore. They waved and flirted with the fisherman in his motorboat a few yards away. He revved his motor and circled the sailboat, flirting back.

Jake thought *apparently Spring Festival tourists are enjoying the river*. He noticed a jogger in black capris and a grey shirt would slow down to a walk and then run again. The dark-haired jogger waved at the models on the sailboat and they waved back.

When his bucket struck a box, he yelled, "Got it!" And he lifted it up. It was exactly ten-thirty. Suddenly, the peaceful Sunday morning was shattered. Shots rang out and Jake slumped over the gears of the excavator. Ed fell to the ground beside him. Davie ran from the building and fell to the ground.

The jogger pounced on the chest like a cat on a mouse. The helicopter lowered to the ground and kept the motor running as the fisherman swerved the motorboat to shore and leaped out. He shoved the chest through the helicopter's open door, then jumped back in his boat and sped away.

The jogger in black laughed almost hysterically. It had been so easy, just as she planned. The girls would return to the house now where Rex would clean up. She would leave on the helicopter with her long-awaited prize. Rex would meet her in New York wanting his share. It could not have worked better.

She reached for the extended hand helping her into the front seat. "Hello, Alana," said Chief Jeb Stanton.

Before she could wrench away, he pulled her aboard and snatched her gun. Zach Beckford slammed the door shut, and the helicopter lifted into the air on its way to the FBI plane at the airport.

An engine on the sailboat sputtered and then purred as it turned from the shore and headed up the river toward the yellow house. The fisherman disappeared around the bend. Two police cars and an ambulance waited in the driveway at 1001 Chattanooga Road. The Coast Guard was on the river near the canal.

As soon as the sound of the helicopter faded, Davie got up off the ground. Ed stood up and brushed himself off. Jake sat back up in the excavator seat. Bernell, Bree, and Kit rushed out of the building and joined the three in celebration. The game was over and they had won! They had videos of the whole event.

Chapter 49 The Fish Box

Sunday about 1 pm, April 14

As prearranged, the **Wellsly family gathered** at the B.B. Jackson Agency at noon on Sunday. Those who had been to church came straight to the Agency. The others met them. Isaac drove his Silverado truck with the locked tonneau to the back door. Safely inside the truck was an old fish box that had not been opened in fifty-eight years.

Bree held the door open while Jimmy and Davie carried the old fish box that had been in the truck since Thursday evening when Davie had found it.

It was a much-anticipated occasion. Bernell laid her hands on the box, remembering her daddy. She had seen him bring it full of fish to the old back porch many times. They'd clean the fish at the pump shelf, pumping that handle as the water gushed. Then they'd wash the fish box and their dad would take it back to the boat. Now it was about to reveal the contents their dad had stashed on that fateful night in 1955.

A crowbar was needed to pry it open. Isaac had come prepared. Everyone held their breath as Davie worked the crowbar and the lid creaked and squawked until it lifted.

Bernell's jaw dropped and she burst into tears.

"My word," said Isaac.

He pulled out gold and silver chains, several pieces of gold-rimmed china, jewelry boxes with broaches and bracelets, and one more thing. All Bernell could see was that strand of pearls.

"Aunt Bernell, you said you had dibs on a strand of pearls, so I guess they're yours."

"You don't understand, Davie." She said as she wiped her eyes. "These *are* my pearls. Jack gave them to me after we got married. He bought them in the Philippines. I've worn these many times."

She fingered the pearls lovingly. "They went missing. I never knew it was Roger Riddick who stole them. How could I not have guessed?"

She laid them against her neck and Lillian fastened the diamond clasp. "Well, you have them back now. And they are perfect. You look beautiful."

Bernell wiped the corners of her eyes and smiled. "I feel beautiful. I did not expect this. I'm thrilled to get them back. Jack would be so glad."

Isaac was looking around for something else. "Where's that jar of diamonds?"

"There's no jar of diamonds in here," Davie said. "This is all of it."

Lillian said, "Isaac, are you absolutely sure no one has opened the box until now? They could have left this and just took the diamonds. That's all they wanted anyway."

Isaac said, "Of course, I'm sure. You saw how hard it was to open."

"But there is no moonshine jar of diamonds," Davie said.

Isaac looked at Bernell. "Where's that letter Daddy wrote? He mentioned diamonds."

She went to her files, pulled a copy of the letter, and read aloud:

Dear Ramey. I am writin this in case sumthin happens to me. Roger Riddick sent Frizele and Winton... smudges, then, *mill again. When I said no, they tried to get me to join Riddick's operation.* The next few words are illegible, then *after they tried three times they,* another smudge, *mill and showed me,* the next word is illegible."

She looked up. "Is this making sense to y'all? There are a lot of smudges."

"Yes, keep going," Isaac said. "But just say 'blank' where the smudges are."

"Okay," Bernell continued:

"They took me on Riddick's boat and BLANK-BLANK jewelry and a moonshine jar of diamonds."

"There it is," Isaac said. "He did say it, a moonshine jar of diamonds."

"Maybe he was being metaphorical," Bree said.

"Daddy was never metaphorical," Bernell answered her. "When he said something, he meant exactly what he said. So, somewhere there is supposed to be a moonshine jar of diamonds."

"Wonder why he called it a moonshine jar?" Davie asked.

Lillian answered, "A moonshine jar was nothing but a canning jar. Bootleggers put moonshine in them. Some people called them fruit jars."

"I guess he was being more dramatic," Davie said.

Isaac put his hand on Davie's shoulder. "Nope, I expect they had moonshine in jars on that boat. He mentioned them drinking it. They smuggled everything."

"Oh," Davie said. "Okay."

"Should I read the rest?" Bernell asked Isaac.

Lillian answered, "Yes, I want to hear the rest of it."

Bernell continued:

They said it's a drop in the bucket. I could make millions BLANK. I pretended to be interested. They wanted to celebrate BLANK-BLANK moonshine BLANK drunk, I got a flour sack, crammed the stuff in it. I hid it in my boat under the nets in my fish box. When they left, I came here to the landing and buried my fish box just a hundred feet from river's edge at the end of our road BLANK big rock chiseled cross BLANK bushes.

"Oh," Davie interrupted. "That was how we found it. I found that rock in the bushes Thursday. It's way deeper than it looks. When I saw it, I knew that was the rock he was talking about. I called Daddy and Grandpa. We waited till everybody left and I used the excavator and moved the rock and dug till I struck something. Daddy parked his truck up close. We pulled the fish box up and loaded it in Grandpa's truck. Grandpa locked the tonneau lid and went home. I pushed the dirt back, then me and Daddy went to see Chief Jeb."

"And it stayed in the garage until an hour ago," Isaac assured them.

"Smooth!" Kit said.

"Okay, read on," Lillian said. "I thought there was more."

"There is a little," Bernell started reading again:

"I'm giving that stuff back to its rightful owners. The men or BLANK-BLANK-BLANK, garage sale. I wanted you to BLANK. Love, Antry."

"What did he mean by the men or something garage sale? And what did he want her to do?" Jenny asked.

Bernell said, "Well, the last one is a short smudge. It could have just been 'I wanted you to know.' But what's with the garage sale?"

"And something else about the men," Kit said.

"The men or, the men or what? The men or Riddick? The men or women? The men or somebody else?" Jessica asked.

"You reckon it was something else about the moonshine jar?" Davie wondered.

Bree laughed. "The men or the moonshine jar has a certain ring to it."

Lillian took the letter out of Bernell's hand and put her glasses on. "Let me look at it." She studied it for a minute. "I don't think it's men OR something. Men is not a separate word. The 'or' looks like it was supposed to be connected."

"Menor? Minners?" Davie asked.

"That would be minnows" Jenny corrected him.

"I don't think it has anything to do with fish," Isaac said.

"It *is* a fish box." Davie reminded him.

"Well, what are we going to do with all this stuff?" Jimmy changed the focus.

Bernell suggested, "I can put it in our vault. We can write up something, advertise items found, and let people identify the things that were stolen. The police department should do it, though, not us."

Jimmy agreed. "And we don't need to identify exactly what's here. People should have to describe it."

"Would you have answered an ad and identified your pearls?" Isaac asked.

She shook her head. "I don't know. It's been so long ago. Maybe if the ad was more specific and said pearls, I would think of mine. I would say, they have a diamond clasp with Italy stamped on the bottom. They are South Sea pearls and the strand is 18 inches long."

"Then it would take a professional jeweler to verify that," Jessica said. "South Sea pearls are very expensive, but not everybody can recognize them. You might have to involve Del Vecchio's."

"Some of it might have come from there," Lillian said.

"I'm pretty sure it did," Isaac agreed.

Jenny spoke up. "So it's going to be nearly impossible to get stuff back to its rightful owners, even though that's what he wanted."

"Especially since it's been almost sixty years," Kit observed. "And some people might have reported it to their insurance company and been compensated. And some could have died. And you can't reimburse the insurance companies because you don't even know who they were, and some insurance companies have gone out of business, too. I mean sixty years is a long time."

"Ugh!" Davie said. "Sure is getting complicated."

"We could just give it to a charity," Lillian suggested. "The Manor at the Salvation Army could sure use some work. And it's way too small."

"I think that's the best idea," Bree said, then held up both hands and backed off. "Although, I shouldn't say anything. Just speaking as an objective bystander."

Bernell looked at her. "Not at all. You are part of the family. And by the way, congratulations on what your Dad did this morning." She did a high five with Bree.

"Yeah, that turned out good, didn't it?"

Isaac said, "I want to commend you all on that major coup. When Jeb called me and said he had information that would wind this all up, I had no idea he'd pull it off so smoothly."

Kit asked, "Y'all want to see the video?"

"I do," Jenny said. "I prayed the whole time in church. I don't even know what the preacher said."

Lillian nodded, "You and me too, honey. I never prayed so hard in my life. I was so afraid there'd be a hitch and the shooters would use bullets. I could just see Davie getting killed over this, and it was not worth it. Not worth any of us getting killed over. Most especially if they've not stayed as close to the Lord as they need to. That's what was tearing me up."

Davie's face turned red. They all knew of his fiasco in Chesapeake now, and they were worried.

"Grandma, you don't need to worry about that anymore. Me and God's got that worked out. I'm sorry I got so caught up in that life, and, well, you know. I've been reading my Bible and praying and I had a long talk with Rev. Rutherford and he prayed with me. I feel like God has forgiven me. I hope you all will."

Jessica put her head against his. "Of course we do."

He looked at his dad. "Even though I was baptized when I was twelve, Rev. Rutherford is going to baptize me next Sunday. I wanted to renew my commitment."

"Hallelujah!" Lillian threw up her arms. Davie let them all hug him, and he sheepishly looked at Jenny whose face was wet with tears. But her eyes were not stormy blue-gray. They just looked happy and sparkled.

Davie smiled. "So if that had been a real bullet, it would have been okay. But I'm glad it wasn't. And Jake and Ed were real troopers playing along with that. We probably ought to give all of this stuff to them." He motioned to the treasures on the table.

"They will be paid well," Isaac said. "And they'd probably rather have the money." Everybody nodded and talked together agreeing.

"That must have been some informant?" Lillian said, "I mean for Jeb to have such trust in that operation and call Zach in."

Bree said, "Yeah. That was one of Dad's pilots. Dad pulled him off the job and fired him. All that man knew was that Zelda Midget was shipping a package to New York and she paid him to pick it up at Davie's boat place on Sunday morning. But he knew he wasn't supposed to do that. And he didn't know she was planning to hijack the helicopter either. Dad decided he'd take the shipment. He wanted to fly again anyway."

"And guess who got hijacked!" Kit laughed. "And we got it all on tape."

"I was really nervous waiting," Bree said. "When I called Dad and said NOW, he said, 'Yeah, she just called,' and he swooped down and opened the door. When the man shoved that box in the helicopter and ran back to the boat, and Alana climbed in, my heart was pounding." Bree grasped her heart with both hands. "I was afraid she would shoot him."

Kit laughed. "Jeb yanked her in so quickly, she didn't know what happened. I wish I could have gotten a better shot of her face."

"You got enough to put her away," Isaac said. "That and, of course, whatever the informant told Jeb."

Lillian said, "I'd sure love to know who the informant was. I want to thank him—or her. I know God sent whoever it was though. God works in mysterious ways."

"I'm hungry," Davie said.

Lillian had a solution. "We can run around to the restaurant."

Isaac thought better of that. "We've got all this stuff to put away. And I want to see the video, too."

Lillian was quick with another solution. "Okay, I'll just call it in and have them bring us a buffet around here."

"That sounds good," Davie said, and they all agreed.

Kit put the video on her laptop and projected it on a screen. It was short but dramatic. As soon as it was over, everyone started picking up the items on display and Bernell laid the jewels in the vault. Jimmy and Isaac carried the empty fish box back to the truck.

"So the digging mystery is over," Bree said as she helped Kit pack up the laptop. "But there's still that issue of counterfeit money that's cost y'all thousands of dollars." She directed her comment to Isaac as he sat down at the table.

Kit asked him, "What will the bank do? Alana's estate should make that good. But what kind of fight would that be?"

Isaac leaned back in his chair and rubbed his face. "Well, all the items they got can be repossessed. I'll get out a warrant. We won't be out that much. Jenny, why don't you send a bill to Jo Swan at Renoir's address for the entire amount of the cushions?"

"Good idea!" Jimmy said and Jenny agreed. She was still ticked off at the way Jo Swan had acted.

Davie said, "Right now I'm more worried about Mike Riley."

Everyone knew exactly why. Despite his relief at the digging being over and Alana being caught, there was still the mystery of the missing Smythes. And Davie was still the main suspect in the murder of the man in the white suit.

Although Kit and Bree had made an amazing discovery that was escalating the investigation, there was still no answer in sight. And Officer Mike Riley had not relinquished his determination to nail Davie.

"That's crazy," Davie said, as he slumped at the table. "I guess I'm reaping what I sowed."

"I don't think so, Davie." Jessica sat down beside him and put an arm across his shoulder. "You screwed up. You made a big mistake. But you have not killed anybody!"

Lillian said, "We're still praying, Davie, and God's still working. We didn't think this morning would happen. But it did. God didn't bring us this far without going all the way. Just keep trusting him."

A knock on the back door meant their food had arrived. "That will help," he said and everyone laughed.

Chapter 50 Reprieve, Review and Regroup

Monday morning, April 15

Monday morning came with great relief to many in Claxton. The Spring Festival was over and had been a huge success. Tourists were leaving town. The beauty shop was closed. The Wellsly's were still basking in Sunday's victory. The buried treasure was found, the digging was ended, and Alana was gone.

To say that Sunday had been a stressful and hectic day would be a gross understatement, from the morning drama thru the massive cleanup. Floats were dismantled and borrowed props returned. The pigs on Jimmy's float got out and had to be caught. Davie helped George and Isaac deliver the sailboat they had gone together and donated for the raffle. It was like Christmas for the Willoughby kids who won that boat. Jenny helped her boutique staff return the few things they didn't sell. She carefully counted the register receipts and made sure no cash was counterfeit. Everyone crashed by the end of the day.

Monday was a reprieve. But with Carolina and Paul Jason home for the first time in three months, Jimmy and Jessica wanted the family to join them for brunch. The previous days were rehashed because it was still on everyone's mind. Caroline said to Paul Jason, "Our life is so boring."

Davie said, "Ours used to be."

Isaac said, "I'll be glad when it is again."

The Agency was open. Bernell knew that somewhere there was another person who had driven that green car with blood on it. Now there was a red shoe, and there was that briefcase with $10,000 in it. It seemed that everything had a connection to Davie and Smythe's yacht though. If that money was intended for him, would he get it? And where would he deliver the yacht? It could not stay at the plant. So Davie's troubles were far from over.

"I felt so sorry for him yesterday," Bree said.

"Yeah, me too," Kit agreed.

Bernell reminded them, "Thomas and Adam are still in Chesapeake on their manhunt. According to their report, they've consulted with hundreds of people and found very few clues. But they are keeping me informed. When I added the search for Martin Morgan Montegue to their task, Thomas said he assumed that at some point, the two cases would coincide. I told him that was what I was expecting. It's just too ironic."

The Smythe's house appeared vacant. But there was no 'for sale' sign. The property taxes had been paid. The post office no longer delivered mail there. No papers piled up. There was no telephone service.

Thomas and Adam had snooped around the house diligently. The heated pool was cold. The electricity was off. There was an antique car in the garage along with two other expensive modern vehicles. They could only see that by standing in a chair from the pool. The guys debated breaking-in but didn't dare, since Bernell had admonished them to stay clean. They had talked to the local police who said there was no problem in that neighborhood. There was no missing persons' report for those people. The police guessed that the Smythes were just away, maybe on a cruise.

In the conference call, when Thomas and Adam gave Bernell that information, she agreed that was feasible. But then she threw in the missing Montegue and they were back to square one.

"We're all working on that murder," Bernell said. "But there has to be something in Chesapeake. Where did he live? She gave them the address from the license. Did he have a family? Has he been reported missing? What was his job? What was his connection to Jeffry Smythe, and why was he carrying $10,000? Kit and Bree are working on the documented data, but ask around and see what you can find."

"Okay, boss," they accepted the challenge and had an idea. They had not yet told her about the Triple M brochure.

"And one more thing," she said. "Find out what you can about Jamie Sampson. We have a picture that looks like her with Montegue."

"So we've got another missing person?" Adam asked.

"No," Bernell told him. "We know where she is; we just don't know how she's connected to the Smythes."

"No problem, boss."

The Best Western Hotel had become home. The ladies at the front desk were friendly and pretty. They thought Thomas and Adam were with the FBI and respected the confidentiality of their work. But they were not oblivious to the charm of those two hunks and more than willing to help.

In Claxton, Joliet Swan was arrested as an accomplice in Alana's scheme, but in a plea bargain was released under her father's recognizance. A move that was driving Renee Renoir mad.

Sampson and Summerlin were arrested when they reached the boat garage after their Sunday morning sail. They were charged with attempted first-degree murder, attempted armed robbery, criminal mischief, vandalism, trespassing, and recklessness because of the bodily harm to Rebecca Wilson and Bud Littman, all as accomplices to Alana Frizelle. They were assigned a court-appointed lawyer who advised them to opt for plea bargaining. They jumped at that chance. Jeb let them return to the yellow house under their own recognizance, but with the security of nice ankle bracelets while they awaited sentencing.

Nobody, not even Summerlin and Sampson, knew the extent of information Jeb had received from an unknown informant who was now being protected for obvious reasons.

Jeb understood that the FBI would put the informant in the witness protection program with a new name and credentials. But as yet, he had not released the person's name.

Bree convinced Jeb to let her study the fingerprints that had been found on the green car. He knew what they had learned from the Oceana Hotel and agreed that there needed to be more investigation.

But she wanted to force Riley into clearing Davie. She decided to work with him in such a way that he could take the credit. He had already indicated there were other prints. She knew he had not followed through. He had just jumped to a conclusion immediately once he saw Davie Wellsly's name pop up. It was too easy to stop there.

Bree told Jeb, "When a person's life is in the balance, it's a mistake to act too hastily."

Naturally, he agreed. The red shoe was her first shot. She brought it in a plastic bag to Riley at the police department. "I found this on the parking lot where the oar was found that killed Martin Montegue. I was wondering if it had fingerprints on it."

He looked at her suspiciously. "Really? It was on that parking lot?"

"Yeah, it was near the rocks at the bulkhead, kind of to the side. I figured you'd want to check it out."

"Let's go back there," he took the bag. She followed him to the fingerprinting room. He dusted the red shoe and entered the print in the data file. In a matter of seconds, the name Jamie Sampson popped up.

"Whoa!" she blurted then caught herself. "Well, this doesn't prove anything. I mean you can't convict a person based on a fingerprint. Let's do some more checking. What about the oar? Do you still have it in here?"

"In the evidence room," he said. "I'll go get it."

As he left the room, she pumped her fist. "Yes!"

As soon as he returned with the oar, she knew it was the match to the one in the fishing boat. She didn't say anything. He ran the test, and as he had said before, Davie's name came up. In seconds, two other names came up. One of them was Jamie Sampson.

"Hey. You see that?" He pointed at one. "Same as the red shoe."

"Wow. I didn't expect that," Bree said. "Do you know who Jamie Sampson is?"

"One of those ladies. She was in jail yesterday. They let her go this morning."

Bree frowned. "Is there any way possible that while she was here she could have touched this oar?"

"No way," he shook his head.

"We need to speak to the Chief," Bree said.

"Well, he assigned this to me, and I think he expects me to handle it," Riley seemed annoyed.

"Okay, then, maybe you could go find her. Arrest her and bring her back here." Bree took a chance.

"I, well, it's not that simple, you know."

"Yes. But Chief Jeb might have a suggestion since he just released her."

He sighed. "You're pretty smart."

"You're pretty smart, too. I'm just older."

He blushed. "And headed toward the chief's office."

"Well, what do you know about that?" Jeb was shocked when he saw the results. "She's supposed to be at the yellow house. But she won't be there long."

"Should I bring her in?"

"Bring her in for more questioning."

As soon as he left, Bree said, "Chief, we've got pictures that Jenny took at Jeffry Smythe's party. In one of the pictures, I'm 99 percent sure it's Jamie Sampson dancing with Montegue."

"Strike three. This is going to be interesting." He leaned back in his seat and said, "Retirement's looking good, Miss Bree."

She laughed. "You're not going to retire. You're too good."

He smiled. He always loved to hear that even if he sometimes doubted it.

"You think I could listen in while you question Sampson?" Bree was counting on him to agree.

"I don't see why not." He rearranged some papers on his desk. "Mike will be back in about twenty minutes. He's a good cop. Wet behind the ears, but he's learning fast. I saw what you did there. Thanks."

Bree shrugged. "I decided it was the best way to handle it. I have some other items from the parking lot I need to share with you. It's been so crazy the past few days, and you were inaccessible, but we did not want to release this to anyone but you." She handed him a folder of pictures. "Bernell put this in the vault."

"What have you got here?" The chief furrowed his brow as he scanned the pictures. "Oh, my goodness. Look at that cash. Where'd you get this? That's not more counterfeit, is it?"

"Oh, we didn't think of that," Bree sat up straight. "But, no, I don't think so." She tapped the picture showing the briefcase with the initials MMM.

"Martin Morgan Montegue, well, well, well. What do you know? So where did you find it?"

"Same parking lot, in the water almost under the building, wedged in those sharp rocks. You familiar with that parking lot?"

"Behind Lee Fish Market? I've parked there, but never really paid much attention. I know it connects to a little pier, and there are some fishing boats usually docked there."

"Yes, and by the way, Friday when Kit and I were there, one of those boats had only one oar. We used it to dislodge that briefcase from the rocks. So I figured the other one is the one you have here. Mike showed it to me and it matches."

"Very interesting," the chief continued studying the pictures, "You think this man was here to see Davie?"

"We think so now," she nodded. "We think Smythe must have sent him. We don't have any proof. I wonder how much Jamie Sampson knows, though."

"We'll soon find out. I hear Mike out there now." He got up and opened the door. Jamie Sampson was sitting in a chair by Edna's desk.

"Let's go to the interrogation room," he beckoned Bree.

Chapter 51 The Red Shoe

Monday, April 15

Sitting in the interrogation room, at that same table, once again answering questions, Jamie Sampson was obviously nervous. She paid no attention to the one-way window with Bree on the other side but answered the Chief of Police anxiously.

"I thought we were done with all this." She looked him in the eye curiously.

"Didn't Officer Riley tell you this might not have anything to do with Zelda?"

"He didn't really know. He said you have my fingerprints on something."

Jeb set the red shoe on the table. "You recognize this?"

She laughed. "Cheap shoes. I bought them in Boca Raton. Yes, I recognize it. Where'd you find it?"

"I think you might know," he looked at her quizzically. "You don't lose a shoe like this without knowing it, do you?"

She put her elbows on the table, bit her bottom lip, and propped her head on her hands looking down a minute. Then she looked up and said, "I didn't kill him."

"Oh, so you do know where we found it. And you know why you're here."

"Yes, but I didn't kill him."

"What happened in the parking lot?" He leaned in, attentively. "Maybe you should start from the beginning. You did know Martin Morgan Montegue, didn't you?"

Her lip trembled. "He was a nice guy. I met him at a party in Chesapeake, Virginia. I used to live there."

Bree's jaws dropped. She took out a pen and pad and started jotting notes.

Jeb showed a heightened interest in Sampson's revelation. "Did you know Jeffry and Julie Smythe?"

"Not really. I worked at the Yarrows Yacht Club and got acquainted with people."

"Were you a waitress?"

"No, I was a hostess. I had to maintain a friendly rapport with members and guests. The Smythes were very friendly and had a lot of parties. Yes, they invited me. And that is where I met Monty. He was their accountant."

"Hmm," Bree muttered to herself. "We read that he was a lawyer."

"So you and Monty became more than friends?" Jeb speculated.

She leaned back and looked up at the ceiling. "We became friends."

"Let me get this straight now. Zelda hired you, or solicited you, to participate in her 'game,' so you came to Claxton with her. Isn't it ironic that Martin Montegue came to Claxton at the same time?" A statement rather than a question. "Did he follow you here?"

"No, it is not ironic. He was here on business for Jeffry Smythe."

"Well, it seems ironic to me. Unless, there was some connection between them all, and you."

"You're losing me, Mr. Stanton. What do you mean by 'them all' and me?"

"I'm just trying to establish whether Alana Frizelle and Jeffry Smythe knew each other."

"To be honest, I think everybody knew Mr. Smythe. As I said, he threw a lot of parties. But I don't know who Alana Frizelle is or who she knows. Zelda did not share any information with us about her other friends. You have told me more about her than I ever knew. I only knew her as Zelda Midget. Are you going to do the same thing with Mr. Smythe and Mr. Montegue?" She was beginning to be a little defiant.

"Okay, okay," The chief decided he needed to take a different tactic. "I just need you to tell me what happened on the parking lot. We'll get to all that other later if there is any need."

Sampson relaxed. "Monty had my phone number, and we talked on the phone. He was divorced and I was divorced, and we both just wanted a friend. So we talked a lot. Even after I went to Boca Raton. I could not tell him about the game because it was supposed to be kept secret. So I did not tell him where I was going. And I did not know he was coming to Claxton."

"So that was ironic," Jeb said.

"If you say so," she appeased him.

He nodded. "Go on."

She took a deep breath. "Jo and Jackie and I had lunch at the Gristmill Restaurant one day. Zelda had told us to look around there because our first job would be there. While we were having lunch, Monty saw us. He couldn't believe I was here. And I was surprised to see him. He came over and talked with us. I still couldn't tell him why I was here, so I just told him my friends and I were on vacation and one of them wanted to stop by and visit her father. It was the truth. I was on vacation from my job."

Jeb listened to her intently and decided he believed her story. "So after you ran into each other...?" He waited for her to continue.

"He said he would be here a couple of days and maybe we could get together. He'd like to take me to a nice place he had heard about on the waterfront, Lillian's Riviera."

She paused, bit her lip, and said, "I liked Monty. Jackie and Jo said do it. They'd cover. He didn't know what they meant, but I did. I told him I would meet him there. So that is what I did. And I wore those red shoes."

Sampson paused, and her expression saddened. She put her head down on the table unexpectedly and sobbed. Jeb frowned. Bree waited. Riley just shook his head slowly in disbelief.

Always compassionate, Jeb patted her on the hand. "I'm sorry. Just tell us what happened." He pushed a box of tissue toward her sensing that she had not killed Martin Montegue, at least not deliberately. Bree was also convinced.

Mike Riley who had been sitting at the table listening was not impressed by this suspect.

Remembering her experience with Kit at that bulkhead, Bree now projected that Montegue's death had been an accident.

Sampson regained her composure, and with her head bowed, and her fingers fidgeting with a tissue, she told how she and Montegue had left the restaurant about ten-thirty. "Monty had parked in the fish market parking lot next to the bulkhead because Jo said that would be a good place to pick me up. She had been there before."

Jeb listened attentively.

"Jackie and Jo took me around there on the fishing boat. One of the rules of Zelda's game was that no one could know where we lived. I had to sneak out to meet Monty. She thought we were scouting down the creek preparing for our digs."

Jeb nodded, assuming that was true because the timing matched up. She continued. "Actually, Jackie and Jo were, but they dropped me off behind the fish market."

She paused remembering the evening, then started again, slowly at first but picking up momentum as she talked. "We were the last ones to leave the restaurant. It was dark when we walked back. A man in a white suit was standing by the car, but I couldn't see his face. It was not well lit." She paused as though trying to remember.

"What did he do?" Jeb urged her on.

"He demanded that Monty give him the briefcase. Monty said 'what briefcase' and he said 'the one under the front seat.' When Monty refused, the man grabbed me. He said he would shoot me if Monty didn't give it to him."

When she stopped, the chief said, "Go on."

She took a deep breath and began again. "When Monty saw the gun, he opened the door and pulled out a briefcase and threw it at him. The man cursed him and shot. I think it struck Monty but Monty lunged at him. The man shoved me against the rail and it fell, and I landed on the sharp rocks and cut my arms and hands."

She stretched her arms out and opened her hands to reveal the marks. Then she put her fingers to her temple and closed her eyes.

"Take your time," Jeb wanted to hear these details.

"Monty came after me, but the man snatched him away, Monty wrestled him down. By then I was on the pier and there was a boat with an oar sticking out. I grabbed it and swung it. Monty yelled 'go, get out of here.' I thought I was going to fall again, but Jo and Jackie rowed up just in time. They saw what was happening, Jo grabbed me and yanked me down in the boat. Jackie started the motor and backed us out. I kept looking back, and I could see one of them running to the car. I couldn't tell if it was Monty or the mugger. I still don't know."

Bree was jotting a note: *Jo Swan could verify this.*

Jeb sat silent for a minute after she finished. Officer Riley decided he had to speak up. "Miss Sampson that's a pretty good story. You think we can really buy that?"

Bree was on the other side of the glass nodding. "I can buy that," she said to no one.

Officer Riley was not aware of the briefcase being found. But Jeb was. That certainly gave her story validity that Riley did not know. This could also explain Sampson's fingerprints on the oar, and they were probably on the car.

"So now we have two men in white suits," Riley said. "Incredible."

"A lot of men wear white suits," Jamie said.

"I don't," was Riley's reply.

"Okay, Officer Riley." Jeb held up his hand to hold him at bay. "We have a story we have to check out. The car was found with blood on it near Pine Ridge Road. Who left it there? Are there any prints on the steering wheel? Can you find out whose blood it is?"

"That's where we found Davie Wellsly's fingerprints," Riley reminded him.

"We've been through all that. We know why Wellsly's prints are there. His wife's prints are probably in the car also. Which would further solidify their story. And besides, we have their registration at Oceana Hotel verifying that that was the car they used. So let's get off that wagon."

Officer Riley said, "Just one more thing. Have you thought about it that Wellsly could be the mugger she's talking about? His fingerprints are still on the oar and on the car."

The chief gave Riley an evil look, and Bree dropped her jaw. "I can't believe that guy." Now she was angry.

Chief Jeb chose to ignore Riley's last comment and turned his attention back to his guest. "I'm sorry Miss Sampson. We have some work to do. We do have a dead body we thought was Montegue. But you have raised some important questions."

Riley reminded him. "We have a wallet with his name in it."

"But it was found on the parking lot, not on the body," Jeb said, just about to lose his patience.

Jamie brightened. "Are you saying it's possible that Monty was not the one in the river?"

"We may have jumped to a conclusion."

"But some people said it was Monty. I wanted to try calling him, but my phone got lost in the water, and I didn't know his number. It was programmed in."

"Fortunately—or unfortunately--the body is still at the morgue because it has been unclaimed. I want you to go see if you can identify it."

Sampson winced and her stomach churned. She was about to be sick.

Bree made a note to get Thomas and Adam on the alert for a missing male about 5'10 in Chesapeake. *It had to be someone who knew Montegue was carrying that much money and followed him here. He might have worn a white suit intending to impersonate Montegue. He must have come from Chesapeake. How would anybody here know he had that much money on him? How did the mugger know it for that matter?*

And then that leads to a string of other questions. Bree's mind was ticking a mile a minute. *If Montegue is alive, where is he? Did he drive the car to Pine Ridge Road? And then what? Why did he abandon the car? And for crying out loud, where is he? Did he kill the mugger? Or did Jamie Sampson kill the mugger? Was the body in the river the mugger?*

Chief Jeb told Officer Riley to make arrangements for Sampson to identify the body, and take her down there, then take her home and get back with him.

He opened the door to the side room and told Bree to come to his office.

"What do you make of all this?" Jeb pulled out a chair for her and then sat down in his chair behind the desk.

"WOW!" Bree said. "I did not see that coming. But judging from my own experience on that parking lot," she showed him marks on her hands and wrists, "I can see it happening just like she said. But what now? We can't get one thing solved before there's something else." She shook her head. "But somehow, it's all connected."

"I don't suppose we can blame this on Alana, can we?" Jeb joked.

Bree laughed. "You know, she IS the one who brought Jamie Sampson here."

"Humph, you're right. Unfortunately, it's not that simple though."

"Right. The Bible says every tub's got to stand on its own bottom."

"What?" He did a double-take. "What did you say?"

She laughed. "I heard somebody say that one time, and I thought it was funny. I've been waiting for a chance to use it."

He laughed. "The Bible does not say that." Although Jeb had been raised in a Christian home, he had to go through a war before he gave his heart to the Lord. But he knew that was not in the Bible.

"Not like that anyway," he laughed again.

"Feel better?" Bree winked at him.

"It always feels good to laugh," he said. "Now that's something that IS in the Bible. A merry heart doeth good like a medicine. I heard my mama say that a million times."

He sighed and got serious again. "Well, kid, we've got some work to do."

"Yeah, I know. And we've got to get Mike Riley on board. He seems intent on pinning this on Davie."

"I may have to take him off this case. He's being too biased and narrow-minded."

"Let's work around him. He's got nothing we don't have." She stood up. "Wait till Bernell and Kit hear about this."

She turned to go, then turned back. "That briefcase with the money. Want us to bring it over here?"

He scratched his head. "Nah, it's safe."

In the front office, Riley had his suspect wait with Edna until he called the morgue. They were more than willing to accommodate. It didn't take but thirty minutes.

Jamie steeled herself for the horrible moment. When they entered, she was visibly shaken, but then slumped and sighed with relief, shaking her head. "It's not Monty."

For the first time, Riley was moved and put his arm around her shoulders to guide her back out.

In the squad car, he looked at her, a pitiful, broken woman. "I'm taking you back to the house, but don't leave town," he cautioned.

She looked at him and smiled. "Find Monty."

"Find Montegue. Find the Smythes. Find a mugger's identity. Find a moonshine jar of diamonds—add that to the list." Bernell said as Bree filled her in on the events of the day and updated her file on the man in the white suit.

Chapter 52 Davie's Surprise

Tuesday Morning, April 16

On Tuesday, Davie's Landing sported a whole new look with a lush green lawn and pink azaleas blooming along the edge of the front parking lot. For an extra spring touch, tall, yellow daffodils bobbed in the cement planters on each side of the driveway entrance.

A flag pole had been erected beside the rock with the chiseled cross, and a new flag fluttered in the April breeze. New white letters over the entrance said *WDGW OARS & BOATS.*

Jeffry Smythe commented on the positive changes as he drove up and parked in the area in front of the office. Julie agreed it looked nice. "They must have spruced it up for their Spring Festival," she speculated.

Davie was standing at a file cabinet when they entered his office. He looked up and did a double-take. He was torn between belting Smythe on the spot or getting down on his knees and thanking him for showing up. He did neither.

Smythe extended his hand for a handshake and Julie greeted him with a hug which was typical. Davie was full of questions but speechless at this heart-stopping surprise.

Smythe said, "So sorry about the mix-up, Davie. When I left Montegue in charge, I figured he would have taken care of everything by now, but apparently he hasn't. We got home expecting to see our new Wellsly Yacht at the club and when it wasn't there, we checked. Couldn't get up with Monty, so we decided just to run down here and check on it."

Julie laughed. "We didn't run. We hopped a plane and rented a car." Davie glanced out the window. It was a black Mercury Grand Marquis from Hertz at the airport.

Still, Davie was tongue-tied. All the things he had been through in the past few weeks and these people were looking sharp and dapper, without a care in the world, and laughing apologetically about the INCONVENIENCE.

He opened his mouth to speak but motioned for them to sit down. He laid his hand on the Bible which now happened to be on top of everything else and silently thanked God for this unexpected turn of events.

Finally, he could speak. "What a surprise! I've tried to reach you. I thought you were dead."

They thought he was joking.

"I have wanted to apologize for running out on the party." He started, but Julie shushed him.

"Not a problem. It got out of hand. It wasn't your fault. Sometimes we invite too many people. We have to start being more selective." And she gave Jeffry a look that meant just that.

"Duly noted," Jeffry gave her a look in return and smiled at Davie. "Well, let's get this thing done. It's a beauty out there, isn't it?" He could see his yacht on the river through the side window.

Davie pulled Jeffry's file from the cabinet beside his desk and handed it to him.

"Ten grand. My check still good?" He grinned.

"I hope so," Davie responded and thought *Dear God, I hope so.* "That includes delivery. You say you want it delivered to the Yarrows Yacht Club at Chesapeake?"

"That's our club."

Davy hit a buzzer on his desk and Alex Wolf came in from the back. He grinned and stuck out his hand, greeting the Smythes. "Long time no see."

"Yeah, sorry about that," Jeffry quipped as he stood up.

Davie handed Alex the order for delivering the yacht. "Think your guys can get started on this today?"

"How about if we leave tomorrow morning? They're in the middle of some projects right now, but we'll pull out tomorrow morning. I thought I'd go along. We've done some test runs, but I want to stay with it until it's safely docked at Yarrows."

"Fine," nodded Jeffry.

Davie agreed; Alex shook Jeffry's hand again, nodded at Julie, and took his leave. As soon as he was out, Davie said, "Have a seat. We need to talk."

"Sounds ominous," Julie said as she sat back down.

"It's about Montegue, isn't it?" Smythe jumped right in.

"Do you know anything?" Davie wanted to know. "I mean where he is? What happened to him?"

"All we know is that his ex-wife called and said he had not paid his alimony this month. He's usually on time. They have no children, but he provides for her well--even though she's such a bi..."

"Jeffry!" Julie Smythe interrupted him.

"Anyway, after her lawyer got up with us, we knew something must be wrong. We checked the club, and the yacht had not been delivered, so we knew then that something bad must have happened. We wanted to get this cleared with you and then see what we can do about finding him. I can't imagine. He's always been so faithful and trustworthy."

"The police are looking for him now," Davie said.

"Police, Oh, my goodness, what has he done?" Julie cried out.

Davie shook his head. "No. Nothing like that."

He explained about the man in the white suit that had been found in the river, and how they had thought it might be Montegue, but that now it has been determined it wasn't him. That person was probably a mugger who may have attacked Montegue, and now Montegue was missing.

Jeffry and Julie sat with mouths open trying to digest the unfolding story.

"What can we do?" Smythe leaned in with his elbow on Davie's desk.

"Our police, Chief Jeb Stanton, is working closely with B.B. Jackson Agency, downtown, to get this resolved. They started yesterday as soon as they learned that the man in the river was not him. You need to check in with them now. You might have some information that would be helpful."

Smythe looked at his watch. "Our flight back is scheduled for tonight at eight o'clock, but yes..." He looked at Julie.

"Where do we go?" she asked Davie.

He wrote down the Agency address. "Go all the way back up Big Creek Road and turn right on Claxton Boulevard. Go five miles and you'll see it on your right. Brick building. The front door says B.B. Jackson Private Investigating Agency. It's a couple of blocks from the police station. I recommend seeing her first. It's less hectic. I'll call Mrs. Jackson and let her know you're coming. They'll get up with the chief."

Jeffry and Julie Smythe hastened out the door on their next mission. Davie leaned back in his chair, let his arms fall by his sides, and took a deep breath. "Thank you, God," he said aloud. Then he sat up and dialed Abby.

Chapter 53 – Connections

Tuesday, April 16

When Abby handed Bernell the name of the couple coming in, she buzzed Kit and Bree immediately. "Get your papers together we're about to hit pay dirt. Jeffry Smythe has turned up. He and his wife will be here in a few minutes."

"How did that happen?" Kit asked. "Did Thomas and Adam find them?"

"No. They just walked in Davie's office down at the plant and acted like nothing had ever happened."

"How could they? Where've they been?" Bree sat down with a folder of notes she had prepared.

Kit sat down beside her. "Do they know where Montegue is? Did they pay Davie? I wonder how that went."

Bernell said, "They paid him with a check. They are looking for Montegue. They say they didn't know he was missing. We'll get some scoop from them in a few minutes. But the first thing I want to know is if there is a connection between him and Alana Frizelle. That will answer a lot for me. You got that folder on the corporation ALANAKIN ASSOCIATES?"

"Got it," Kit said. "I did a little research, but I want to see what he says. A lot can be hidden in corporations and foundations. Tons of money can be funneled through them. Sometimes they're caught. Sometimes they're not."

Abby brought a well-dressed middle-aged couple through Bernell's office and into the conference room. They were especially youthful looking for a couple supposedly retired. He wore a dark blue suit with a white shirt and a red tie. His blondish hair did not show any gray. Her dark hair had a touch of stylish blonde frosting. Her red shirt and white pants made them look like a patriotic poster.

"Mr. and Mrs. Smythe, this is Mrs. Jackson, Mrs. Griffiths, and Mrs. Ingles." She pointed at each of them. "They've been doing work on the case you're here about."

As the Smythes sat down, they reached across the table to shake hands. "Julie," Mrs. Smythe corrected as she shook hands with each of them.

They responded: "Bree." "Kit."

Mr. Smythe said, "Jeffry."

Bernell did not mention her first name but got right down to business. "I understand Martin Montegue works for you?"

Mr. Smythe looked at his watch. He was just as eager to get this over with. "He has been with us for fifteen years."

"Is that with the corporation or you personally?" Bernell asked.

"The corporation? Oh, I retired from the corporation five years ago. Monty worked there also, and when I retired, I suggested that he join me in some business ventures. I wanted to make a few investments and I needed a good, solid lawyer. He took over as my business associate, sort of lawyer/accountant. He's got a good head on him, and I have always known him to be faithful and loyal. A very trustworthy friend. Now I am stumped at this situation."

"What is the name of the corporation you were CEO of, Mr. Smythe?" Bernell seemed more interested in his past than the present.

"ALANAKIN ASSOCIATES," He said simply.

"Allen Aiken Associates?" Bernell repeated slowly the way he said it.

"Yes, Alan Akin was at Harvard when I was there. He started his company even before he graduated. It was no time before it grew into a major marketing firm in New York, and he asked me to join him. I practically ran it until five years ago. Are you familiar with it?"

"No, that's why I'm asking," she looked him in the eye. Bree and Kit looked at each other and almost snickered but held their composure.

Smythe described the corporation. "We did marketing and advertising, promotional work. We distributed logo items, things like your pens and pads here, and the candy in your dish. You probably have the magnifying glasses and pens that function as flashlights since you're a detective agency. Who did these for you?" He picked up a handful of mints with the B.B Jackson P.I. Agency logo. "Looks like Marcum and Sills? They do a lot in this area."

Bree raised her eyebrows at Kit and jotted down *magnifying glasses and pen flashlights.*

Bernell was taken aback. "Umm, no, it's a smaller company out of Nashville. Have you heard of Alana Frizelle?"

"Is that a marketing firm?"

"No."

He looked at his watch. "I don't understand. We're short on time. I thought we were talking about Montegue's disappearance. Is there a connection?"

"That's what I'm trying to find out, Mr. Smythe." Bernell had not smiled yet.

Kit interrupted. "We need to establish credibility and trust."

Bree added, "Trust is critical in our business, as I am sure it is in yours."

"Yes, well, back to what I was saying, I have trusted Montegue with everything. When we left, unexpectedly, on that last cruise, I trusted him to finalize the deal with Davie and get the yacht delivered, but something has gone awry."

"How can you have an unexpected cruise?" Bernell asked cynically. She still wasn't completely on track.

Julie spoke up with a laugh. "At a party in January, our friends asked us to join them and we hadn't planned it, but we don't ever do anything spontaneous, and I said, 'Jeffry, let's go. You only live once!' And, well, he finally capitulated. He'd had a few drinks." She laughed. "The next morning, he said 'what have I agreed to?'"

Smythe spoke for himself, "It was totally out of character for me." He looked at Bernell. "And...well," he looked at his wife. "You see? This is what happens."

Okay, he's clean, Bernell relaxed, finally satisfied that he was not in cahoots with Alana. Although she would never be totally convinced of anyone's sanctity from the deceitful Alana.

She motioned to Kit and Bree to take over and find out what they could about Martin Morgan Montegue, his habits, his family, his job, his acquaintances.

They would leave no stone unturned. Even Jamie Sampson's name came up as a hostess at the yacht club who had become a good friend of Montegue. Jeffry wasn't sure about her past. "But she was very friendly, and seemed like a nice lady." Julie was a hundred percent in agreement.

"Does he always wear a white suit?" Kit asked.

"Heavens no!" Jeffry and Julie both laughed. Julie answered. "He has a full wardrobe of colors. He always looks nice."

Bernell looked at her watch. "I understand you have a flight at eight. We'll contact you. Are all these numbers now working?" She showed them her list of numbers. "We wouldn't want a repeat of Davie's experience."

Smythe read the list, nodding his head. "Yes, these are all correct. The house is open now. Everything's back on. You guys find Monty. If everything's alright, we'll throw a party and celebrate. And I insist that you all come—you too, Mrs. Jackson."

Bree and Kit exchanged snickering glances.

Julie Smythe smiled and agreed. "God forbid this turns out badly."

"Amen to that," Kit said. Bree and Bernell made it unanimous.

The Smythes were hardly out the door before the phone rang and Abby buzzed Bernell. When she picked up the phone, Thomas said, "Good news! Jeffry Smythe has returned to the living. We haven't talked to him yet, but we wanted you to know he's home."

Bernell laughed. "Never mind, Thomas. He just left here. I think he's a big fat jerk, but at least he's paid Davie and that ordeal is over. And get this. Bree has also learned that Montegue might not be dead, but he is still missing. It's a long story."

"You want us to come back?"

"No. Talk to Bree." She called Bree to the phone and Bree filled him in about the mugging and the still missing Montegue. She gave him her projected description of the mugger. "See if you can find out who that is. I have a hunch it's somebody in Chesapeake that followed him down here. Montegue was carrying $10,000 in cash."

"FWEET WHEW! Thomas whistled. When he hung up the phone, he winked at Adam. "How about a trip to Triple M today?"

"Finally! I'm ready! I told you we needed to go there, but you were scared we'd get in trouble." Adam teased.

Thomas whacked him on the back of the head. "AIGHT now! It wasn't Bernell I was scared of. It was you! I was afraid YOU would get us in trouble."

Adam grinned.

Chapter 54 And They're Off!

Tuesday morning, April 16

Again it was a lovely ride through the countryside where Adam and Thomas had admired the horses. When they reached the roadside stand where they had stopped, Thomas slowed down. It was closed. "Guess we won't be asking them anything today," Adam said.

Just past the stand, Thomas turned into the driveway that led up to the main building, a white plantation-style mansion with round columns and a porch across the front.

"Just out of curiosity," Thomas said, as he turned into the driveway.

"You're kidding," Adam said. "Are you going up there?"

"Just reading that sign," he pointed to the 4 x 8 white sign posted at the driveway entrance.

Seashore Farms in blue foot-high letters. Below that in smaller letters was J. J. Smythe Associates then an address and phone number.

"J. J. Smythe," Adam read. "That's the man we've been looking for."

Thomas laughed. "Ironic, isn't it? We were right here and could have asked those ladies Friday if we had seen this sign."

"But you got more interested in that brochure and we went back the other way."

"Well, I don't reckon there's any need to worry about him anymore. Bernell talked with him today, right there in her office."

Adam's phone pinged--a message from Bree. He held it up for Thomas to see a picture of a man and woman dancing. Her text said, "Jamie Sampson and Martin Montegue?"

"Bernell said Montegue worked for Smythe." Thomas took the phone and studied the picture. His phone pinged and he had the same message.

"There's a car turning in behind us," Adam said. "You're going to have to drive on up there."

Thomas crept on up the driveway and parked, but he didn't get out. He faced Adam. "Okay, they thought he was dead, but now they think he's not. But is he back here or down there?"

"Sounds like they think he is still there, but Bree thinks the mugger was from here. You know they expect miracles, don't they? I mean, how are we going to find out who a mugger was in Claxton, just because she thinks he came from here?"

"Honestly, I don't think it's their job to find out who a mugger was."

"Nor ours either."

"I do think Bree gets carried away. Are you getting the feeling we're wasting our time here?"

"Bernell might if she knew we went to the beach this weekend."

"We were working. Just because we had fun at the beach doesn't mean we weren't working. We picked up right much info from Gloria and Karen Saturday."

"Yeah, we did ask a lot of questions about the people in the area. Gloria didn't know much, but Karen was pretty savvy. She used to work at the yacht club and had heard of the Smythes but didn't know anything much about them. We didn't ask her about Montegue. And we didn't know anything about Jamie Sampson then. Maybe we should ask her about them when we get back to the motel. We can show her this picture now."

"You know, If Montegue worked for Smythe, and Smythe owns this place, we have to go in there." Thomas was already opening his door.

Adam crawled out of the passenger side and the two climbed the steps to the veranda. "Sure feels like the Old South doesn't it?"

Thomas just said, "It's a beautiful place."

Inside, the high-ceilinged lobby was just as beautiful, but the theme was more Western with pictures of horses and trophies on shelves. A gift shop on one side had a variety of horse memorabilia and a rack of assorted brochures.

"Is this a hotel?" Adam whispered.

"No," the lady behind the counter whispered back. Adam laughed. "Oh, sorry, it just looks like a hotel lobby."

"Actually, this is the lobby where people check-in when they come thru. But it's not a hotel. We have people spending a week at a time here on the ranch to learn to ride. We have week-long sessions, but some people just come in for the day also. Are you gentlemen interested in lessons?"

Adam and Thomas were both shaking their heads. "I didn't think so," she responded. "You look more like…"

"We're looking for Mr. Smythe," Thomas interrupted before she could make any more guesses. Adam looked at him and wondered, *what is he up to? He knows Smythe is not here. He's in Claxton.*

"Oh, are you from the IRS?" The lady with a name tag that said GALE was determined to keep guessing.

Thomas and Adam both laughed. "That's the first time we've been mistaken for the IRS," Thomas said.

Adam had no idea where Thomas was headed but jumped in. "Actually we are looking for Martin Montegue, but we heard that he worked for Mr. Smythe and thought he could tell us where to find him."

Thomas nodded thinking *that was good.*

Gale laughed. "I was joking about the IRS. No, Martin Montegue does not work for Mr. Smythe. They're partners. Just up the road is Triple M Bar and Grill. Mr. Montegue runs that. Or rather he owns it. Someone else runs it for him. You could go on up there. Just about a mile. It's a good place to eat, too."

"Triple M Bar and Grill," Thomas repeated. "Oh, I've heard of that. It's an Off-Track Betting place, isn't it?"

She looked at him a little suspiciously. "Yes. It's legal. But don't go in there and say you're from the IRS. You'll clear the place in one minute."

"Really?" Adam asked innocently, "Why?"

She laughed at him. "Well, you're supposed to report what you win from gambling to the IRS, aren't you? I'm sure those guys don't."

"I bet they lose more than they win. So they could deduct that."

She looked at him wondering just how young he was. "It doesn't work that way, does it...?"

"Johnson!" Thomas said because she was looking at him and searching for a name. "That's what I've heard. That's why I don't gamble. This is Adam. Adam Brothers. He's older than he looks, but he's never gambled either."

Adam pretended to be angered. "Do you have to tell everything?"

Gale laughed. "No problem. I didn't hear a thing. So what is it, really, that you guys want?"

Busted, Adam thought.

Thomas was serious. "We really are looking for Mr. Montegue. We did not know he owned the Triple M. We'll go on up there. Thank you. You've been very helpful."

"Anytime," she said. "You fellows have a nice day. And Good luck!"

Back in the car, Thomas said, "I don't think we handled that very well."

Adam buckled his seatbelt. "Yeah, we went in unprepared. But I think it worked out okay. I'm never going in there again though."

Thomas backed up and headed the car back down the driveway. "You know, it makes a little more sense now, Montegue having so much cash with him. I bet those betters bet with cash all the time."

Adam said, "Yep. That does make sense. But then I'm too young to know anything about gambling."

"Get over it," Thomas said. "Let's go in there and eat and figure out what to say to the manager."

"What if we just tell the truth?"

"That's an option," Thomas agreed. "But we will not mention that Montegue had a lot of cash on him—and we're not from the IRS!"

Thomas pulled into the spacious parking lot which was about half empty. Mid-afternoon on a Tuesday was not a busy time for a bar and grill. A good time for them to be here.

When Thomas and Adam stepped inside, they were ignored. A half-dozen men sat at the lunch counter yelling at four televisions mounted on the wall above the menu. A man in a red plaid shirt yelled, "Go Jack go!" bouncing on the seat as though he were riding.

Next to him, a man in a white shirt and red tie, with his shirt sleeves rolled up, was pounding his fist on the table. "Come on Bonnie Baby!" Words at the bottom of the screen indicated a live thoroughbred race from Florida's Gulfstream Park.

Adam and Thomas stood and watched, unnoticed. The eyes of everyone in the room were glued to the television screens, all showing the same thing. A whoop and holler and the race was over. One man blurted an expletive, and others began moving around grinning or shrugging defeat.

Through an arched opening, Adam could see three pool tables in an adjacent room. Television screens were on the walls in that room, too. In all, Adam counted forty TVs streaming content from the race. A few bettors sat at high-top tables, a few were at the bar. One patron had his own seat cushion. A couple of tellers accepted bets as men shuffled through a line. An ATM sat between the tellers' windows.

Some people at regular other tables were reading pamphlets. Thomas picked up two from a rack and handed one to Adam. They sat down at a regular dining table and studied schedules and printouts of race statistics, horse and jockey names, past performance times on dirt and turf tracks. They were not familiar with the horse racing jargon but it was fascinating.

Adam picked up a food menu. "This I can understand," he told Thomas.

A cheerful, dark-haired girl with a black skirt and a white apron came over, said her name was Rose and asked if they would like to order something. Her white cap matched her apron and both had Triple M embroidered in black.

Adam ordered a Mile-High Hamburger which was really just six inches high but loaded. Thomas ordered a Sloppy Joe that was just about as thick. As they munched on their food, they observed the patrons and listened to the cheers and groans.

There was something addictive about the excitement and high emotion of the Triple M. When the waitress brought their check, Thomas laid down a twenty for the tip and asked if she could tell him if the manager was here.

"Are you IRS?" She asked coyly.

They laughed. "That's the second time today we've been asked that," Adam said. "No, we are not."

Thomas opened his badge showing that he was a detective from B.B. Jackson Investigations. She backed off, afraid to say anything else.

Shaking his head, Thomas said, "It is okay. Nobody's in trouble. We're just looking for someone."

She motioned her head to a man wearing a cowboy hat sitting alone in the front corner of the restaurant. "Wilson Cranston."

A friendly looking gentleman with a short white beard, he looked a lot like Colonel Sanders of the chicken fame. Except for the hat. On his table was a stack of pamphlets like the one they had been reading. He was talking on his cell phone, then laid it down.

Thomas and Adam worked around to his table and Adam stuck out his hand. "Hi. Mr. Cranston, I'm Adam Del Vecchio, you've got a great place here. This is my partner Thomas."

Mr. Cranston shook their hands. "Gentlemen, what can I do you for?" They liked him immediately which made their next part easier.

He motioned for them to sit and pushed the stack of pamphlets out of the way. "I take it you're not here to place a wager."

Adam laughed. "I never have, but it sure looks fun."

Thomas gave Adam an evil eye. "Mr. Cranston, we're looking for Martin Montegue," he said as he opened his badge to identify himself.

"I thought you might be," Mr. Cranston pulled out a pipe. "Can't smoke in here, but I can chew on it. You mind?" They smiled and shook their heads.

"You're the fifth one in a week looking for Monty."

"Really!" Adam and Thomas chimed.

Mr. Cranston sighed. "Yeah, that ex of his has had detectives out here. She came once herself, and then yesterday Jeffry Smythe came looking him. I didn't tell any of them anything. What's your story?"

Thomas flipped his phone out with the picture of Jamie Sampson and Montegue dancing, and before he could say anything, Cranston said, "That's what I figured."

"What do you mean?" Thomas asked. "Do you know her?"

"That's Jamie. They've been seeing each other and when he didn't come back, I figured they'd run off together. Where'd you get that from?"

"Our client was at one of Smythe's parties and took the picture. This was just one out of a bunch of pictures. But when he was supposed to meet them and went missing, they asked us to find him. They were worried about him."

Cranston squinted at both Adam and Thomas long and hard, and finally said, "There's more to it than that. What happened?"

Thomas and Adam looked at each other and nodded. This was a smart man. It was time to tell the whole truth. What they knew of it anyway. They opened up.

Cranston listened intently and nodded occasionally as they talked, then said, "You say he is alive then?"

"Yes, hopefully. But they can't find him. For a while, they thought he was the body pulled from the river, but Jamie has identified the body, and it was not him. She didn't know who it was, but it was not him. It was the mugger who had tried to rob them."

"I told him he should not carry that cash."

Adam's eyes widened. "You knew?"

"Course. He's my buddy. He's my boss, but we're friends, too. You say they were mugged? Hmm. There's a guy that's been hanging around here. He lost a bunch of money on a wager. He got mad and accused Monty of rigging a race. Which is absurd because we don't have anything to do with the races. We just stream them. His name is Cully Solomon."

Thomas jotted down *Cully Solomon.*

"I'd lay odds he followed Monty out of here."

"That's exactly what Bree guessed," Adam said to Thomas. "Smarty pants."

"He hasn't been around in a couple of weeks. I figured he'd got over it."

"Any idea where he lived?" Thomas asked.

Cranston raised his arm and snapped his fingers. "Hey, Rosie." She came over to take his order. Instead of ordering food, he said, "Run back there and see if Margie can look up Cully Solomon's address."

"Sure, anything else?" She poised her pen to write. He shook his head and motioned her to go.

Thomas and Adam looked at each other with raised eyebrows, somewhat impressed. "Sweet," muttered Adam.

"Now what?" Thomas closed his phone and put it in his pocket.

"Let me know what you find out about Solomon." Mr. Cranston reached into a brass horse cardholder and pulled out a business card for each of them.

"What about Jamie?" Adam asked as he slipped the card into his pocket.

"She's a good girl. Got in a little trouble about ten years ago. Drugs I think, but she's been clean ever since. I'd put her up against that strumpet he was married to any day."

Rosie returned and handed Mr. Cranston a yellow note which he handed to Thomas.

"So what do we do now?" Adam looked at Thomas.

"We go to 1107 Bay Street," Thomas said, reading the note.

They stood up; both shook Mr. Cranston's hand and expressed their gratitude.

Adam said, "You've got a super place here. And the food is great, too."

"I know." Cranston nodded and smiled.

He winked at Thomas and then said in a serious tone, "Please, do get back up with me about Monty." He stressed, "Any time, day or night."

Thomas assured him he would and gave him a card with their numbers also.

As they slipped back in the car, Adam said, "Wow! That was good food and a good meeting! I like that fellow."

"It's five o'clock, call Bernell and tell her where we are," Thomas said as he punched the Bay Street address into the car's navigation system.

Five miles away, it was a modest neighborhood. The house at 1107 was locked. Thomas noticed mail spilling out of the mailbox. He didn't touch it.

Adam spoke to the neighbor who was watering flowers while her little boy was riding a tricycle up and down the walkway.

She had not seen the neighbor in a couple of weeks. "He keeps to himself. He's in and out of jail. You might want to check there."

"Thank you," Adam said and waved goodbye to the little boy who waved back.

There was no Cully Solomon at the jail, nor the hospital. It was eight o'clock before they called Bernell back.

"Stay there," she said. "I've got one more mission for you."

Chapter 55 The Good Samaritan

Wednesday morning, April 17

Lillian opened the mailbox and noticed a bill from the hospital. Neither she nor Isaac had been. She figured it was for the gentleman from the homeless shelter. "YIKES!" She showed it to Isaac. "Merry Christmas," Isaac said.

"Well, God expects us to share our blessings. It's sort of like the Good Samaritan in the Bible isn't it?" It made her feel good to make that comparison. Isaac agreed. "Yeah. That's exactly how it is. What do you know about that man? Anything?"

"Only that he had a concussion. He's recovering from that, but he still does not have his memory back. And they don't know who he is. At the hospital, they call him John Wellsly."

Isaac laughed. "I don't know why that struck me funny. Poor fellow. Couldn't they identify him from his fingerprints?"

"Bree says not unless his prints are in the database. And obviously, they're not."

"Oh, you talked to her about him?"

"The next day after Davie showed us Jeffry Smythe's picture and we decided it was not Smythe."

"Well, you reckon our John Wellsly could be the missing man now? Montegue?"

"I think two plus two is four, Isaac. I'll go up to the hospital and see what they know. They won't tell me much over the phone. Even though we're paying for it. Isn't that something?"

A knock on the door interrupted her, but before she could open it, Davie came it. "I just wanted to stick my head in." He was all smiles.

"Yes, I know you're the happiest man in Claxton right now," Lillian hugged him.

"Maybe so. You got any Mountain Dew?" He opened the refrigerator.

"In the pantry," Lillian pointed to the back of the kitchen. "I'll get you a glass of ice. Get me one, too. Isaac, you want one?"

Isaac shook his head, but he sat down at the table. This had been the Wellsly conference room for years even before Bernell built her agency. It was still a good place to hang out, sunny and cheerful, with an Italian provincial table that could be expanded to seat twelve, but today it would only seat six.

Lillian set a plate of homemade pretzels on the table along with the two glasses of ice.

Davie set the two Mountain Dews on the table and took a chair on the side next to the window. "I just wanted to come see you. I feel like I did that day ten years ago when everything was over and Rev. Rutherford took George and the boys."

"I'm sure you do. I feel sort of like that too," Isaac said.

"We had us a little prayer meeting last night," Lillian munched a pretzel. "It's like prayers are being answered all at once. They arrested her Sunday, and you got the fish box that was buried, and now Smythe has dropped out of the sky and even paid you. It's praise time."

"I got a call just now," Davie said in a serious tone.

"Oh, no, what is it?" Lillian laid her pretzel down. Her first thought was Mike Riley and his accusations.

Isaac squinted at Davie waiting for the other shoe to drop. He also thought about Mike Riley.

"Well, I wanted to get your advice." He opened his bottle and poured the Mountain Dew on ice. "A man at Yarrows Yacht Club called me. They are so impressed with Jeffry Smythe's yacht that he wants me to build him one."

"Oh. What a relief. You had me scared for a minute." Lillian chomped down on her pretzel and Isaac chuckled.

"Well, he hasn't even seen it yet. All he has is pictures. Julie took a lot of pictures yesterday after they talked with Aunt Bernell. And she was showing them to her friends this morning at their club. Now they want to plan a christening party Friday. And they want me and Jenny to go."

"Hmm." Lillian poured her drink on ice and watched as it fizzed. The last place she wanted Davie to go was back to Chesapeake to a party.

"The yacht won't even get there until tomorrow," Davie said.

"They seem like impetuous people," Isaac concluded.

"Does that mean you think I shouldn't go Friday?"

"What do you want to do? What does Jenny want to do?" Lillian quizzed him with her fingers crossed under the table.

"Neither one of us wants to go." Davie sat back and looked at his grandparents. "I think they should not rush things that much. They don't even have it; something could go wrong on the trip up there. Alex will let me know when he arrives. He and Pete and Billy are going to fly back or else rent a car." He shuddered to shake off a thought and blew a long breath. "Besides, I'm not even supposed to leave town yet."

Isaac sympathized. "I know. That car and all. But I have faith that that's gonna all be over by Friday. Just let the Lord handle it. Bernell is working on it. You've done all you can."

"Yeah, but it was me that got us into that mess."

He sipped on his Mountain Dew. They didn't say anything. He'd confessed everything, he'd made things right. He'd been accused of murder and even though signs pointed to his innocence, the officer was still not convinced. Finally, he said, "I know what to do now."

"Care to tell us?" Isaac probed with a glint in his eye. He already knew.

"We're not going to Chesapeake for a long time. I just wanted to see if you thought I should go as a business thing. But you know what? I'm not going, even if everything is cleared up by then."

Isaac beamed at his grandson. Lillian patted him on the hand. "Good decision. There'll be plenty more boats you can build. You've learned a lot from this one."

"You got that right!" Davie blew another sigh.

Isaac said, "You will build more yachts. But you don't have to start on one this week. Make a file, evaluate this project from beginning to end. You've had some ups and downs. You had to expand your building and hire more workers. Now that that's done can you keep them on? Do you need all that building? Do you even know how much you profited from it?"

Davie shrugged and shook his head. "Not really. I'm getting low. I've had to cut some back on their hours. It makes me feel bad. And I feel bad that I may have to let Alex go now that the project's done. But what are you gonna do?"

"You need to plan better Davie. I think you went into this without a real plan. You've been flying by the seat of your pants, so to speak. You need to evaluate. Next time you'll go in it with your eyes wide open. I expect you will get calls from that group up there in Chesapeake, and, no doubt, from others that the Smythes show off to. But be prepared to do it from a strictly professional perspective. Have you been watching your Aunt Bernell? She knows how to run a business."

Davie grinned. "You do too Grandpa. Look at the Gristmill Restaurant and the whole resort out there."

Lillian and Isaac looked at each other remembering the origin of that venture. For the next few minutes, they reminisced and told Davie about the dream they had, and how they asked God to reveal what He wanted them to do. How they had put out a fleece, and God started making things happen. How Lillian's mother had not spoken to her for so long and disapproved of their marriage, and how one day, out of the blue, she called and everything started coming together. They had prayed so long for reconciliation between Lillian and her mother, and only God could have moved like that. And how he had led them every step of the way, and their restaurant had been the first in Claxton to serve all races with no discrimination.

"So what you're saying is you can't go wrong if you let God be the head of your company, right?"

"That pretty much sums it up," Isaac and Lillian agreed.

"I'm gonna put Alex in charge of evaluation and planning. He can help me with that."

"How strapped are you financially?" Isaac was always ready to help.

"More than I'd like to be. We made a lot of money. In all, he's paid me a little over $2.4 million. But we have spent a lot of money. I had to contract the engine and electrical work. I didn't make anything on that. And I hired on more specialty help. It's gonna be hard to keep Alex on, but I think you've solved that. I'll put that last ten thousand from Smythe into saving Alex's job. Maybe in a month or so, we'll get another yacht. In the meantime, I'll do what you said. I'm sure Alex has wondered, but I've been in such a state we haven't talked about it. He may already be looking for another job, and I'd hate to lose him. I'll call him today and mention this."

"And don't forget to put God in the executive seat," Isaac said.

Davie laughed. "I guess that position was vacant. But it's filled now. I've been praying about what to do, and here I am talking with you, and it sounds like my prayer is being answered in ways I hadn't even thought about."

"God does things like that," Lillian said. "And like Isaac told you, that murder suspicion is going to be cleared up soon. I'm trusting for that."

Chapter 56 Hospital Visit

Wednesday afternoon, April 17

When Davie left, Lillian brushed her hair and put on a little makeup, and headed to the hospital. She didn't know where to go but asked for the room of John Wellsly. The attendant scanned the patient list and handed her a hall pass with the number P-456. "Hmm, Psychiatric Division," she noted.

She had no idea how she would handle this. Up the elevator four floors and down the hallway, she wished she had brought flowers or something. She should have stopped at the gift shop. She never liked to go anywhere empty-handed. But here she was, empty-handed to visit a stranger and possibly..."

She tapped on the door and a voice said, "Come in."

Half sitting up with the hospital bed raised at his back, he opened his eyes to see a graying lady in sensible navy shoes, with navy pants, and a light blue top that matched her sparkling eyes.

"Hello," she extended her hand, greeting him with a smile as though he were someone special.

She couldn't be staff because she wasn't wearing a badge or carrying a chart. For a moment he wondered if that could be his mother. He would not have recognized her either.

Automatically, he reciprocated with his right hand.

"John Wellsly?" she asked.

"That's what they're saying," he answered.

"I'm Lillian Wellsly," she introduced herself. He was taken aback. "Are you my mother?" he asked.

She laughed. "I have only one son, and his name is Jimmy, but I guess, in a way, I'm at least your guardian."

He lost his smile. She picked up on the confusion. "It must be awful not to remember your real name, nor how you got here."

His smile returned. "It is very frustrating."

"I understand you had a big lump on your head. That's some shiner."

"They said I had a concussion, but it is better. I don't have bad headaches anymore."

"You're certainly looking better than you were the last time I saw you," Lillian said.

"Where did you see me?"

"At the Manor—ah—the homeless shelter. I volunteer there, and Mr. Harmon told me about you. We called the hospital, and since nobody knew your name, we gave you one."

"Well, I do appreciate it. Am I related to John Wesley?"

"Oh, you know about John Wesley?"

"And Columbus and George Washington. I just don't know about me."

"Well, ain't that a crock!" She said with her hands on her hips.

He laughed. She thought, *he hasn't laughed much lately. That's good for him.*

She relaxed her hands. "Our name is similar, but, no, we're not the Wesley's. We're the Wellsly's. Close but no cigar."

He laughed again. *Oh, good,* she thought.

A nurse tapped on the door and came in. "Time for your medication, Mr. Wellsly. Oh, "Hey, Aunt Lillian."

Lillian turned around. "My word, Kenzie. I thought you were still in pediatrics."

"I graduated," she said. "When I took off a few years to have Milly and get her into preschool, I lost my place. They put me up here when I came back. But I love it here, too. I get to meet the sweetest people."

She smiled big and offered her patient a paper cup with water and a pill, which he took dutifully.

He had watched their interchange and said "Everybody knows each other but me."

"Now, now, Johnny, be patient. You'll get it all back soon. I have it on good authority."

"Who?"

Kenzie pointed upward. "I've been praying for you."

He smiled a half-smile and said, "Thanks."

Lillian followed Kenzie out and asked, "Do you know anything? What are they doing to help him get his memory back? Can you tell me anything?"

"He has been assigned to Dr. Rosenberg. She'll be meeting with him tomorrow. We hope she'll be able to help him."

Back in the room, Lillian said to the patient, "I hear you're getting a wonderful doctor tomorrow. She's a good person. I highly recommend her. Have they been feeding you good?"

He laughed. "You must be a Jewish mother."

Lillian was astonished. "Oh, my, gosh! I am!" She was speechless for a moment. He chuckled at her reaction.

Oh, good, he's laughing again, flashed through her mind.

She had intended to ask him some questions, mention Jeffry Smythe and see if it triggered his memory. Suddenly, she realized she might be getting ahead of God. All God wanted her to do was help him relax. Take the edge off the fear and confusion that he must be going through.

"Well, I'm glad to see you progressing," she said honestly. "I'll tell Mr. Harmon. I don't know if you remember him or not, but he was the bearded guy at the shelter that helped you."

"I remember him. I thought I was in the hospital and he was the doctor. Only he looked more like Santa Claus."

"Oh, somebody else you remember, Santa Claus." He laughed out loud.

Her heart bubbled with joy at seeing him experience that emotion.

"Well, I can't stay; they'll be running me out. Could I pray with you before I leave?"

He shrugged. "Sure." She put her hand on his shoulder and prayed, "Dear Heavenly Father, I pray for this gentleman we have named John Wellsly. He has lost some of his memory. But I know that you know who he is. I pray that you will continue to heal his injury and heal his mind. Restore him to himself. Restore his memory, restore his life. Restore his friendships. Most of all, I pray that you will open his heart to receive you if he hasn't already. Save his soul and secure him into thy kingdom. In Jesus' Name. Amen."

When she opened her eyes, she noticed his eyes were glazed as though his heart had been touched.

"Thank you," was all he said.

"I'll check on you again tomorrow," she said.

Again, he said, "Thank you," but he had a big smile.

Before she left the hospital, she stopped by the gift shop and ordered a huggable teddy bear to be sent up to John Wellsly P-456, with the note, "From your friend, Lillian."

*

On her way home, Lillian made an impulsive decision and stopped by the Agency without calling. She had to wait. She chatted with Abby a while then relaxed at the mesmerizing aquarium until Abby finally told her Bernell was coming out.

It was after five o'clock and Bernell's usual vitality had been zapped. It had been an arduous day. But she forced a smile and invited Lillian into her office.

Lillian sat in the chair Bernell offered and started telling her about her day. "Today instead of going out to the Manor, I went to the hospital to visit one of our homeless. I wanted to tell you about him. And also let you know that Zoey has been assigned to him starting tomorrow."

Bernell looked puzzled. "Is this a new case you're talking about, Lillian? You're killing me. I never worked so hard in my life."

Lillian laughed. "No. It's not a new case. I didn't want to jump to any conclusions, though."

"Okay. What's up?" Bernell resigned herself to taking on yet another case before she could get a break from the last ones.

Lillian started, "When I went to the soup kitchen on Wednesday of last week, he had been there since the Friday night before. Mr. Harmon had been taking care of him. That was the same day Jimmy saw the man in a white suit at the Gristmill Restaurant."

Bernell's ears perked up, Lillian continued. "We got him to the hospital. He had a concussion. It's been a week now and he still does not remember who he is. We named him John Wellsly because we had to take care of the bill."

Bernell laughed. "You named him John Wesley?"

Lillian laughed. "No, John Wellsly--like us. I signed him into emergency."

"Oh," Bernell laughed, then stopped. "Wait, go through that again."

Lillian rephrased, "We have a homeless man at the hospital who showed up at the shelter on Friday night--twelve days ago—with blood on his head, a concussion, and no memory of who he is."

"Martin Morgan Montegue. Hallelujah! Lillian." She jumped up, energized, came around the desk, and hugged her sister-in-law.

"I think you've broken our case. Did you say Zoey will be with him tomorrow?"

"Yes, that's what Kenzie told me today. I didn't tell her anything about what's going on, she may know, but I didn't bring it up. She was busy. But I figured you'd know what to do now."

"Yes! I need to call Zoey. I also need to get Bree and Kit on it. Bless you, my sister."

Lillian smiled as she stood up. *It's all coming together, Lord. Bring his memory back and let's get this thing over with. Thank you for what you are doing.*

She turned to leave and said to Bernell, "I'm going home now. I'll be praying God gives you the strength to get this resolved. I'm sure He will." Bernell flashed that familiar smile. "I'll call you."

Chapter 57 Dr. Zoey Rosenberg

Wednesday evening, April 17

Kit and Bree were almost at the back door leaving for the day when Bernell stopped them. "You ain't gonna believe this!" They hadn't seen her this excited since Sunday. Without further ado, they met her at the conference table eager to hear what had brought such change.

"Bree, I think you're gonna want to get up with Jamie Sampson. Might have to get Jeb's help on that. Or maybe they have access to the van, I hadn't thought about that. Anyway, you handle Jamie Sampson."

She looked at Kit. "Kit, pull those pictures Jenny and Davie brought us. Enlarge the pictures of the people at the party, especially the ones with the man we think is Montegue and anybody that could be recognizable if a person knew them."

"What am I gonna tell Jamie Sampson?" Bree wanted to know. "What's got you so rejuvenated? An hour ago, I thought we were going to have to scrape you off the floor."

Kit laughed at Bree's description but nodded. "Yeah."

"Oh, sorry, I did to you the same thing Lillian did to me. Guess it runs in the family." She laid her hands flat on the table with her fingers stretched out – no nail tapping. "I think Lillian's found Montegue!"

"I didn't know she was looking," Kit said.

Bernell laughed. "I think God puts Lillian in places to get things done. It's always been that way with her. You know she volunteers at the Salvation Army Soup Kitchen."

Kit nodded. "Yeah, at the old Magnolia Manor." Bree listened. The Magnolia Manor was before her time but she knew about it.

"The same day Jimmy saw the man in the white suit at the Gristmill Restaurant, this man showed up--about midnight--at the manor with a concussion. Mr. Harmon took him in and took care of him. He didn't know it was a concussion, but when Lillian went on Wednesday, he talked with her about him and they got him to the hospital. He's been there ever since. The man still does not have his memory, but I think it is Montegue. I don't have a picture of him." She pointed at Kit. "That's why your pictures are important."

Bree said, "And Jamie Sampson needs to go up there and see if that's him. Also, Davie's got to remember where he was Friday night. That will give him the alibi he needs to get Mike Riley off his back. I told Jenny that today. I couldn't get up with Davie. Well, this is good news, ma'am!"

Kit said, "If you want to go on home, Bernell, we can take it from here."

"No, I'm going to call Zoey first and find out what she suggests. She would probably want to see the pictures, too. I was thinking if he sees them it might trigger his memory, but I don't know. Zoey's the expert. Anyway, I'll call her. Y'all get on with your part."

Bree called the police department, "Edna, is Chief Jeb still there? I've got something important to tell him." She was put on hold.

Kit set up her laptop with the file of photos from Jenny and Davie. A daunting task in itself with almost a thousand pictures, but she started scanning and making selections to print.

Abby came to the conference room. "Aren't y'all gonna take a break for dinner?"

Kit pointed at them. "Bernell is on the phone with Zoey, Bree's on hold for the chief, and I'm printing pictures. We think we've found Montegue. Have you already locked up the front?"

"Yeah, I locked it behind Aunt Lillian. But I didn't want to leave y'all still working. Is there anything I can do?"

"Yes," Kit nodded. "Somebody's got to call Davie and Jenny. They need to know this."

"Sure thing." Abby started to her desk and Kit used her cell phone to call her husband. "Hon, I'm gonna be late, can you call in a pizza for dinner? We've just got a breakthrough in that Montegue case. I've got a ton of pictures to print. . . Yeah, we think he's a patient at the hospital with amnesia. I'll call you in a little bit. Thanks. Hon. You, too."

"Abby," Bree called out, holding her hand over the receiver, "You mind calling Tony?"

"Sure thing," Abby yelled back and went to her desk to call Bree's husband and Davie.

Bernell came back to the conference room. "Zoey said, yes, she'd love to see the pictures tonight if she could. She's still at the hospital."

Kit beckoned her to the laptop. "I've got the printer going. But I can email her some and let her look at them on her phone. That would be instant. I can still keep printing. She'll probably want Montegue to look at some pictures to see if he can recognize anybody."

"Oh, wait," Bernell said. "Don't print those with Davie on the diving board. And don't send them to her either. I don't know if she knows about that, and I sure wouldn't want her to find it out like this."

Bernell sat down. "Oops." Things were getting complicated. "Yeah, if they haven't talked to her, they need to. If Montegue's memory comes back, he might even mention that. And I know Davie would not want that."

She sighed. "I'll have to call him. Tell Abby." She went back to her office.

*

Jenny was setting the table when the phone rang. It had been wonderful to be free of the worry about Julie and Jeffry Smythe. They were still celebrating.

"Oh, hey, Aunt Bernell," she said when Bernell spoke. When Jenny hung up, she went to the den where Davie was watching television. "We've got a little dilemma," she said carefully.

"Oh? What now?" Davie asked, fearing what she would have to tell him.

"All your family knows about our fiasco at Chesapeake and they're okay. But, you know, we never did tell my family."

"I was hoping we'd never have to," Davie said.

"Well, listen to this." She proceeded to update him on the developments at the Agency. "And now Mom has been assigned to him and it will probably all come out about that party, and the DUI, and jail. What are we going to do?"

"Be sure your sins will find you out," Davie said. "I just have to call her and tell her. Ugh!"

"She's still at work at the hospital. You want to call her, or should we go down there, or what?" Jenny sat down beside him.

"Let's get it over with," he said.

"Well, you want to eat first, don't you?"

"No. I want to get it over with. Call and ask her to wait for us there. I'd rather tell her by herself. She can tell your dad."

Jenny laughed. "I know what you mean." She called her mom.

In twenty minutes there was a tap on Dr. Rosenberg's office door. She figured it was Jenny and Davie but couldn't imagine what the urgency was. Until they finished their story.

She smiled as she listened, then winced, then clenched her jaw, then frowned, then blew a long sigh of relief.

"Mom I thought you could keep a poker face when you're listening to people," Jenny said.

"Yes, other people. But you dragged me through the mud. I could feel your pain and fear. My heart almost stopped. You're my daughter and Davie's my son-in-law. I'm thankful to God that I am hearing this from you instead of hearing from a patrolman that you're dead on the highway up there. Thank God. And that's all I'm going to say about that."

"No, you have to tell Dad."

"I will."

She paused then said, "So this man, you think is Martin Montegue is connected to Jeffry Smythe who owns the yacht you built. And you have been charged with his murder, but now that he is found alive, the charges have not been dropped?"

Davie just nodded. Jenny explained, "Officer Riley still thinks Davie is involved because nobody knows what happened. His regaining his memory is a key to solving everything. We never met him that we know of, but he is in the pictures that I took."

Zoey said, "So the plot thickens."

They sat silent a minute digesting the weird circumstances. Finally, Zoey stood up and came around to the front of her desk, closer to Jenny and Davie. She leaned against the desk and looked at Davie. "Thank you, Davie, for coming forward like this. It took a lot of fortitude and grace. I'm sure it was very humiliating. In fact, I expect you've suffered a lot of emotional pain in the past couple of months."

Davie slumped in his chair. "Like you wouldn't believe."

"We had to tell you, Mom. Can you imagine counseling a patient and learning that he had just got your son-in-law out of jail?"

When that sank in, Dr. Rosenberg went back around and sat down in her chair. She leaned forward with her elbows on the desk and her thumbs propping her chin. "Maybe I should step aside and let another doctor take this patient."

Davie winced. "And then, if the hospital wants to know why? What then?"

"Oh, no, Mom," Jenny said, "I hadn't thought of that. You have to stay on it."

They all sat quietly for a couple of minutes, mulling the circumstances. Davie sat slumped, feeling like he'd been tried and convicted. Jenny laid her hand on his leg in an attempt to console him. Finally, Zoey spoke. "I can't let Bernell down."

She looked at the clock on the wall. "I want you to do something."

Davie and Jenny both sat up as she explained. "It's visiting hours. I want you to go up to P-456—that's his room. Lillian visited him today and I've heard it made a difference in him. Go up there and just say, something like 'My grandma came to see you today.' Both of you go. Don't ask him anything. Just be friendly. If he recognizes you, it could trigger a memory. I'll stay outside at the nurse's station. Just take a minute or two."

"Ugh!" Davie said. Jenny kicked his foot. "Okay. Let's do it," he said as he got up.

When John Wellsly saw the nice-looking young couple tap on his open door, he beckoned. "Come in."

"Hey," Davie said.

Jenny smiled and stuck out her hand, then Davie did the same.

"I'm getting popular," John mused. "Third visitor I've had today, not counting all the nurses and doctors. You're not a doctor, are you?"

"No," they both said and shook his hand.

"I run Burgundy Blue Boutique," Jenny said, "a decorating and art store."

"Nice," he smiled as though he understood what that was.

Davie said, "I build boats."

John nodded again. "That's nice."

There was no sign of recognition, just awkward silence, and Jenny said, "You're wondering why we're here."

Davie took the cue. "My Grandma. She came to see you today, and, well..."

John laughed as though he understood perfectly. "Your Grandma--the Jewish Grandmother. I understand. Tell her I enjoyed meeting her today. Look. She sent me this."

He picked up the teddy bear and squeezed it. It said, "I wuv you."

They laughed. "That's my Grandma," Davie said.

Jenny said, "Well, we better go. We just wanted to say hi."

"Tell your Grandma hi back," he said. And they left, waving as they went out the door.

Zoey was close by listening. When they left the hospital room, she turned and headed down the hall. They followed her.

In the elevator, she said, "You did great. Just enough to plant a thought. Davie, it was good saying you build boats. That could trigger something. I'm proud of you both."

That certainly helped make up for the beaten-down feeling he had before they went upstairs.

She shut the door behind them when they entered her office then sat back down in her chair. They did not sit down.

"I'm not going to say anything about all that you told me," Zoey said. "I am a professional. I am going to proceed as one. He is my patient. He appears to be doing well. He has a good attitude." She smiled as she talked. "Your Grandma was a big boost for him today. And this little encounter was good. This just might be a win-win all around."

Davie looked at Jenny. "I'm hungry."

"Right. Mom, we need to go. We came up here as soon as Aunt Bernell called because--well you know."

"Yes, and Davie, you don't know how much I appreciate it." Zoey got up and hugged them both. "Things will get better. I feel it. It's already started, hasn't it?"

Davie smiled. "Yeah, I guess. Thank you for being understanding, Miss Zoey."

"We'll get through this," she patted him on the back which made him feel better.

Chapter 58 Relief

Wednesday evening, April 17

On the way home, Davie finally relaxed. They rode in silence. All the past few weeks had been such pressure, he felt like he had aged thirty years. Sometimes he had felt like he was going to have a heart attack. *I guess a guilty conscience can do that* he thought. Learning that Montegue was alive—or at least that they thought it was him—felt better than having Alana arrested.

He remained quiet as Jenny finished getting dinner on the table. It was still hot. *The crockpot is a modern miracle* he thought as he enjoyed his late meal. It felt good to fill an empty stomach and even better to have the weight off his shoulders. At least for the most part. He knew there would be a process, but now Riley had to back down.

"You know what?" He sounded as though a great thought had just struck him.

"What," Jenny asked.

"Now Riley can't accuse me of killing him. Hahaha. That's the best thing about it."

Jenny went to the refrigerator and pulled out a lemon meringue pie. "We can celebrate that!"

She handed him a huge slice of pie on a blue dessert plate and cut herself a smaller piece. Davie loved anything lemon.

"Yum! You know you're catching up with Mom and Grandma."

She laughed. "I have a long way to go, Davie, but that's the best compliment I've ever had."

Then out of the blue, Davie said, "I still think there's a moonshine jar of diamonds somewhere."

"I wouldn't be a bit surprised," she agreed.

He told her about his visit with his grandparents today and how wise he thought they were. She could not disagree.

"I'm keeping Alex on," he said. "I called him today. They've made good time. They were off the coast of Norfolk. You know, I hadn't mentioned anything about what he would do next, because I didn't know. I was dreading having to let him go. But after talking with Grandpa, I figured it out."

"Oh?"

"Yeah, and when I mentioned it to Alex, he sounded relieved. Guess it's been weighing on his mind, too."

"I can imagine. So what are you going to have him doing?"

"Evaluating and planning. We don't have any idea how much we made on that yacht. I mean we haven't kept it separate or anything. All Mack does is accounting. He doesn't analyze anything."

"Sounds like you've put some thought into it," Jenny put their dishes in the sink. "I'll finish this later. Let's go crash in the den a while. We haven't sat in there for days."

He picked up a knife and followed her. Before he sat down, he used the knife to extract the black listening device from the lip of the aquarium. "I guess she won't be listening to this anymore."

He went back to the kitchen, and Jenny could hear the garbage disposal grinding something foreign. She laughed and it felt good.

Chapter 59 The Mystery Man

Thursday morning, April 18

Jamie Sampson did not want to wait until Thursday morning to go to the hospital. But Zoey had gone home and the hospital would not allow late visitors. Bree consoled her. "Sometimes you just have to wait. I'll pick you up at seven-thirty. I think we can get you in there by eight."

Bernell called Zoey at home. "You see any reason Jamie Sampson couldn't go in to see the mystery man in the morning?"

"Not at all. Seeing her might bring him back. And that's all we want. I'll call the nurses' station and alert them." That's all it took for Bree to have clearance.

She arranged for Montegue's breakfast to be brought in by Jamie. As word spread, the whole ward was anticipating the outcome. The mystery man had been there a week with no visitors and no recollection of who he was.

A chaplain had visited him every day. And nurses and doctors had been in and out. He had seen no one else until Lillian showed up. Then Davie and Jenny. He did not know them.

Bernell decided that Bree should take the briefcase, empty of course, but Zoey had agreed that it could help to trigger his memory. She also suggested that Jamie wear what she wore when he last saw her if that was possible.

"It had blood on it and was torn. I just threw it away," Jamie fretted. "I couldn't let Zelda see it."

Bree ran home and found a blouse in her closet that was similar to what Jamie described and it fit. It was a red silk button-up blouse she wore over black slacks. Jeb let Bree get the red shoe and her outfit was complete. Everybody was eager for the mystery man to be revealed.

Bernell had created quite a stir among hospital and law enforcement officials now that she had a projected identity of the mugger. Jeb said Forensics would be working on that. If necessary, they would bring in Mr. Cranston from Chesapeake, who had agreed to come if they called.

When Jeb asked, "Why are you so persistent in identifying the mugger?"

Bernell replied. "Because I want to clear Davie and your deputy is determined to pin this on him one way or another."

"Well that's not going to happen," Jeb said.

"I know," Bernell said. "I'll see to it."

On a different matter, Jeb asked, "Have you heard anything from Thomas and Adam about that other?"

"I told them last night. It's 7:45 A.M. I doubt they've had time to do much yet," she said.

They all laughed, which helped to break the tension. Jeb said "I'm just so anxious to get this over with. I don't think I've slept since March."

Zoey said, "You need me to prescribe something."

"It's tempting, but no," Jeb said. "I think these bird dogs are going to flush it out soon. I've got a hunch."

Bernell agreed.

Jamie Sampson looked super nice in her red blouse and black skirt as she walked down the hall beside the breakfast wagon. Bree was with her, carrying a briefcase. When the wagon stopped outside Montegue's door, and the orderly tapped, a voice said, "Come in."

Bree went in ahead and pulled the adjustable table out for the food. Jamie carried the tray and set it on the table. "Is this high enough?" she asked him.

"Yes, that's fine," he answered. Bree laid the briefcase in a chair where he could see it. He noticed it but didn't say anything.

Obviously, there had been no instant recognition. As planned, Jamie said, "How long have you been up here, Monty? I was glad when they said I could come see you."

He looked at her and smiled, but it was obvious that he did not recognize her. "I'm not sure how long I've been here," he said. It did not register that she had called him Monty.

Bree said, "I wanted to find out where you will go when you're discharged. You'll soon be well enough to go and we don't have a plan yet."

He looked at her blankly. "Well, maybe back to the Manor? I remember Mr. Harmon. And my Jewish grandmother goes there."

"Okay." Bree made a big display of picking up the briefcase so he could see it. "I'll make a note of that. You have a good day, Mr. ah, Sir." She didn't want to confuse him with more details. Zoey had said, "Don't overdo it."

She left and Jamie stood by the bed looking at him as though she wanted to hug him goodbye, but just said, "I have to go. We'll visit later."

He looked as though he wanted to ask her something but didn't. On impulse she kissed him on the forehead and left, closing the door behind her.

In the hall, she burst into tears. She and Bree joined the others in the conference room. "He didn't remember me," she said sadly. "But that is Monty. No question whatsoever. Did you see the horse tattoo on his left bicep? He told me he got that when he went into the horse business five years ago. He owns Triple M in Chesapeake. Mr. Cranston runs it for him. Mr. Cranston is a very nice person. I've always liked him. Maybe if he came to see him, it would help."

Zoey said, "That's a possibility. But let's don't be too hasty. Let Monty, as you call him, absorb this encounter. He'll think about it all day. The nurses have already told him to buzz as soon as he recalls anything. He follows directions well. I'll be right here all day. Thank you, Jamie, for coming. It may be more helpful than you realize."

Bree told them how she handled the briefcase. "He might remember that later too," Zoey said. "Every case is different, but we'll see."

Bernell said, "Thanks for coming, Jamie." She looked at Bree. "I'll see you in the office later. At least we now know that this is Martin Morgan Montegue."

"Yes!" Jamie confirmed again. They all commented, grateful for this positive step.

Bree took Jamie back to the yellow house which they both had come to hate. She was sorry to have to leave Jamie there. The gray van was still sitting in the driveway. They both inadvertently shuddered when they saw it, and then caught each other's eye and laughed.

"Jackie won't drive it."

"What do you mean?"

"She goes to the library a lot. She's a reader. But she walks over there. She won't drive the van."

"Because it has that wheelchair lift on the back?"

"Maybe."

Bree had an idea. "Did Zelda have an invalid sister? I heard that was the reason for the wheelchair lift."

"Yes. We had to meet Zelda at Crest Lawn Rest Home in Chesapeake to come down here in the van. She said her sister had been with her a month and she was bringing her back for a while. Her name was Wanda. But we never heard anything about her again."

"Could I ask you a question? I mean, I haven't read any transcripts, so I don't know what the FBI asked you, but just out of curiosity, when did Zelda first get you in on her game?"

Jamie did not seem to mind Bree's questions. "Nobody else has asked me that. The end of January, in Florida."

"You mean she was in Florida then?"

"Yeah. We knew she was a nurse and looked after an invalid sister. She was driving the van then. She said her sister was in the hotel. She met us on the beach. She had been watching us and thought we would be perfect in her game. She made it sound really fun. It was like it was a TV show. Sort of like "Survivor" or something. We just had to keep it a secret. I know when they tape a television show, the contestants are required to keep it a secret until the show airs. So we just thought it was like that. And we had to go through training."

"Training?"

"At a firing range in Norfolk. She said it was just to develop a skill. We had to meet her at the nursing home parking lot to show her our credentials. She said we would leave there on March 25th at noon. Somebody had to drop us off at ten or we could leave our cars in the back parking lot. Mine's there now."

"Did you ever suspect that she wasn't on the up and up?"

"Not until we had been here a while. She changed. Then we got scared, but we knew we couldn't get out without her catching us. That morning when the helicopter picked her up, we were so scared. We just knew she had planned to kill us. I've never been so happy to see a cop in all my life. That's what Jackie said, too." She laughed a little.

Bree had to leave. "Well, I wish you luck, Jamie, in getting cleared of all this."

"Thanks, I just hope Monty gets his memory back. I miss him."

Bree smiled and touched her hand. "He will."

She watched Jamie go up the driveway and open the back door. "There's such a spirit of evil here," she said aloud and shuddered again.

As soon as she got on Claxton Boulevard, she called Bernell's cell phone. "You in the office yet?"

"Just walked in the door, why?"

"Well, sit down." She shared the information she had just learned. By the time she got parked and into the conference room, Bernell and Kit were at the conference table waiting.

"I talked with Thomas," Bernell said. "They're on their way to Crest Lawn Rest Home right now."

"This is going to be interesting. Think we ought to get Jeb in on it? I mean, I know he would want to. The FBI has sort of kicked him aside and taken over, but I think he did a better job than they have. OOPS. No offense, Kit."

"None taken. George is retired, you know. He's commented on how some of them these days are not as good as he was."

"That's true," Bree said and they laughed.

Bernell called Jeb. "You got time to come over here a minute? No, I'm not going to beat you up. Just come here."

She hung up grinning. "Silly man. He's on his way."

She looked at her watch. "Wonder what's happening in Virginia?"

"It's been ten minutes, Bernell," Bree laughed.

Chapter 60 Petals in the Wind

Thursday morning, April 18

At the hospital, Dr. Rosenberg answered her phone. It was the nurses' station by Montegue's room. "He keeps asking questions. He probably needs to talk with you." Zoey looked at her calendar. A consultation was scheduled for ten o'clock. She had thirty minutes. "Can you bring him down here to my office?"

She opened the blinds to let in the April sunshine. A dogwood tree was blooming a few feet from the window. Petals drifted in the breeze. It was the kind of day you wanted to be outside. She pulled the string raising the blind to the top. She could see some patients being walked around on the grounds. It was enclosed but spacious and the blue sky and sunshine made it feel like all outdoors. *I might get someone to walk him around out there,* she thought.

A nurse wheeled the patient into the room. "Thanks, Missy. I'll call when he needs to go back. Give us a few minutes."

She had Monty sit where he could see out the window. She believed in prayer and sunshine.

He didn't waste any time. "Who was that at breakfast?"

"Well, I wasn't there so it's hard to say. Someone on staff?"

"One lady acted like she was. But the beautiful blonde in the red blouse. I know her. I just can't place her. But when she was there, I just felt like she belonged there. She even kissed me on the forehead before she left. I wanted her to come back, but she didn't."

Zoey stood up and walked over to the window. She watched the petals floating on the wind. "You feel like one of those petals?" she asked him.

He watched a minute. "Pretty much. I've lost my grasp on reality." He watched the white blossoms dancing in the breeze. "The girl in the red blouse is one of those petals too, isn't she?"

Zoey smiled. "Well, I don't know about that. As I said, I wasn't there."

He watched the petals, then got up and walked over to the window. "Could I sit out there?"

"Sure. Those other people walking around are patients also. And nurses, of course. Or family. I see some family, too."

"I don't have any family."

"I'm sure you do, you're just away right now."

"No, I don't have any family. We never had any children and I'm divorced. My parents live in California. I never see them. I have a brother in Chicago."

"Oh, really? Then you do have a family. Would you like to see them?" Zoey was shocked at this line of discussion. "I thought you couldn't remember any of your past."

"Well, you know my Jewish grandmother?"

"You mean Lillian?"

"Yes, I know she's not my grandmother, but she's...ah, you know, the one last night. She's his grandmother. I had a grandmother like that when I was a boy."

"In California?"

"No, Chicago."

"Oh, so your brother in Chicago lives where you grew up."

"Yes, well, not in Chicago, but in the country, a couple of hundred miles west. We had horses."

Zoey remembered the horse tattoo on his bicep that Jamie mentioned, but he was wearing a robe now and she could not see it. She didn't mention it.

"So, you grew up on a farm near Chicago, and your parents went to California, and your brother stayed there. Where did you go?"

"I went to New York. I lived in Manhattan, and I had a job at the World Trade Center. But that was a while back. Before they bombed it. Well, they rammed two airplanes in it and the towers fell. I was so glad I had left when that happened."

"Where were you then?"

"I don't know. It's like a dream. I was not in New York and I was glad, but I don't remember where I was. And then I met that beautiful lady in the red blouse. I know that was her this morning. I just can't remember who she is."

"Are you sure you weren't dreaming this morning?"

"Maybe. But it was a good dream. Except for the other one, annoying me about where I was going to go when I leave the hospital. I don't want to go back there. I want to go home."

"Where is home?"

He put his hands over his face and rubbed his eyes, which hurt because of his injury. "I don't know. You're a psychiatrist. I see by the diploma. Can't you hypnotize me and make me remember?"

"Sometimes that works. Especially if a person experiences something they want to forget. You don't seem to fit that description. Unless you're suppressing something from your time with your parents? Not implying anything, just putting it bluntly, because it sometimes happens. What was your childhood like?"

"Fine. We talk. They just don't want to come east and I don't want to go west."

"Then maybe you could meet in the middle. Your brother would probably like that."

"That's a good idea. I'll call him."

He closed his eyes. "Oh, but I don't know his name. Jeffry. No. That's somebody else. It'll come to me. Then I'll call him." She smiled.

"Would you like to spend more time with the lady in the red blouse?"

"I would love to."

"I think that can be arranged. I'll get a nurse to take you back to your room. Get a nap, or just relax. I'll see what I can do."

"Thank you, Dr. Rosenberg."

Zoey buzzed the nurses' station. Montegue walked back over to the window. "Could we sit out there?"

"That's what I was thinking," she said. She handed a note to the nurse, who glanced at it and nodded.

Chapter 61 Crest Lawn Rest Home

Thursday morning, April 18

Pulling out of the Crest Lawn Rest Home parking lot behind the ambulance, Thomas called Bernell. "Chief Jeb was right. When Adam and I got here we asked to see Wanda Riggs and they directed us to her room."

Thomas and Adam were on the car phone both telling their experience at the nursing home. Bernell was in the conference room with Bree, Kit, and Jeb. She put the guys on speaker. Adam said, "I told them she was my aunt. She had called me saying she was dying and wanted to see me."

The office lady said, "I didn't know she was dying. She pointed us to the right hallway and said 'turn left and go to 321.' "

Thomas said, "When we got there, we just went in without knocking. Her husband was bending over her with a pillow and stood up real quick. She was so near gone, he probably didn't need to do that anyway."

Adam continued. "He said, 'I'm fluffing her pillow, trying to make her more comfortable.' "

Thomas laughed and said, "Adam kept pretending she was his aunt and said, 'Aunt Wanda, it's me, Adam. Can you hear me?' She was so lethargic, she couldn't respond. Her husband told us, 'Get out of here or I'm calling security. My wife is sick and doesn't need to be disturbed.' "

Adam said, "When we ignored him, he stood up and opened his coat enough we could see his gun in a holster. And then Thomas stood up and opened his coat a little so the man could see his gun in a holster. It was a Mexican standoff!"

"Hold on a minute," Thomas said. He was in tight traffic and needed to turn into the hospital driveway. The ambulance was already at the door.

Adam passed along that detail. Then he continued to recount the incident. "He thought I was a kid or something and didn't notice me. I punched 911 on my phone and stepped out the door. Right down the hall was a fire alarm which I thought was lucky. I pulled it and ran like the dickens to the front entrance. Everyone was running around. Patients were trying to run with their walkers. It was really funny."

"And you have a sick sense of humor!" Bernell said.

"Well, it stopped Riggs from killing his wife," Adam retorted.

"But he got away," Thomas said. "He ran out another exit."

Adam added, "The EMT's tried to resuscitate Aunt Wanda and rushed her on out to the hospital. When we were leaving, I saw the firetruck pulling in. I don't think anybody knows what happened."

"So you're saying Riggs got away?" Jeb asked, shaking his head. "Drat."

"For now," Thomas answered. "But he'll get caught. Law enforcement was everywhere."

"Okay," Bernell said, "Go on in the hospital and tell authorities what you know. They need to see if she's been poisoned."

"Right, we'll get back to you."

"We'll be here. Good luck," Bree ended the call.

Abby had joined Bree, Kit, and Jeb listening to the scenario.

"That was a close one wasn't it?" Bree commented.

"I guess Wanda can thank Montegue for saving her life," Kit said.

"How's that," Abby asked. "And who is Wanda?"

"That's what you get for being late this morning."

"One hour?"

"A lot can happen around here in an hour," Bernell said.

"Don't I know it! The doctor said my hand is better, though." She stretched her fingers farther than she had been able to.

"Great," Bernell said and stroked Abby's crippled fingers. "Bree, want to fill her in?"

Bree turned to Abby. "Okay, when I took Jamie Sampson back to the yellow house after she visited with Montegue this morning, we talked a little bit. I asked her about Zelda's invalid sister. Mainly because I didn't even believe there was a sister. I was surprised when Jamie said her name was Wanda. As soon as I left, I called Bernell and she called Jeb. Jeb already had suspicions, and that confirmed it. He made a few phone calls."

Bernell said, "I thought Alana had killed Zelda and taken her place, but there never was a Zelda Midget."

"What about that funeral?" Abby asked.

"No body!" Bree said.

"Nobody what?" asked Abby.

"There was no *body*. It was all staged to make it look like Alana had died," Jeb said.

"I knew it!" Kit said

"So that explains why I couldn't find anything else on Zelda Midget," Abby surmised.

"Yep," Jeb explained. "It was Alana pretending to be Zelda Midget pretending to be a nurse at the prison."

Bernell said. "I figured something like that."

"Right," continued Jeb. "The warden schemed with Alana to get her out of prison, then get rid of his wife, thinking he would leave the country with Alana and the diamonds."

"How'd you figure out all that?" Abby asked.

Zeb answered. "The warden created a file for a nurse named Zelda Midget. Then he let Alana pretend to be the nurse, then they faked Alana's death and got her out, and Zelda had to quit her job."

"Because it was the same person," Kit said.

"There were too many coincidences," Jeb explained. "Alana died and Zelda quit at the same time. Somebody in authority had to make that happen. But why? When I heard that the warden was on vacation, and the administrative assistant couldn't find a file on Zelda, I started investigating. That's when I learned that the New York prison system had no record of an employee named Zelda Midget."

"I wonder how he did that," Abby was curious.

Jeb reminded her that Alana was in solitary confinement and there was very limited access to her by others. But the warden can see anybody.

Abby said, "So then you figured that Zelda was Alana."

He leaned back in his chair and didn't say anything. Then he finally said, "You know I can't divulge a confidence."

Bree said, "We know there was an informant about the plan. But I think you already knew it was her."

He was reticent to speak, but finally leaned forward and said, "Well let's just say I gained a new respect for Louis Renoir."

Bree squinted at him suspiciously. "I wondered why you were so lenient with Jo Swan."

"Did he know Zelda was Alana?"

He held up his hands to stop the questions. "That's all I'm going to say about that."

Abby observed, "I guess by claiming to be a nurse, and taking care of an invalid sister, Zelda created a wholesome image."

Bernell nodded. "That was probably the plan. She created that game to find the diamonds, but her plan was full of flaws. For one thing, she had too many people involved."

They all laughed. "Too many cooks spoil the broth," somebody said.

Bree squinted at Jeb. "But Jeb, you didn't know about Wanda until I told you this morning."

"When you said Wanda was in Crest Lawn Rest Home in Chesapeake, it hit me. I had learned that Warden Rigg's wife's name was Wanda. Then it came together. Alana was supposed to get rid of Wanda, but she hadn't finished the job. So, yes, Abby, Wanda Riggs can thank Bree for saving her life."

"Not just me, all of us," Bree said. "Especially Thomas and Adam. That Adam is a character."

"Don't be talking about my buddy," Abby surprised them. They looked at her curiously, but she got up, opened the hallway door, and headed toward the front. "Gotta go to my station."

"Hmm," Bernell smiled. The phone rang and Abby came back in. "It's them again."

Bernell punched the speaker button on the phone. Thomas was already speaking. "Doctor says Wanda Riggs has been getting doses of arsenic for some time, but she will be alright eventually." Kit and Bree did a high five.

Adam said, "They caught Riggs, and he's spilling his guts."

Jeb and Bernell did a high five.

"He's in custody for attempted murder," Adam added.

Thomas said, "But listen to this. An officer told me there's a rumor that the warden was involved in a scheme with a known criminal. Helped her escape. They were going to kill his wife and leave the country with diamonds the criminal stole. But then she was arrested and he had to get rid of his wife because she knew too much."

"That would probably make a good movie," Kit said, and they all laughed.

"You want us to come home now?" Adam asked.

"Unless you want to take a couple of days and enjoy the beach." She was half-joking.

"I'm ready to come home," Adam said.

"I will stay here if that's alright," Thomas said. "I've kind of got a thing going here. I'll see you Monday."

"But you've only got one car," Bernell said.

"I'll hop a red-eye to Atlanta and Abby can pick me up," Adam suggested. "If that's okay."

"That'll work, just let me know the time," Abby grinned at Bernell and sashayed back to her desk. Everybody laughed at the new Abby.

"Woohoo," Bree said.

"I've learned that God sends special people into your life when you need them most," Bernell observed.

Chapter 62 Into My Heart

Thursday afternoon, April 18

Zoey watched the petals dancing on the wind and thought how appropriate. It always felt good to be able to help a patient. This one was interesting, but she felt confident that he was recovering. The nurses' station called; they did not have any information on reaching Jamie Sampson. "I don't either. Bernell did all that. Call B.B. Jackson Agency."

When Abby answered, she sent the call to Bree. Bree spoke to Bernell. "The hospital wants Jamie Sampson to go back out there. Should I go get her, or should she drive that van—she does not want to drive it."

Bernell shook her head. "Go ahead. But it's not our responsibility to transport them around."

"I know," Bree agreed. "What do you think of me calling Jeb and see if he'll send someone?"

"He's just left here. Wish they'd called ten minutes ago."

"She doesn't even have a phone. Hers is in the river. Those ladies have got to get their life back," Bree noted.

"Well, it's not our place," Bernell said.

"It's a pitiful case," Bree said. "They probably don't even have any money."

"Yeah, they can't use that counterfeit anymore," Bernell said. "You know what? They're Jeb's prisoners. He should take care of this."

"You know, I don't think Zoey even realizes that these are the ones that broke into Jenny and Davie's house—her own daughter's house," Bree said.

Bernell sat down. "Oh, gee whiz. I hate this. Well, Montegue needs his memory back. Davie needs to be clear of these folks. What do you think?"

"I don't know what I think. But this is what I know. They were charged with attempted first-degree murder, attempted armed robbery, criminal mischief, vandalism, trespassing, and recklessness. They could have all gone to prison. And still could. Their hearing for sentencing is tomorrow at 9:00 A.M. John Frederick is waiting for Davie, Jimmy, and Isaac to decide whether they want to press any charges. He says they could."

"And I could understand completely if they are not willing to just drop it," Bernell said. "In the meantime, we have to decide what to do."

"Let me go. I'll go out there and pick her up. I'll talk with her about some things. And besides, she has my blouse."

"Go ahead," Bernell nodded.

Bree stepped into her office, picked up her purse, and a Bible she kept in a drawer. She made a snap decision to stop by Walmart on the way. She picked up a TracFone and paid for the month. She used the name Jamie Sampson. She bought a modest phone, figuring it would be replaced soon, but right now, Jamie had nothing and she needed one.

When she arrived at the house, she tooted the horn and then went up to the front door and knocked. She cringed remembering the history of this house. Jamie opened the door, still wearing the red silk blouse and a black skirt. She looked like she had been crying. Bree certainly could understand that. "Can we talk?" she asked.

"Sure, come in," Jamie motioned for her to have a seat. "Can I get you something? Tea or a soda?"

"No," Bree shook her head. She felt like she would suffocate, but she didn't know where else they could go to talk. She focused on the carpet. At least it was new. The old one had a bloodstain at the foot of the stairs. "Is Jackie here?" she asked.

"No. She's still at the library. She practically lives over there."

"Umm," Bree uttered. She remembered when Giorgio practically lived over there. She closed her eyes a minute and breathed a silent prayer. *Oh, God, help me. There are evil spirits here. I rebuke them in the Name of Jesus. Dear Lord show me what to do.* She stood up. "Jamie. Our Mystery Man at the hospital wants to see you again."

"Oh, does he remember me?"

"No, not yet. But Dr. Rosenberg wants you to go back. She sent me to pick you up. Grab your purse."

Jamie laughed wryly. "I don't know why; there's nothing it in. But for looks," she picked it up.

"We'll put something in it," Bree said.

Jamie followed her to the car and got in on the passenger side. Bree climbed into the driver's seat. She was thankful for the ample seating and breathing room in her Lincoln Town Car. She had always liked driving a big car. It felt safer, and today she appreciated it more than ever.

Jamie started to buckle her seat belt, but Bree said, "Just a minute." She reached into the backseat for the Walmart bag and handed it to Jamie. "This is for you. You needed it today."

Jamie looked at her curiously as she opened the package. She smiled. "Is it already working?"

"Yes," Bree explained. "It has unlimited minutes for a month, a smartphone. But probably a cheaper version than the one you lost. You've needed one today though."

Bree punched in the number on her own phone and Jamie's phone rang. "Answer it."

Jamie smiled like a kid. "Hello?"

"Hi, this is Bree Ingles. You have my number in your phone now. Save it, and you can use it anytime."

"Aww," tears pooled in Jamie's eyes and slid down her cheeks. "You didn't have to do this. I'll pay you when I can--if I can."

"No need," Bree said and hung up the phone. "But I have something else for you. I told you that you would need that purse."

Jamie put the phone in her purse and looked up to see a Bible Bree was handing her. "What's this?" she asked. "I mean, I know what it is, but why?"

"Jamie, with all the charges against you, if you have to go to prison, you could spend years there. I know about the plea bargain, but Davie and Jimmy could still press charges. Two people were injured, and Davie's house was ransacked. So, I don't know."

Jamie's expression told Bree that she understood and feared just that. But she said, "We didn't go with her in that house."

"I'm glad to hear that," Bree said. She wanted to say something positive. "But even without that, it's bad enough."

Jamie bowed her head and nodded.

Bree continued. "One thing I know is that in prison, they let you read the Bible. People come in and hold services and pray with you. Jesus has saved a lot of people in prison. I guess it takes that for some people to stop and realize there is a God who loves them."

Jamie kept her head bowed. "I never prayed until now. For the past few days, I've done nothing else. I keep praying, please don't let me go to prison. I don't know if God hears me or not. It doesn't feel like it."

"Have you asked Him to forgive you for what you've done?"

She looked at Bree. "A thousand times."

"Because you were caught or because you are truly, truly sorry," Bree asked gently.

"Both."

"Have you ever read anything in the Bible?"

"Not really. When I was little, I went to Vacation Bible School at a church near us. But that is all."

"Let me show you something." Bree deftly turned the pages to John 3:16."

"Ever heard this?" She read aloud, "For God so loved the world that he gave His only begotten Son, that whosoever believeth in him should not perish, but have everlasting life."

"Sounds familiar, but I don't know what it means."

"It means that Jesus Christ, God's Son, died on the cross, to save you and me, and we will have eternal life if we believe in him. Because when they killed him on the cross and put him in a tomb, he rose again and ascended to Heaven, and we will do the same thing if we believe in him."

"And that's why we have Easter."

Bree was impressed. "That's exactly right! So you have heard."

"Well, I just thought Easter was a myth though. Or just another holiday like Christmas and Halloween."

"Christmas is when we celebrate the birth of Jesus Christ on the earth, and Easter is when we celebrate his death and resurrection."

"His birth on the earth?"

"Even before he was born to the Virgin Mary on Earth, He existed. He was God's Son in Heaven. But people were so bad on Earth, Satan was destroying them, but God wanted to save them, and He sent his Son to preach to them and teach them to love God. And Jesus preached and healed people and he had a following, but then they killed him on the cross, and God said he would save everybody who believed in his Son."

"That's kind of confusing."

"It is confusing if you don't believe. But when you believe in Jesus and pray to God in Jesus' Name, then God will answer your prayers. Just remember Jesus saves. That part is not confusing is it?"

"Jesus saves."

"Yes, Jesus saves and God forgives us all our sins when we ask Him and believe in Jesus."

Bree continued, hoping to say the right thing, "It's wonderful to be a Christian, Jamie. You always have a friend and a guide. He will always be with you to help you and lead you in the right direction. And at the end of your life, no matter how young or old you are, He will take you to Heaven. If you don't believe in Jesus, then I'm sure you have heard of the other place."

"Hell."

Bree was quiet. She wondered if she had explained this clearly. She had never felt good about her ability to witness to adults. It was easier to teach little children. Adults have a harder time accepting Christ on faith.

"How do you know all this is true?" Jamie asked, not cynically, but seemingly in earnest.

"Only by faith," Bree said.

"I might not have faith in anything," Jamie said sadly.

Bree thought a minute. "I have faith in you."

"What do you mean?"

"I believe you are truly sorry for the things you got involved in. I believe you have love in your heart for other people. I believe that you want to live the rest of your life better than this. And I believe that the only way you can do that is to believe in Jesus Christ, God's Son."

"Wow."

"I also believe that all you have to do is take the first step. Accept Jesus and he will multiply your faith. You will see how he helps you. That doesn't mean that you will never, ever, have a bad thought again or be tempted to do something you know is wrong. It means that you will have someone in your heart that is stronger than you are, and He will help you do the right thing if you believe in Him. When I was little we sang a song."

And Bree started singing slowly, reverently, in a clear, soft voice "Into my heart, into my heart, come into my heart, Lord Jesus. Come in today, come in to stay, come into my heart, Lord Jesus."

Tears streamed down Jamie's face. She nodded and her lips trembled. Bree sang it again slowly, softly, and Jamie cried. Finally. Jamie looked up at Bree and smiled. "I believe." The tone of her tears changed to rejoicing, almost laughing.

Bree squeezed her hand. "Me too. You won't ever forget this moment, Jamie. That is what it feels like when Jesus comes into your heart. Jesus saves you."

Jamie asked, "How do I keep this?"

"I am giving you this Bible. Read it. Get another one if you like the print better. But read it. It is your guide. Read these first books of the New Testament." She showed her Matthew, Mark, Luke, and John. "Pay attention to the red letters. They are Jesus's own words. Read in the Psalms." She flipped to Psalms in the Old Testament.

"Learn about David, he wrote the Psalms. Read the first book." She flipped to Genesis. "And learn about how God created the earth, Adam and Eve, and the Garden of Eden."

She flipped to Acts. "Read about Saul on the Road to Damascus, and how God changed his name to Paul, and how he preached and led people to the Lord. This is your handbook. Read it. Keep His words in your heart."

She handed Jamie the Bible. "And call me anytime day or night. Find a church where you can be with other people who love Jesus. Where a minister will preach the Word of God. It's a wonderful life, Jamie. No matter what comes your way, you will have Him in your heart and He will help you. You have taken the first step. I will pray for you to keep going. You will never, ever, regret it."

Jamie twisted around and hugged Bree and sobbed, "Thank you. Thank you for everything."

Bree patted her on the back. "You're welcome. Now let's go see Monty. Someday, maybe you can tell him about Jesus."

Jamie pulled away and buckled her seatbelt. She kept glancing at Bree and smiling. She held the Bible to her chest as though it were a lifeline.

Bree opened the console and pulled out a pack of tissues, took one for herself, and handed the packet to Jamie.

Jamie took them and laughed. "Thanks."

In the hospital parking lot, they paused to freshen up then headed for Dr. Rosenberg's office.

Zoey noticed Jamie's eyes immediately. "Is everything alright?"

"Yes," Jamie said. "Yes, everything is alright."

Bree winked at her and said, "I don't think you need me. I understand you'll be here a while. I'm running back to the office. Call me when you're ready to go back to the house."

"Okay," Jamie said.

Zoey nodded approval. "Thanks, Bree. I'll call you."

"Or I can." Jamie patted her purse and smiled. Bree smiled, too.

Back in the car, Bree called Lillian. "I need you to help me pray for something." Then she told her about Jamie.

"Oh, yes, praise the Lord. I will, Bree. That's wonderful. I'll pray right now."

As soon as Bree arrived at the office, Abby told her that Chief Jeb was trying to reach her. "He said to call him. He has another mission for you. It sounded important."

Chapter 63 Memory

Thursday afternoon, April 18

A nurse wheeled Montegue wearing hospital pajamas and a robe into Zoey's office where Jamie was waiting. He smiled when he saw her and stood up. But Zoey motioned for him to have a seat. Jamie was already seated and looking puzzled about the wheelchair.

Recognizing her concern, Zoey said: "It's just hospital policy." She spoke to the two of them. "I'd like you to talk some more. You may have known each other before this. If not, you can just enjoy the fresh spring air outside." She pointed to the window and they could see the dogwood tree blooming.

"Does he have to go out in the wheelchair?" Jamie asked.

Zoey shook her head. "No, you can just walk around. There are plenty of benches out there, and picnic tables. Just enjoy the outdoors and get acquainted." She felt like her patient was on the verge of a breakthrough and hoped that this might bring him out of the amnesia. It was an experiment anyway.

"Come with me." She led them down the hall to the exit and gestured across the greening lawn and parklike area evidencing spring. Red, pink and yellow tulips bloomed in beds by some of the trees. Several dogwoods would gently rain petals with a puff of breeze. White benches invited patients and friends. A few sat at a picnic table on the far end. A couple strolled a path that wound through the area.

Monty pointed at a white wrought iron bench with a filigree back that said welcome. As they sat down, Zoey gestured to her left. "That's my window. You know how to find me. I'll be in there for a while."

Jamie and Monty sat down on the seat. There was a moment of awkward silence, then Jamie opened her purse. "I just got a nice gift."

She pulled out her phone and explained. "I had lost my phone and someone gave me this."

"That is nice," Monty said as she handed it to him. He handled it familiarly, then gave it back.

She laid it beside the Bible then said, "I have something to tell you."

"Okay," he said and waited.

"I might have to go to jail."

His jaw dropped. "What?"

"I have done some very bad things, Monty. I didn't tell you because I was supposed to keep it secret. Now I know why. The woman I was working for got arrested. And we got arrested, too. Now I might have to go to jail. So this might be the last time I see you for a long time, or maybe ever. I want you to know that even if you never remember me, I will always remember you. I have had a wonderful time being with you, talking, and just being myself. You've been a good friend."

All the time she was talking, she kept one hand in her purse touching the Bible. Then she pulled it out. "I got another gift, too."

Monty did not know what to say, he just listened. If he had been a good friend to this beautiful lady, he was glad. He squeezed his eyes shut and tried hard to remember. But his mind was blank. He admired her and let her talk. Just as in the hospital room earlier, it felt right being with her. Her green eyes twinkled when she smiled. He liked that, but she seemed very serious now.

"Have you ever heard of Jesus, Monty? I just learned about Jesus, today. I never knew Him before. It feels so good to have Him in my heart. I've got a lot to learn, but she gave me this Bible. I never had a Bible before. But she's so pretty and so confident, and she sings pretty, too."

Monty didn't know who the other "she" was but decided just to listen. He could almost feel the joy she seemed to be experiencing.

"It felt so dark and sad in my heart. And all I could do was cry. But then I felt something else..."

She stumbled for the words. "Something peaceful," she looked around and gestured upward. "Like the sky."

He looked up. The sky was perfectly blue and without a cloud. "That's nice," he said and wished for that spirit of freedom.

He saw when she put the Bible back in her purse, and he heard a knock or a thump. Something loud. He looked around. There was nothing making noise. Petals drifted silently downward and landed at their feet. He reached down and picked up a dogwood blossom with all four petals intact. He studied it. The outer edge of each petal was reddish-brown and crinkled like it was damaged. There was something about that, but he couldn't remember what it was.

He heard that knock again, like a whack on his head. This time he jerked around.

"What's wrong?" Jamie asked.

"I don't know," he said. "I think I'm getting that headache."

"Oh, I'm so sorry! I've been talking too much. I'll take you back in." She stood up.

He pulled her hand. "No, it's stopped now. Please keep on. I'm enjoying hearing you talk. You seem happy."

She sat back down. "I think I am, Monty. Even though tomorrow morning . . ." she trailed off, looked away, and bit her lip.

"What is tomorrow morning?" He asked.

"The hearing."

He looked at her closely. She had cried a lot. He could tell. His heart went out to her. Whatever she was going through must be as bad as what he had been through, but she was content about it now.

He watched her as she seemed to be tottering between newfound happiness and deep sorrow. He guessed the tears were bittersweet. He wished he knew how to protect her and take away the sorrow.

She leaned over and reached down to pick up a dogwood blossom from the ground, and her hair fell around her face. He thought she was falling and grabbed her. "I'm okay," she said and sat back up.

For a second the blue sky and sunshine were gone. It was dark. All Monty could see was Jamie falling and the sound like a gunshot. He felt that knock in his head like before.

Then it was light again, and he felt the soft breeze and noticed the dogwoods waving gently and the blue sky overhead.

She looked at him worried that she had upset him and stood up again to take him back.

"No. I'm alright," he said. "Keep on talking to me. I need to hear you talk."

She smiled and sat back down, then sighed. "I don't know what else to talk about Monty. I wish you could remember. She laid her hand on his. "Thank you for being my friend."

He noticed her hand. She was not wearing a ring. He heard that knock again and a thought struck him. *I want to put a ring on that hand one day.*

Had he ever said that to her? She didn't act like it. Maybe he had thought it. He watched her slip her hand back in the purse as though she wanted to touch that Bible again.

Suddenly he heard his mother's voice. "Don't go, Marty, please, don't go."

Marty? He shook his head, trying to shake off that feeling, and squeezed his eyes to shut out the image, his mother standing at the door as he left in anger, his father standing behind her.

Suddenly he opened his eyes and said to Jamie, "I have to go."

"Okay." she stood up.

"No," he reached her hand and pulled her back down again. "I don't mean in there. I have to go home."

"Back to Chesapeake?"

"No, to the farm."

"Seashore Farms?"

"No. Home. Where I left my mom and dad. I have to go back to my father." His voice was shaky but urgent.

She looked at him. "You're scaring me, Monty. You told me your parents were dead."

He looked at her with sudden recognition. "I was hit in the head with a baseball bat."

"No, it was not a baseball bat. It was an oar. Did I hit you?"

He remembered! Her heart leaped. She didn't know whether to be happy or scared. "I thought I hit that other man."

"Cully Solomon!" Montegue blurted. Then with deep emotion, "Oh, Jamie. I thought he was going to kill you. I couldn't let him kill you. I love you."

"You love me?" She repeated with a smile in her voice. "I love you, too." He threw his arms around her and kissed her and in that embrace all his memory flooded back.

And she could tell. Because she had dreamed of this moment but never let on. In her heart, she knew that this was right.

They laughed and wept together. "I'm so glad you're back," Jamie said. "When I thought you were dead, I was so sad. Then they said you weren't dead, but you were missing. I was still sad. Then they said they found you, but you had amnesia. I wanted to see you, but I was scared you would never remember me. I've missed you."

"I'm never letting you go again," he said with his right arm around her shoulder and his left hand holding hers. He looked at her tear-streaked face. "Will you go back with me?"

"Yes. I mean, no. I can't. I mean..." she dropped her head. "Tomorrow. . ."

He surprised her. "My mother always told me to trust God and pray."

She blinked and smiled. "Tell me about your mother, Monty." On impulse, she pulled the Bible out and laid it on her lap. This was the second time today she had been told to trust God and pray.

"I've seen my mother like that a million times," he said. "She used to read it to my brother and me."

"Aww, I wish...What about your dad?"

"My father was very strict. He didn't want us to do anything but stay on the farm. My brother was okay with that, but I wanted to go places, see the world. In school, I was smart. I applied to Columbia University in New York and got accepted. I had a scholarship. My dad was angry. He said no son of his was going to that heathen place."

She squeezed his hand as his voice faltered. He continued. "Mother said, there are colleges in Chicago. But I wanted to go to New York. My father said, if I left, I'd be on my own. I left anyway, with only enough money to get there. I got a part-time job and struggled. But I saw money everywhere. I saw success. And I was determined to get that. My mother called me some at first, but she couldn't tell my father. She said he would be mad at her, and he was too hurt. I haven't talked with her in a few years."

"Oh, no, Monty! That hurts. That's awful. That's so sad. I know they want to hear from you."

"I've thought of it a few hundred times. But then I always remembered how mad my father was, and I lost my nerve."

Jamie surprised herself. "They want you to call."

"I can't call them now. I lost my phone. When I get home and get a new phone, I'll call them, and if they will let me, we will go."

"No." She pulled her new phone out of her purse. "Do you remember the number?"

"After fifteen years?"

She opened the keypad and held it for him.

He punched in numbers that came automatically to his mind. "But that was the number at home when I was growing up. They would not have that number now."

"Hello?" He heard a man's voice and hung up.

"Why did you hang up?" Jamie asked.

"I don't know. I didn't know what to say."

"Was it your dad?"

"It was a man. But he sounded old."

She took the phone back and pressed redial. When the voice answered, she said, "Hello, Sir. This is Jamie Sampson at Claxton Hospital and Rehab Center. I wonder if you could tell me. Do you know a Martin Montegue?"

The man's voice cracked, "Is my son dead?"

"No," she said. "He wants to talk with you." She heard the voice on the other end say, "Oh, Lord. Thank you. Jesus," as she handed the phone to Monty. She got up and walked away.

If she never did another good thing in her life, she was glad that she had done that. She remembered where she got the phone and closed her eyes. "Thank you, pretty lady."

It was ten minutes before she heard him say, "Goodbye. I love you Dad."

She walked back to the bench and he seemed different. Like a weight had been lifted. He smiled up at her and pulled her down on the bench beside him. She hugged him, happy to see his miracle. She had never known that feeling before.

"We're going home," he said.

She let him talk. He seemed to have forgotten about tomorrow. She wouldn't remind him now. She just held his hand, and smiled, and listened. She felt joy for him and his parents. She could only imagine. He chattered on.

"I can sell Wilson the Triple M. He likes you. He's told me so. I can keep my shares in Seashore Farms. I could move my law practice to Chicago. Mama was so happy, Jamie. All she could do was laugh and cry and praise the Lord. Dad was happier than I ever heard him. He said, 'come today,' but I told him I have to get out of the hospital first. I told them I got hit on the head accidentally and had a concussion, and I'd been thinking about them and I met this wonderful girl, and I want them to meet her. And they just cried and talked at once. Thank you, Jamie, for making me call."

She said, "I didn't make you. I just handed you my new phone."

Word spread through the hospital, and many congratulated Zoey on helping the Mystery Man to get his memory back. She told everyone who mentioned it, "I didn't do it. It was an answer to someone's prayers."

When Jamie told her about the phone call and the conversation with his parents, Zoey said, "Sort of like the prodigal son in the Bible, isn't it?"

"Okay," Jamie said and made a mental note to look for that in her new Bible.

Even if tomorrow--I will always have this, she thought. *Whatever happens, I will always have this.* An unexplainable peace settled in her heart.

Chapter 64 Testimony

Thursday evening, April 18

As his doctor, **Zoey Rosenberg had posted a note** at the nurses' station to call her immediately if the Mystery Man regained his memory. She indicated that the Police Department must be called because impending criminal charges were possibly connected to the man's injuries and disappearance.

Fortunately, Zoey was the first to learn of Montegue's breakthrough and called Chief Stanton herself.

Needless to say, he was ready and told Zoey that Montegue had to be questioned.

She said, "Do it here. He is my patient and he has not been released. In fact," she said, "meet him in my office. And I think Miss Sampson needs to stay if that's okay."

"Perfect," Jeb agreed. When he left the police station, he told Edna he was meeting Montegue at the hospital. "We don't need to get Officer Riley involved in this. I've sent him on an errand."

Thanks to the Jewish grandmother, a box had arrived at the nurses' station about three o'clock for John Wellsly. Lillian had recognized that he was about the same size as Jimmy and decided no one should be stuck in a hospital gown all day.

She spoke to Jessica, and they put together an outfit of Jimmy's clothes. A red golf shirt and gray slacks. They laughed at his potential embarrassment when they threw in a pair of navy blue, silk boxers with Merry Christmas written in red. She retrieved his shoes from the Manor and bought a new pair of black socks. She took the package to the hospital and sent it up by Kenzie with a note, "To John Wellsly."

Montegue swallowed his pride and dressed when he was presented with the package. He didn't expect it but was glad to be able to put on something less humbling than the hospital garb, in spite of the embarrassing Christmas gift.

Jamie had to hang out in the waiting room until they were both brought to Zoey's office at five o'clock.

"You look nice," she said when she saw him.

"Even with the black eye, that you gave me, that's turning green now?" He smiled and took her hand. She was as beautiful as ever.

"Even with the black eye," she said. "I'm sorry about that."

Jeb noticed the different demeanor in Jamie Sampson and attributed it to Montegue's being found. He did not know about her gifts from Bree.

Seated in Dr. Rosenberg's office, after introductions, Jeb asked Montegue, "Can you just tell us what happened? Do you recall being in the parking lot behind Lee Fish Market on Friday night, March 29th?

"I think I do. Feels like last night to me now, but it's been three weeks, hasn't it?"

"Almost," Jeb said. "You took a pretty good whack on the head, didn't you?"

Montegue rubbed the side of his face lightly. "Yeah, but it wasn't from the mugger. This girl can pack a mean wallop. When she swung that oar, I should have ducked, but I didn't see it coming."

"I'm sorry," Jamie said again.

Jeb surprised them. "It might have saved your life. I guess the mugger didn't want that woman coming after him."

They chuckled lightly and broke the tension of the moment. Jamie was a little uncomfortable. She was sorry she had hurt Monty, but she was glad she had stayed in shape.

Montegue said, "He did get off me, and I was able to get up and run to the car."

"Did you see what happened to him?"

"No, I just started driving."

"And left Jamie?" Dr. Rosenberg asked.

Jeb suddenly realized this was a mistake. Dr. Rosenberg did not know who Jamie was. *This is getting complicated* he thought. *Thank goodness I came instead of letting Riley in here.*

No one spoke for a moment. Jamie didn't know what to say. Montegue didn't know what to say. Suddenly he remembered what Jamie had told him under the dogwood tree. She had been arrested. He had wanted to protect her. Remembering that night again, he heard himself yelling for her to 'go, get out of here,' but he did not know where she went. She just disappeared.

"I got in the boat..." Jamie started to speak, but Montegue interrupted her. He put his hand to his head and said, "I'm sorry. I have such a bad headache. It hurts to think. Could we postpone this? Or get me something for my head?"

Dr. Rosenberg jumped up. Her patient was not as well as she thought. "Yes." She looked at Jeb. "Let's get him back to his room. I may have rushed things. I knew you needed to complete your investigation, and I called you. But this has been a tremendously stressful day for him. I'm sorry."

It dawned on Jeb that it was Dr. Rosenberg's son-in-law who was being charged with Montegue's murder, and she was eager to have Davie cleared. She wanted this over as much as he did.

He stood up. "You're right doc. We've all been so anxious to get this over with, we might be acting too hastily. Let me get back with you tomorrow. In the meantime, Mr. Montegue, you rest and do what the doctor says. We want to get you back to Chesapeake, but we want you well."

"I agree," he said. "Could Jamie stay a while?"

Dr. Rosenberg hesitated but then answered. "I don't see why not if she will just sit quietly. Maybe the cafeteria can bring her something, and she can have dinner with you if you feel like it."

He nodded. "I'd like that. Thank you."

"I'll tell the nurses to take care of it," she said.

"Thank you," he said again as Zoey buzzed for a nurse who came in with a wheelchair. Jamie walked beside him as the nurse wheeled him back up to P-456.

Jeb said, "Dr. Rosenberg, I just realized, Davie is your son-in-law. Don't you worry about him anymore! The charges will be dropped as soon as I get to the office. And I'll hear the rest of Mr. Montegue's story later."

"Thanks, Chief. You're right. I've been very concerned about what's happening to Davie and Jenny. And I do want it over with."

She stood by the door as they all left. When she closed it behind them, she leaned against the door and blew a sigh of relief. *Oh, what a tangled web we weave.* She felt sorry for Davie and Jenny getting into this mess. *He'll certainly grow up after this experience*, she rationalized. He was a good boy, and mature in certain areas, but he had been so naïve on other things that got him in trouble. "Dear Lord, please help my children get out of this mess," she prayed.

Jeb thought as he walked to his car, *I have to get to the bottom of this, but I will speak to Montegue alone, somehow. At least I can let Bernell know we've got this started.*

When he called her, Bernell said, "Somebody has to take Jamie back to the house. Think you could handle that?"

"I'll send someone," he said. "But not Riley. I can't send Riley. But she'll be up there another hour or so."

In room P-456, as soon as the door was closed, Jamie asked, "Why did you do that?"

"I don't know. I was afraid you would be in trouble. You told me something that didn't make much sense today. But you said there is a hearing tomorrow. I just felt like I had to protect you."

Jamie did not know that Dr. Rosenberg was related to Davie Wellsly. Neither did Martin Montegue. He had never met the man who built the yacht for Jeffry Smythe. And he didn't know it was the same young man who came to his room last night. He still did not know.

Jamie said, "Why don't you just tell me everything that happened and I'll write it down, and you can give that to the police. Maybe that would work."

"We could try that," he said.

They sat in the hard chairs in the hospital room facing each other. He would not get back into the hospital bed even though she suggested he should.

She admired his new outfit. "You look nice. You look like yourself now."

"I feel like myself." He looked down at his red shirt and grey slacks. "I had a flight bag with clothes in it. I don't know what happened to it. I have to thank my Jewish Grandmother for these."

Jamie had heard about the Jewish Grandmother but she only knew her as the lady who worked at the homeless shelter because that was all that Monty knew.

"I'm so glad about your talk with your father."

"He told me he loved me and missed me. He said he was sorry he tried to stop me. I told him I was sorry I left like I did. I was young and stupid and wanted my own way. He said if he had it to do over again, he would support me. I said if I had it to do over again, I would not leave."

"I bet that was a tough thing for your dad to admit," she sympathized. "And maybe you, too."

"I could have gone to a school in Chicago." He closed his eyes. "Why are we so stupid when we're young?"

He picked up her hand. "I'm going back now. I want to see them. Will you go with me? I want to get a ring on this hand." He kissed her fingers.

She smiled. "That will be nice. Did I say yes?"

"I hope so," he said. "Will you marry me, Jamie?"

"Yes," she leaned in for a kiss but straightened quickly as a knock on the door announced the arrival of dinner.

Dr. Rosenberg stopped by the nurses' station. "I'm leaving for the night." She scribbled a prescription for Montegue's headaches as needed. "I think his headache was from the tension of the moment and all the emotional upheaval of today. If it continues, give him this. I believe, though, that a good night's sleep and he'll be good as new tomorrow. If so, I'm expecting to release him. Chief Stanton is sending someone for Miss Sampson."

She stuck her head in P-456 and told Monty and Jamie the same thing.

Chief Stanton decided he would go himself. He had an idea. When he tapped on the door at six o'clock, he had Martin Morgan Montegue's wallet with his driver's license and other important ID.

"You feeling better?" He asked the patient.

"Much better." Montegue smiled. "The nurse said you were coming for Jamie. Can you bring her back in the morning?"

"Don't you have the keys to that van?" Jeb looked at Jamie.

She took a deep breath and nodded. Monty did not understand her reluctance but Jeb did. "Use it. You'll be alright."

She swallowed and laid her hand on her purse. She could feel the Bible still there. She nodded. "I will."

Jeb turned to Montegue. "You'll be glad to get this." He handed him the wallet.

Montegue opened it and grinned. "That's me. Finally, I'm back!" He held up his insurance card. "I'll show this to the nurse and get my records changed from John Wellsly to the real me. I can never repay everybody for what they've done. But I can start."

Jeb had to say, "Knowing Mrs. Lillian and Mr. Isaac for the people they are, when they hear the story about you getting up with you folks that will be pay enough for them. I'm sure you have been in their prayers, and they didn't know a thing about you."

Montegue looked at Jamie and nodded. "I knew they had to be special even before. I will contact them." Jamie smiled.

Jeb said, "Okay. Let's get a nurse in here. I'll be right back." Jeb stepped out and was back in a few seconds with the head nurse, Mrs. Randall.

She was all smiles. "Wonderful news about you today. I understand you have an ID for me?"

Montegue handed her his driver's license and insurance card. "Can you take care of this and get me documented as myself? It's not fair for the Wellsly's to pay this bill."

She took the cards. "Certainly, I can do that." She looked at the driver's license. "Mr. Montegue, we'll get some papers in here for you to sign right away."

As soon as she left, Jeb turned to Montegue. "I thought if you felt better now, you might want to go ahead and get something on record so we can close this case."

Montegue looked at Jamie and smiled. "This is even better."

Jeb pulled a digital voice recorder from his pocket. "I'll let you tell us what happened, we'll record it. I'll get Mrs. Randall back in here to be a witness. No questions. You can just tell us what happened."

Montegue nodded. "Okay. We can do that. That will be okay with my doctor, won't it?"

"I'm sure she will be pleased. Especially if we have your nurse in here to make sure I'm not harassing you. I'll record it on my phone also and send that to Dr. Rosenberg immediately and I'll tell her Mrs. Randall is here."

He held up the digital recorder. "This will be for our records at the department. And I've got a form right here," he pulled an envelope from his pocket, "that you can sign and it will all be over."

"Wonderful," Montegue said. "And Jamie can stay in here, too. Right?"

"Certainly. She's already made a statement. She can just sit here and listen."

In a minute, Mrs. Randall, returned with a handful of papers for Montegue to sign. Jeb mentioned his plan and she agreed, she would be glad to help.

Montegue got up and stood by the bed to talk. Jeb laid the recorder on the rolling bed stand.

Montegue began talking. "My name is Martin Morgan Montegue. I live at 1235 Creekside in Chesapeake, Virginia."

He paused a minute to figure out what to say. "I own the Triple M Bar and Grill which is an Off-Track Betting Center. People come in and eat and place bets on horse races that are being live-streamed through television. It is all completely legal. Recently one of our patrons lost a lot of money, and then he accused me of rigging the race. I have no way of doing that. He accosted me, but my Manager Wilson Cranston was able to throw him out."

Jeb nodded approval, understanding the reason for this information.

"I came to Claxton to pay off the yacht my partner bought here, and since we deal with a lot of cash, I decided to bring the ten thousand dollars he owed in cash." He paused and then said, "That was a stupid decision, I know."

He looked at Jamie. "I do stupid things sometimes. But I hope I've learned."

He looked back at Jeb. "I brought it in a briefcase, but I didn't think anybody saw me get it out of the safe."

He paused to gather his thoughts. "When I got here, I ran into Jamie and asked her to have dinner with me at Lillian's Riviera. She met me at the parking lot behind the fish market across the street from there because she came there in a boat."

Jamie nodded agreement with that. He continued. "When we finished eating and left the restaurant, it was about 10:30. It was dark because there wasn't any moonlight. The streetlights weren't very bright. The only light on the parking lot was at the steps that led down to the pier where a few boats were docked."

Jeb scribbled on a pad *add more streetlights at waterfront area.*

Montegue continued. "A man in a white suit was waiting by my car--the one I had rented at the airport. A green foreign car, I can't tell you the brand, but I remember the color. It was green, sort of between a chartreuse and olive, I believe, from Acme Rentals."

Jeb nodded recognition of the car and smiled remembering how Jenny had described it.

"I recognized the man as Cully Solomon," Montegue continued. "The same man who had accosted me at the Triple M. He demanded I give him the briefcase. As I said, I didn't think anyone knew about that. But he had a gun and grabbed Jamie and threatened to kill her. I didn't have a weapon or anything. I got the briefcase out and instead of handing it to him, I threw it at him, hard. It was dark enough I couldn't tell where it went. It must have made him mad. He pushed Jamie and shot and lunged at me. I wrestled him to the ground and then I got hit on the head with something like a baseball bat. But I've learned since that it was an oar from one of the boats."

Montegue paused, staring at the floor as though seeing the story unfolding there. "Cully scrambled up, and I thought he was going after Jamie. I yelled for her to run, to get out of there.

"When I got up off the ground, I could see her falling into the boat with some people, and I heard the engine as the boat left. I knew her friends had picked her up."

Jamie didn't say anything but nodded, agreeing with that statement, and Montegue continued.

"I ran around the car and started it up. In the car lights, I could see Cully climbing on the rocks after the briefcase. I was sick that I had lost all that money, but I was bleeding and my head was killing me, so I drove off.

"I had to get to a doctor. I thought I had seen a hospital, but I turned in the wrong direction. Everything was closed, but I kept driving. When I got out of town, I knew I had gone too far and I stopped to turn around. The car stalled and then I couldn't get it started.

"I got out and started walking. I must have walked for two hours. When I saw that building with lights on, I thought it was the hospital. A man helped me upstairs and gave me a bed. I passed out then, and I don't know how long I was there.

"When I woke up, I was here at the hospital, and I couldn't remember anything. After a few days, I started remembering things from way back like when I was young and going to school. But I couldn't remember who I was, nor how I got here.

"When Jamie came in, I started remembering more. Then today, outside under the dogwood tree, Jamie was talking, and it all came back. I remembered us being attacked and then I remembered everything that happened before I passed out. That's all I know to say now."

Jeb turned off the recorder. "That just about does it. That's pretty close to what Miss Sampson told us. She did not know the mugger though."

"Umm," Montegue said, and sounded as though he had another thought.

Jeb looked at him. "You got something else?"

"No, I was just wondering about my briefcase. I saw one like it in here. Was that mine?"

Jeb did not know, but Jamie did. "I know about it," Jamie said. "Miss Ingles thought if you saw it, you might remember."

"I did notice it and was curious about it, but I couldn't connect it until now. What happened to my money?"

Jeb knew that one. "Your money is safe in a vault. You'll get it back. You've provided enough information, it's evident that it's yours. And your initials are on the briefcase. I'll send this to Dr. Rosenberg and call her. I expect by tomorrow afternoon, you'll be on your way back to Chesapeake."

Mrs. Randall stood up. Jeb laid a form on the table and asked her, "Can you sign that you witnessed Mr. Montegue giving this statement?"

"Certainly." She took the pen he offered and scribbled her signature, then she patted Montegue, on the back. "You've been through a tough time. Congratulations on surviving it. I'll come back later for the hospital forms."

Jeb thanked her. She said, "Happy to be doing this." She nodded at Jamie and slipped on out to the nurses' station.

"What's going to happen to Jamie?" Montegue asked Jeb.

Jeb was taken aback by the question but answered honestly. "I don't know. The Wellsly's still have the option of pressing charges. It's in their hands, and of course the judge's. He has to pass sentence. I understand the hearing is at nine o'clock tomorrow."

He looked at his watch. "It getting late now. We'd better go." He looked at Jamie. "You ready?"

"Wait," Montegue said. "The Wellsly's?"

Again Jeb realized that Montegue did not know the whole story. Was it his place to tell him?"

Jamie spoke up. "I'm sorry Monty. I told you today. I just didn't use any names."

"Oh," Jeb made a quick recovery. "Wellsly is a very popular name around here. Almost like Smith," he laughed.

"Oh," Montegue said as though he understood.

Jamie stood up to leave. Montegue stopped her, and asked Jeb, "Could we have just a minute alone?"

"Sure, I'll be right outside."

Jamie's eyes were wet and her chin trembled as she watched Jeb leave and then looked up at Monty. He pulled her close and said, "No matter what happens. We will get through this. I am not letting you go. I will be praying all night. Promise you will let me know the minute you know anything."

"If I'm allowed," she said in a small voice. She kissed him goodbye. He held her hand until she had to pull away. She could not look back.

Jeb drove her back to the yellow house without speaking, but as she got out of the car in the driveway, he said, "Good luck tomorrow. Call if you need me."

"Thank you," she smiled weakly as she shut the door.

When he got back on the road, Jeb pulled out his phone. Anxious to hear from Bree after sending her on that mission this afternoon, he called her.

Her story was as amazing and fulfilling as his. Finally, the case of the man in the white suit could be wrapped up. He had one more task.

Chapter 65 Tough Decisions and Forgiveness

Thursday night, April 18

When Bree heard the details of Montegue's story, she was thrilled to have played a role in what seemed like a miracle. She had not understood herself doing what was so out of character. But she called Lillian to tell her and thanked her for praying; and, of course, Lillian said, "God works in mysterious ways."

Bree did not see a problem with telling Lillian about her afternoon. Which also got Lillian's happy exclamation, "Yes! Thank God for that, and thank you! I will pass that along. Thank you, Bree."

At the same time, Isaac, Jimmy, and Davie were sitting at her dining room table discussing the drama of the past three weeks.

Jessica and Jenny had taken Caroline and Paul Jason to the airport in Atlanta and wouldn't be back for a couple of hours. Lillian had prepared dinner for the men. She listened as she cleared the table but did not contribute to the conversation.

They had an important decision to make about their options for tomorrow. Isaac told Jimmy and Davie, "This morning, all the things they bought from me with counterfeit money were returned. When George got to work, he called me. Sitting at the dock in front of the store was the boat, the lifesavers, and oars. He counted it up, and every item they had bought was brought back. There was a note that simply said, 'I am sorry. J.S.'"

Jimmy asked him, "Had you filed a warrant for repossession?"

"No, not yet. Hadn't had time. And get this. Nancy told me there was an envelope in the mailbox at Jane's beauty shop with five-hundred dollars in it. It was wrapped in a sheet of paper with a note that just said, 'I am sorry. J.S.' I don't know if it was the same person or not."

Lillian set out three dessert dishes with lemon meringue pie. Davie grinned. "Thanks, Grandma."

Isaac told them, "I have no charges to file. No one was hurt on my property, though they could have been, no real damage was done."

Davie laughed. "Well, guess what. When I got to the plant this morning, the boat the red-haired lady bought was sitting on the landing. It had a note just like that. It just said 'I am sorry. J.S.' "

Jimmy said, "That's interesting. Weird that they all had the same initials. Well, nothing was brought back to me, but yesterday, I received a letter from Louis Renoir with a check."

Isaac raised his eyebrows. Davie asked, "What'd he say?"

Jimmy opened the letter and read it aloud:

> April 15, 2013
>
> Dear Mr. Wellsly,
>
> I sincerely apologize for the trouble caused by my daughter, Joliet Swan, and her friends, Jamie Sampson and Jackie Summerlin. Please accept this check in the amount of $3,200 for payments they made at the Riverside Hotel and Resort with money they did not realize was counterfeit.
>
> They have been arrested and could face prison. My daughter is in therapy and working through this traumatic time.
>
> Again, I apologize for this inconvenience and hope that you will have compassion on Jo and her friends.
>
> We look forward to enjoying your wonderful restaurant and resort in the future as we have in the past.
>
> Sincerely

L J Renoir

"I deposited the check today and it was good." Jimmy added, "Knowing the pride in that family, I'm sure it was hard to do that."

"Oh, yeah," Davie said. "Jenny got a check from him too--for the cushions. She sent Jo Swan an invoice and I guess he paid it."

"Sounds like a lot of restitution going on," Isaac said.

Jimmy mentioned Rebecca and Bill. "I don't know what they will do. They have a right to sue; they could sue me. But so far, they have said just pay their medical bills, and we have done that. What the insurance company didn't cover, Uncle Benny and I have."

"When people hook up with the devil, they sure can leave a lot of destruction in their path, can't they?" Isaac observed. "Davie, what about your house?"

"It cost me a little to have the door fixed," Davie said. "They didn't steal anything. It was just frightening, and a lot of aggravation. I've been so mad I could choke somebody."

He pushed his empty plate away and rubbed his stomach. "That was good Grandma."

He continued his analysis of the situation. "I was determined to make whoever did that pay. When John Fredrick said we could press charges, even though they had a plea bargain, I was glad, and I was planning to do that."

He looked around at them all paying attention. "But Jenny and I talked last night. And, well, if everyone can forgive me, and God can forgive me, I guess I should forgive them."

"So, that's it then?" Isaac asked.

But Davie wasn't through. "Jenny reminded me that the Lord's Prayer says forgive *us* as we forgive others and that sort of stopped me in my tracks. I have to forgive them if I want God to forgive me. So, I'm not pressing charges for anything. I'm gonna try to not think about how mad I was. And I really am thankful to God for forgiving me."

Isaac smiled and patted Davie on the back. "I think you made the right decision."

He looked at them both. "I can call John Frederick then?"

"Yeah," they told him.

When the judge answered the phone, Isaac said, "We're not going to press any charges."

John Frederick said, "Okay. What I'm going to do then is give them five years' probation, with a warning that if they so much as get a speeding ticket, I'm throwing the book at them. And that goes for all three of them." He read their full names. "Jacquelyn Boggs Summerlin, Joliet Marie Renoir Swan, and Jamie Rose Madison Sampson."

"I think that's fair," Isaac said. "Do we need to go up there tomorrow?"

"No. Not unless you just want to."

"No, you handle it. I'll pass this along to Davie and Jimmy. You're a fine judge, Freddie. We're proud of you. I mean John Frederick." They both laughed.

The judge said, "Thanks, I appreciate you, too. And you have a good night."

Isaac had jotted notes while John Frederick was talking. He handed Davie the note with the full names on it. Davie said, "They sure got long names."

Jimmy looked at the note. "Right, William David Greyson Wellsly." They all laughed.

Isaac turned to his son and grandson. "Well, it's over boys."

"Except for one thing," Lillian said. "I'm glad you all made the decision you did." She told then them about Bree's incident with Jamie today and how the Mystery Man had regained his memory, and it turned out to be a Prodigal Son story.

"I hope we can hear more about that," Isaac said. "It's just amazing how God works, isn't it?"

They agreed. Then Lillian told Davie, "There's more. Officer Riley has held out that you were involved somehow and would not relinquish his stance. But after today, he's done. Bree says you will get word officially tomorrow. You will be exonerated. Bree just told me everything."

"But nobody's told me." Davie worried. "And that Riley has even said I was the mugger. That hurt, and it makes me mad as fire."

"Try to be patient, son." Jimmy patted him on the arm. "We've come this far. God will not let us down. We have to trust Him."

"I know I brought it all on myself." Davie couldn't let go of the guilt. "And they have not proved who the man in the white suit was. If you listen to that DJ, I contrived the whole thing. And the police department is covering up for me."

Jimmy said, "I heard that he said today on the radio, he was running for mayor and he was gonna clean up this town."

Isaac stepped in, "He's riding on the high of his popularity at the Spring Festival. Satan is always going to have somebody to come against you. Just pray, Davie, and put on the whole armor of God. You know what the Bible says. In the King James Version, Ephesians 6:11 says, 'Put on the whole armor of God that ye may be able to stand against the wiles of the devil.' "

Lillian picked up the Bible she kept on the counter and turned to the next verse, "Stand therefore, having your loins girt about with truth, and having on the breastplate of righteousness."

Jimmy added the next verse without looking. "And your feet shod with the preparation of the gospel of peace. You know what that means. Study, pray, go to church, stay prepared."

Lillian read aloud, "Above all, taking the shield of faith, wherewith ye shall be able to quench all the fiery darts of the wicked." Then she said, "That's all this is, Davie, fiery darts from Satan."

Isaac quoted the next verse, "And take the helmet of salvation, and the sword of the Spirit, which is the word of God."

Lillian and Jimmy said at the same time, "Praying always with all prayer and supplication in the Spirit."

Davie said, "Y'all have all that memorized. I've read it but I can't quote it."

Isaac smiled, "Yeah, the scripture says, hide the Word in your heart, and we've always tried to do that. It helps in times like this to be able to draw from God's Word."

The phone on the wall interrupted their discussion. Lillian said, "Excuse me," and got up to answer it. It was Chief Jeb looking for Davie. "He's here, hold on," she said and handed the phone to Davie.

Jeb was so pleased to be able to say, "Good news, Davie. You have been exonerated. You're free of all suspicion. Paperwork is signed, sealed, and delivered."

Davie said, "But not to me. I don't have anything that says that."

Jeb said, "Okay, let me tell you everything that's happened today. Are you sitting down?"

"Yes, at Grandma's table," Davie answered.

"Okay, today after I learned the name of the man in the white suit, I called the coroner. You know how slack he's been, just depending on Officer Riley and, well, you know how that went. Anyway, today he decided to go to the crime scene. I had Officer Riley take him, and I called Bree and asked her to meet them out there."

Davie said, "Okay." He remembered Bree's experience.

"Bree showed them both how she and Kit found the briefcase, and she also showed him where her hands were cut from the sharp rocks. Then Jones decided that could explain the cuts on the man's hands."

"Duh," said Davie.

Jeb continued. "Jones came to the office tonight with pictures he took of the rocks and the boats out there. He says he knows now what happened. He said when Cully was jerking on the briefcase, he fell backward, and his head struck the bow of a boat that is still out there. He has a close-up picture of the boat with traces of blood on it which he says is consistent with the wound that killed him. He finally said that the man was not struck with an oar. The blood on the oar was not his."

"That's good then, isn't it?" Davie asked.

"Yes, but wait. You'll like this. While Bree and Riley were out there, they searched around for the man's gun. I fault Riley for not doing a better job of that. He's been knowing since Monday that there was a gun involved. When they searched the area today, Riley found the gun himself!"

"Really? Where'd he find it?" Davie asked.

"Just at the edge of the water on the rocks under the pier. Riley ran a check and found that the gun was registered to Cully Solomon in Chesapeake, Virginia."

"Chesapeake, Virginia!" Davie exclaimed.

"Yes, but there's more. Bree also found a wallet. It was coming apart because it had been wet, but the laminated driver's license was still intact. When the coroner saw it, he recognized the picture as the man in the white suit. He admitted that that was him.

That also coincides with Montegue's testimony, and the report we got from Thomas and Adam after they talked with Mr. Cranston in Chesapeake. So, you don't need to worry about Officer Riley, or Coroner Nick Jones, or DJ Reeves, or anybody else for that matter. It's airtight Davie. It's over."

Davie was still not satisfied. "I want to believe it. But I need something in my hand that says I am free."

Jeb was so sure about it that he had relaxed and even called Dr. Rosenberg. But Davie needed proof in his own hands.

"Give me your cell phone number," Jeb told Davie.

Davie quoted it. "Check your phone," Jeb said. "I took a picture of the document that is being filed here. I'll hold while you look."

Davie's cell phone pinged. He handed his grandmother the house phone and picked up his cell. Finally, he saw the picture of the file titled Man in the White Suit. He read it aloud. "Name, Cully Solomon. Death by accident. Slipped from rocks behind Lee Fish Market on Waterfront St., March 29, 2013."

On three lines were signatures: Coroner Nick B. Jones, Chief of Police Jeb Stanton, and Investigating Officer Mike W. Riley. Stamped in a big circle on top of all the details was CASE CLOSED, April 18, 2013.

Davie had not cried in a long time. And he wouldn't now. But he didn't remember when he had come so close. He could feel his body lighten and sat up straight for the first time in weeks. Almost involuntarily, his hands went up. "Yes! Thank You, Lord!"

Jeb heard him and laughed. Lillian thanked the Police Chief graciously before hanging up, and then she joined the others laughing, crying, and praising the Lord.

After a couple of minutes, Davie's phone pinged again. It was a text from Officer Riley. "Sorry, Mr. Wellsly, I was just trying to do my job. You're free to go."

"Can you believe this?" Davie asked and read it to them.

"Are you going to respond?" Isaac asked.

"No," Davie said.

Jimmy said, "Jeb probably made him do that. He's not been happy with Riley's handling of this from the beginning."

Davie said, "He knew I didn't do that, and he was just trying to pin it on me. And I didn't have an alibi because I was working at the plant that night by myself. Between him and that DJ, they have tortured me every day for two weeks."

"Accusing you of things you didn't do," Lillian said.

"Right," Davie said.

"Just like they did Jesus," Lillian said.

"Right!" Davie said, then winced. "Wait, what?"

Nobody said anything. Davie sat there torn between holding on to his anger and letting it go. Finally, he texted something and laid his phone down. Then he got up and went to the pantry to get a Mountain Dew.

Isaac picked up the phone and read aloud, "I forgive you." He raised his voice and said, "Bring me one, Buddy."

A tear ran down Lillian's cheek. Jimmy pursed his lips, then smiled and winked at her. Wiping his eyes from the joy of the moment, Jimmy said, "Mama you are full of good news tonight!"

Davie and Isaac laughed and clicked their glasses, "Amen!"

Lillian looked at the clock and decided now was as good a time as any. There had been so much going on, and she hadn't been absolutely positive at first, but now she was. And she really wanted to do this right. "Well, if you all have time, I do have one more thing," she said.

Isaac wondered, *what has she got up her sleeve now?*

Davie said it aloud, "What have you got up your sleeve, Grandma? You look like the cat that swallowed the canary?"

"Except no feathers," Jimmy said, and they laughed.

"It can't get any better than this though," Davie said, holding up his phone. The impending heart attack he had felt for days was gone. There were no words to describe his relief.

"I could use another piece of that lemon pie," he said.

"Of course," Lillian said and set the remainder of the pie on the table with the pie server. Davie helped himself and offered a piece to Isaac and Jimmy. They declined, so he took it all.

Lillian reached up in the cabinet and pulled out a pint canning jar, and set it on the table. "Davie this is a moonshine jar."

"Okay, what do you want me to do with it?" he asked with his mouth full.

"Don't talk with your mouth full," she admonished.

"Just hold on to it. I'll be right back."

Chapter 66 One More Thing

Thursday night, April 18

Davie finished his pie, put the empty dishes in the sink, and then sat back down to hold the jar. Lillian returned from the living room carrying the brass menorah that Mother Ramey had given to her many years ago.

She set it on the table and looked at her grandson, "Davie, your great-grandmother Ramey gave me this. When my mother saw this on Isaac's mother's buffet, she made the assumption that Isaac's family was Jewish. Of course, Mother was very pleased. They had met Isaac and liked him. I had been Isaac's nurse for a year in the hospital, and he kind of liked me."

Isaac grinned and rolled his eyes, and she went on with her story. Jimmy figured he had heard it, but he didn't think Davie had.

"Isaac arranged to have both our families for Sunday dinner at his mother's house, so he could ask for my hand in marriage. He wanted my parents' approval first, so he stood up and made a toast and thanked them for raising such a wonderful daughter. Of course, that made them proud. Then he told them what he had in mind, and, of course, they approved, and we had a celebration."

Davie sat there twirling the canning jar between his hands. Lillian sat down, pulled up her chair, and crossed her arms on the table.

"A few days later, Mother learned that they were not Jewish and she went crazy. She accused Mother Ramey of tricking her. Of course, that was not true. I told my mother that Isaac's mom had bought that just because she thought it would look nice on her buffet. She never meant for it to fool anybody."

Davie stopped twirling the jar and listened. Even though Jimmy had heard the story, he was attentive. Of course, Isaac knew it all, but he wondered why Lillian was telling it now.

"Mother forbade me to see Isaac again and told me I had to give his ring back. She had been impressed at the beautiful diamond ring and said 'that's a keeper.' But it didn't matter anymore since he was not a Jew. Well, I didn't give it back. I didn't wear it around her, but I never gave it back."

They noticed that she was still wearing the ring.

"About two years later we did get married. Still without my mother's permission, although my dad had relinquished and given us his blessings. My mother was mean about it for a long time, but we prayed and prayed."

Isaac sat, nodding his head, remembering the story she was telling.

"Nobody knew how much Isaac hated working at the gristmill, but me. Then one night, Nana and Asher Ingles were having dinner with us and got the idea we should build the Gristmill Restaurant and serve both Jewish and Southern cuisine. There were a lot of Jewish people in the area but no good restaurants serving Jewish food. Both our mothers were fantastic cooks in their own right, and Asher thought that would be a big hit."

Isaac helped her tell the story. "We didn't think we could do that without them. So we put out a fleece like Gideon in the Bible. Only we said, if this was God's will, then we would get both our mother's participation."

"I guess that was a long shot," Davie said.

Lillian agreed. "Yes, it was. Mother Ramey agreed to it right away. She was excited about it, but she said we'd never get Elizabeth in on it. That's what we were afraid of, but we still prayed and waited for God's guidance."

Isaac reached for the Bible still on the table and turned to the story about Gideon in Numbers, Chapter 6, as Lillian talked.

"I wanted reconciliation with my mother more than anything, but she would not talk with me. Then one day, out of the blue, she called me. We knew it was God." Isaac nodded, remembering.

Lillian continued. "When I went to see her after she called, I was so thrilled to see her, I didn't even think about the restaurant idea at first. It had been months since I had seen her, and we just talked about everything and caught up. We both had some forgiving to do. She forgave me for marrying Isaac. I stopped blaming her for my father's death and told her how sorry I was for the hateful things I had said."

She reached for a napkin from the white wrought-iron holder as she talked. She wiped a spot on the table left from the pie.

"When Mother and I got to talking about what we had been doing lately, I thought about our restaurant idea. She was impressed with that and WANTED to help. I didn't even have to ask her. So I knew that was what God wanted us to do, and He had brought my mom around. Of course, I had been praying for that, even when no restaurant was involved. But, you know, it was the fleece. And God did it just like we had asked. Just like He did for Gideon in the Bible."

Isaac said, "Then Lillian's mother and my mother became best friends and were best friends for the rest of their lives. Forty some years."

"I didn't know that part," Jimmy said. "I thought they had always been friends."

"Not those first few years," Isaac said. "That's why the idea of having a Jewish restaurant was so odd. We needed her help and God knew that."

"That's a good story, Grandma," Davie said. "You mentioned it to me the other day."

"I didn't tell you this part though." Lillian smiled and watched him closely as she spoke. "My mother made an assumption when she saw this menorah at Isaac's house. But I told her Isaac's mother bought this at a garage sale just because she thought it was pretty."

Lillian watched the three men as it started dawning on them. Jimmy furrowed his brow, Davie's jaw dropped, and Isaac leaned back in his chair and looked at her sideways.

Davie said "Men or... garage sale. Grandma, what are saying?"

Lillian got up and retrieved a screwdriver from the utility drawer and laid it on the table. "Sunday night, Jimmy brought this menorah back from using it on his float in the parade, remember?"

"Yes," they all nodded.

"It hit me. I remembered that she got it from a garage sale, and then how Mr. Antry's letter mentioned "menor and garage sale.' And nobody knew what he meant. It had to be this. I had always noticed that the menorah was a little heavy, and I got to thinking. I turned it every which way till I found a tiny little screw. This screwdriver fits. You want to do the honors?"

Davie couldn't restrain his smiles.

"Hold it up for him, Jimmy," Lillian instructed.

Jimmy held the menorah steady. Isaac watched as Davie turned the screw. The screwdriver slipped, and he started over. Finally, it stuck, and he made a few turns. The base loosened, and Davie twisted it slightly. A piece of glass fell out. Then another.

Lillian pushed the jar under the opening in the menorah base, and diamonds started pouring out like marbles. Some bigger than others. When the last piece fell into the jar it was full. Davie shook the menorah, but it was empty. He couldn't stop grinning.

He picked up the jar. "Wow, that's heavy."

"A MOONSHINE JAR OF DIAMONDS," Isaac announced. "Just like Daddy said."

"What are we gonna do with this?" Davie asked.

Jimmy was speechless. He had watched the whole operation without saying a word. "I want to feel them," he said. He poured a handful in one hand and then poured them back in the jar. Then he did it again in the other hand.

He laughed. "Who'd have thought, Mama? Can you believe this sat on that flatbed out there in the garage Friday and rode down Claxton Boulevard with the pigs, and everybody pushing, and shoving, and throwing things? And then it sat there in the garage all weekend until I brought it back to you Sunday night. This is incredible. Absolutely incredible. Makes me right nervous."

Davie said, "And you grew up, in this house, with that sitting on Grandma's bookcase."

Lillian said, "She gave it to me for my birthday one year because I had admired it. And she knew that I was a Jew, and it might mean more to me than it did to her. Jimmy was about three."

Isaac said, "Lillian, the first time I saw you, I knew you were a diamond. You were already polished and perfect. When your mother forbade me to see you again, I thought I'd lost you forever and my life was over. But being the diamond you were, you cut through all the chains that kept us apart. You've always been my moonshine jar of diamonds, Lillian."

"Oh, you." Lillian pecked him on the cheek and blushed, even after fifty-eight years.

Davie said, "Now that was a *metaphor*. But like Aunt Bernell said, these are real!"

Lillian said to Isaac, "That menorah was already in your mom's house and your daddy used it to hide those diamonds."

"Yep," Isaac said, "But I didn't know it. I never even knew where she got that from. And no one ever would have guessed what was in it, if you hadn't figured it out."

"And if your dad hadn't written that letter. And he knew she got it at a garage sale."

Isaac turned to Davie. "And that's the rest of the story about the origin of the Gristmill Restaurant."

Davie laughed, although he was distracted by the game he was playing with his dad, running diamonds through their fingers and playing like kids with a new game.

"Look at the rainbows," Davie let them catch the light as he poured some back in the jar.

"Some of them are almost blue," Jimmy said. He lined some up and used a roundish one like a marble to shoot them to Davie.

"I'm afraid you boys aren't going to be able to keep those toys," Lillian said. "But I guess you can play with them while they're here."

Isaac said, "We've had them since 1955."

Jimmy said, "I bet when your daddy put those clues together, he figured if they found the fish box, at least they would never find these."

"He got that right!" Davie said. "I'm glad he wrote that letter, or we wouldn't have found them either." Then he wondered. "You reckon it was him trying to let us know that night when the mirror crashed? That's why we found it. Gives me goosebumps."

"And was that Bruiser howling that night?" Isaac questioned. "Sure sounded like him."

"Or God directing it all," Lillian said, "to get our attention. If He can use a donkey, he can use a dog. And if he can part the red sea, he can break a mirror."

Davie shivered. They paused a minute and reflected on that possibility. "Maybe God wants these used for something good," Isaac said. "Weren't they part of the diamonds stolen from your Uncle Ivey's jewelry store in that heist in 1955?"

"That is my understanding," Lillian said. "So they're his, or my brother Jacob's now."

Davie said, "But the insurance company would have paid, and they would belong to the insurance company now."

"They were not insured," Lillian said.

"Not insured!" Jimmy was appalled.

"He thought they were. There was a mix-up. He hadn't been with that company long enough, or the premium was late, or something. I didn't know, l just remember they wouldn't pay, and Uncle Ivey almost died over it. That's why when part of them were found, and the FBI traced them to his shipment, Uncle Ivey was so glad to get them back."

"So this is the rest of them," Isaac said. "After all these years, and it was Daddy's intention that all that stuff go back to its rightful owners."

Lillian went to the phone and dialed her brother's number. "Jacob, I know it's late, but you've got to hear this."

She was on the phone for ten minutes while Davie and Jimmy continued playing with the diamonds. "I could pour all these in the bottom of Jenny's aquarium and nobody would ever know," Davie said.

After a few minutes, Lillian asked Jacob if she could put him on speaker and he agreed to tell them what he had just told her.

"About three weeks ago, I had a weird dream. Or nightmare. I dreamed God was in my room. He was so bright, I was almost blinded, but He told me not to be afraid. Then He held up a jar. It looked like it was full of crushed ice and He poured it out. Then I realized it was diamonds. Being a jeweler, of course, I knew they were priceless, and I started picking them up. They were rolling everywhere.

"Then God said, 'Stop. They are for Lillian.' "

"At first I was angry and said, 'No! They're mine! I own the jewelry store. They were stolen from my father. They are not hers. They are mine!' "

"Then the diamonds disappeared, and God said, 'Where are they now?' I said, 'I don't know. You hid them.' "

"And God said, 'That's right. I've been saving them. Now, tell Lillian, you want her to use them.' And I woke up and the room was dark."

"Wow," Davie shivered. "What did God look like?"

"Nothing but light. I couldn't tell. But His voice was like music."

"Did He say anything else?" Davie asked.

Jacob said, "No. He disappeared. I woke up and it was three o'clock, and I couldn't go back to sleep. Then a few days later, I heard about people digging holes on your land, and I wondered if they were looking for the diamonds God was talking about."

Lillian said, "Yes they were. But God took care of that!"

"Well, I'm glad. You know, I had decided it was just a nightmare. I attend New Covenant Church, but God never spoke to me, and I never dreamed about Him before. Now, Lillian, you're telling me you have a jar of diamonds just like I dreamed about?"

Lillian was astounded. "I believe so. Yes, Jacob, and they're your diamonds. They were stolen from Uncle Ivey, and now they've been found."

Jacob said, "No, Lillian. God told me they are for you to use."

"But how? I don't know a thing about diamonds like that."

"Grandma, are you gonna disobey God? That's not like you," Davie observed.

It was one of those rare times when Lillian was speechless.

Jacob said, "I'll work with you, Lillian. God must have already shown you some things that need to be done, and you've been praying about it, but you would need a lot of money to do it."

"That's very true," she said as she began remembering all the things she had prayed for lately. The needy, the homeless, the soup kitchen, and so many things she had a burden for beyond her means to accomplish. "I guess the scriptures are really true. I've always believed Matthew 21:22. 'All things, whatsoever ye shall ask in prayer, believing, ye shall receive.' "

Isaac said, "John 15:7, 'If ye abide in me, and my words abide in you, ye shall ask what ye will, and it shall be done unto you.' "

Lillian said, "I've been quoting that a lot lately, And also John 14:13: 'Whatsoever ye shall ask in my name, that will I do, that the Father may be glorified in the Son.' And there are so many more. I always knew that. I just never expected it to happen like this."

Davie said, "But Grandma, you always tell us God works in mysterious ways."

Jacob said, "It's getting late, Lillian. Call me tomorrow. We'll get together. I think God's got some work for us to do. And I thought we were both too old for this."

Davie laughed at that. "Don't ever tell my Grandma she's too old for anything."

As he spoke, the front door opened and Jessica and Jenny came in laughing about something on their trip. Jimmy and Davie jumped up to greet them. "Wait till you hear what you've missed tonight."

Lillian told Jacob she would call him tomorrow and said good night.

Everyone started telling Jenny and Jessica bits of the good news. Lillian got out some dishes, and set sandwich ingredients and a chocolate cake on the table.

"Might as well eat while we catch you up. We've got a lot to tell you," she said.

Davie pulled a chair up for Jenny. "You're gonna love this!"

Jenny and Jessica were speechless, listening to all the cheerful banter and wonderful news.

They didn't know that all the items bought with counterfeit money had been returned. Jenny only knew of the check she had received in payment for the cushions.

They were glad to hear that Montegue's memory had come back and he was able to clear up all the mystery surrounding the man in the white suit. And he had reconnected with his parents which was another story.

Finally, Jessica said, "So many prayers answered. His mother has prayed so hard. I can't imagine how bad that must be, losing your son for so many years."

They were especially glad to hear that Mike Riley finally had to back down—and had even apologized. If you could call it that.

Jessica and Jenny were almost as thrilled as Davie when he told them about Jeb saying the case against him was closed.

Davie showed them on his phone the picture of the Case Closed File.

"All that is wonderful news, what we have been praying so hard for," Jessica said.

Finally, Jenny pointed at the jar in the middle of the table and gave Davie a questioning look. "But you haven't mentioned that."

"Oh yeah. That's a long story," he said. "Grandma and Grandpa will tell you about that. It's a moonshine jar of diamonds."

ADDENDUM

Monty Montegue and Jamie Sampson returned to Chesapeake together and married in a chapel with both families present.

Jackie Summerlin and Rex Richards left together for parts unknown. Some said they were getting married in Florida. Others speculated they were going to Nevada. Only Chief Jeb Stanton and the FBI ever knew.

The yellow house was condemned and donated to the Claxton City Fire Department who used the house for fire training and burned it down to the ground.

The Italian cypress trees were removed to build a new fire department with two shiny, new fire trucks that were donated to the city. A basketball goal was erected beside the parking lot.

The Del Vecchio Foundation was established with funds available for interest-free loans and grants for any person or organization in the city or county who needed financial assistance.

New Covenant Church for all People announced plans to build a new sanctuary on the north lawn and add a fellowship hall and more Sunday school rooms where the old building was.

The First Baptist Church on Chattanooga Road received a large, anonymous donation for their building program in honor of Roy and Tiffany Fields.

Magnolia Manor was remodeled and expanded. Mr. Harmon was given a full-time job as caretaker of the property and private quarters for life. A staff was hired to run the soup kitchen daily.

A new scholarship fund was established at the university for students entering the Forensic Science program.

The City Library received an anonymous gift to establish a trust fund to hire a full-time computer instructor.

And few people ever heard about the moonshine jar of diamonds.

ABOUT THE AUTHOR

Having earned degrees in English, Psychology, and Education Administration, Dr. Ramona G Kearney has always been a writer. She has published numerous short stories, articles, poems, and reviews. *MOONSHINE JAR OF DIAMONDS: Buried Secrets at Big Creek* is her fourth novel in the Oars Series.

Previous books include:

OARLOCKS AND BAGELS: Rescue Me

BROKEN OARS: Van Gogh, Diamonds, and the Garden of Eden

OARS IN THE WATER ~ Music, Mayhem, and Murder

OARS IN THE WATER: ANA'S STORY - Prelude to Music Mayhem, and Murder.

Dr. Kearney is a mother, grandmother, and great-grandmother to a brilliant, talented, and awesome family.

Made in the USA
Columbia, SC
20 January 2021